A TRIPLE-NOVEL UNLIKE ANY EVER WRITTEN BEFORE

By the gloom of electric lights, stunted and misshapen beasts scrabble for their lives in blasted landscapes of poisoned canals and grotesque vegetation. But this is no alien world. This is Earth, or used to be.

Now it is Tartarus, shut off from the face of heaven, from the sky and the stars, by a huge platform which completely envelops the world. Living in a technological utopia, the inhabitants of the platform have long forgotten that other men still live in the grim underworld that they abandoned.

But one man descends to the depths. He discovers that under the accelerated evolutionary conditions of this hothouse underworld a whole new ecology of grossly mutated life-forms has emerged. Now the True Men share their environment with rat-men, cat-men and gigantic waterworms . . .

Brian M. Stableford

THE
REALMS
OF
TARTARUS

DAW BOOKS, INC.

DONALD A. WOLLHEIM, PUBLISHER

1301 Avenue of the Americas
New York, N. Y.   10019

FIRST PRINTING, JULY 1977

1 2 3 4 5 6 7 8 9

PRINTED IN U.S.A.

Contents

I. THE FACE OF HEAVEN

1

The stars stood still in the sky, as they always had, as they always would. They shone with a steady pearl-white light. Each one was perfectly round. They were not evenly distributed in the sky. They clustered above the land that was called Shairn, and they grew hardly less dense towards the east, where the lands of the Men Without Souls stretched away from Cudal Canal farther than the eye could see from Amalek Height. To the north of Shairn was the Swithering Waste, and in those skies the stars were set farther apart, and farther still as one went west of north, skirting the great wall of iron. Ultimately, in the far west of north, were the blacklands, where no stars shone at all except for a single line which curved away into the darkness: a road of stars. No one followed the road of stars, not because no one was curious as to where it might lead and why, but because the blacklands sheltered creatures which preferred to stay away from the lightlands and from men of all kinds, and the men were afraid of them.

To the west and southwest of Shairn the stars shone brightly enough, but those were bad hills, stained with poison and incurable disease. There were nomad paths—allegedly safe paths—across the hills, but only the Cuchumanates dared use them unless need forced fugitives to take the risk. To the south itself was more good land—the land called Dimoom by the Children of the Voice.

Chemec was crouched on top of the hill called Clauster Ridge, sheltering beneath the umbrella of a sourcap from the light of the stars. Clauster Ridge was by no means the impressive peak that Amalek Height was, but it brought Chemec far too close to the stars for him to feel truly comfortable. He felt that as he watched the Livider Marches which stood unused between the ridge and Cudal Canal, so the stars kept watch on him. But someone had to keep watch—someone always had to keep watch in these troubled times. Old Man Yami was getting old, and the young Ermold across the canal was aching for a fight and a chance to take a few skulls. For any reason, or for no reason at all.

In fact, with the sourcaps all around him, Chemec could hardly *watch* at all, but he took a liberal interpretation on his duty, and he had every faith in his nose. The fashion these days was to train eyes rather than noses, but Chemec could never really come round to the idea of counting the stars his friends in the great war of life. They were, at best, neutral. Whereas odors . . .

He was listening also for movements in the fields of asci which carpeted the gentler slope of the ridge behind him. If anything edible went by, he might as well catch it, and he definitely did not want to be caught unawares by one of his own people. The wind—a gentle enough wind—blew direct from Walgo. It always had and it always would.

When he caught the signal, it came sharp upon the wind, like a tiny stab in his sinuses. It was a cold smell, and a weird smell. A smell that was distinctly alien. It came to him with such a shock that he imagined a shadow rushing on him from the east, and he leaped to his feet, swinging his stone axe out of the cradle of his arms and into readiness for attack. But the shadow was nothing.

He moved with a strange sideways shuffle, something like a crab. One of his legs was bent, the bone having been broken when he was very young. He had learned to live with the deformity. He had the reputation of being a lucky man. When he wanted to move quickly he scuttled like a spider, and one could never quite judge his direction while his head was bobbing and his shoulders weaving.

The sharp smell was a liar. Nothing was close at hand. Whatever it was, it was out of sight. But it *was* coming, slowly. Chemec waited, wondering and worrying, ready to stay or run as the event might demand.

Something new, to him, meant something terrible.

2

The stars stood still in the sky. Pearl-white light. Every star perfectly round, no matter how close his imagination soared, no matter how far it crept, huddling into the mud and the foul earth. Always the same stars. Always still-standing, white-shining. Always.

Carl Magner, sweating in his sleep, dreaming a dream which, for him, was filled with horror and mystery, had no possible idea of what those stars might signify, and why. He only knew that they seemed to be perpetually falling upon him, threatening him and taunting him with a cold, steely anger.

Magner liked stars. Real stars. Stars which shone weakly, pin-point stars which wheeled their way slowly across the night sky and faded in the west when dawn came. He felt an attraction to those stars. They meant something to him—something real and safe and ultimately knowable if, for the time being, unknown.

But while the stars wheeled Magner slept, and his sleep took him into the world of alien stars which acted as stars should not.

They were the stars of Hell.

Carl Magner had no real understanding of his nightmares. There was no one who could help him to understand. Nightmares no longer existed as signs and symptoms and real phenomena. No one—except Carl Magner—had nightmares. The word was a label that had become a lie. There were no nightmares, supposedly. Carl Magner was alone. There was no one to help him, no help to be offered.

In fleeing the fall of the stars, Magner kept company with all manner of strange creatures—creatures whose names were also lie-labels, but whose being may once have been real, or at least hypothetical. He could name them—most of them—but he could not understand them. He had no pre-conceived attitude appropriate to them, nor any chain of logic which might help him decide.

They were the creatures of Hell. True Hell. Real Hell.

Not Dante's Inferno, but Euchronia's Tartarus. The Underworld. The world beneath the bowels of the Earth.

Knowing as he did that Hell was real, and knowing that there was no conceivable doubt of that fact, Carl Magner had little alternative but to accept the revelations of his dreams as realities. Because dreams were extinct, the unreality of dreams was by no means axiomatic. It did not even seem probable to Carl Magner. He looked upon the experiences of his sleep as an extra sense—an ultra-sight. There was no other way he *could* think of them.

Given that Hell was real, given that the nightmare experience was real, Carl Magner had no alternative but to think that the urgency of the dream, the madness of the dream, the fierceness of the dream, and the fearfulness of the dream were meaningful. The feelings of fear and compulsion were purposeful. Magner thought—and what else could he think? —that the dreams were not only trying to tell him something, but trying to make him act on it. He alone, of the millions of men who inhabited Euchronia's Millennium, was prey to this compulsion, this fear, this need.

There was something messianic in the very fact of his perennial nightmare.

In Magner's dreams, the Underworld was filled—positively *filled,* or it seemed so—with people. People living under the stars, *trapped* forever under the cold light of the alien stars. It was their terror which Magner felt, or so he thought. It was their compulsion.

He hardly sensed the people as individuals at all. He was aware of them *en masse,* as a unit, as a gargantuan hive organism, perpetually growing, and dying by degrees. But it was essentially human. He sensed the people of the Underworld as a whole race, but it was definitely a human race. Magner could identify with those people—he *was* identified with them. In his sympathy, he identified his fear with their fear, his nightmare with their nightmare.

Magner, in his sleep, was enmeshed in a gruesome, gluesome phantasmagoria of images which forced him to react. He could not exempt himself from the sensations of feet in sticky earth, lungs filling with dead, fetid air, gullets sucking up filthy water, any more than he could exempt himself from the terror. In his dreams, he was never clean, because excrement of all kinds was *always* close to him. He sweated constantly. It was hot, and worse than humid. It was glutinous.

Often in his dreams he found himself running—from the

falling, staring stars, from the fluttering, screaming (?), nightflying moths, from the multicolored, shinyskinned, click-clicking crabs. But the running was so slow, his limbs so gummed down, his environs so thick and turgid, that he never got anywhere at all. The creatures of the eternal night kept coming. Eternally.

They never caught him, save by degrees.

The worst thing of all—absolutely the worst—was the fact that he passed so easily from the Hell-world of his nightmare to the real world of his waking life. The one faded into the other with a casual smoothness like the changing of images in a holoreceiver. The world of his inner, secret life and the world in which he lived as one of the infinitely privileged of Euchronia's Millennium were not merely close. They overlapped.

At best, they touched. At worst, they were one and the same Earth.

Carl Magner believed, deeply and sincerely—and what else *could* he believe?—that his nightmare was a message and a command. He believed that the people of the Underworld were asking . . . demanding . . . his help.

3

Chemec followed the four aliens along the contour of the hill. Their incredible stink was still filling his nostrils, but he had already become used to it, and it was no longer painful or sickening. It was, in the final analysis, only slightly unpleasant. Its pervasive quality made him feel exposed. He felt that he would not be able to smell a harrowhound at close quarters. This scared him, though he must have known that the smell would send a harrowhound running.

In consequence of his fear, Chemec walked with his ears pricked and his eyes—normally quiet and idle—flicking furiously from side to side. Sometimes he brought both eyes forward at once to focus and give him stereoscopic vision, but that was little enough use in the dim outdoors—he considered it a child's trick, or a device for reading by lamplight.

Superficially, the strangers resembled men. Men Without

Souls, chiefly. But their clothing was not man-like, if it really was clothing. They were hairless—bald as eggs. They had bulky packs on their backs and they carried things— not axes, not spears, nor knives, but most definitely the produce of Heaven Above. But there was more to their presence here than a visitation from Heaven Above. They were more alien than that. They wore masks, but not painted man-masks after the fashion of the Ahrima. Small masks, with eye- and nose-pieces. They moved like nothing on Earth, walking high and slow, with no semblance of care or caution.

Their strangeness was frightening to Chemec. He stumbled once and disturbed a flight of ghosts. They fluttered madly up into the air and a big bat swooped out of nowhere to snap one of them into its mouth. The rest clicked softly as they spiralled back into the shelter of the silkenhairs, swaying in mid air as their huge papery wings jockeyed for position.

The aliens saw neither the flight of the ghosts nor the swoop of the bat, although no real man could possibly have remained unaware. Chemec could even smell the incident, despite the scent of the aliens. The panic of the ghosts had oozed from their pores into the night air—a warning to all who lurked nearby. But not the strangers.

A few moments later, the aliens did come to a halt— suddenly—and Chemec's heart seemed to recoil as he thought that they might have known he was following all the time. But he was not *that* old—his heart did not stop, and his body froze into perfect stillness. He might have smelled of fear . . . just a little. But he was entitled to that, while he was dogging the footsteps of the unknown.

But the strangers had not seen Chemec. Instead they had seen Stalhelm, for the first time, nestling in the valley beyond the hill. They had not realized it was there, despite the fact that the slopes on which they now walked bore the unmistakable signs of human usage. Chemec realized that the aliens were idiots. They were crippled in the senses—lame in the very being.

While he was still, a crab walked from the shadow of a cranebow and crossed his path. It was only a few feet away, and he could have picked it up, ripped away its claws and cracked its shell between his teeth in a matter of seconds. But he let it go. He often did. He thought of himself as

Chemec the crab. Bent-legged Chemec, who preferred other meat as a matter of distinction and self-pride.

The strangers moved off again, walking straight toward Stalhelm. The villagers knew by now that an enemy—they had to be presumed enemies—was approaching, and they would also know that Chemec was following. They would be sure that he was doing his job, holding his stone axe ready for action. Twice, or maybe more, Orgond and Yewen had brought up the idea of his being made Star King, but he had always been ready to be tested, and he had always passed the test, bent leg notwithstanding. Even Old Man Yami was something of a friend to him, despite the fact that he was crippled. But there had to be limits on friendship for the Old Man. The only certain thing in life was the fact that the Old Man would one day be the Star King, and the Old Man was ever more ready to submit someone else to the test in his place. Nobody wanted to be starshine when his closest friend was sitting by the fire. Friendship had limits.

The strangers walked all the way to the earthwall as if they expected the gates to be opened before them and the people of the village to come out crying welcome. But the gates remained firm, and half a hundred arrows were already notched to bowstring. The warriors of Stalhelm waited, but they were anxious, and when the smell took over their nostrils they would be keen to kill. The aliens had no chance at all of life. If they had not worn masks . . .

Yami, brave Yami, testing his own patience and his own courage, because he was full of confidence, let them come to the very threshold of his village.

It was a fine and beautiful gate that opened the way into Stalhelm, sown with the bones of a hundred and fifty men, with every skull set in the wall on the grand curve. Every skull was an honest one—or no man would admit otherwise, if it were not so. (In Walgo, so Chemec and every man in the village firmly believed, they sowed their gate with the bones of their own dead. Even their women. But the men of Walgo had no Souls, by definition, and so—to them—it probably did not matter.)

The strangers muttered among themselves as they stood before the skull-gate. Chemec was astonished to hear that they spoke his own language. Real Ingling. He could understand every word they said.

How, he wondered, could aliens know the language of the Underworld? Even the men of the Underworld could not *all* speak Ingling—not good Ingling, at any rate. The Cuchumanates, for instance, had only a few words, and the harrowhounds had some foul barking-language that was exclusively their own (or so it was said).

Chemec moved closer to the strangers, confident by now that they were practically deaf and without the sense of smell, and they would not know that he was right behind them unless they turned round. They did not turn, but they did stop talking before he had caught the real thread of what they were saying. The great gate of Stalhelm was opening, just a crack.

Chemec had not expected it. He stopped dead, and waited.

Old Man Yami . . . brave Yami . . . came out. Only Camlak, hardly more than a boy, was with him. Yami felt the need to stand a test. Perhaps it was wise, bearing in mind the rumors about Ermold's bloodthirst. It did seem that much time had gone into memory since the last Communion of Souls. Yami was preparing in advance for the inevitable challenges. He was dressed in his Oracle clothes, and he was emptyhanded. (But his boy-son Camlak carried a long steel knife. Heaven-sent tool to carve Heaven-come meat.)

A row of faces gradually filled itself in along the earth-wall, fleshed faces mingling with the ice-white skulls. A few children climbed bodily on to the stockade, greedy for the sight and smell of some Heavenly blood. It was probably the only chance they would ever get.

Yami sat on the ground, and indicated that Camlak should sit beside him. Camlak, who was studying the art of leadership in preparation for the day when he would try to take the Old Man's place, took up his assigned position with alacrity, showing no fear whatsoever.

The bone-woven gate oozed shut behind them.

Chemec crouched, eager to see with what kind of mockery the Old Man was going to taunt the strangers before they were slaughtered.

The strangers squatted in a semicircle, waiting for Yami to speak.

"We have come here from the world above," said one of the strangers, pointing, first at himself and then at the sky, as if he thought that Yami was a fool.

"I know that," said Yami calmly.

"My name is Ryan Magner," said the stranger.

"And what have you brought to give us?" demanded Yami.

"We have come to talk to you," said Ryan. "We want to learn about you."

Yami laughed, sharply at first, and then authoritatively, until the warriors on the wall, and the women behind it, and the children swarming everywhere all took up the note and screamed their derision.

The laughter went on for a long time.

4

In his dreams Carl Magner was drowning. He was dying, and he knew it. The pressure of . . .

The pressure was intolerable.

Waking, Carl Magner preserved his fear. He was really afraid. Afraid in reality. Something was very wrong.

He knew the secrets of Hell. He did not know that the stars stood still in the sky beneath his feet in the same way that he knew the stars above his head were distant suns, but nevertheless . . .

The consequences of the knowledge were by no means equivalent. He knew about the excrement and the hothouse effect and the radioactive waste and the wrecked world of prehistory. One way or another, he knew. Such knowledge was not censored from the learning of the citizens of Euchronia's Millennium, but only from the myths. *The Marriage of Heaven and Hell* was complete and plucked clean out of the closets of his mind. He had drawn some inspiration and a vestige of understanding from a study of Blake, but in the end his need to misread and misinterpret the original and twist it to his own purposes had proved unconquerable. He believed in his own fourfold vision, not in Blake's.

Carl Magner was still afraid.

The pressure was forcing him to . . .

5

At the end of the second dark age, when the coldness of imminent exterminability became just a little too much to bear, and the clothes of madness too thin to wear (the second dark age is also known as the age of psychosis) it became clear that the world was irrevocably lost. The surface of the Earth was ruined.

The Euchronian Movement became the only significant form of protest against the extinction of knowledge, culture, civilization and other things which human beings might then have called humanity. The Movement specialized in cold equations—for years it had been quoting cold equations as recruitment propaganda and protest against the continuing furious spoilage of the world. In the end, the cold equations became simultaneous, and combined into a single absolute equation. The world was dying. A new world would have to be built. The Movement put in hand plans to construct a shell which would enclose the entire land surface of the Earth: a gigantic platform upon which a new civilization could be built from first principles.

The idea was ludicrous. The equation, however, was capable of only the one solution. In addition, the idea of starting afresh was both exciting and attractive. Most telling of all, it came to represent hope. The Movement adopted a political attitude of casual optimism and continued to play its figures icy cool. It might take a million years. But things might get easier as time went by. Perhaps five hundred thousand would suffice.

The Plan (The Euchronian Plan) got under way. Earth and Earth's humanity did not possess the technology required to raise the platform, nor could they imagine where they were going to get the necessary power. But they began work anyhow.

Even as a gesture, the project was a worthwhile endeavor, and even as a failure it would be quite some gesture. There was no shortage of manpower placed at the disposal of the Planners. The operation began at a thousand points all over the globe. The Movement gobbled up governments and nations, and took over a dispirited world by bloodless revolution. The whole human race, insofar as it was organized, became Euchronia. The rebels were neither expelled nor hated, but merely ignored, as though they had forfeited their humanity.

Work went on, calmly, implacably. Progress was made. And the end remained quite patently impossible. It was not so much that the project was beyond all human ambition and ability, merely that time was so completely set against them. They had not the time to learn because they had not the time to live. The world could not support their effort. The exhausted world simply could not meet its deadlines.

Sisyr's starship arrived on Earth during the first century of the Plan. It was pure coincidence. Reason (cold equations) said that a technology which could build starships could also build a new world, and so Euchronia asked Sisyr for help. He considered the problem in all its aspects and finally declared that the job could be done and that he would take the responsibility on a contractual basis.

He sent a message back to his own people asking for supplies and for technical assistance. The message took decades to cross the interstellar gulf, the supplies and assistance took centuries. In the meantime, Sisyr and several generations of Euchronians collaborated in revising the Plan, educating the labor force and discovering new potentials in the wasted lands of Earth. There *may*, at this point, have been a hypothetical choice between building the new world and reclaiming the old. If so, the commitment of the human race to Euchronia was such that no choice ever became obvious.

Sisyr and a small army of helpers of his own kind supervised the construction of the platform over the next few thousand years. By the time it had grown to cover the Earth's land surface, most of the aliens had gone back to the distant stars.

Sisyr remained to coordinate the rebuilding of a viable civilization on that surface. He assisted in the modeling of the Earth's new surface, he collaborated on the scheme of land management, and he provided designs for the entire pattern of the maintenance of life. The social system itself was designed by the Movement, but it was designed to fit the world and the environment which had been built largely to Sisyr's specifications.

In return for his services, Sisyr was allowed to make his

home on the remade Earth. He remained isolated from the Euchronian community, but pledged to keep its laws. He built himself a palace and retired. Some eight or nine hundred years before the Euchronian Plan, in its final form, came to fruition Sisyr had ceased to take any active part in it. Starships called at Earth three or four times each century, but they called on Sisyr, not the people of Earth. The people of Earth had nothing at all to do with starships once all the necessary aid from the star-worlds had been delivered.

Sisyr's contribution to the Plan resulted in its successful completion in a little over eleven thousand years—a short time, comparatively speaking. The Euchronians, of course, claimed the triumph as their own—as, indeed, it was. Theirs had been the vision, theirs the labor, theirs the will. Sisyr had only lent them time which they needed badly.

Sisyr, like the Underworld the Euchronians had left behind, remained known to every citizen. But only as a fact, and an irrelevant fact at that. He had no part in the mythology of the New World.

The Euchronian Millennium was finally declared, and the people became free of their total obligation to the Plan. They were released, to enjoy its fruits, to make what they would of their new life. The Movement did not claim that the society it had designed was Utopian, but it did claim that it had Utopian potential. All that was needed to make perfection was the will of the people. The society was designed to be stable, but not sterile. Euchronia's stability was dynamic stability. Neither perfect happiness nor perfect freedom was immediately on tap, but Euchronia did what it could, and waited—with casual optimism—for the reheated equations of life and death to work themselves out.

The completion of the Plan had demanded—indeed, the whole philosophy of Euchronia had demanded—that while the Plan was incomplete the people should remain single-minded, working together to the same end. The Movement had helped single-mindedness along somewhat, by devious means which seemed to have excellent results. When the Millennium began, the hegemony of the Movement retained those same devious means in order to assist society in its first, difficult years of freedom and readjustment.

The single most remarkable fact about Euchronia's Millennium, about Euchronia itself and its leaders in particular, was the apparent blindness—willful blindness—exhibited with respect to the wider contexts of existence. They lived in a thin stratum, paying no heed whatsoever to the realms of Tartarus below, nor to the infinite universe above. But they lived in the early years of the Millennium in the heritage of eleven thousand years of narrow-mindedness, in which the only fragment of existence which mattered was that thin stratum. It took time for them even to begin to realize that such tight boundaries could not contain them.

6

The strangers tried to communicate with the Old Man, but he was not interested in communication. He was not interested in their questions or in their reasons. He was interested primarily in showmanship. The aliens were merely the means to his end.

He exposed himself to them, and they did not kill him. He laughed at them, and they were patently hurt by his laughter. Then he made silence fall, and he began to put his patience on show, knowing that the silent waiting would ultimately hurt the invaders as much as the laughter.

Chemec knew that when the silence had stretched far enough, Yami would have the aliens killed. There was no possible question about that. Chemec saw no other way. Nor did the warriors at the wall. There were some inside who *did* see things another way, who might have wished that the demands upon Yami were not as they were. The readers, undoubtedly, saw the advantages implicit in making friends with the men from Heaven. They would have wished to do just that. But they knew as well as Yami did that life was simply not like that. There were ways of doing things which had been well tried.

Outside the gate the boy Camlak probably had more sympathy with the readers' point of view than he had with his father's. He was studying statecraft carefully, but he was still at the stage when he thought that the Old Man was obeyed because it was simply right that others should obey him. He had no conception of the delicate matters of deciding fitness to rule and make decisions. Decisions came hard to Camlak because his judgment was always crowded with motives and reasons and possibilities. His head would have to be clear of all that before he was allowed to take Yami's place.

The silence which Yami had made grew old, and finally died.

"I am Yami," said the Old Man. They were the only words he spoke. He knew the value of words and the majesty of simplicity.

The strangers had grown visibly uneasy once their initial attempts to kill the silence had faded away into muttering confusion and final bewilderment. When Yami spoke, they relaxed as if some wonderful thing had happened. They smiled beneath their macabre masks. One of them reached forward, his hand open as though he wished to take hold of Yami. The Old Man remained still, and stared the hand away as though he were outfacing a snake.

The alien withdrew his hand. "I'm sorry," he said.

The great gate opened again behind the sitting men. Evidently Yami had been playing a prepared part. The end had been decided before he had stepped out of the gate. The strangers sat, quietly and comfortably, seemingly content, while the young woman Myddal fetched bowls of warm liquid, one by one, and placed one in front of each of the aliens. Eventually, she gave the last bowl to Yami. It obviously contained something different because it was not steaming. The strangers saw this, and even though their minds were crippled they evidently suspected something. But the one who had called himself Ryan Magner sipped from his own bowl and signaled with his hand. The others did the same.

Yami drained his bowl, and watched while his victims did the same. Then he laughed again—not loudly, this time, nor insistently. No one joined in. It was the laugh of a private moment—a gesture of personal satisfaction. The laugh was low, and it bubbled over the Old Man's tongue.

"It's poison, Ryan," said one of the strangers, bitterly. Three of them—all except the leader—knew then that they had been murdered. The leader would not admit it, though he must have *felt* it to be true, by now.

"You bastards," said one of the men, as they all struggled to rise. Only one actually managed to make it to his feet.

As the man stood tall, Chemec raised himself to the full extent of his three feet ten inches and reached up to kill the man. He was careful to smash the spine below the atlas vertebra, so as to preserve the skull unblemished.

7

Burstone dragged the heavy suitcase along the catwalk to the head of the ladder which descended into the depths of the pit. The steady throb of the great machine filled his ears and blotted out the soft footfalls of the man who was following him.

When he reached the ladder Burstone secured the case to a chain which dangled from a wide axle. He pushed it clear of the catwalk and began to wind the handle on the axle, paying out the chain. The lamps which were arrayed in a long line beside the ladder (for the benefit of the maintenance men who occasionally had to attend the machine) were dim and yellow, and the suitcase soon became a blur in the half-light.

Joth paused to wait for Burstone to finish lowering the case. He was perhaps forty or fifty yards away, and he held himself flat against the body of the machine. He was not quite invisible, but Burstone showed no inclination to look back—he had no reason to think that anyone might follow him down here. Hardly anyone ever came down this low. The machine never went wrong and routine checks were made only twice a year or thereabouts.

Joth was sweating quite heavily. He could feel the heat of the machine through the thin cloth of his shirt, and his own flesh seemed to be very hot, glowing with insistent excitement. He had expected it to be warm down here, but he had not expected anything of the quality of his own reaction. The pressure of his heartbeat sent thin waves of nausea through his body. He could not explain himself.

Burstone was also hot, but he had been through this operation a hundred times before. His reactions to what he was doing and how were qualitatively somewhat different from Joth's, but it was in the integration of his psyche with the physiological symptoms that the real difference lay. Joth was experiencing a mixture of fear and excitement, and to him it was raw sensation. Burstone's mixture of feeling was rather more complex, and he was savoring the delicate blend and balance. To him, this was *good*. This was the fulfilment of a real purpose.

It would have been impossible to hear the soft bump as the suitcase hit bottom, but Burstone knew almost to the inch how much of the chain to let out. He was ready for it to go slack, and he wasted no time. The economy of his motions, the fluid efficiency of the whole enterprise, provided a fair measure of the kick. He heaved himself over the edge of the catwalk, placing his feet comfortably into the metal rungs of the slender ladder, and began to descend comfortably and easily.

Joth moved to the head of the ladder. He gripped the rail of the catwalk hard on either side of the gap, squeezed, and then eased his body forward so that he could peer down into the abyss. It scared him. Height, darkness, uncertainty—all these things were relative strangers to his senses. He had every right and reason to be frightened. He waited for a full minute longer than prudence demanded, gathering his courage and determination, before he followed Burstone into the depths.

He could feel the beating of his heart, and it seemed to be racing ever faster by comparison with the deep, steady beat of the machine. He did not know the purpose of the machine. He took machines for granted. Machines were everywhere, and no one asked how they integrated themselves into the complex web of function which supplied human need in almost every way. Machines were the substance of life itself.

Burstone reached the bottom. He was alone in a tiny pool of light, surrounded by an illimitable darkness. Hiding in the darkness was the machine, and machines parasitic upon it, and machines parasitic upon them. There were pipes and wires and bolts and welds. He knew almost nothing about their outlay or their role. He had never felt the need to explore at this level. This level was dead, with nothing to offer a connoisseur's curiosity. Electronic anatomy and mechanical physiology were not his subjects any more than they were Joth's. What Burstone was interested in was life, and life was a long way below him yet.

With complete assurance, needing no light, Burstone moved away from the foot of the ladder, dragging the suitcase behind him.

By the time Joth reached the foot of the ladder Burstone was long gone. Joth cursed his reluctance to descend and crushed a suddenly flowering urge to retrace his path. The anxiety which had made him cling with such fierce determination to the ladder at every step now held his hands tight, and it took a real effort to make them let go and leave him standing on his own feet. He realized now that he was at the very bottom of the world, and the knowledge that space and the Underworld might be only mere inches beneath his feet made him think that he was in imminent danger, somehow, of falling *through* the floor. He strained his ears, but he could hear nothing. He knew he would have to use his torch.

Even by the dim light of the lampcell set in the side of the machine he could see which way Burstone had gone. There was only one blurred pathway through the thick-layered dust—one worn clean by many journeys, but only one pair of feet. And a suitcase.

Joth switched on his torch. It was a tiny device, with a crystal as small as an eyeball. The beam it shone was pencil-thin. It would have been invisible to the human eye. He set out to follow the path through the dust, hoping that Burstone would have already passed on to the next stage of his descent, but certain in any case that the other could not see the tiny glow that was following him even if he cared to look back.

Ahead of him, Joth saw a quick flicker of light which died away to a soft glow almost imperceptible to his retuned eyes.

At the end of the pathway in the dust was a circular hole in the floor. A cover which had been clamped to it had been removed to one side. Another windlass was positioned beside the hole—bigger and stronger than the one which Burstone had used to lower the suitcase from the catwalk. It was whirring softly—operating automatically. Joth guessed that the strong double chain which unwound with leisurely steadiness supported a cage or basket of some kind, in which both Burstone and the suitcase were riding. They were on their way to the Underworld—to the surface of the ancient Earth.

Joth switched off his torch. The soft pearl-white glow which limned the black rim of the hole surprised him. He had always thought of the Underworld as being pitch dark. He reached up to adjust his eyes, setting them to take the maximum benefit from the light of the Underworld's stars.

He got down on to his hands and knees and crept close to the lip of the hole. He looked into the Underworld, from the viewpoint of one of its own stars.

He could see a long way . . . hills, forests of weird fleshy plants, intermingled with others of a squatter, more varied nature.

Wilderness, broken and confused, but most definitely not dead. Very much alive, even rich. But he could see no sign of human habitation. Except, perhaps, for the low and even ridge which ran alongside a stretch of water away to his right. That might . . . just *might* . . . be a wall.

Far below him, the cage was still descending.

Joth nodded, reassuring himself that all was well. Then he readjusted his eyes, switched on the ultraviolet torch, and looked around for somewhere convenient to hide.

8

Burstone and Ermold haggled for an hour or more—though the time meant little or nothing to the man of the Underworld. Two warriors from Walgo, Fortex and Theogon, gave some desultory help to Ermold in his arguments, but were really only along for the ride.

The girl, on the other hand, was something different. Burstone had never seen the girl before. She was tied to Ermold —actually, physically tied. The cord was round her neck and his wrist. Occasionally, when she thought Ermold wasn't paying any attention, she would pick at the cord with her fingernails. Ermold usually caught on and swatted her within a minute or so. Once he kicked her.

From Burstone's point of view, the haggling was virtually a waste of time. It always dragged on too long. But he stood to gain nothing by it—the price he received for the goods in the case went to the supplier. So far as he was concerned, the material transaction was just an exchange of garbage. He was in it for quite different reasons. For the experience, in fact.

The girl was interesting. The girl could make this whole trip worthwhile. Her presence did something for the occasion, though none of the men ever mentioned her or referred to her presence. Burstone never touched her, never attempted to talk to her and never asked any questions about her, but he was aware of her, and aware of the cord which attached her to Ermold, which she seemed resolved to break. Ermold was breaking her in. He was a sadist.

The warrior had aged quite noticeably over the last couple of intervals. It seemed such a short time ago that he had been, by Burstone's standards of judgment, a young man. Now he was past middle age. Time moved faster in the Underworld, if it could be said to move at all. Men aged faster, packed up their lives more economically, wound up their existence more tightly.

Ermold's voice was cracked, he punctuated all his sentences with curses, and his temper seemed inordinately short. Burstone carried a gun, of course, but he knew that Ermold and his men were fast enough to have him in slices before he could kill one of them. So he was frightened. He fed on that fear, as if it was his only pleasure.

Burstone gathered from the excess of bitterness and nastiness which flowed out of Ermold that the chieftain was sick of the whole silly business. But both men knew that Ermold couldn't do without Burstone, and in the end he had to accept Burstone's terms. If there had been any alternative at all . . . but there wasn't.

So Ermold fingered the sharp edge of his knife—a knife which Burstone had provided for him—and thought dark thoughts, indulging himself in crude fantasies of what he might do to the man from Heaven . . . but dared not.

In the end, however, the deal was completed, and the two parties went their separate ways. Burstone took his parcel, Ermold made Fortex carry the heavy suitcase.

Hauling himself back up to the Overworld was a long and laborious job. The hoist was properly counterbalanced and the machinery was in perfect order, but Burstone had seen a gradual deterioration in the performance of the machine over a period of time. Whether the decline was due to a failure of the operating mechanism or a failure of his own patience he was not sure. He was not mechanically minded.

Up at the top, in the roof of the Underworld and the deepest cellars of Euchronia, Burstone carefully secured the hoist and clamped the circular cap over the hole. He lit a flicker briefly to make sure of the exact direction of the path back to the ladder. It was a cursory, almost unnecessary gesture motivated by long habit. Normally he let the flame sputter for only a couple of seconds. This time, it lasted longer while he noticed the second set of footprints which led away from his doorway into Hell.

Then, giving no indication of the fact that he knew some-one else was there, or that he cared, he walked away into the darkness.

9

Half an hour later he came back. The hoist was down, the cables were slack. He wound the cage back up again, and found to his utmost satisfaction that it arrived empty. He secured it for a second time, clamped down the cover, and ignited his flicker for a couple of seconds. Then he walked away. This time he went all the way back up to the sunlit spaces of the civilized world, wondering whether his route was still viable.

Whoever had followed him was trapped in the world below. It was some time before he would be making another trip, and the spy would undoubtedly be dead long before then. The only problem was whether anyone else knew about him and, if so, why they were interested.

10

The Underworld did not, of course, begin all at once. The eclipse of the old surface by the new was a gradual affair, taking several thousands of years. What is more, the plat-form which was to become the Overworld was started in several sections. Thus the perimetric borderlines between the two worlds were both extensive and slow-moving.

Gradually, the life-system of Earth moved across those borders. Under each section of the covered world some kind of ecosystem survived from the ancient world. The surface was already spoiled and communities of organisms had been in a state of dynamic imbalance for some time before the light of the sun was gradually cut out. The extra pressure imposed by the theft of the sun was great, but not ultimately decisive. When the sections of the platform joined up, so did the two struggling—and not necessarily similar—communities which had grown beneath them. The comingling of the communities induced competition and complementation, and assisted the evolutionary adaptation of the new whole.

Homo sapiens was the species which adapted most easily to the new régime, and by his active interference he encouraged and assisted many other species to do likewise. Not all men belonged to Euchronia. Some preferred their own concept of freedom—freedom from a plan which would demand their total commitment and pay them—individually speaking—absolutely nothing. There were a good many men who regarded the New World as a dream—castles in the air—and who thought it both right and wise to commit themselves to the Old World, and to dedicate themselves to making what they could of it.

Despite a certain amount of mutual dislike and resentment, a good deal of trade went on between the Euchronians and the Groundmen for many centuries while the platform was under construction. Without the food supplies, and to a lesser extent the mineral supplies provided by the men who were committed to the ground, the early years would have been far more difficult for the Planners. But as the platform grew it grew over the lands which were used by the Groundmen—and it swallowed up the lands of the cooperative just as it swallowed up the lands of the hostile. For many centuries there was a bitter war fought on the expanding frontiers of the Overworld. The Men of the Old World thought they had dealt fairly with Euchronia, and that the theft of their sun was the harshest of evil treatment. The Euchronians believed that the Plan was all-important, that there could be no compromises, and they offered the only compensation they had to offer to all those on the ground—the opportunity to join the Plan. Most of the Groundmen refused, and most of them migrated before the advancing world of darkness, until there was nowhere else left to run, except to the islands which were too tiny to interest the Planners. Many of the islands were already incapable of sus-

taining human life—there was a poor living to be made
from the desolated sea—and many more became so as the
hordes descended on their shores. Some island colonies were
successful, but for the vast majority of men there were only
two choices which mattered: Heaven and Hell. When the
platform finally closed its grip on the world, the larger number capitulated, and ascended to Heaven and commitment to
the Plan (which was still millennia away from completion).
A substantial number, however—perhaps a surprising number—stayed with the Old World, accepting the pale electric
stars as a permanent substitute for the garish sun. Their
motives were many, and usually mixed. Bitterness and
sheer hatred for the Planners were prominent, but not
paramount. The dominant reason for the human race refusing to quit the Old World was a commitment to it and an
identification with it that was as powerful as the commitment
of Euchronia to its Plan.

The Old World was past redemption in terms of the human civilization which had grown up in it. But that did not
mean that life was doomed to extinction, nor even that there
was any realistic possibility that life would become extinct.
It merely meant that most of the old species had to die, and
that hitherto unimportant species would become vital to the
system, and also that new species would have to be discovered. A whole new contract for the interaction of life
with environment had to be drawn up and negotiated—
negotiated largely (but not entirely, thanks to the presence
of man) by trial and error.

The lowest stratum of the biotic hierarchy, the stratum of
primary production, underwent the greatest changes. The
priority enjoyed by photosynthetic forms was lost. Plant
evolution virtually abandoned the angiosperms and reverted
to a more primitive state in order to rebuild. The stars were
vital in that they allowed the bridge a small extra margin,
but in the end they were quite useless as sources of energy
(save to a few fugitive species of little importance). Their
only real function was to provide for the senses of much
higher organisms—man, in particular.

Obviously, it was the fungi and the nonphotosynthetic
algae which proved most readily adaptable to the new conditions. They underwent an evolutionary renaissance with
great alacrity.

The specialists of the second stratum—the primary consumers—went the way of their diet. The generalists, how-

ever, simply reordered their personal priorities. Man had no chance at all of saving the cow, the sheep or the hen, but he could and did save the pig.

In the higher strata, the percentage devastation decreased serially. Secondary consumers tended to be much less particular than primaries, and had an advantage because of the relative success of some primary species. The more secondaries that were successful, the easier it became for the tertiaries. There was change in the higher regions of life's hierarchy—of course there was change—but there was a relatively low level of extinction. In terms of appearance, change was slow but eventually drastic, but in terms of evolutionary continuity there was nothing like the cataclysmic reorganization suffered in the lower strata. Only the specialist insectivores and some of the carnivores disappeared from the scene that was visible to the naked eye. Microbiotically, things were slightly more complicated, but the principle remained the same.

The omnivores were in no real trouble (in terms of racial survival) at any time. Any species which had survived the rigors of the second dark age was unlikely to be troubled by the roofing of the world. Man's ancient allies the cat and the dog both survived—but independently of man. His ancient rivals, the rat and the cockroach, also survived—indeed, they thrived.

Extinction was responsible for very few of the changes which took place in the tertiary strata. Adaptation, on the other hand, demanded that vast changes in behavioral patterns—and often vast changes in physical form—must take place.

Under the circumstances of such a vast reorganization evolution was permitted—forced, in fact—to work very quickly indeed. The rate of evolution, not just in one or a group of species but throughout the life-system, passed into tachytelic mode.

Evolution by natural selection can be immensely costly. In order to replace erstwhile-useful genes by now-useful genes, vast numbers of individuals in a number of generations have to die. The load on the species becomes tremendous. This demands great fecundity and the acceptance of a very high mortality rate. When unusual requirements are placed on a species the gross numbers of that species inevitably shrink. The more the numbers shrink the faster the turnover of genes proceeds. But there is a threshold beyond which the species cannot replenish itself no matter how fast its rate of evolution. At or near that threshold the evolutionary process is capable of incredible bursts of change. Below it, extinction becomes inevitable and the species dies amid a truly frantic burst of adaptive attempts. If, however, the evolutionary burst at threshold is successful in providing a whole new schema of adaptation *without* taking the absolute numbers of the standing population too low, the evolutionary burst is followed by a rapid increase in numbers, during which selection still continues to foster a rate of evolution faster than the "normal" horotelic mode characteristic of a stable species in a stable environment. Relatively rare species with a high degree of genetic homogeneity existing in ultra-stable environments may slip into the third mode of evolutionary pace—the bradytelic—whereby change slows down drastically and the species retains little capacity for change.

During the thousands of years that the Euchronians were taking their Plan to ultimate completion the tachytelic evolution which embraced the entire Underworld life-system completely changed the face of the lower Earth. A few thousand years is a very brief interval in evolutionary terms but the circumstances were highly unusual, and the process was—to some extent—stimulated and guided by the efforts of mankind. Man himself was by no means immune from the changes he helped to bring about, and the human race—or races, to be strictly accurate—which survived in the Underworld were very different in many ways from the race which survived up above. Even this race—Euchronian man—underwent some evolution during the millennia of the Plan, for the circumstances of that race also necessitated a rate of change somewhat higher than horotelic.

By the time the Euchronian Millennium began, the Underworld had slowed in its evolutionary progress. But the stable horotelic rate which was becoming characteristic of that world was by no means the same as the horotelic rate in the Overworld. In the Underworld there was still a régime of rigorous competition demanding evolutionary divergence. In addition to that there was an extra, and by no means insignificant, load imposed by the high frequency of mutation. The radiation output of the Overworld was directed downwards. Radioactive wastes were disposed of down below, and though they were carefully packaged the rate of leakage was high.

Man—omnivorous, intelligent and at the very highest level

of the biotic hierarchy—changed least of the species at that level, and even the human race suffered a tripartite sub-speciation. The species which changed most were the semi-intelligent species which had cohabited with man the concrete jungles of the age of psychosis. Such species had been under considerable adaptive pressure for some centuries before the advent of Euchronia's Plan. Under the new régime that pressure burst the conceptual barriers which hindered mind development, and three species quickly evolved intelligence of an unusual order.

While the Euchronians began their new life after the Plan had been brought to a successful conclusion, the people of the Underworld were still faced with a fearsome struggle for existence. While the one world settled down to embrace total stability, the other remained in a state of virtual chaos.

11

The Marriage of Heaven and Hell by Carl Magner became available at all household lineprinters and the usual public outlets within a matter of minutes after the job of coding it into the cybernet was complete. The information that the book was so available took a little longer to circulate, and even then there was no mad rush to have a look at it.

Many people misinterpreted the use of a well-known title by William Blake. It was by no means uncommon in Euchronia's Millennium for people to write long commentaries on, and even new versions of, prehistoric literature. After all, the essence and the meaning of ancient works had changed completely in the light of brand new Euchronian perspectives, and there was an eleven-thousand-year gap in the more abstract realms of cultural studies to be intellectually bridged. The assumption that Magner's work was intimately connected with Blake's was not unnatural. It is entirely possible that some of the men and women who did read the book soon after publication actually misread the whole text on the basis of that presumed connection. It is not inconceivable that given a decent interval and a certain amount of wayward luck Magner might have become something of a literary phenomenon, hailed as a genius in some quarters and viciously slandered in others.

But the *avant-garde* missed their chance (or Magner missed his). It was not too long before it was realized that the work stood by itself, that what it proposed was real, and that Magner actually meant what he said. This revelation caused something of a stir, but it was a stir of an entirely different kind.

The book gave a detailed account of life in the Underworld as it was lived by the human race. The account was possessed of a strange kind of hysteria, and the images presented lacked overall coherency though they had undoubted force and individual clarity. Many readers came to the conclusion that Magner was, if nothing else, a consummate artist. The bizarre and the terrifying were not common in the literature of the Euchronian Millennium.

The book also presented a strongly worded argument to the effect that Euchronia was guilty of extreme inhumanity in that it chose not to share its wealth with the men on the ground. Magner claimed that Euchronian civilization should not have shut the door on the Underworld when the platform became a single unit. He claimed that the opportunity to join the Movement should have been made available throughout the history of the Plan.

He further claimed that the citizens of the Euchronian Millennium had a moral obligation to throw open the doors to the Underworld, to resume commerce with the men on the ground, to supply their needs, and to allow them—if they wished—to leave the Underworld and take their place in the sun. "We have no right whatsoever," wrote Magner, "to deny the people of the world below the Face of Heaven."

12

It was some two weeks after publication that the Magner affair began to get off the ground. The man who initiated the *cause célèbre* was Alwyn Ballow, a software processer for the holovisual network. He took it to Yvon Emerich, who was *the* major influence in the live media.

Emerich was a busy man. He was a man with a burning need to *keep* himself busy, to burn himself out. He had a great deal of energy to expend and he expended it all outwards, sending it worldwide throughout the network, throwing his sound and fury into every household which cared to switch him on. The sheer power of his extrovert determination was enough to command him a vast audience. He had innumerably more enemies than friends, but his enemies loved him more than his closest allies. He had nothing to offer friends but everything to offer enemies—people luxuriated in the charisma of his attacks, and he attacked everybody, tearing down all points of view with equal verve. No one really suffered from an attack by Emerich simply because in the *laissez-faire* world of the Millennium no one had the level of commitment necessary to suffer destruction at his hands. Argument was a gladiatorial game, in which the loser changed his ground and everybody enjoyed the show.

Ballow was scared stiff of Emerich, but he was willing enough to absorb his fear if he could start something in motion. He confronted Emerich and came straight to the point.

"The Marriage of Heaven and Hell," he said.

"What about it?" demanded Emerich.

"Have you read it?"

"You know damn well I never read anything. I know what it's about. What the hell would I want with it?"

"It's good."

"Call Sauldron. He's an arts man."

"Not that sort of good," Ballow persisted. "Good for a run. It's got one hell of a bite—the first real bite we've seen for a long time. Could be the biggest ever."

"The man's a lunatic," said Emerich shortly—though the fact that he was prepared to argue meant that he was prepared to listen and take note—"and you can't make a big thing out of a lunatic. In the end, a lunatic will make you look a fool. Every time. No percentage."

"No," said Ballow. "This proposal might be insane but it has mileage. It's going to attract some pretty hot discussion at *all* levels. If we can get in now we can carve up that discussion and feed it. It'll go right to the top, and I mean the top. The Eupsychians will take it up purely as agitation, but it's not really a Eupsychian thing. It goes deeper. When this gets to the Hegemony they're going to find that it's hot. It can't be ignored and it can't be laughed off. Heres and his cohort have been retreating toward the wall for forty years or more now and it won't take much more to break their back. This could be it, if it's blown up enough. Somebody somewhere is going to try, and try hard. And we ought to be in there to feed on it. This is our meat, Yvon, provided it's handled right."

Emerich stared at the other man for a few seconds, and then made up his mind. "Okay," he said, and cut the image. The voiceprinter screen faded to dull gray. Emerich remained staring at it for a few seconds more. He was hooked. He would have to chase it if only to find out what the hell Ballow was talking about.

He requisitioned a couple of copies from his desk unit, and scanned the first few pages as they fluttered out of the lineprinter. He grimaced dramatically, and dropped the printout with distaste. He reached for the voiceprinter again. He would have to find someone to read it for him.

13

Having predicted that something was going to start as a result of Magner's book, Ballow was fully committed to doing everything in his power to start it, and thus justify his prediction. He began calling his valued acquaintances in all fields of work as soon as Emerich cut him off. Nobody he called had read the book, and few of them would bother to catch up on it as a result of his recommendation. But most of them would be prepared to talk about it if it was going to become a big talking point.

Within a matter of hours Ballow had precipitated something of a rush on *The Marriage*. Lineprinters in the most unlikely corners of the world were busy clicking out copies at a furious pace. Not many of the copies would be read from beginning to end, but everybody who intended to involve themselves in the debate wanted to have some familiarity with the shape of the work and the style of presentation.

There was something of a snowball effect when the

cybernet made it known that there was expanding interest in the book. The controversy grew by leaps and bounds as individuals selected standpoints and prepared for argument. The promotion of the book to a position of some importance was almost entirely a matter of fashion. It was all something of a game. In the wake of the Euchronian Plan there was not much else it could be. *Everything* was a game, now the Plan was done with. When a single-minded people lose the objective of eleven thousand years of completely focused purpose, it takes time to rediscover anything like a *range* of purpose and endeavor. The whole of life and action is reduced to triviality, and the whole structure of social action has to be rebuilt from the ground up.

The citizens of Euchronia's Millennium had to *evolve* into their new circumstances, and in the strategic absence of virtually all basic social pressures, that evolution was not something which could take place overnight. There had to be some form of struggle to find new things to *need*—not simply to want—and the context of that struggle made it a very difficult one. Euchronia became a world of children and eccentrics the moment the Plan was laid to rest. The Hegemony of the Movement were not surprised—they accepted that a long period of adjustment would be necessary. Indeed, they welcomed the fact, because it gave them a chance to plan the kind of adjustment which would evolve, and it gave them time to fulfill their aim of shaping a stable society. Their work on the physical environment was over, but their work on the human factor was only just begun. By the time that Magner's book was published they had made very little progress indeed (some would have argued that they made none, or less than none) but they were prepared to be generous with time. They still had faith—perfect faith. Again, that was the legacy of eleven thousand years' commitment.

Thus, though Ballow was not an important man, he found it fairly easy to make an issue out of Magner's ideas. If he had not, someone else would have. They were, when all was said and done, rather revolutionary ideas. The fact that virtually no one took Magner seriously in the beginning did not handicap the progress of his work towards popularity (notoriety, at least). And it was inevitable in a world which so desperately needed *some* kind of ideological commitment that he should gradually begin to win supporters.

The snowball grew, and Magner moved ponderously into the political arena.

14

Rafael Heres was by no means pleased when Enzo Ulicon took it into his head to demand an instant discussion of Carl Magner's *The Marriage of Heaven and Hell*.

"I'm in the middle of a game of Hoh," he said, his tone making it quite clear that he resented the interruption.

"Postpone it," said Ulicon.

"I'll lose all semblance of control over the situation," said Heres. "What about the others? They aren't going to take kindly to the interruption."

"Rafael," said Ulicon, "you're the Hegemon. You can't fit the running of the world into the interstices of your social life. There's a storm brewing."

"Don't be ridiculous," said Heres. "This business of opening the Underworld is a farce. It's all under control. It's just a nonsensical argument thrown up to confuse the *real* problems we have to face."

"You aren't going to solve *any* problems playing Hoh," Ulicon pointed out. "I have to talk to you. This is urgent. It's not just talk any more. This thing is touching one of the most fundamental of our problems. *The* most fundamental."

"What do you mean?"

"Interrupt your game and I'll tell you."

Heres, reluctantly, phased himself out of the game, leaving the other players to carry on without him or to let the game go cold while they awaited his return, as they pleased. When he was alone—switched out of the other call circuits, that is—he gave his full attention to Ulicon. He was still wearing his displeasure prominently.

"What is it?" he snapped.

"I've been trying to find out where Magner gets his information," said Ulicon. "He's pretty close-mouthed about it. There are no sources offered in the book or in any of the associated material."

"Magner's son went down there."

"He didn't come back, so far as I can tell. Nor did any of the others. I've conducted a fairly thorough search. If they were using the net they'd be easy to find, but they're not. They could be in Sanctuary, but every source I have says that they aren't. There are four of them—and it's not easy for four men to stay unfound up here. Everything suggests that they went into the Underworld and are still there. In addition, Magner's other son—the younger one—has also slipped out of sight. You may remember the fuss there was about him when he was a child. Anyhow, he's gone too. But Magner hasn't contacted either of them since we first mounted our watch."

"Are you saying that he made it all up?"

"It's a possibility," said Ulicon, "but no, I'm not saying that. I heard a rumor which was much more significant, and I've checked with Magner's doctor. He wouldn't tell me anything directly, but with police help I got some records out of the net. Magner has been consulting his doctor regularly for twenty years. He complains of bad dreams. Nightmares."

"That's not possible," said Heres.

"It's possible, bearing in mind what Magner went through with regard to his younger son. But rumor says that Magner's picture of the Underworld comes straight out of his dreams, and if that's so it's a fact we can't ignore. It's a fact with some rather weighty implications. We need to find out for certain, but what's more important is to decide what we have to do if it *is* true."

"Nothing," said Heres. "It's absurd. It can only be a freak even if it's true. We're hardly likely to have an epidemic of nightmares."

"I'm glad you're sure," said Ulicon. "But it still needs checking."

"You want a meeting of the close council?"

"Naturally."

"Couldn't we keep it between ourselves?"

"Rafael, it's bad enough the close council keeping secrets from the Hegemony, without keeping secrets from one another. All right, I know this will give ammunition to Eliot, but believe me, if the implications of this are as bad as they might be, then Eliot has a strong case. We have to work this out. All of us."

"When?" said Heres.

"Tomorrow. A forgathering. This can't go through the net. We need to talk off the record. But in the meantime I'm going to do some prying and I advise you to do the same. Emerich's on to Magner and there's going to be a splash soon. If this business of dreams crops up and Magner *isn't* the only one, then we have a very big headache indeed. You see?"

Heres saw perfectly clearly. His mind was already working on the point. The implications of Ulicon's argument were deadly, not only to his own personal position, but to the standpoint of the Euchronian Movement.

15

The basis of Euchronianism is the philosophy that better things lie ahead. The Euchronian Movement was founded on the principle of directing change, not on a small scale, but on the largest scale possible. The Euchronian Movement preached the doctrine that to design a model society and predict that it would one day come about was simply not enough. The Movement demanded commitment—commitment to an ideal state which lay so far in the future that no man would live to see it, nor his children, nor his children's children—only descendants so remote that they might number half the human race. The Movement demanded ultimate sacrifice in the name of a goal which could only be a racial goal.

William Blake's "prophetic books" offered the first Euchronian philosophy.

Karl Marx's social science offered the first Euchronian doctrine.

Fundamental to Euchronianism is the intellectual transcendence of pure selfishness. Euchronianism is not necessarily religious, nor is it necessarily socialist. It is, however, necessarily altruistic.

16

Cudal Canal, for the whole of its length, marked the boundary of the land of the Men Without Souls and the land of the Children of the Voice which had come to be called Shairn. It was a natural boundary, and one which nobody was particularly keen to dispute, but over the centuries walls of earth and stone had been erected on either side to emphasize it and to allow some sort of defense of it if the need arose. The canal itself was a vile place—its water was undrinkable and even the crabs would not use it—and the land on either side of it was diseased and swarming with flying insects. It was land that was crossed only by wanderers and invaders. But once now and again it became necessary for a meeting to take place in the neutral territory—a meeting between the Men Without Souls and the Children of the Voice. The former usually came out from Walgo, the latter from Stalhelm.

The Men Without Souls often hit hard times, and when times became too hard they had no alternative but to turn toward Shairn for food. The Children of the Voice managed crops on a large scale and rarely went short of food, even when the migrations threatened to starve them of meat. In peaceful times the men from Walgo would trade regularly with Stalhelm, offering fish and tools for grain and bricks. But times were rarely peaceful, and Ermold of Walgo was by no means a peaceful man. Trade had ceased during the time of his reign, and the meetings by Cudal Canal were rare —forced by necessity upon Ermold's people.

Because Ermold's people were the ones with the dire need the meetings at the canal usually resulted in the better side of the bargain going to Stalhelm. This only made Ermold hate such occasions all the more. When he desperately needed Shairn's grain he had to pay not in fish or other standard trade goods, but in Heaven-metal and Heaven-sent books. Because Shairn had no independent source of such things, and because the Children of the Voice were lovers of books and efficient tools, such things were always in high demand. But the Children of the Voice were prepared to go without if need be, and could afford to. The pressure was always on Ermold, and he resented that. Often he would try to raid Stalhelm and steal supplies rather than buy them, but such fighting was always costly and bitter, and the invaders rarely managed to carry off anything like what they needed. It had become clear to Ermold that it was easier and better to trade with the Children of the Voice first and *then* raid—to steal what he could and to make him feel better anyway. Stalhelm knew of this thinking, and they made him pay all the more in consequence. It was accepted in Stalhelm that while Ermold ruled there would inevitably be the worst of bad blood between the peoples on either side of Cudal Canal.

Ermold and his men had to cross the filthy water to attend the meeting, and they spent some time making sure that they could do so without getting their feet wet—and that they could get back in a hurry if need be.

The chieftain of Walgo positioned three or four of his best men behind Shairn's wall, supported by a rough and ready pontoon, and then he went forward into Shairn, accompanied only by Fortex and—of course—the girl named Huldi, who was still secured to him by the cord.

He watched the Children of the Voice coming slowly down-hill towards him.

"Filthy scavengers," he muttered. "Filthy, disgusting little beasts." Ermold was not a very big man by the standards of his people, though he was broad and immensely powerful. His height was closer to the average of the Children of the Voice, and the worst insult that could be hurled at him was well-known among his people. He had killed people for calling him "Shairan" and he would probably have gone berserk if he had heard anyone use the word "Rat." The insults of his elders during his childhood probably had much to do with his deep-seated hatred of his neighbors.

"That gray meat they bring will be full of cockroaches," he said to Fortex. "It's what they wouldn't eat themselves. And they think it's good enough for *men*. I'll have a few skulls before this affair is quit. If I could only get near Old Man Yami . . ."

"He's not with them," said Fortex, in a low voice. "It's his son. Camlak. I wonder whether he's killed the old one."

"That one!" snarled Ermold. "A coward if ever I saw one.

If *he's* Old Man in Stalhelm we won't need to go hungry for a while. I could eat him alive."

"He'll not be Old Man," said Fortex glumly. "He'll be here under orders. When Yami's finished they'll get a new leader. A strong one."

"They don't have that much sense," said Ermold. He was optimistic only by virtue of the strength of his hatred.

The girl was picking at the cord with her teeth. His attention had wavered. He kicked her in the belly and checked the strength of the cord.

Fortex wondered—privately—what the Shaira were going to think of Ermold having to keep his woman on a string, but he would never have dared to make such a thought known.

There were six men from Stalhelm, and each of them carried a basket filled with dried asci from the gray-green saporshafts which they tended in some of their fields. In Ermold's lands, they grew wild, but the supply was almost gone. Six baskets was little enough to distribute among the people of Walgo, but there would be more in time and time after if things went well today. A meeting of this kind could drag on and on before a serious squabble developed. Terms of exchange were always agreed at the first encounter, but they rarely held good forever, or even for long enough for Ermold to lay in anything of a store. Something always went sour.

Ermold half-turned. "Bring the box," he commanded.

The suitcase was passed over the wall, and Fortex stepped back to collect it. It no longer contained all that it had when Burstone brought it into the world—some of the knives and implements would never find their way into Stalhelm, the books and the rest of the steel would have to be eked out and supplemented with such junk as Ermold thought he could pass off.

Huldi began biting at the cord once again.

Camlak came forward from his party and stood some six or ten feet away from Ermold. The warriors from Walgo stood up, stretching themselves to the full extent of their height to emphasize their superiority. Huldi stood up too. She was bigger than Ermold. He jerked the cord and made her fall back on to her haunches.

"Where's Yami?" demanded Ermold.

"Sick," said Camlak.

"Sick of a steel blade," suggested Ermold.

"Just sick," insisted Camlak, refusing to be intimidated by size or anything else. Porcel and the other warriors were watching him closely. This might well turn out to be something of a test.

Ermold let out a sound that was midway between a laugh and a belch. He threw the suitcase at Camlak's feet. "That's worth twenty baskets," he said. "You can take away the books one at a time and bring more gray meat. Later, we'll bring you more. Just keep the meat coming."

Camlak opened the case and inspected the contents.

"Six," he said. "You want more than we brought, you bring more. I take it all now."

Ermold went into the old routine. It was new to Camlak but the younger man obviously knew what to expect. He had inherited little enough from his father, but he did have patience. And from his own point of view as well as the point of view of his people, he could not afford to take less than he might get. Ermold tried hard, but got nowhere. The trouble was that Ermold *expected* Camlak to take less than his father would have, and when the young man proved just as obstinate Ermold became very angry.

The haggling grew intense, and then fierce. A genuine gap was open between each man's final price—or what each man thought his final price ought rightly to be. Camlak had every intention of sticking by his—he was prepared to take the asci home if he had to—and Ermold's temper boiled as this became more and more obvious.

Meanwhile, Huldi had gone to work with a sharp stone, and had succeeded in scratching apart most of the threads in the cord which bound her. While she sawed she wondered exactly what she was going to do when the string finally parted. She knew that she could only take rebellion against Ermold's anger and lust so far, and that in the present circumstances the simple fact of getting free was liable to be more than far enough. She had to run fast, and she had to have somewhere to run. She dared not go back toward Walgo while Ermold lived, and so it seemed that she had to cross Shairn—or persuade the Shaira to shelter her. That was not unknown—there were always odd Soulless Men and Hellkin hanging around the towns of Shairn, and in Central Shairn they would hardly be likely to hold it against her that she came from troublesome Walgo. Ermold's trouble was limited in scope.

While she sawed she looked speculatively at Camlak and

his followers, and flicked occasional anxious glances back at Fortex. She could sense a fight building up and she knew which side she was on. She only hoped *they* would realize it fast enough.

The rope parted just as Ermold was in the process of yielding to his temper. It was an unfortunate coincidence that at the very moment of parting he was jerking his right arm in a gesture of anger and petulance. The loose end of the rope flipped up into the air and distracted Ermold at the crucial second. His knife was already half-drawn, and the one time that momentary surprise is invariably fatal is when it catches a man with his weapon half-drawn.

Camlak got to him first. The small man had a knife up his sleeve, and he didn't even have to stand up. The blade was in Ermold's abdomen just below the navel before he had time to think. It was a vicious wound, but the knife was far too small for it to be mortal. Ermold went down in a heap and lay still, waiting for the arrows to fly over his head. Camlak was already hauling out a deadlier weapon and the other warriors were coming forward.

Ermold howled.

Fortex howled too and launched himself on Camlak, brandishing a great stone axe. Ermold's spare warriors popped up over the wall, bowstrings stretched. Fortex landed beside Huldi, but his attention was completely fixed on Camlak. That was a mistake. Huldi sprang up and brought her left arm round in a long arc. The sharp stone carved a gaping hole in the side of Fortex's neck, and his carotid spouted blood.

One of Walgo's bowmen caught a spear in his right eye and was hurled backwards into the water. It was a blow directed by sheer fortune. The other Men Without Souls unleashed their arrows harmlessly, counted up the odds, and fled, bounding back across their pontoon and making for Walgo with all possible speed.

Camlak was astonished. He stared at Huldi, holding his long dagger as if he had half a mind to run her through. His mind was made up by Ermold, who grabbed him by the ankles and upended him before leaping to his feet, hurling his own knife at the nearest of Camlak's men, and taking flight. No doubt he would have loved to kill Huldi before he went, but there was no time. Nor was there any chance of getting back to his own side of the canal. He set off along the Shairn bank in the shadow of the wall. A couple of arrows followed him, missed, and then he disappeared with a crash into a tall clump of clawreeds.

Porcel and the other warriors never paused to wonder if they should await orders from their Old Man's son. They were after Ermold like a pack of hounds. They knew he was wounded and the thought of his being allowed to get away and recover from his wound was patently intolerable.

Camlak was the only one who stayed. He got to his feet and stared warily at Huldi, who was still there, waiting.

"You're not going after him?" she said.

Camlak shook his head. "I've got what I came for."

He picked up the suitcase, and carefully fastened the locks. He sheathed his dagger, and set out for Stalhelm—walking slowly. Huldi followed him. As they walked past the group of baskets filled with gray meat, Camlak kicked them over.

A swarm of flies was not long gathering over the meat, and over the bodies.

17

Julea sat at the dressing table, inspecting herself critically in the mirror.

She looked too young to have sent her brother to his death. One of her brothers. The other had gone of his own accord.

Downstairs, she could hear the argument beginning. She bit her lower lip, and continued adjusting her hair. The argument had begun so many times, by now, and had never yet reached any semblance of an ending. Tonight's version, at least, was to be private, and one had to be thankful for that.

Somehow, she could no longer see her father as the hero of the affair. She believed in him, after a fashion, but she could no longer commit herself in any way at all to the storm which was building up around him. There had been a storm before, shortly after she was born. She had grown up in the shadow of that storm, alongside Joth. Joth was dead now. She had sent him to follow Ryan, and he had. It must have been madness on her part. She must have known, underneath, that he would meet the same fate, whatever it was.

She looked at herself in the mirror, and accused herself of murder.

The charge wasn't fair, but the guilt still massed in her mind. She had lost so much, in a world where loss was so rare, and so immaterial. No one else could possibly understand how she felt.

While Carl Magner angled for one more convert, his daughter played out her private melodrama.

They were saying that her father was mad, and she had begun to listen to them, if not to believe them. She felt some guilt about that as well.

When she had finished attending to her hair she sat still for a few moments more, still fascinated by her own tragic image in the mirror. It was trying hard to be an alien face, to cast itself in the role of accuser or accused so that her feelings could be polarized at least in her illusions. She felt almost as though her identity were shattering slowly. All the things which had conspired to maintain it were dying or dead.

Carl Magner was one of the dying. His sons were the dead.

She had bad dreams herself now. But nothing like her father's. Just disturbed dreams, in which images of Ryan and Joth and the world competed for her guilt and erased her part in the fabric of being.

She simply could not understand what was happening. Worse, she had no idea *why*.

She blanked the mirror and went downstairs.

18

Abram Ravelvent was one of the cognoscenti. He was a scientist—a man of knowledge.

Knowledge is not wisdom, and nowhere was that more obvious than in the character of Abram Ravelvent.

He looked old—his hair was gray, his complexion dark. His skin had the visual texture of horn. Yet he had fifty more years in him yet, if he was careful and moderately fortunate.

He was barely turned ninety. The look of antiquity was cultivated—it had been carefully brought out over the years, matured, remodeled, set hard and firm. The look of the all-knowing. The look, also, of the verbal *chevalier,* the argumentative artist.

Ravelvent had no influence save for his personality, but nevertheless he would be one of the most valuable additions to the Magner bandwagon if he could be persuaded to climb aboard.

He was at least willing to be persuaded, but he had come armed with arguments which he believed to be infallible. He intended to refute Magner's case entirely, just to show that he could do it. Then, if the prospect seemed attractive, he might become Magner's ally in the campaign to have the Underworld opened.

His infallible argument, fairly simply stated, was that *The Marriage of Heaven and Hell* could not possibly be true.

19

"Why not?" said Magner, brusquely. "Explain to me. Why not?"

"It's a naïve picture," said Ravelvent. "It simply does not take into account the rigorousness and the essential alien-ness of any life-system which could survive in the conditions as they must be down there. Without light, the primary energy-source is likely to be heat. What you are proposing, therefore, in your portrait of life as lived by the people of the Underworld, is the evolution of an entirely thermosyn-thetic plant-kingdom to the level of complexity and efficiency required to sustain higher life-forms in a mere matter of eleven thousand years. It's simply not possible."

"There's an alternative energy source," said Magner.

"These 'stars' that you mention? Really, one can hardly put much credence . . ."

"Waste," said Magner. "The waste of the Overworld. Our civilization exports millions of tons of raw waste into the Underworld every year. Organic waste of all kinds—waste which is replete with reclaimable energy."

"We reclaim a lot of it," Ravelvent pointed out.

"Not so," said Magner. "We reclaim metals, phosphates, nitrates and a few other minor things which are convenient and cheap to reclaim. But with atomic power, solar power and tidal power in relative abundance we don't need to exploit the waste as an energy source—and that's the way in which the Underworld will exploit it. We take back a very tiny fraction indeed of what we export, as a glance at the figures available through the cybernet will assure you."

"But even if that *is* so," Ravelvent protested, "the principle remains the same. You're proposing an evolutionary proliferation which just isn't possible. You're hypothesizing the death of virtually everything of the old régime, and the growth of an entire replacement system. All right, even if that could happen, even if it has happened, one simply cannot imagine the kind of continuity you imagine to have taken place in human society.

"Look closely at the kind of life which you suppose these people to be living. You imagine them to be loosely grouped into tribes, inhabiting small towns, buildings made of . . . what? Earth? Mud? Brick? Anyhow, they seem to have agriculture on some scale. They live peacefully for the most part, though they are a strong people. They hunt, but for the most part they use their weapons defensively against large carnivores whose description defies classification. They have other enemies, too, which you also seem to find some difficulty classifying. Humanoid creatures, larger than men, warlike, sometimes masked, sometimes naked, sometimes clothed, sometimes *furred*. What are all these strange beings supposed to be? There is no explanation in your book. But never mind that. What is the sum total of what we have here? An image of man as a kind of noble savage, heroically struggling to maintain a primitive social organization and even primitive social ideals of peace and prosperity against the terrible threats of a hostile environment.

"But this hostile environment does little more than threaten. Most of its threats seem to be ghostly creatures with no sense to them at all. Giants and ape-men. What are they supposed to be? Mutants? . . ." He paused for a moment, but Magner did not seem anxious to enlighten him at this particular juncture. "Your account makes a strong psychological appeal. It may even make some kind of psychological sense. But scientifically, it is nonsense to suppose that life in the Underworld could be anything like this. If there *are* men alive down there, then they *do* live in an implacably hostile environment. The sheer dereliction of the environment must make searching for food a full-time operation. The notion of agriculture, townships, tribal organization . . . all these are quite out of the question. Man was and is a product of environment. The men of the Underworld were functionally designed to live in an environment which has very little, if anything, in common with the present environment of the Underworld. The idea of their maintaining the same kind of existence is patently ludicrous.

"If there are men in the Underworld today—and I feel obliged to say *if*—then we cannot rationally imagine that they have anything in common with the men of prehistoric ages, let alone with ourselves. They would not merely be primitives and savages, they would—quite literally—be animals. They would be forced to spend their time providing the bare necessities of survival—food and fecundity. They would be no more human than cattle or, if you would like a more appropriate example, wolves. If they work in groups, the groups are packs and not tribes."

"You paint a very harsh picture," said Magner.

"It is a realistic picture," insisted Ravelvent.

"You seem to have virtually no faith in humanity as a species or the human being as an intelligent, adaptable creature," said Magner.

"Faith! What has *faith* to do with it? We cannot decide what the Underworld is like on the basis of faith. We cannot determine the nature and the abilities of man by wishful thinking. There are *facts* to be taken into consideration. Hard facts which we know to be true. Even as a speculative exercise, we must make full and complete use of the facts in sketching a picture of what life might be like in the world below. Complete fidelity to known science is an absolute necessity in any *proper* use of the imagination. I *know* that the account you give of the Underworld in your book is the product of your imagination purely and simply because you have used that imagination badly. It is an imagination undisciplined by fact. If we *are* to open the Underworld—and I do not believe that proposition to be unreasonable—then we must have a realistic idea of what we are likely to find.

"You seem to think that all that is necessary is for us to throw wide our gates, and the men of the Underworld will queue up to desert their world. Perhaps that is so. It can hardly be doubted that they would find our world a more attractive proposition than theirs, provided that they could stand the sunlight. But you seem to assume that the story ends—happily—there and then. That is patently ridiculous. If these creatures—and I say creatures quite deliberately—come into our world they will not do so as citizens of Euchronian society. They will do so as predators and scavengers—as beasts. In prehistoric days they gave accounts of feral children—men reared as beasts—and they said that such children could not be reeducated to human ways. They could not even be made to walk like men. You are proposing that five hundred generations of feral children can be accepted into the human race just like *that!*

"If we open the Underworld, then we must do so both forewarned and forearmed. We cannot do so in order to deal in any way whatsoever with the people of the Underworld. Our chief priority must be to explore, to discover, and to evaluate. We are far more likely to find that the rigors of the Underworld are breeding creatures which are a potentially deadly threat to us than men which we can communicate with. We must know about the Underworld, and we cannot afford to turn our backs to it forever. But we must recognize that these anthropocentric ideas of yours are nothing but a tissue of dreams."

Ravelvent stopped, unaware of the effects which his last remark might have had on Carl Magner.

Magner made no immediate reply. In the final analysis, he had nothing with which to argue save conviction, and that was one thing which the people of Euchronia's Millennium could not accept. They did not even know what it was.

"We must send people into the Underworld," said Magner. "A proper expedition *must* be mounted, as soon as possible. This is the first priority. When it returns, then we will all know that what I have said is *true*. Every last detail. I know that there are men in the Underworld who live as I have *seen* them living. We have no right to withhold from them the Face of Heaven."

"I think," said Ravelvent, "that when the truth *is* revealed, it will be closer to the picture that I have drawn."

20

The basis of Eupsychianism is the philosophy that a better life is to be sought inwardly rather than outwardly.

Eupsychianism is, implicitly, the alternative to and the enemy of Euchronianism. Whereas Euchronian ideals are directed toward collective man, favoring the group rather than the individual, Eupsychian ideals are intrinsically self-centered and self-limited. Euchronianism is an extrovert philosophy, Eupsychianism is introverted.

The essential difference between the two opposing philosophies is not a matter of the extent of freedom, but of the very meaning of freedom.

A Euchronian would claim that a man is the product of his environment, and that the enrichment of a man is attainable purely and simply by the enrichment of his environment. A Euchronian would argue that the perfect freedom is the freedom to manipulate and shape the environment, the freedom *of* the environment.

A Eupsychian would say that the whole essence of man is the power to transcend his environment, and that capitulation to the forces of the environment is equivalent to the destruction of humanity itself, or at least the subjugation of that humanity to purely mechanical external demands. A Eupsychian would argue that the only true freedom is freedom *from* the environment.

Paradoxically, a Euchronian Utopia would probably be very little different in appearance from a Eupsychian. The difference would lie in its direction of development. The society of the Euchronian Millennium is by no means anathema to the Eupsychians, who form the principal (minority) opposition to the political arm of the Movement proper. The difference between the factions is to do with attitudes to people and the functional design of social institutions rather than with the mechanical components of the civilization. Both factions admit to the machines as the ideal means of providing for the basic needs of survival. But the Euchronians are dedicated to stability—to the management of collective mankind, while the Eupsychians reject any such notion with disdain. They reject all forms of political and social management.

It would be naïve to imagine that the split between the factions as it is reflected in Euchronian society is quite that clear or quite that orderly. Citizens come in all shades of opinion. Not everyone would call himself a Euchronian or a Eupsychian, and two men who accepted the same label might have very different views—not only at a trivial level, but in terms of basic priorities.

However, in the context of the Euchronian Millennium, the polarization of political attitudes may be said to fall along the defined spectrum.

The Euchronians, for the most part, regard the Eupsychians as traitors. There is some justice in this—the Euchronian Movement planned and built the civilization in which they live, and built it by means of absolute dedication on the part of the Plan's participants. In the eyes of the Euchronians, Euchronianism has proved itself absolutely.

The Eupsychians, on the other hand, see the Euchronians as having become redundant on the day the Millennium was declared. There is some justice in this too—the society of the Millennium is ultracomfortable, but it must be admitted that there is a surprising amount of unrest and unhappiness. Despite the fact that no citizen of the Millennium lives in a state of deprivation there is a significant crime rate, and crimes of violence are not uncommon—though the violence involved is usually at a trivial level. Violence against the machines which provide for the populace is also surprisingly common—and this is occasionally not so trivial. The Eupsychians claim that now the priority is no longer survival but freedom, then true freedom must be encouraged, not the Euchronian version. On the other hand, the Euchronians would counter this argument . . .

The debate, of course, continues.

21

Joth was panic-stricken.

He was moving through perpetual night, timelessly, going nowhere, with no motive for going.

He had no sense of direction, no sense of distance, no sense of speed. It might almost be said that he had no sense of being. He was not afraid.

Joth had no instinctive reactions. Instinctive reactions had been withheld from him, deliberately and strategically. Instinct would have allowed him to be afraid. It would have given him a context for fear, and the physiological component of the emotion would have mobilized his resources for a fear-reaction. He would have run, but behind his running there would have been an urgent, fear-stimulated consciousness.

Without instinct, Joth was in the grip of panic. There are reactions which go deeper than conditioning, deeper than instinct, deeper even than reflex. Conditioning and instinct are both properties of mind—of mental organization, however primitive. A dog has instinct, a bird has instinct, a fish has instinct. Below mind, there are still mind-like reactions, An amoeba has tropisms, a mollusc has tropisms, even a plant has tropisms. These things too have some component of function in them, of reason. In that sense, Joth's panic had some semblance of reason. When mind is inadequate—totally inadequate—to deal with situation-stimulus, then mind must step aside and allow something deeper to assume control of body. Joth's mind had recoiled when he found himself trapped in the Underworld—recoiled all the way. It had simply denied all responsibility, refused to have any part in determination of events. Joth's actions had passed into the control of something different—something more basic than the essential *him,* his identity.

Joth ran. Hard. He was outside time and outside sensory perception. His ego was in a well of utter, ultimate loneliness. Perhaps beyond space also, isolated from the universe itself. Nowhere. In the oceanic, transcendental regions where the soul lives (if men have souls).

His heart pumped at a furious rate, his muscles sucked up energy at the very limits of their capacity. His limbs levered his body through space without any regard whatsoever for the strain on the ligaments and membranes.

He felt no pain. Yet.

His eyes reflected the gleam of the stars, but did not see. Even so, his headlong flight failed to bring him into collision with any of the pillars which supported the sky, or with any of the impenetrable clumps of vegetation which dotted the ground between them.

Eventually, however, there had to come a time when the body could no longer put up with the demands which were being made upon it. It simply could not meet them. When that happened, Joth collapsed, and he lay still.

Again, the interval was timeless.

When he came to, his mind was once again in his brain. This time, he opened his eyes and he could see the stars in the sky, pale and still. He knew where he was.

He could not move. His whole body was being eaten by pain. He lay face upward in inch-deep mud and slime, and he could feel the wetness all over his back and his legs and the back of his head. There were cockroaches moving over his body, but he could do nothing. He was helpless.

It was as though he was newly born for a second time. He could remember the world above, and he knew who he was. There was no amnesia. But he had lost his connection with the memories. He had lost mental continuity. The legacy of the whole of his life—more than twenty years—was suddenly incomplete, inadequate, insane. The facts remained, but all the meaning had somehow drained out of them.

Tears began to ooze from the lachrymal glands in the corner of each eye.

A cockroach, wandering across his face, had to struggle hard to escape when it almost fell into the pit of his open mouth.

22

Ermold was running. There was, perhaps, just a hint of panic about *his* headlong flight, but it was panic which shared control of him with honest fear and cold rationality. The leaf-bladed dagger which Camlak had flicked into his belly had hurt him badly, but it had done him no permanent damage, if only he could win free to let it heal. The big danger was that running might rip the wound farther and farther open, spout more and more blood from its orifice, and ultimately make it into a mortal blow. No vital organ had been touched, but a hole in the belly was a hole in the belly, and Ermold needed time.

He knew exactly how many men were after him, and he knew that it was no use making any sort of attempt to reduce the odds unless he could get them well and truly strung out. Arrogance assured him that if he could take them one at a time he could dispose of all five. He would have to, if he was to get away. He could hardly hide while he was spilling a trail out of his guts, and the prospect of help arriving was remote indeed.

While he ran, he sustained himself with thoughts of what he could and would do to Huldi and Camlak when he recovered. In order to make those fantasies into fact he *had* to survive, and his indulgence was no mere whim. He was feeding his need, fueling his determination.

Objectively speaking, he had very little chance of getting away. But circumstances are rarely defined objectively. The odds are never what they seem. Probability is a measure of a mechanical universe, not a human one.

He did not attempt to cross the canal. Climbing the low wall would not be difficult, and gaining his own territory would no doubt reduce the advantage enjoyed by the rats, if only in a psychological sense, but he simply dared not dive into the poisoned water with an open wound in him. That *would* be fatal.

He placed his faith in the length of his stride and the innate superiority of man over false man. The innate superiority was a myth, but it was faith that counted and not truth. The length of his stride, however, was an important factor. The Children of the Voice were fast movers, but they were built for short-distance work, not long cross-country chases. While Ermold ran he stayed ahead of his pursuers and gradually, he did begin to string them out. He tired, and they tired, and the battle condensed, temporarily, into a battle of Ermold's wound-affected endurance versus the Shairan warriors' natural endurance.

As the clutching hands of fierce pain and the weakness of lost blood reached out to claim Ermold and put an end to that phase, forcing him to turn and stand, fate intervened.

As he blundered round a cluster of pepper-squab stalks his foot was snagged by a creeper, and he was brought heavily to the ground. The fall jerked the wind out of him and tears blurred his eyes. When he blinked and focused them again he found that his own face was mere inches away from another.

And the other face was made of shiny steel.

23

Porcel was too far behind Ermold to see him fall, but he slowed down as he came up to the pepper-squabs because of the smell. He knew something was behind the cluster, but he could not for the life of him think what it was.

He did not stop, but he allowed his body to relax into a crouch, with his dagger arm extended before him, ready to tackle anything.

As he came round the corner the steel face was thrust forward into his own. The surprise was just too great. He bounded backwards, hesitated, and then ran.

Ermold dropped Joth's limp body back into the mud and peered through the curtain of creepers after the fleeing warrior. He saw Porcel meet the next man, and the next, and he knew that once all five were gathered together they would pluck up the courage to approach. He glanced down, and saw that Joth was squirming slightly, beginning to recover some vestige of control over his limbs.

Ermold kicked him, but not very hard. "Get up!" he hissed.

But Joth couldn't.

Somewhere, not too far away, a harrowhound howled. Ermold cursed beneath his breath. There were enough hunters abroad without new ones trying to get into the act. But he knew that the harrowhound's nearness might work for him as well as against him. It would worry the Shaira as well, and they wouldn't be keen to split up again.

He reached down and hauled Joth to his feet, shaking him to try and jar some sense into his brain. Finally, Joth could stand. By this time, though, the warriors of Stalhelm were coming forward again.

Ermold shoved Joth forward, steadied him, and then shoved again. Then, without bothering to find out what effect, if any, Joth would have on the advancing Children of the Voice, he turned and ran. The rest had done him little enough good, but he hoped fervently that he would not need the power of his legs much longer.

24

Joth staggered no more than six paces before slumping forward again. He fell first on to his knees, and then toppled forward face-first into the mud. Moments later, he felt himself being turned over.

His consciousness was still seeping back with tortuous slowness. It was without surprise and without wonder that he looked up at the ring of faces inspecting him.

The creatures were small. Pygmies or dwarfs . . . perhaps goblins. Their faces were more beast-like than human, but Joth could not for the moment pin a name to the beast. Their noses were large, their eyes small black beads. Their teeth were closely packed inside their mouths. Their ears were tiny and rounded, mounted oddly—too high, too far apart.

He tried to speak, but he was unable to produce any sound other than a low groan which—when he forced it—came out something like a cat's purr.

He gave up the attempt. One of them passed a hand over his face, feeling the metal and the plastic flesh-substitute which, in collaboration, provided the whole structure of his cranium, his eye sockets, his nose and his cheeks. Only his lower jaw and bottom teeth were real—those he had been born with. His eyes were metal orbs, but they functioned as eyes (better than real ones) and they connected to optic nerves which were his own. The olfactory organ, however, was not functional. He had no sense of smell.

"It's a mask," said one of the weird creatures.

"No," said the one who had run hands over his face. "It's real."

Joth realized that they were speaking English. As the faces peered closer he saw that they were covered in sleek gray fur. The fur and the fact that they spoke combined to give him a fleeting sensation of paradox. Then he lost consciousness.

The Shaira argued among themselves for a few moments, and then came to a decision which might have been motivated more by fear of Ermold than by concern for or interest in Joth. They picked him up by his ankles and his shoulders, and they carried him away in the direction of Stalhelm.

25

Joth Magner was probably unique among the citizens of the Euchronian Millennium. He was one of the very few members of that society ever to have faced a serious crisis. Not only did he face and survive such a crisis, but he had no choice in the matter. It was forced upon him.

He was probably the only man of his age to have struggled for continued existence over a considerable period of time, and to take that struggle as it came, as a matter of course. He was one of very few who had to come to terms with difficult circumstances and physical hardship. Not by choice, but by something akin to necessity.

When Joth was less than a year old a malfunction in a household cyberunit possibly assisted by some interference at the hands of the older infant Ryan, caused a panel of the unit to explode in his face. He suffered extreme damage to his eyes and his skin was burned away over a considerable area of his scalp and cheeks. Because of the relative softness and flexibility of his skull-bones, and the fact that his brain had not yet grown to fill the skull cavity Joth's frontal lobes suffered relatively little damage. Nevertheless, it seemed an open-and-shut case so far as the euthanasia board was concerned. Infancy counted against him severely in that he had no voice in the decision and he was considered to be below the threshold of social consciousness.

The strenuous arguments of his father, however, delayed the board in coming to a terminal decision. Carl Magner proved dogged, stubborn and extremely determined. By sheer refusal to entertain any arguments in opposition, and inordinate vehemence in putting forward his own opinion over and over again, he prevented the board from making a ruling. While the board was in session, of course, surgeons worked to keep the child alive and to repair the damage done. In the end, with the aid of a clever lawyer, Carl Magner stalled the board long enough for the situation to have changed so materially that the decision went the other way. The baby was permitted to live.

For many months Joth was sightless and quiescent, and even Carl Magner must have wondered whether he had done the right thing in forcing the euthanasia board to bring in a negative verdict. There was a certain amount of public criticism of the board and of Magner's lawyer. Relatively little was said about Magner himself, for whom excuses could obviously be made. But controversy ran high for some time until it was extinguished by the surgeons and a series of educational experts who contrived to prove that the boy was neither physically deficient, nor mentally retarded, nor psychologically aberrant. It was not until Joth was four years old that he finally stilled all arguments as to the rights and wrongs of his specific case by demonstrating his ability to use his artificial eyes effectively, and his brain as well as any child of his own age.

The experience undoubtedly had an effect on Carl Magner, but that was measurable. The effect which it had on Joth, however, was quite unknowable. He grew up to be an intelligent, adaptable and apparently ordinary member of Euchronian Society—ordinary, that is, except for his rather striking physiognomy. But the Euchronian standards of personality assessment were tailored to Euchronian assumptions and criteria. The differences that existed between Joth and other men went somewhat deeper than that. He *was* different, and he knew that he was different. He had paid a price for his individual survival that no other man of the Overworld could evaluate, or even imagine.

Perhaps the accident also made an impression of some kind on Ryan Magner. He was three when the accident happened and only he ever knew whether the explosion was partly his fault or not. But even if not he was at an age to be affected by constant contact with Joth and constant awareness of Joth's difficulties.

The accident which led to the death of Joth's mother had happened some months before the explosion and was totally unconnected with it except insofar as it might have affected Carl Magner's state of mind relative to the euthanasia board. However, it is significant that the family had to endure misfortune that was quite out of proportion with the ordinary flow of life in the Euchronian Millennium.

Whether the incidence of Carl Magner's nightmares had anything to do with the stress placed upon him by either accident or their consequences was not known even to the man himself. It seemed possible, to him and to his doctor.

The adult Joth owed his existence to endurance in conflict. He, in collaboration with others, had fought for life and health throughout his most impressionable years. In a sense, Joth *never* laid down his arms in that struggle to survive. More than any other man of the Overworld, including the most devout Eupsychians, he felt self-contained and somehow detached from his environment. He was not really a misfit, because he adapted perfectly well to his circumstances.

But in different circumstances, the difference between Joth Magner and his contemporaries could, and did, prove crucial.

26

The close council met in Heres' house, taking advantage of a chamber which was totally isolated from the cybernet. Nothing of what they said went on to any kind of record.

They were discussing a secret which, though not theirs alone, was theirs to protect as they saw fit. Heres was determined to keep the secret. Eliot Rypeck wanted to reveal it to the world. It was a difficult decision, considering that the close council had no theoretical executive power. Theoretically, the close council had no right to exist.

"You're firmly convinced," Rypeck asked Ulicon, "that the origin of Magner's data is his dreams?"

"That's not possible," said Clea Aron. Heres gestured with his hand to keep her quiet.

"I am," said Ulicon.

"And are the dreams accurate?" Rypeck followed up.

"We don't know. We have no up-to-date information. Offhand, I couldn't tell you how to get into the Underworld, though I don't imagine it's difficult. We must send someone to find out, if we can find anyone willing to go. This is something we need to know."

"I'm not so sure that the truth or otherwise of Magner's visions is a point at issue," said Heres. "It's the visions themselves that we ought to be concerned with. One thing we *do* know is that this man has complained of bad dreams over a very long period of time. What we want to know first and foremost is why. Is he immune to the i-minus agent?"

"How do you suggest we test him?" said Ulicon.

"Did you get anything from the doctor?" countered Heres. Ulicon shrugged and shook his head.

"Wait a moment," said Rypeck. "Isn't it more likely that we'll get useful information from Magner himself? We could ask *him* instead of conspiring to get information by all sorts of devious means."

"We can't do that," contributed Acheron Spiro. "Magner's book is a strong attack on the Movement itself. He has set himself up in extreme opposition to us. We can't ask him to explain his dreams because we're worried about them."

"Our hands are tied somewhat in the matter of making inquiries," said Heres. "We can't tell people what we want without letting out the secret we're trying to safeguard with the answers. We have to get the answers without exposing the fact that we're interested."

"This is ridiculous," said Rypeck. "Surely it's clear by now that the i-minus effect is totally and utterly failing to counter the unrest in society. The agent doesn't work—we already know that, or we should. It's time to stop playing games with it and bring it out into the open. If Magner is immune, then maybe others are too, and we have a possible explanation of why the agent hasn't had the effect we've been hoping for. But think of the possibilities which are opened up if Magner *isn't* immune, if the i-minus agent is working perfectly. In that case we might have something entirely new to deal with, and something vitally important. If Magner is mad, we must know *why* he is mad. I don't think we can afford to play this down, to pussyfoot around it, to hesitate and argue and finally fail to reach any meaningful decision. This could be something we ought to know about *now*—something we ought to have known about years ago. And we have to find out."

"Not at the cost of the i-minus plan," said Heres. "You say that things are going badly for us despite i-minus, and I agree with you. But I think that i-minus is all that's standing between us and total breakup. Eleven thousand years have gone into the building of this world and eleven thousand years of responsibility rests on our shoulders."

"That's just my point," interposed Rypeck. "It shouldn't rest on our shoulders."

"But it does," said Heres. "Like it or not, we have charge of the i-minus project as it was handed down to us through thousands of years of closed council. To make the project public is to go half way to destroying it. We simply do not have the *right* to betray the Movement in this way, without full knowledge of what we are doing."

"I say that we are betraying the Movement by keeping the secret," said Rypeck. "The whole concept of a close council is alien to the principles of the Movement, and it's patently ridiculous that six members of the Hegemony, including the Hegemon, should participate in one."

"But nevertheless a council exists," said Heres, "and we are that council. We cannot dismiss lightly a decision which was taken so long ago and which has served the movement so well for so long. The i-minus effect *has* worked—it worked for generations. Without i-minus, the Euchronian Millennium might not exist. If we cannot cope with the responsibility that we have to deal personally with i-minus then we run the risk of destroying Euchronia."

"All this is a rather haggard argument," said Ulicon. "The question is what we do about Magner. It may turn out that we have to reveal or even abandon i-minus. But let's fight about that when we come to it. And we can't come to it unless we first make every effort to deal with this matter as it lies. We have to make an effort to come to terms with the situation and get ourselves into a position to end it. We want to know three things: Is the i-minus effect still working? Is it working on Magner? Is the input into Magner's dreams an accurate statement of reality? The first is relatively easy to answer, but will take too long. The second is more difficult. If, however, we assume that the answers to the first two questions are both 'yes' then the third becomes absolutely vital. If the first two answers are 'no' then the answer to the third must surely also be 'no.' Doesn't it make sense to mount an expedition to the Underworld at the earliest possible opportunity?"

"I think there's more to consider than that," said Clea Aron. "We shouldn't be obsessed with the i-minus aspect of this affair. It has other implications as well. We mustn't overlook the direct challenge to Euchronia because we're aware of certain deeper issues. Magner wants dealing with purely and simply on political grounds. This plan needs squashing."

"Hardly," said Leul Dascon. "Why should we allow ourselves to look foolish by deigning to take it seriously? I've talked to Abram Ravelvent about this and he assures me that any men in the Underworld will be little better than savage wild animals by now. Much better to produce our own counterproposal to sterilize the Underworld completely—wipe out all its vermin. If we're actually going to send an expedition down there we'll need some sort of reason."

"It would be foolish to take up any such definite stand," said Heres. "I think the opposite angle would be better. Officially, we don't believe a word of what Magner says, but out of the kindness of our hearts we'll send someone down to have a look. We can pretend to have a certain sympathy with him while assuring the world that it's all a fuss over nothing."

"I think Magner could be troublesome," Dascon persisted. "We shouldn't offer him any kind of encouragement."

"Nobody will encourage him," said Heres. "We'll just use him as an excuse to mount our explorations—*all* of our explorations. Luel—you'd better take charge of mounting the expedition. Enzo—keep following up the medical aspect. Find out all you can about Magner's dreams and i-minus effects. Clea—you can handle the media. Acheron and I will handle the Hegemony and the political aspects of the argument. Eliot, you'd better find out what you can about the Underworld from the cybernet. Luel's team will need information as well as equipment."

"You do realize," said Ulicon, "that if there *is* something in the Underworld transmitting ideas into Magner's head, then we might have to face the fact that Earth has two worlds and not one."

There was a brief period of silence.

"I just want to make it clear," Ulicon carried on, "that the implications of Magner's book go a long way beyond our perennial squabbling over the crime rate and the i-minus problem. After eleven thousand years, we may have to confront the fact that the old world didn't die after all, and that something down there might actually pose a threat to us. I say this now because I don't think there's a single one of you has really absorbed this idea, and I think we ought to get used to it. The Underworld *is still there.* Remember that."

27

Later, Heres ran the whole argument back through his mind, looking for an answer. The important thing, of course, was not to let any part of it get out of hand. Rypeck could be handled—Rypeck had been handled for years. The man lacked a positive side to his character. Argument would never convince him, but it would not be necessary to keep him from acting. Rypeck was not the type to act.

Ulicon, on the other hand, was more difficult to assess. He too was a man who would appeal to the group for justification rather than take any kind of independent intiative, but he would make his appeal on a rather different level. Rypeck dealt in dilute arguments. Ulicon seemed to be dealing in not-so-dilute scare stories.

Any kind of a scare had to be avoided at all costs. That went without saying. But the suggestion of a scare was not necessarily a bad thing. A threat to all helped to unite the group, provided that it could be dealt with in the right way, by the right man. When it came down to it, Rypeck and Ulicon could both be given a role to play in Heres' scheme of things. Ulicon was the man to pose a question, Rypeck to agitate on the basis of the question. Heres, though, was the man to act and answer the question, and by so doing deal with both kinds of opposition. Spiro, Aron and Dascon would thus remain solidly behind him as always, their faith constantly reinforced.

Since the Millennium had begun, the administration represented by Heres and his predecessors had faced no threat to their power except for the Eupsychians, who were really only a fake threat. Under the current régime Eupsychianism had no chance to spread (so Heres believed) and no chance to topple the Movement even if it did. The *real* potential threat was the threat of strife within the Movement itself— such strife as would undoubtedly occur if the matter of the close council and its purpose were to be made public. Heres' first priority was controlling the close council.

Heres regarded the Magner affair, so far as it had gone, as a regrettable inconvenience of strictly temporary concern. Given time, the man would disappear along with his ridiculous ideas. Once the man was out of sight, he would be easy enough to put out of mind. Another of Eliot Rypeck's arguments would go stale, and Enzo Ulicon would abandon his worries about the Underworld. The balance would be restored—another victory for stability. Heres believed, absolutely, in stability.

He also believed quite sincerely in the i-minus effect, which was supposed to control dreams. The fact that Magner was an exception (apparently) to the i-minus rule did not frighten the Hegemon—he believed that every stable situation has room for a handful of misfits, and that stability is enhanced rather than threatened by the visible presence of such wayward factors. Heres, in fact, was quite willing to remain in blissful ignorance of *how* Carl Magner was beating the system in this respect.

Somewhere behind all these attitudes lies the true key to Heres' character. One might describe him as "megaloid"— inferring that he was power-oriented without necessarily being mentally aberrant. In Heres one can definitely see a man who would seek fulfillment through control, control of both environment and situation. This is not to say, however, that Heres had Eupsychian tendencies—quite the reverse. His ideas of control involved a scale of consideration not permitted by a Eupsychian philosophy. He was a lover of pattern and balance, and his efforts were directed to the overall maintenance of pattern rather than to the grasp of personal power of determination.

As Hegemon of the Euchronian Movement and one of the close council Heres sat at the apex of a vast pyramid of executive responsibility. He was not really the most powerful man in the world, and his influence over the vast arena of social action was in many ways the most indirect. But he was the fulcrum of the system. His movements might not cause the biggest ripples, but his ministrations served to damp down most big ripples before they had a chance to grow.

Heres was a vain man—any man with such a degree of self-confidence is necessarily a victim of vanity. But this is one of the so-called "qualities of leadership." Any Hegemon is essentially a vain man. Heres was also an intelligent man, but it might be argued that he was *too* intelligent—that his intelligence was so massive as to prove unwieldy when brought to bear on specific problems. Heres' mind was a mind perennially locked in high gear. Whereas most men despair of the practicality of thinking of two things at once, Heres found difficulty in restraining himself to one. Heres' intelligence lacked small-scale utility. He would throw himself wholeheartedly into the most complex matter and come up with *the* solution of dazzling brilliance. But only the most complex matters. Where smaller things were concerned, he was a fumbler. Like a physical giant who cannot help knocking things over, Heres was a mental giant who was also mentally clumsy.

He was also a dedicated master of the game of Hoh. Hoh, played by novices, can be a competitive affair. Played by experts its competitive aspects are buried in a bewildering range of possibilities. The ideal game of Hoh from the viewpoint of the connoisseur—and far and away the most difficult to play—is the game where *all* the players win. In this kind of game all the players must play with one another as well as against one another, and must unite against the random factors in the game. (When a Eupsychian plays Hoh he almost always tries to end up the sole winner of the game. Such strategies, while perfectly valid under the rules, are frowned upon as simple-minded and contrary to the real spirit of the game by virtually all purists and experts.)

In completing a study of Heres' character it must be noted that he was not a good leader. In many ways he was not a leader at all. He had charisma, and commanded a good deal

of respect, but he was not very efficient. He was clever—
but like a driver who takes his corners late he needed to be
clever. He was not really good because he was not really
safe. The Magner affair illustrates this. While others were
worrying Heres was merely observing. It would not occur to
him to act decisively at this stage. He had every confidence
that if things got worse he could bring off a mental riposte
of startling elegance, but the fact remains that if another
man were in control the problem might not have been allowed to develop in the way it did. Many men close to him
were aware of this failing in the Hegemon's character, but
there was nothing, really, that they could do about it.

Except worry.

28

Huldi's reception in Stalhelm was a poor one. The Children
of the Voice, especially those who could be termed neighbors of Ermold, harbored no affection whatsoever for the
Men Without Souls, despite the fact that some of the things
which enriched their lives came from Walgo.

When Camlak brought her back, not as a captive for
ransom but as a fugitive seeking protection, the women of
the village were amazed, if not appalled. The women had
lived long by Yami's ways, which were hard ways. Life as
they knew it tended to be ruled by the principle: if in doubt—
kill. Camlak made it known that Huldi had killed one of
Walgo's fighting men, and that she hated Ermold as virulent-
ly as any Shairan, but those were not reasons which the
women would accept as sufficient to permit Huldi the freedom of Stalhelm. Hellkin were welcome enough in the village, and there had been times when Men Without Souls
passed freely in and out of the gate—as they undoubtedly
did in the villages of western Shairn. But the women were
ruled by memory and by habit, and Camlak's choice did not
rest easily with them. Camlak had always been something
of an enigma.

The Old Man's son installed Huldi in his own house when it
was clear that she would not be accommodated elsewhere.

There she was made welcome, after a fashion, by Camlak's daughter (by the woman Xyli) Nita. Camlak's present woman, Sada, objected to the intrusion in no uncertain terms, but dared not show her displeasure in full measure while Camlak was present. Eventually, however, Camlak went to confer with Yami and the elders in the long house, and some of the spite was allowed out.

After a few insults Sada left to work and to talk with the other village women, but Nita stayed. She was old enough now to work, and should, perhaps, have been out in the fields, but she enjoyed a certain latitude by virtue of being kin to the Old Man.

Nita was fascinated by Huldi. In the present troubled times she had never actually seen a woman of the Soulless Ones. She had never been close to a living Man at all, though she had seen plenty of warriors' heads brought home to adorn the skull-gate. She was amazed to discover how tall the stranger was. One got no real idea of size from a distance (and none at all from skulls). She could not imagine that the girl really needed so much body to support a head which did not seem unduly massive.

Nita had heard from the women that the inhabitants of Walgo were child-eating giants only one step removed from the ultimately horrifying Ahrima, but Nita had always been ready to discredit such talk because it lacked Camlak's endorsement. Everyone knew that the old women lied about almost everything. The sheer size of Huldi was enough to keep her suspicions awake in some degree, but for the most part Nita's attitude to the newcomer was not unfriendly.

Huldi squatted in a corner when Camlak left her, ready to defend herself if necessary, but she relaxed once Sada had gone, and discovered that she was very tired. The elation which had followed her success in winning free of Ermold was evaporated by now, and she was afraid. It was all very well to think of running away to Shairn while Ermold had her on the end of a leash, but the fact was something else entirely. She was alone now, with no idea of what she was or what was going to happen to her. She had to pin her faith on Camlak because there was no alternative, but she could not possibly know the degree to which that faith might or might not be justified. The only refuge from fear which was immediately available was sleep, and to sleep she went, while Nita sat and played with a handful of sticks in the opposite corner of the room.

Later, Yami came in—without Camlak—to look at her. No sooner had he crossed the threshold than Sada was behind him.

"You should kill her," said Sada.

Yami did not reply, but simply stood there, looking at the girl with his pale, rheumy eyes. Sada dared to let loose a short, hissing sound which expressed something of her contempt for the man who was old in fact as well as in title. It was time that he was replaced. She had hoped Camlak would do it, but by now she was half-convinced that Camlak would not even if he could. She was disillusioned, and felt betrayed by circumstance. She had grown to hate Camlak, considering him only half a man. Camlak tolerated her anyway, which made her conviction all the stronger.

Yami looked at Huldi, and he wondered. He did not understand. He had reared Camlak to be a leader, and he had failed—or so he believed. Perhaps he had been half-hearted in his determination. No man looks forward to being deposed by his son, no matter how deep his faith in the way the world works, and in the ultimate inevitability and rightness of that way.

"I ought to kill her myself," muttered Sada.

Yami laughed at her derisively. He did not bother to turn and face her.

"Well?" said Sada. "What has he brought her here for?"

"To be a wife instead of you," said Yami coldly. The suggestion was mildly obscene.

"He's mad enough," she mumbled. "Mad enough to take a beast to his bed."

"Shut up," said the Old Man.

"I'll see her dead," Sada promised herself, audibly. "I'll see her dead."

Yami turned to spit at her. "You only kill babies," he said. "You see them *all* dead."

Then he turned on his heel and went to the long house. Sada watched him go, with a savage glare in her eyes. She had borne her children, but they were all dead. Only one of Camlak's children lived, and that was his by another woman. She had killed no child—to think of such a thing was impossible. It was the deadliest insult Yami could throw. Yami blamed it all on her. She blamed Camlak. A man should have more than one child, and no woman should die childless.

Sada grabbed Nita by the scruff of the neck and shoved

her out of the house, telling her to go to work. She might have attacked Huldi then, or even fulfilled her threat of murder while fury blinded her to the consequences. But she was distracted by something which was happening outside. There was a commotion which grew quickly. Porcel and the others were coming back. At the thought that they might have Ermold's head Sada rushed out to join the crowd.

29

"Is it true," Nita asked Huldi, "that you have no Soul?"

Huldi was busy making a meal of the scraps which had been left after Camlak had gone back to the long house. She had been given a share in the meal but she thought it wise to guard against the future. She looked up at the shadowed form of the girl-child, not sure that she should answer, or even that she *could* answer.

"Is it true?" persisted Nita.

"No," said Huldi, not knowing whether it was truth or lie, and not caring greatly.

"Why do we call you Men Without Souls?" asked Nita.

"*We* don't," countered Huldi.

"Everyone else does," claimed the child.

"They don't," Huldi contradicted her flatly.

Nita thought that there was no point in quoting instances. She was obviously not on the right track. "What do you call yourselves?" she asked, instead.

"Men," said Huldi, shortly.

Nita pondered this revelation for a few moments. "What do you call us?" she asked. "We're men, but we call ourselves Children of the Voice."

"You're Rats," said Huldi.

"Why?" asked Nita.

It was an unanswerable question, and it threw Huldi out of her stride for a moment while she tried to examine the possibility of finding an answer. She was tempted to say: It's what you are, but that didn't seem to advance the argument at all. In addition, to call someone a Rat was the ultimate insult in Walgo. Perhaps she should be more careful and less honest.

"I don't know," she said, finally.

"What's your name?" inquired Nita.

"Huldi."

"Why did you come here?"

"There was nowhere else to go."

"Are you going to stay?"

"I don't know."

Nita considered this series of answers with all due seriousness, and decided that they were not really adequate. She tried to figure out a way of demanding a better answer, but couldn't find one. Then Huldi went on.

"I wanted to get away," she said. "They would have killed me. I tried to kill Ermold. I would have killed him, if I could. I wanted to get away from him. I don't know what I can do now. I can't live on my own."

"You could," said Nita.

"No." Huldi shook her head.

Nita considered further, and decided that she had had enough of questions and answers.

"I'm going out," she said. "I want to know what's happening in the long house. They have a man with no face, and they don't know what to do. Yami will kill him, but I don't know how."

Huldi simply did not know how to react to this information, so she did not. She simply watched Nita go out of the house. Then she moved back into her corner, wondering what to do—and what alternatives might be before her.

30

Abram Ravelvent came to a decision.

Carl Magner was important. Carl Magner was not so ridiculous as had been supposed.

Ravelvent found a certain amount of sense in *The Marriage of Heaven and Hell*. He still did not believe in it, but he discovered a certain attractiveness in its ideas. On top of that, it was obvious that something was brewing. He had been asked for advice by members of the Hegemony and by Alwyn Ballow. People were taking sides in the Magner affair.

Ravelvent decided that he was on Magner's side if he was on anybody's. As a man of science—a man without prejudice—he felt no disposition to take the side of Heaven rather than that of Hell. Quite the reverse, in fact. To take the bad end of the case *looked* more objective. It was definitely more promising, from the point of view of wringing out some good argument.

The criteria by which Ravelvent selected his stand may sound somewhat vague—that is because they were somewhat vague in his own mind—but they were sufficient to commit him. He looked upon the whole affair as an academic exercise. Having made up his mind what he was going to prove he set about gathering evidence in a thoroughly scientific manner, by painstaking research. He had no intention whatsoever of going down into the Underworld himself but he offered to lend his advice and his moral support to the expedition which was being mounted.

Ravelvent borrowed Magner's arguments and embroidered them. He disentangled them and reset them into a pattern which was largely his own. He shored up a few of the weak spots with speculative logic and added a few details to help round out the picture. Then he threw his weight into the gathering controversy. It was not too difficult for a man of his argumentative caliber to convince others that there might be something in Magner's book.

There were half a dozen more like Ravelvent. Together, they managed to form a rallying point for all those who had some kind of sympathy for Magner. The Eupsychians flocked to the banner in droves, eager to recruit any idea which might be magnified into a thorn to prick the Movement. There was hardly one of the principal supporters of Magner's cause who lent any real credence to his allegations, let alone any real conviction to his conclusions, but the cause grew anyway. Magner was uplifted—and exposed.

The world, at this stage, was only playing a game. But it meant a lot more than that to Magner. Magner stood to suffer from the way the game went. He had already suffered a great deal. The pressure on him was on a totally different order to anything else in the game. For him, as for his faceless son, it was a game of life and death.

31

Randal Harkanter was the man who was asked to lead the descent into the Underworld. He was by no means Heres' number-one choice—in fact, his selection represented a certain desperation in the whole matter of selection. Everybody was suddenly interested in the Underworld, but nobody wanted to go. Who could blame them?

Luel Dascon, the Hegemon's right-hand man, finally decided that Harkanter was the only reasonable prospect, and approached him.

Harkanter was a big man, over six feet tall, with a strong liking for games of a rather more primitive kind than were popular in the society of Euchronia's Millennium. Harkanter was a fierce competitor, with the attitude of a hunter. At fifty years of age he was starting what could well be a very long prime of life.

He was implicitly Eupsychian in his approach to life, but he was in no way politically inclined. Insofar as the Eupsychians were organized into a form of political opposition he despised them utterly. He was a strong-minded man who believed that he could get what he wanted, and who believed that anyone who couldn't get what they wanted was unworthy of his attention. He had no time for philosophical arguments about the form of society. His ideas and needs were far more basic.

He was a complete misfit.

"A situation has arisen," Dascon told him, "which opens up some rather interesting possibilities. Interesting to us, and to you, in rather . . . er . . . different ways. The question concerns the Underworld."

Harkanter was surprised. Dascon was not surprised by Harkanter's surprise. Harkanter was not the sort of man to pay any attention to matters like the Magner affair. Harkanter had probably never heard of Carl Magner, or *The Marriage of Heaven and Hell*. Or William Blake, for that matter.

"So?" said Harkanter.

"It has been claimed that there are human beings still living on the old surface," said Dascon.

"Rubbish," said Harkanter, positively.

"That is what needs to be ascertained. The question has been raised, and no matter how ludicrous it may seem, we need direct evidence to answer it. It has been suggested that the Overworld be opened to allow some kind of commerce between the platform and the surface. The idea is causing speculation. We need facts to counter that speculation."

"What's it to me?" Harkanter wanted to know.

"We need a man to lead an exploratory party into the Underworld. It's a job for which few enough men have the qualifications. Everyone's interested, but nobody wants to take the trouble to find out."

"Send a contingent of police," said Harkanter.

"It's not a police job. The police are no more qualified than anyone else. We have half a dozen scientists whose appetite for facts is strong enough to reconcile them to the idea of taking a look down there, but they'll need someone to look after them—someone they can trust to make sure they come to no harm. You qualify. I think you'll find the experience stimulating."

"Why don't you just stamp on the whole argument?" asked Harkanter. "Issue a flat statement that no life exists down there."

"We can't," said Dascon.

"Too many people want to argue. The Eupsychians?"

"Partly. But we *do* want to know the truth ourselves. It might be important."

Harkanter laughed. "You want *me* to help you squash some Eupsychian propaganda."

"Why not?"

The big man shrugged.

"You are interested?" said Dascon tentatively.

"So are you," retorted Harkanter, "but there's nobody in the Hegemony going to spend a fortnight sightseeing in the sewers. Why should I?"

Dascon smiled politely. "It's your kind of challenge, Randal. Isn't it? Wouldn't you envy anyone else who got this particular patch of limelight? The first expedition into the nether world for . . . what? . . . five thousand years? Perhaps more. Certainly, it will involve contact with a certain amount of dirt—but you've always despised people who won't dirty their hands. It may involve a certain amount of *danger*—

but you can handle yourself and you're proud of the fact. There isn't that much opportunity for this kind of excitement nowadays . . ." Dascon allowed the sentence to fade out gracefully, prompting Harkanter's imagination to take up the thread of the argument.

It already had.

"There's not a lot of excitement to be found grubbing around in the sewers," said Harkanter. "I don't go out to find excitement: I go out to make it."

"Will you do it?" asked Dascon, easily, confident that Harkanter was well and truly hooked by now.

"I'll do it," said the big man. "I'll get some stuff together and provide a couple of extra hands to help keep your tame scientists safe from the crocodiles, or whatever. I guess I'm a fool but if it's going to be done it might as well be me. It'll be dark down there, I suppose?"

Dascon shrugged elegantly. "I would imagine so," he said. His voice sounded suddenly distant. He had said what he had to say. After he had closed the circuit he took out a handkerchief and wiped the palms of his hands. His smile had vanished without trace.

32

There was a long period of sickness and delirium. Joth lay on a bed of straw in the best room in Camlak's house. Camlak had saved him, Camlak accepted responsibility for him. Joth did not know how close he had come to death in the long house.

Even as it was, he was close enough to death. His mind was rarely in possession of his brain for more than a few minutes. He had fever after fever, and both Nita and Huldi spent long hours by his side trying to cool him. Sada would not help. She no longer lived in Camlak's house.

They fed him broth made from gray meat and the flesh of various beasts. At first his stomach rejected them all, and whatever they made him swallow he would instantly vomit back. But they made him take water to replace what he sweated off, and gradually they were able to enrich the water with some kind of sustenance. The period of adjustment was long, but in due time Joth became accustomed to the food of the Underworld and he recovered from those diseases which took hold of him. Occasionally he would speak or cry out, and there were many occasions when tears would flood from his eyes as he sobbed helplessly. In the early time his skin swelled and broke out into rashes perpetually as his exposure to alien proteins caused reactions in his flesh.

Gradually, however, the sharp smell which marked his body as alien dwindled and was lost, and his body adapted to the new environment.

The adaptation of his mind made some progress over the same period, but long after he was taking food regularly and sleeping without fever his consciousness retained the alienness that his body had rejected.

The time was hard for Camlak, Huldi and Nita, because what they were doing was, in a sense, just as alien as Joth. It was not the way that life was lived among the Children of the Voice. It was not Yami's way. In a different time, perhaps Camlak would not have been given the opportunity to defy convention and opinion, but Yami was old and ageing faster all the time.

But if it was hard for Camlak to bring something alien into his world, it was ten times as hard for Joth to accept that he had come into that world. He found it difficult to locate himself, almost impossible to rediscover himself. Physiologically, he only had to be rehabituated. Mentally—perhaps spiritually—he had to be reshaped.

Joth was born again in Stalhelm. The world of Euchronia's Millennium, in which he had lived for more than twenty years, faded away as if it had been a dream. It retreated into his memory so far that it became almost unreal. It remained *his* world, insofar as he knew he had come from there, and it remained his insofar as he was determined that he should return to it if he could, but as a real and living world it was largely replaced by a whole new set of precepts and contexts.

The hold which Joth had on his own world—and the hold which it had on him—were naturally slight and superficial. Joth had no instincts.

He was lost, for a time, inside himself. He spent a period of time in nowhere. The people who tended him understood and accepted that, and they allowed him to come back in his own time. The people of the Underworld did not count, weigh and trade in time as did the people of Heaven, who were ruled by the metrication of days and nights. They had a better understanding of time and a more amicable relationship with it than did the people of the Overworld.

When Joth awoke, in the real sense of the word, he found himself occupied by fear. Not panic, but fear. He had found himself a balance. For a long time—subjective time —after his rebirth, Joth could find nothing in his past but insanity. But he was in something of a privileged position. He did know what a nightmare was. He had a label to apply, and a context into which his experiences could be set. It was a good start.

He remembered Ermold—just—but could make no sense of that particular encounter. He remembered the warriors finding and carrying him, too, and could make no sense of that either. But he could also remember Huldi and Nita and Camlak feeding him, tending him, cleaning him and cooling him. This he could make sense of. This he understood. These three individual beings he accepted as his friends, his relatives, his kindred of the new birth. He began to love them without being conscious of the fact, and he continued to love them likewise.

Two worlds met by Joth's bedside, and became caught up with one another.

When Joth finally knew for sure that he was alive, awake and real, Nita was beside him. He looked at her, trying to decide exactly what manner of being she might be. A dwarf. A child of a dwarf-people. A face like an animal, but too human to be anything but the face of a man—a girl, a child.

He searched his mind for something to say, and could find absolutely nothing. He knew that his failure must be written in his face, along with his fear. He looked around, and saw that they were alone in a small room. One lamp burned on a bracket in the wall. The walls seemed to be made of clay or crude plaster, but here and there the surface had crumbled to reveal the infrastructure, which consisted of bricks and square stones cemented together. The ceiling—also, presumably, the roof—slanted gently away from him, and was made of wood with the cracks sealed by the same plaster/clay.

He sighed and relaxed, letting his head sink back. The girl looked at him curiously, and reached out a hand to touch him. His face—the flesh beneath the metal hood—was hot, but not wet. There was sweat on his neck, though.

"The face," she murmured, trying to prompt him to speak.

"I was hurt," he said. "They repaired me. A long time ago."

She accepted that. "The eyes," she said, very quietly. "The eyes can see. But they are only bowls of metal. Metal lids, metal eyes."

"Yes," he said, finding words and glad of the opportunity to use them. "They replaced my eyes. The eyes work well. Better then real eyes." He whispered, as she did, not sure whether it was necessary.

"Better than mine?" she asked. Her eyes were small, wide-set but mobile and keen.

"Perhaps," he said.

"Your chin," she said. "Your ears, your head."

"Some is plastic flesh, not metal," he said. "They did what they could. But the plastic needs a base of real flesh. Where they had to cut to the bone, they had to use metal. The rest of me is real. All save a few scars of plastic. Quite human."

"Are there men in your world who are all metal?" she asked.

He wanted to answer, to reinforce his friendship for the child, but he was by no means sure what answer to give. There were robots in the old world—Euchronia's world— but were they men, by her definition? He decided not, in the end. The robots were never wholly humanoid.

"No," he said. "All men are flesh and blood. I was hurt. I have only been repaired. You understand? The top of my face was burned away."

She shook her head. "We don't repair men," she said. "Who burned you?"

"No one," he told her. He felt no impulse to laugh at her assumption that he had been burned deliberately. He knew that the question was serious. "It was an accident," he explained.

She said nothing for a few moments, looking pensive.

Then she said: "I knew, really."

"What?" he asked.

"That the men of the world above aren't made of metal. Some of the children have been saying so. The women say so. And worse things. It's the old women making up things. I knew better. All the time."

Again, no impulse to laugh. Had this been a human child . . . a child of the Overworld . . . But it *was* a human child, though not of the Overworld. Joth felt a moment of confusion. Was it . . . she? . . . human? Of course, he decided. But in that case, what, precisely, did the word "human" mean?

"How did you know?" he asked. He was not humoring her. He wanted to know. She could help him find out . . . everything . . . She could be his teacher.

"I can read," she said. She said it flatly, not proudly. It was not a boast. Reading, to her, was part of the pattern of life. She could read, therefore she knew. Others, presumably, were not so fortunate.

"Burstone," he murmured. "He brings you books. In the suitcase. That's what he was carrying. But why?"

She didn't reply. She didn't know what he was talking about.

He knew that he ought to begin to question her, to begin the long business of learning about his new world, but he was tired, and he hardly knew where to start. And he was still afraid. Very much afraid. His fear inhibited clear thinking. There was another priority, above that of learning. He had to know whether there was a way out, a way back. If not . . .

He faced the thought of death. Ryan had died in the Underworld. Somewhere.

He said: "The lights in the sky . . ." and paused. He had spoken loudly. She looked around quickly.

"We have no sky," she said, swiftly, as though time might be running short. "We have a roof. Some of them call it the sky, but they cannot read. The stars are set in the roof. The roof of the world. The sky is beyond that. I do not know how far." There was a dullness, almost a sadness, in the words as she spoke them.

He tried hard to see the special significance in what she said, but he could not.

"The lights in the roof," he said. "Do they always shine?"

"Always," she said.

"They have always been there?" he asked.

"Always," she said, patiently.

"We didn't know," he muttered, feeling that some kind of explanation was due. "I didn't believe him. I didn't really believe in the stars. But he was right."

Suddenly, before his mind had time to frame another question, she was gone. She had heard something outside. He looked at the curtain which hung over the doorway, which stirred slightly after her withdrawal.

He waited. He lay quite still. Wondering. Helpless.

33

Porcel was counting his blessings. There didn't seem to be very many. But time was on his side. He had not been forgiven for bringing back Joth instead of Ermold's head, and naturally enough the rumor that he had been frightened out of his wits by his first sight of the man with the metal face had been aired all over the village. But it would die, given time.

Porcel had ambition. He wanted to be Old Man. He didn't think much of Camlak's chances, and in open competition he had a better chance than most of imposing his will. He was a strong man, and a fierce fighter. The Communion of Souls was about due—an attack by Ermold was expected any time. So Porcel was estimating his chances, and thinking of ways to improve them. He had the time to think. Camlak was not in the village, nor were the warriors, for the most part. They were out in the fields, planning and organizing defenses. He had been detailed to stand guard at the long house. Apart from a handful of warriors at the gate there were only women and elders and children within the wall.

Porcel knew that there was no point in standing guard at the long house. It was a purely ceremonial duty. Hence he was bored, and thinking hard. Could he provoke a fight with Camlak? Could he arrange things so that Camlak would *have* to fight him, and on his own terms?

While he was thinking, he saw Nita slip through the skull-gate and make for Camlak's house. He watched her, knowing that she was going to the man with the metal face. Porcel had decided that he hated the man with the metal face, and that it would have been sensible to have lopped off his head while the opportunity was there. He would hardly have been able to claim much credit for lopping a head of a quiescent body, but to have settled the matter there and then would have meant that subsequent trouble could have been avoided entirely. Yami was at odds with his son for taking the alien in, but he was also at odds with Porcel for having brought him in in the first place.

Porcel decided that he would take Nita as a wife. Such a marriage would be desirable if he were to become Old Man, as some sense of kinship between rulers seemed proper. In addition, Camlak would hate the idea and Porcel would enjoy taking some of his hatred for Camlak out on the child. Further to these very good reasons was the ambition of simple carnal lust.

The warrior's eyes dwelt on the doorway to Camlak's house while these thoughts ran round his idle mind, and he began to feel resentment and determination rise within him.

Sada passed him by then, and shot him a quick glance as she did so. She muttered something about there not being a man left in the village, maliciously, just loud enough for him to catch the general drift of her meaning. He lost his temper and stepped quickly toward her. Sada ran away, past Camlak's house and in between two others. Rather than run to catch up with her, Porcel kept walking, straight through Camlak's threshold and into his house. The woman Ayria was there, having taken over the household duties from the disespoused Sada. She looked up in surprise as Porcel strode in.

She ducked the first blow he threw, but was too completely off her guard to dodge the second—a wild, backhanded smash with no real malicious intent but quite some power. It caught the side of her head and knocked her over. She whimpered, completely bewildered by the warrior's behaviour.

Porcel paused, realizing that there was no point in taking out his vindictiveness on Ayria, who had done no one any harm, but the rage of his bitterness carried him away for a few moments more. He looked around, clenching his fist convulsively. Nita came out of the back room to find out what was happening.

She tried to get round Porcel to the door and failed. He grabbed her and lifted her off the ground, his eyes flaring suddenly as his anger found a real target. He lost all thought of consequence and gave way to the full force of his inner fury. He hurled the child to the ground, flat on her back, and ripped her ragged skirt apart. She had no other garment underneath.

Porcel dropped heavily on top of her, pinning her securely before reaching down to dispose of his own skirt.

Ayria backed away into a corner, totally bewildered and settled into immobility, watching without understanding.

But someone understood. Sada, curious as to why Porcel had gone into Camlak's house, had come back to find out. She lifted a corner of the cloth which covered the door and began to laugh. She was delighted by the thought of what was happening.

Nita could not find the breath to scream. The sudden and unexpected assault had left her completely winded. The weight of Porcel's body crushing her seemed to preclude the possibility of any air even reaching her lungs again, and she was convinced that she was dying. She felt Porcel fumbling at her groin but she experienced no pain at all as he tried to thrust into her. All the pain was locked into her chest and head, and she was terror-stricken because it would not come out and let her draw breath.

Even when Porcel's weight was summarily snatched away she could not suck air into her lungs and she had no idea of what was happening. She was simply alone with her terror.

Joth kicked Porcel clear out of the door, sending Sada bounding backwards out of the way. He followed up, and kicked the warrior again, as hard as he could. He felt a quick wave of satisfaction as the blow had similarly spectacular results. Joth weighed more than twice as much as Porcel, and he had long legs. He was not back to peak fitness by any means, but he had power enough.

By the time Porcel realized what was happening to him he was half naked and sprawling in the mud halfway back to the portal of the long house. The first time he tried to rise he slipped and fell back into the glutinous filth of the street. At first, he realized only that he had been hit and hit hard, and his actions were purely reflexive. But then he realized who had hit him, and how. He also realized that he was in full view of half the village. Sada was whooping and an audience would not be long in gathering.

He made a noise that was pure animal, and reached for his weapon. Joth hung back momentarily, unsure of himself, and Porcel found the time to come to his feet and take the long knife from its scabbard. While Joth still hesitated, the warrior launched himself murderously into the attack.

Joth had not expected the little man he had kicked so effectively to transform himself into a ferocious—and very fearsome—beast with a vicious instrument of murder and a clear intention of using it.

In the split second that Joth saw Porcel coming he remembered that he was still exhausted, very stiff, and had never indulged in any form of violence in the whole of his active life.

He would have been stone dead within a second if Porcel had not been so completely driven by mad hatred. The warrior was far, far faster than the man from the world above, and Joth's clumsy attempt to get out of the way would have availed him nothing if Porcel had not been so utterly determined to ram home his point with every last vestige of strength he could muster.

But sheer inertia carried Porcel's point a fraction of an inch past Joth's swerving waist. The same inertia took Porcel the way of the blade.

The two bodies collided, but Joth remained unhurt and more or less unmoved. The relative masses of the two men made it inevitable that it was Porcel who was thrown off balance to sprawl once again in the dirt. Joth won a precious second or so to scramble away. He made the best possible use of it.

But there was no possibility of escape. Joth couldn't run. Porcel whirled as he rolled right back to the doorway of Camlak's house, and then he stopped deliberately, allowing himself the luxury of two seconds to collect himself and to control and discipline his anger. He decided in that brief space of time exactly how he was going to begin carving Joth into small slices.

There was one instant in which Joth met his murderer's eyes, and read all the malice and the hate therein. Somewhere at the back of his mind he noted, with some wonder, the intense humanness of Porcel's registered emotions.

Then Porcel's mind went absolutely blank. He collapsed silently in a ragged heap. He fell on top of his knife, but it did not pierce him.

Huldi stepped out of the doorway, still holding the cooking pot she had hit him with. She looked round, fearfully, at the circle of eager faces.

Sada was laughing.

34

Eliot Rypeck was a small, excitable man with an unusual combination of mental proclivities. On the one hand he was a man who could pay excessive attention to trivia (something of a collector's quirk) and on the other he was one of the few men who had a genuine understanding of the way in which man and the cybernet were potentially capable of establishing a quasi-symbiotic collaborative relationship within the context of mechanized society. Because of this, he was something of a two-sided coin. His determined opposition to the perpetuation of the i-minus project beyond the Plan and into the Millennial society itself reflects the *second* side of the coin—the basis of this particular conviction was the belief that man should be allowed full scope to adapt himself wholly to the new environment of the cybernet. While the instinct-suppressor was in use, he believed that this could not be achieved.

Rypeck was not expert in any particular field, but with respect to any specific topic which happened to attract his attention he was capable of very rapidly picking out significant factors and gaining a good working understanding of it. His affinity with the cybernet was only a good working relationship after this fashion, but by the standards of the early Millennium it was remarkable.

Heres and Rypeck were natural enemies to some extent. The form of their personalities was such that they clashed inevitably over method and manner. Rypeck was an older man than Heres, and became a member of the close council before Heres joined it. Heres would not have permitted a man like Rypeck to be coopted into the council once he became Hegemon, but once a secret is shared, there is no way of taking it back. A member of the close council, once inducted, was a member for life.

It might be argued that it was Rypeck who should have been Hegemon and not Heres. Again, this reflects the difference between their characters. Rypeck would have been a more efficient administrator, but it was Heres who com-

manded the following. In fact, had their positions been re-
versed both Rypeck and Heres would probably have found
the situation intolerable.

Like Heres, Rypeck was an excellent Hoh player. His
basic assumptions and strategies were different, but he
worked toward similar ends, and his play was only marginally less masterful than the Hegemon's. Hoh provided an
important touching point for their minds and personalities.
It enabled them to get along together. Hoh was important
in the lives of both men.

35

"I have to confess," said Rypeck, "that I'm frightened."

Heres regarded the image in his screen soberly. Though
there was no animosity in his expression he could not keep
it out of his voice.

"There's no need for melodrama," he said.

"I am *frightened*," insisted Rypeck, "by the extent of our
ignorance."

"Well then," said Heres, "I suggest you set about alleviat-
ing some of that ignorance by telling me what you're talking about."

"I'm talking about dependence on the cybernet," said
Rypeck. "Not the old, old argument about where would we
all be if the net stopped working—I'm talking about a different *kind* of dependence altogether.

"Quite apart from its operational functions the cybernet
provides us with a central data storage system. That, of
course, is one function that the cybernet is uniquely equipped
to handle. It is at this point that we ought to see the perfect
partnership of man and machine. The machine provides
data storage, sorting and processing facilities while the man
provides creative thought and purpose.

"You know all about the controversies concerning machine intelligence and the possibility of the machine's being
able to provide the human element of the partnership itself.
But you've probably not considered an alternative problem."

"Get to the point," said Heres.

"The point is," said Rypeck, "that instead of worrying about one element in the partnership crossing the gap and fulfilling all functions by itself, we ought to be worrying about the gap becoming so wide that the functions cannot be fulfilled at all."

"You don't make sense," said Heres, drumming his fingers on the console of his desk unit.

"Let me put it this way," said Rypeck. "The machine isn't duplicating human functions—but the human is *failing* to duplicate, in any meaningful degree, the machine functions. We are becoming too specialized as providers of creative thought and purpose. The cybernet provides us with a supremely efficient data store, but in order to use that store we must retain some sort of idea of what it contains and what processes may be used in order to exploit it properly. The cybernet is infallible. It never forgets. But this does not mean that *we* can forget everything we ever knew. In order to use the data in the net we have to know it is there. The partnership cannot work if neither element in it has any conception of what the other can contribute. The gap becomes uncrossable.

"Because we rely on the cybernet to be our memory we have become an ignorant people. Not only that, but we do not even realize that we are ignorant. Because the cybernet knows everything, we consider that we do too. But what use is information in the cybernet if we do not know it is there, and would not know its relevance if we did?"

"Eliot," said Heres, "I'm busy. Did you call me to argue about a purely theoretical point or have you actually got something to say?"

Rypeck sighed. "Yes," he said, "I have something to say. I want to say that we are ignorant, and that our ignorance frightens me. But as that's not what you want to hear I'll tell you some other things instead.

"I've been trying to find out what we know about the Underworld. I expected to find that we know virtually nothing. I never gave a moment's thought to the Underworld until this matter came up. I assumed it had been ignored ever since the platform was completed. I was wrong. There is a good deal of information about the Underworld in the net. Some of it is very disturbing information.

"Firstly, there is life in the Underworld. Secondly, it isn't absolutely confined there. Spores from the Underworld plant kingdom and microfauna of all kinds flow constantly into the lower regions of our own world. The machines at the lower levels are equipped to deal with this constant invasion and do so most effectively. Almost nothing is manifest on the surface itself because these organisms are not equipped to compete effectively with surface organisms. But a number of species now established on the surface undoubtedly originated in the Underworld after the separation. There are no less than forty different kinds of automatic devices specifically designed to cope with the invasion of Underworld organisms in the lower levels. They are efficient. Within limits.

"The Underworld is illuminated by several millions of electric lights set in the ceiling of that world—on the under side of the floors of our lowest levels. Their power consumption is not great compared to the power consumption of our own lighting facilities, but it is significant. Thus there are several facts for you to think about. The Underworld is alive, and it is alive—at least in part—because we keep it alive. It is not completely separate from us and it never has been. Enzo told us all at the close council meeting to remember the Underworld—to remember that the world the Movement abandoned is still there. I say that remembering is not enough. We should never have forgotten the Underworld.

"Rafael, I have been working on this for a matter of days. What else is there that I ought to know? What else is there in the net that I might be able to find—if I knew what to look for? This is more important than the Magner affair. It's more important even than the Underworld. We haven't *begun* to count the cost of the eleven thousand years of the Plan, in terms of knowledge which we have lost and which we are making almost no effort to recover. We're as innocent as newborn children, Rafael, can't you understand that?"

"You're getting upset about nothing," said Heres flatly. "I advise you to think about it for a while. What's the point in coming to me with a lot of garbled nonsense like that? We need the information about the Underworld now, and it's there to be recovered. All you have to do is recover it. Just get the facts, and forget the rest."

"That's just the trouble," said Rypeck. "We have forgotten the rest."

Heres made a gesture of annoyance and switched off the screen.

36

Rypeck was not the only one who went digging for information in the cybernet and found more than he bargained for. Alwyn Ballow conducted some research for Yvon Emerich, preparatory to exposing Magner to the cameras. And Abram Ravelvent went in search of knowledge partly for its own sake and partly for the benefit of Harkanter's expedition, which was getting together very slowly and in no apparent hurry.

The degree of success which they enjoyed in searching out facts was various. Ballow did not get very far, but he did manage to find out about the lights. Ravelvent found out about the lights early on in his study and was inspired to investigate the flow of energy from Overworld to Underworld in rather more detail. In this matter he found a great deal more than he bargained for. A study of the energy budget over the Overworld covering a period of ten or a hundred years would probably have told him nothing. But Ravelvent, unlike Rypeck and Ballow, was pursuing a rather broader picture of the possible basis on which life in the Underworld subsisted. He dealt in thousands of years. With the calculative facilities of the cybernet there was no reason why he should not. Over a thousand years, even the tiniest discrepancies show up. And once he had located one discrepancy he began to locate more, and more.

Ultimately, he was forced to the quite fantastic conclusion that export from the Overworld to the Underworld was not merely a matter of light energy and waste products. A steady trickle of materials of many kinds had been working its way into the Underworld for years. Not only the years of the Millennial society, but also the many long years of the Plan. In the days when every last ton of usable metal and every last scrap of paper should have been under strict control no less than in the days of present affluence there had been a steady drain of material into the world below. Manufactured goods had been continually exported, albeit on a microscopic scale, consistently since the day the platform was complete. Someone was—and had been for a very long time—supplying the Underworld with metal and with paper and with plastic. Weapons, tools and books.

Ravelvent was forced to conclude that it was the Movement itself which was responsible. There seemed to be no alternative. But whoever was directing the supply, it was obvious that the machines of the Overworld were supporting not one world, but two.

37

Porcel woke up with a sick headache. He was somewhat surprised to find that he was still alive. Had Camlak arrived back while he was unconscious, there was every chance that he might not have been. But Camlak was not back, and he had been removed from where he fell by some of the women. He was now in his own house.

He decided almost immediately that there was no time to be wasted. There was no longer any problem about provoking a fight with Camlak. The problem now was to enlist support in making a formal affair out of the fight. Matters were coming to a head. The Communion of Souls would be declared soon, and then the bickering would start. Yami's time was over and someone had to succeed him.

Porcel went out in search of support. He expected it to be easy to come by, but he was wrong. It did not take him long to find out who it was that had hit him over the head, and with what. His standing in the village had fallen catastrophically. It was hardly any fault of his own that he had been felled from behind with a cooking pot, but that was what had happened, and his public image was in ruins.

His temper, which had started out bad, got worse.

38

Yami emerged from the long house to confront the assembled people of Stalhelm. He was dressed in his ceremonial robes, and he was already deep in the trance state. The Chief Elders lined up behind him. They, too, were in trance, but they would have no part to play in the Old Man's declarations. They were present purely and simply for show. It was Yami and Yami's soul that mattered.

Before the Old Man came out the crowd had been making a good deal of noise. Camlak had returned only minutes before, with the main party of the warriors and virtually all of the field-workers, the stone-workers and the gatherers. Talk was flying back and forth across this large group with great speed and verve. But Yami silenced them all with a gesture, while he took up his position squatting on the high throne-stone. There he waited, until his audience settled.

"The Communion of Souls is beginning," intoned Yami, in his Oracular voice. "We must make ready."

There was a long, pregnant pause. The audience waited for Yami to proceed to the important business. The Sun had to be chosen, and the Earth, and the Star King. And the testing had to be determined.

Yami let the silence drag on. This moment, in itself, was a kind of test. This was the moment when names formed on every tongue, when every mouth had to taste the name it held, and decide whether to swallow or to shout. This was the moment when ambitions had to be weighed carefully, and either discarded or committed to the test.

Finally, Yami spoke again.

"Who will name the Star King?" he asked.

This time, there was no pause. Porcel stood up from where he crouched beside the throne-stone, and said flatly, "I name Yami."

Yami, in trance, was not permitted to react. He was not present in his own person, but in the person of his Gray Soul, and in the person of the Old Man. If he accepted his own name, as he might well be bound to do, then he would

wake from the trance state not as the leader of his people
but as their victim.

Not one of the elders challenged Porcel's declaration. They,
too, had come to a decision in this matter, and they agreed.
But Camlak, for one, was determined that the matter
should not rest there.

"I name Porcel," he said, without rising from where he
crouched at the back of the crowd. Porcel did not bother to
react. He knew, as did the elders, that Camlak's call could
not be accepted. Yami was an ancient, at the end of his life.
Porcel was a warrior. If anyone were to be named who
had any real chance of being Star King instead of Yami,
then it would be an elder, or perhaps a reader. Not a fighting man.

But there was no other name. It had already been settled
between those who mattered that Yami's time was over.
Even Yami would have accepted that. He loved life as
well as anyone, but he knew as well as anyone the way in
which life was lived—and from that there could be no freedom.

"Yami is named Star King," said the Oracle, speaking his
own name without a trace of emotion. "Who will name the
Sun?"

This time it was bent-legged Chemec who sprang to his
feet beneath the high stone.

"I name Porcel," he called loudly. This time there was a
reaction in the crowd. Some laughed, others made vague
sounds of agreement.

The reader named Orgond then nominated Camlak, and
this nomination too was greeted with mixed sounds of approval and derision.

There was a pause, while the people waited to discover
whether anyone else wished to declare his ambition at this
particular point in time. And a third name was offered, and
then a fourth. It was an unusually high number. But neither
Porcel nor Camlak could be said to meet with unilateral approval, and this would be the last chance for a good many
men who were passing or just approaching their prime, and
in whom spirits ran high.

The third name was Yewen, and the fourth Magant.
Both these men were good fighting men, strong and intelligent, but neither of them would have seemed likely candi-
dates. Their ambitions had been nurtured more or less in
secret.

Yami rejected none of the four names. A slight stir ran through the crowd when this was realized. Usually, these matters were settled directly between the aspirants, but the Old Man could hardly order four men into a ring to fight it out. Three dead men was a high price to pay for a Communion of Souls, and the winner of such a complex contest would hardly be able to claim all the credit of victory.

"The names will be put to the test," said Yami, still intoning in a low, smooth voice. "They must face the harrowhound. The one who kills will rise as the Sun."

Camlak felt his heart sink inside his chest. He had known that the time was come to face the crucial test—he had expected to fight Porcel in the ring. This test, however, was an entirely different thing. He would be at a disadvantage in a duel, but that was nothing compared to the challenge of facing a harrowhound. And in this manner of contest, he would have to face it alone. He looked toward the base of the throne-stone, and he found Porcel's face amid the crowd. Porcel was looking back at him. Their eyes met and locked. Neither man knew what the other would do.

Somewhere in the crowd, Yewen withdrew his name. After a pause of half a minute or so, Magant also indicated that he was unwilling to accept the test. Porcel and Camlak both remained silent. If either one refused, then the other would pass the test by default, and would not have to go through with the challenge. Each man waited for the other to refuse, and when each man realized that the other would not they searched for the courage to accept.

Finally, Porcel said: "I will kill the harrowhound."

It was a bold enough step, but one taken in bitterness rather than in courage.

Camlak had no alternative but to declare that he also would attempt to kill the beast.

The ritual then passed on, but as Yami—supposedly entranced—said: "Who will name the Earth?" a faint trace of a smile lingered around his mouth. Camlak was not the only one who believed that the Old Man, condemned or not, had contrived to have the last laugh.

39

All forms of social organization are inherently repressive.

In any society certain "natural" attributes of the human being (that is to say, attributes determined by genetic selection, defined over a matter of thousands or millions of years) must be set aside in favor of "unnatural" social demands (that is to say, demands which are historically recent and selected by nongenetic processes). In order that society should exist and develop according to the precepts of the individuals involved, a certain suppression of "human nature" is absolutely necessary.

As a result of this necessity, it is inevitable that the individual in society should be the focus of a conflict. His instinctive pattern of reactive behavior and his socially conditioned pattern of learned behavior are at odds. The resolution of this conflict may take several forms. If the repression of instinct is total, then perfect adjustment to society becomes a theoretical possibility. Total repression, however, is itself a state of personal maladjustment. Society may enforce conformity by increasing the pressure of repression, but if this process is successful then society becomes an assembly of neurotics. If, on the other hand, society tries to reorganize in order to allow instinctive patterns some limited contexts for expression, the entire social unit will become "neurotic" in that it will always exhibit self-threatening symptoms.

The Euchronian Movement wished to create a stable society. It needed such a high level of organization in order that the Plan could be completed that total repression and conformity seemed imperative. However, the ultimate aim of the Movement was to create a society where repression would be minimal. The Movement therefore faced a dilemma. In searching for a way to sidestep the whole problem, it came up with the i-minus effect.

The i-minus agent did not do away with instincts altogether, it merely prevented them from having any influence on behavior patterns.

Instincts are programmed into the genetic heritage of the individual. But the behavior patterns signified by the instincts still have to be learned. There has to be a process by which the purely physical language of the genes has to be translated into the conceptual language of the mind. An individual learns to behave instinctively in exactly the same way that he learns to behave socially—by repetition and rehearsal. The conscious mind provides one arena for such rehearsal, but *only* for consciously observed behavior—that is to say, social behavior. The conscious mind does not have direct access to the instincts.

There is, however, a second arena in which behavior may be rehearsed and learned, and that is the arena of dreams.

Animal dreams consist entirely of rehearsals of instinctive patterns of behavior. When an animal dreams its brain operates exactly as if the animal were awake and active, except that all motor stimuli to the body are short-circuited by a body known as the pons. If the pons is prevented from carrying out its function by surgery, animals can be observed "acting out" their dreams. Sleeping cats go through the motions of hunting, stalking, eating and the full range of sexual behavior. Everything which an animal does not learn from real experience it learns from "unreal" experience in its dreams.

In animals there is rarely any conflict between the behavior patterns learned from external experience and those learned from internal experience. Animals live the life which is laid down for them in their genetic heritage. They never try to be anything different. The only time that they are forced into conflict is when they are forced to be something other than they were "intended" to be by man. Only domestic animals and animals in zoos tend to become neurotic, and they tend to become neurotic because what they are taught by their manmade environment conflicts with what they are taught by their instincts.

In man himself, however, the situation is very much more complicated. Man *does* try, continually, to be something other than instinct would make him. This is the consequence of mental evolution to the point where the conscious mind obtains means of control and influence over the subconscious. Once a species evolves intelligence and self-consciousness, then its development races far ahead of the slow process of instinctive evolution. The trouble is that instincts can only be reshaped by natural selection—a tortuously slow process—while society can be remolded continuously by will power in the service of the active conscious mind. In the human being, the arena of dreams becomes an arena indeed —a battleground where learning and belief and imagination conflict terribly with the rehearsal of instinctive behavior patterns. In a human being, a dream is at best enigmatic and at worst maddening. All human beings are domestic animals or animals in a zoo—creatures in conflict—and the only answer provided by the power of the mind is repression, which is not a cure but merely an alleviation of the symptoms.

The i-minus agent devised by the Euchronian Movement during the years of the Plan changed all that. The i-minus agent was a selective genetic inhibitor which prevented all forms of genetic translation into the arena of dreams. The *only* input into the dreams of Euchronia's citizens was the input of real experience.

The theory was that this would lead to perfect social adjustment. The theory was only half-right. The citizens of Euchronia dreamed on, and their dreams were not devoid of conflict. But that conflict was muted very considerably indeed, and it was conflict of a rather different kind—a purely intellectual conflict of ideas and opinions.

The i-minus agent was administered in secret to the struggling millions who made themselves subject to the Euchronian Movement—in the food and in the water. In large measure, the i-minus project was responsible for the completeness of the dedication lent to the Plan by the people committed to it. One could not argue that the Plan would have been impossible without the i-minus agent, but it would certainly have taken much longer to complete.

When the Millennium was declared, the custodians of the secret decided that the project should be maintained in the interests of promoting adjustment to the new social régime. They formed a close council and laid down the rule that the council should perpetuate itself by coopting new members to replace those who died. The power of the close council in this matter was to be administrative—other men who were party to the secret (scientists, for the most part, and some civil servants in charge of food production and mobilization) agreed to abide by the majority decision of that council.

It was generally agreed that in order to remain effective

the i-minus effect had to be secret. Otherwise, any individual who cared to do so might exempt himself.

The simple fact was, however, that the Euchronian Millennium did not see any very rapid adjustment to the new social environment. Blocking the instinctive input into dreams was simply not enough to guarantee Utopia—not, at any rate, in a matter of decades. The intellectual conflict continued unchecked, and the society of the Euchronian Millennium continued to reflect that conflict.

On the other hand, had the i-minus project been abandoned, Euchronian society might have been considerably worse off. One does not eliminate conflict by introducing new conflicts. The moral question of whether or not i-minus was justified was, of course, a different one. Opinions varied greatly.

In the meantime, Euchronia's citizens had relatively peaceful sleep, and nobody suffered from nightmares. Until Carl Magner . . .

40

Julea was sitting in the garden, supposedly reading, but not really paying much attention to the book. The sun was high and hot, and she had eaten a heavy meal. She might have drifted off into sleep had it not been for the fact that she was saturated with sleep. She slept long hours these days —as long as she could.

A man's shadow fell across her couch.

"Oh," she said, peering upwards, squinting against the light of the sun. "It's you."

Thorold Warnet sat down on the grass, and reached out a hand to toy with a rose which grew behind the couch.

"Has he come back?" he asked.

"No," she said. "Did you come through the house or climb over the wall?"

He shrugged. "I didn't want to disturb your father."

"He knows far more about all this than I do," she said.

"He doesn't know what I want to know."

"What makes you think I do?" she demanded. "All this is

nothing to do with me. I don't have bad dreams, and I don't write books. I'm tired of the arguments. I don't really have an opinion, one way or the other, and I know that whatever anyone says the Underworld *isn't* going to be opened, so why don't you go argue with someone else?"

"I didn't come to argue," said Warnet. "I came to find out what Ryan knew that he told you, and that you told Joth. That's all."

"If you're sure that's what happened how is it that you don't know what it is that was passed so mysteriously along the chain of communication?"

"Because you haven't told me yet."

"I won't," she said. "Why should I? You're a Eupsychian."

"I'm not a criminal," he said. "Just a heretic. A Eupsychian is as entitled to be interested in the Underworld as anyone else. Both your brothers have gone down there. I know why Ryan went. He was properly equipped and others went with him. He knew what he was doing, to some extent. But Joth made no preparations, and he didn't tell anyone he was going—except you. He had no equipment, and no real reason. That seems odd to me, if not to anyone else. It suggests to me that perhaps Joth *didn't* intend to disappear. Perhaps he only wanted to look at the Underworld. Perhaps he only wanted to know how to get down. Perhaps something unexpected happened. Your father doesn't know. He doesn't know anything. I think you do."

"Why should I tell you, if I haven't even told my father?" she asked.

"Why shouldn't you tell me?" he countered. *"And* your father? Why keep it a secret?"

"Because Ryan told me not to tell anyone," she said quietly.

"But you did," Warnet said, also quietly. "You told Joth."

"Exactly," she said.

"Don't you want to know what happened to Joth?" he asked.

"Nothing's happened to Joth. I'm waiting for him to come back. That's all."

"He might not," said Warnet.

She wouldn't answer that comment. She pretended to look at her book.

"We can help you," persisted the Eupsychian. "We can find out what *did* happen, if you give us the chance. We can find the truth. Or is that what you're afraid of? Perhaps you'd rather *not* face the truth? Perhaps you'd rather pretend?"

"Perhaps," she said, coldly.

"Is your father's book a true account of life in the Underworld?" he asked.

"No," she said.

"But you don't know that. Nobody knows that except Ryan and his companions. And perhaps Joth. Possibly Joth."

"There's no point," she said, her voice breaking slightly into a tremulous whisper.

"Just *tell* me," he pleaded. "Just tell me what it is that led Joth to do whatever he did."

She hovered on the brink of tears. Rather than give way to them, she gave way to the questions.

"Ryan told me there was a man," she said. "A man who had been into the Underworld. Not just once. Lots of times. That's how Ryan knew how to get down into the Underworld. He said this man knew several routes, and used them. He thought it would be safe. But it wasn't. It couldn't have been. I didn't want to tell anybody."

"But you told Joth."

"Yes. And Joth's gone too. I shouldn't have let him go. Not after Ryan didn't come back. He went to find the man —went to find out about him. And he hasn't come back either."

"What's his name?" asked Warnet, softly.

"Jervis Burstone," she said.

41

Carl Magner watched the young man disappear at the bottom of the garden. He was too far away to make out any details, and a little too distraught to care overmuch. Later, however, he went out to speak to his daughter about the visitor.

She explained what Warnet had wanted, but she lied, saying that she knew nothing and had told him nothing. There was nothing which could make her send her father after her two brothers. She hoped that Warnet would find out about

Burstone and make sure that no one else ever went down into the world below.

"I was dreaming again," Magner told her. "The dream is always there. It's only a matter of time before it's there while I wake as well as while I sleep. The people . . . I see them all the more clearly every time . . . I only wish that someone could really understand."

"Yes," she said, inaudibly. "I wish that someone could."

42

Joth woke screaming from his nightmare.

Huldi rolled over and put her hand over his mouth, pressing hard to squeeze him into silence. When she was sure that he was finished she let her fingers go limp, and lifted them slowly.

Joth lay perfectly still, his spine rigid. He let out his tongue to lick the sweat from his upper lip. It tasted of Huldi's hand.

"It's going," he whispered, his tone undulating on the soft whistle of his fast-drawn breath. "It's going. Farther and farther."

"What?" she asked. "What was it?"

"I don't know," he said, fearfully. "I don't know. Already. It's going away. I can't remember. I didn't see. I don't know."

"It's only a dream," she said, putting her fingers back to his face. She touched his lips briefly, then let them linger on his cheek. His face was hot and dry. The only sweat was the sweat that came from her hand. He licked his own fingers and drew them across his forehead. There was water in a bowl not far away, but he could not reach it while his back was still rigid. Somehow, for some strange reason, he dared not move.

"It wasn't the same," he said. "It wasn't the same dream. Not at all. There was nothing . . . nothing at all . . . it was . . . insane. Crazy. I'm going mad."

"It was only a dream," whispered Huldi. "Only a dream."

"Not the same," he muttered.

Camlak drew aside the curtain and stood in the doorway, staring at them. The room behind him was lamplit, but the room which Joth and Huldi shared was pitch dark. Nevertheless, by some complex line of reflection, they could see a glint in Camlak's eyes.

Huldi flinched, fearing that they had disturbed him. But he spoke to them in a low voice, with no hint of anger.

"They came back a few minutes ago," he said. "The harrowhound has killed Porcel. It is time for me to go."

43

Camlak sniffed the air. He made a small sound in his throat, something between a cough and a purr. It was wordless and meaningless, an animal sound. For the time being, he was not wholly a man, because he had retreated into the cave of his mind, so that the Gray Soul could simulate something of the beast in him. Something of the harrowhound. A hunter needs to identify with his quarry. It is what makes him a hunter. Camlak made the animal sound for its own sake. It was not communicative.

The others were some way behind him. Chemec was there, and Magant and Cicon. The warriors of the village come to sit in lofty judgment over their kindred. A judgment from apart, without decision or participation. Only Porcel was not with them. Porcel was already dead.

If Camlak died too . . . well then, the bickering would begin all over again. They would cast dice for the pleasure of taking Yami's head. They would cast dice for Huldi, too, and Joth . . . they would let blood in full confidence because both Porcel and Camlak had spilled all theirs in the test. They would let blood in fear and in hope that they could continue to do so—in the war against Ermold's raiders.

Camlak carried a long knife and a short spear. The knife was beaten metal—soft, tainted Underworld metal which decayed and splintered, not the hard steel of the world above. The spear was tipped with bone—the bone of a harrowhound —and its shaft had been dressed in the blood of a harrowhound. A hunter must identify his weapons with his quarry.

In this fight there would be no help from Heaven at all. Camlak had nothing which was not his own. This was a man's challenge and there was more at stake than life and death.

There was a group of warriors peeling away from the main party, away to the left. Another would begin working its way to the right in a matter of moments. They carried drums and horns—their purpose was not to kill but to herd. They were to make sure that the harrowhound would not run. It was not the way of the harrowhound to avoid a challenge, but the beast had already fought once, and had eaten its fill of the victory. Camlak knew that he had an advantage over the beast which Porcel had not. But that was the luck of the draw. Nothing is decided by fitness alone. There is always the random factor. But the fact that he faced a slower, perhaps less ferocious, harrowhound did not make Camlak's test an easy one. It was still, perhaps, the ultimate test of all.

Camlak had to offer himself to the hunting-beast, to make it clear that they were fighting under rules. The harrowhound would understand. It would know that the fight was one-to-one and that if it won it would be allowed to run free. Until the hunters came again.

Not one of the warriors following Camlak had ever faced such an enemy alone, for all that they were men of courage and strength. In the normal course of events it would not occur to four or five hunters to track a harrowhound to the kill. Ten men might, but any less would content themselves with defending life and property. Even in a grand hunt, when twenty or thirty men might set out to corner and kill a hound, it was accepted that one man or two might die. Many such parties considered themselves fortunate to return home two men short, with only one huge head to show for it.

There could be no possible doubt that Porcel, given the choice, would far rather have faced a man than a harrowhound, even if he considered the advantage to be against him. But Camlak was not so sure. He was not, by nature, a fighting man. He had not the taste for man-killing. Hunting was entirely different, even hunting a man-beast. He would not have felt at ease facing Porcel in a ring. But in confrontation with a harrowhound, he *was* at ease. He had true confidence in the idea that this was *the* way of life. The killing of men—even Men Without Souls, to some extent—

he thought of as Yami's way, which was an altogether different thing.

In a slender gully, where a stream ran slowly, and thin, dry spikestalks pushed their way up from cracks in bare rock, the harrowhound decided to make its stand. It knew what was happening because of the drums. It knew that it was called upon to kill or be killed. It knew enough to select its own ground. It was an intelligent beast, though its world was devoid of how and why and measured time. It was a thinking beast, a calculating beast. It knew the odds, and it knew the odds were in its favor. It waited in the gully, preparing itself for the contest, adjusting its state of mind. Its brown eyes gleamed with tear-reflected starlight. Its tongue lolled from its great mouth, stirring slightly and sliding back and forth across the crowns of its savage teeth.

It was not smiling.

Neither was Camlak, who came slowly up the gully, deliberately relaxing his muscles and his mind, tautening his spirit and trying to attract his Gray Soul out of the wilderness of nowhere and into the battle.

The drums slowed and stopped, and the last mournful notes of the horns died a lingering death. The warriors of the Children of the Voice aligned themselves along the gaping, twisted lips which ridged the gully, and they looked down from their vantage, eager to appreciate the coming conflict. The combatants seemed to be a long time coming to the climactic moment of their meeting. The harrowhound moved not at all, and Camlak seemed as though he were walking through water.

The great beast stood nearly as tall on four legs as Camlak stood on two. Only its head seemed out of proportion (too small) and even this impression was offset by its vast luminous brown eyes. Camlak wore a little armor, but it was only hide and bone—the natural armor of the harrowhound (thick, matted hair) was probably more efficient, and certainly more comfortable. Camlak also carried weapons, but these too seemed little enough compared to the natural weapons of the beast—the knives set in the hound's jaws were as sharp and strong as his, and *alive*. The massive callused paws were frightening clubs.

They faced each other, locked eyes, and showed themselves. Camlak did not stop his slow march forward. He was balanced lightly on his feet, his short tail held rigid, his own tiny jaws held slightly agape.

The beast looked at him somberly, fearlessly. It sensed, somehow, that even the assembled crowd were in the balance. They were not committed to Camlak—they did not know whether or not they wanted him to win.

The harrowhound moved forward, closing the distance between itself and the oncoming hunter in a couple of long, loping strides. It expected the man to pause, or even to fall back, jockeying for position, trying to spy a mark for the spear, preparing a sequence of moves which might inflict a blow without taking one in return. But Camlak did not fall back and try to set himself up to receive the charge. On the crest of a sudden wave of terror, Camlak surged forward.

The harrowhound howled with terrifying volume as it launched itself from its back legs, already too close for the leap to be timed to perfection.

Camlak's soft hiss was lost in the howl, and to the watchers on the ridge it seemed that his body was lost too, disappeared into the belly of the hound as the hunter moved the wrong way.

The head of the beast came down, jaws reaching apart, the whiteness of teeth gleaming in the starlight.

The closeness of the bodies made it difficult to see what might be happening. The warriors expected that Camlak would have plunged his spear into the off-white underbelly of the beast, and thrust his knife up at the threatening head. They knew, as the beast must have known, that neither attack could do any lasting damage. The spear-point would stick in the muscle if it penetrated the hide. It could not get past the ribs to the pleural cavity. The thrust into the mouth might draw blood and cause pain, but the blade could not possibly reach a vital point *via* the skull. But the watchers could not see what Camlak did—they could only guess.

For a fleeting second Camlak believed that he was lost and dead, but he was not. Somehow he avoided the sweep of the massive jaws. He had not lost or broken his spear. He still held his knife. He swung away to one side, out from the shadow of the monster, slashing at it with a frantic sideways stab. The blow cut skin and seared tendon, and when Camlak was clear and the hound came down its leg buckled under its weight. As the combatants drew apart the beast seemed almost to limp.

The warriors fastened their stares on Camlak to see how he was hurt. But Camlak still moved easily—without speed, but without brokenness. Camlak surged into the shadow of the beast for a second time, and this time the beast had little enough grace in its leap. There had been no pause to draw breath, no hesitation of fatigue or fear. The harrowhound's head ducked once, twice, almost pecking at the hunter. Somehow, the teeth missed Camlak both times. The jaws could not close.

Camlak, right inside the beast's spring, thrust this left hand up to the fold of skin beneath the chin and wound his slender fingers into the hair with a single convulsive twist. He pivoted on his arm, keeping his head low, and simply pushed the jaws aside as they reached for him. His knife slashed furiously, and with the same short-armed backhanded stabbing motion he lacerated the flesh of the legs which buffeted him. The point of his spear had gone down into the groin of the animal and the shaft had broken. He had aimed for the muscle of the hind leg and missed.

The full weight of the beast came down on Camlak from directly above, and he was crushed to the hard stone. But he did not relax his grip on the hair beneath the animal's neck, and his own head was still low, still protected by the arm from the dip and snap of the jaws.

As the harrowhound thrashed its legs man and beast rolled. Camlak still slashed with his knife, not daring to make any more positive thrust in case the blade was lost like the spearhead. The beast's teeth finally made contact with the man's shoulder, but they could do no more than rake the flesh. Camlak sank his own teeth into the stripped flesh of the leg he had attacked with his knife. The taste was foul and there was enough hair left to fill his mouth like a gag, but he bit as deep as his jaws had strength.

The hound bayed again.

Camlak took advantage of the roll to get free of the monster before the full weight pinned him for a second time, and he scrambled sideways, regaining his feet on the bank of the stream. His mouth was dripping blood which was not his own. The beast tried to right itself in a single convulsive bound, but one foreleg at least was hurt badly, and it had to turn away and dance backwards or it would have staggered toward Camlak's eager knife. The beast sought the slanting stones at the back of the fault in order to launch itself again but Camlak, still impelled by persuasive terror, had not stood still for a moment. He had come forward while the beast went back, and it was the man who closed the gap between the two.

But this time the monster was not to be caught. Flailing its forepaws, it knocked the little man flying. Camlak was tumbled backwards from the flat stones into the stream. His fingers scraped the bottom as the water soaked into his clothing, and they came free of the surface with a handful of fluid mud and thin weed. As the harrowhound's jaws widened above him, Camlak threw the handful of sodden debris into the beast's face. Then he dropped flat, back into the water. The hound lurched over him, giving vent to a single titanic sneeze. But it had no sooner landed in the stream than it was turning, blinded and maddened.

Camlak grabbed the loose fold of skin and tangled fur yet again, and jammed the blade of his knife upward through the tightly pulled hide into the beast's throat. He pressed as hard as he possibly could, and then leapt backwards, leaving the knife buried. The harrowhound reared up on its hind legs and plunged wildly, missing him by a considerable margin. Camlak looked round for the shaft of his lost spear. He found it and went for it, and the weight of the beast came down on him as it bounded the same way. The collision was almost accidental, and the jaws closed on air, but Camlak felt his left arm break as he was hurled to the ground again.

Nevertheless, he was free and clear, and the beast was still half-blind. Its breathing was cut off and it was furious. It leaped again, and once more Camlak evaded the leap, and this time he had the shaft of the spear in hand. As the monster came at him again he dealt it a heavy blow on the skull, which seemed to have no effect at all. Once again, the hunter was knocked flying.

The hound blinked its eyes clear, but it was still leaping without pause, and it missed again. As it landed it was seared by pain from the wounds in its leg and in its groin, both of which it had aggravated considerably by its frantic movements. It staggered and fell forward, and as it sagged on to the rocks it turned the knife in its throat. Camlak hit it again and again with the stick, and though the blows did no damage at all, the beast gave way beneath them.

Camlak, exhausted though he was, found the strength and the presence of mind to hurl the stick away and pick up a sizeable rock from the shallow bed of the stream. Though he had to pluck it out of the water one-handed he managed to raise it high above his head and then bring it down edge-first on to the back of the harrowhound's head.

The beast was already choking, and it was hammered to the ground by the blow.

Camlak followed, recovered the stone, and hurled it down again on the beast's head.

The harrowhound would not die, but it could not rise. It had to lie, twitching and uselessly snapping its jaws, while the new Old Man of Stalhelm smashed it slowly with the flat stone.

It still had not died when the warriors came into the gully to accept the verdict of the test. Camlak sagged into Cicon's arms, but after a few moments rest he was able to stand again and walk back to Stalhelm. Chemec the cripple was allowed to carry the harrowhound's head, after they had managed to cut it off with steel knives.

His arm was broken and his body was covered with bruises but Camlak was undoubtedly the leader of his people. The time had come for the Children of the Voice to learn Camlak's way.

44

Enzo Ulicon made very little progress at all in finding out more about Magner's nightmares. As data accumulated his early suspicions were confirmed, but he made no significant discoveries. The need for diplomacy in approaching medical sources, and the need to be evasive in pursuit of what he actually wanted to hear, slowed him down and made him tired.

He checked cases of dream disorders going back some centuries, but discovered that the number of cases where no clear pathological reason for the disorders had been traced were very few and in no way helpful. He could find no convincing evidence that anyone else was suffering, or had suffered, visions of Hell during their sleep.

His scientific advisers, familiar with both the theory and the practical application of the i-minus effect, offered him ideas, but nothing concrete. In the end, he had only logic and suspicion to guide him in reaching the most tentative of conclusions.

"There's no evidence to suggest that Magner is a genetic freak," he reported to Heres. "And in his waking life he appears to be quite ordinary—or did, until the dreams started to get the better of him. I think it's real, Rafael. We're not dealing with brain damage or with instinctive resurgence. This is something else. It's real, and it's meaningful, if only we can figure out what the meaning might be."

"You think that Magner's a telepath?" said Heres.

"I do."

"Can you prove it?"

"No. But something's getting into his head and we can't find any source for it inside him. It has to come from outside. The question is, where? And how, and what does it mean?"

"That's a lot of questions," said Heres. "How about some answers?"

"Guesses," said Ulicon. "It's all we have."

"Go on."

"All right. Number one. The source of the trouble is probably the pons. Magner awake doesn't suffer from visions—at least, he hasn't so far. Thus the visions come to him via some process active during sleep. The pons is the body which decouples the motor responses from the dream-simulation. The pons *might* be the receiver in the telepathic link. What kind of radiation is involved we obviously have no idea. The cytoarchitecture of the pons might offer us some suggestions. That research will take years, though.

"Another guess. If we assume that the input into Magner's dreams *is* coming from outside then it seems like a good working assumption to say that it's coming from where Magner thinks it is—the Underworld. Someone—or something—down there is transmitting. New question: are they doing it deliberately? If so, is their message beamed specifically at Magner or is he the only man capable of picking it up? Personally, I find the idea of a deliberate transmission hard to swallow. I don't think that Magner's picking up messages at all. My guess is that it's some kind of leakage. He's getting vast assemblies of incoherent images which build in his mind to the visions he's written down in his book.

"The big hitch in all guesses is just this: what contribution is Magner making to the organization and interpretation of this input? How much of what Magner has written is raw input and how much is his personal reaction to it? We have no possible way of making a guess at this point. Not without another subject or another input. We have no basis at all for any sort of comparison."

"It's just not convincing," said Heres.

"I know," said Ulicon. "Don't you think I realize that? I wish it were convincing. I wish we had a few more puzzling facts to help make a pattern. I wish we had a few more definite data to help us rule out some of the possibilities. But we just don't have enough."

"So what do you think we should do?"

"Nothing. What can we do?"

"I agree," said Heres. "Nothing. But you know that some might not see it that way. The important thing is to avert any kind of a panic. We don't want to be rushed into action by something we can't understand, and which might turn out to be completely meaningless. Our top priority, as I see it, is to get on top of the whole thing so that we *can* do nothing. We have to squash the whole affair."

"Publicly, yes," said Ulicon. "But whatever we do in public we mustn't allow this thing to drop in private. We can do nothing as yet, but I'll bet my life on the fact that sooner or later this plot is going to thicken. Tomorrow or next year or Heaven knows when, there'll be another Magner, or another message, or another problem entirely. This thing is only just beginning, Rafe. You and I might not see the end, but we'll sure as hell see more than we've seen so far."

"But in the meantime," said Heres firmly, "we have to keep everything under control. We can't afford to let this thing blow up out of all proportion until we know more about it. Much more. We need something to divert attention from Magner. Either that or a way to silence him."

"That's up to you," said Ulicon. "But if I were you I wouldn't turn my back on the Underworld just at this moment. I'd worry. I *do* worry."

"I worry too," Heres assured him.

45

Later in the day, Dascon contacted the Hegemon with news of Randal Harkanter's party, which was just about to leave for the Underworld. Heres hardly listened to what the other man said. Whatever Harkanter's small expedition discovered, it was hardly likely to add much to the solution of the problem, which, if Ulicon was even half-right, had moved into an entirely new dimension.

For the first time in his life, Heres felt the strange sensation that beneath his feet there was a gulf, and that if he did not tread lightly the floor might crumble beneath him and send him hurtling into the abyss.

Rypeck was frightened, and that was something Heres could ill afford, especially since it seemed there really might be something for Rypeck to be frightened *of*. If Rypeck took things into his own hands and talked about the i-minus effect it would be the end of his political career.

Heres knew that the interests of stability had to be placed first. The interests of the community—Euchronian interests. Fear of the Underworld simply must not be allowed to spread. There were factions which would undoubtedly benefit from such fear, and which might even try and foment anxiety. It was by no means a good thing that the expedition to the world below was in the hands of a man like Harkanter, who was something of a scaremonger even over and above his heretical leanings. And there was Emerich, too. Emerich *fed* on the ripples in the Euchronian pool—he was a glutton for strife and distrust. If only Emerich could be replaced by a man with a greater sense of responsibility . . . but it was in the very nature of the media that they existed to shock and excite and stimulate. Emerich's part in the drama of life was altogether too popular to be threatened. An Emerich would only be replaced by another Emerich. That was the way of life . . .

Heres worried, all right. But he would find an answer. Some kind of answer. There was always a way of sweeping the dust under the carpet.

Always.

46

The outstanding thing about Camlak was his toughness. In Stalhelm he might find those superior in strength, in courage and in intelligence. But there was no one else with Camlak's refusal to bend and his capacity to withstand pressure of *every* kind. In a sense, he was like his father, but while Yami's toughness and inflexibility had thrived on a policy of destroying all conceivable threats, Camlak's rested on a carefulness of a rather different kind. Camlak was not a destroyer.

The key to Camlak's character was an unusual predilection for doubt. He withstood the pressure of education; he refused to accept common opinion and custom. He would not admit that precedent was adequate justification. Camlak *had* to be tough, to have survived with his doubt. Under normal circumstances a fighting man cannot afford doubt—in the struggle for existence certainty is usually a powerful survival factor. But doubt is the doorway to discovery and Camlak's discoveries, assisted by a certain serendipity, kept him ahead of the race. He survived. He was not well liked, because he was not well understood, but he commanded some sort of respect.

The Children of the Voice were not, by and large, a cogitative people. Evolution had given them intelligence, a high degree of sentience, and the capacity for conscious, rational thought which is the road to self-change. But the use to which the Children of the Voice had put these gifts tended to be rather narrow. In the early days of their "rise" as a species they had been overimitative of the True Men and in the latter days they were overdependent upon the beings which they called their Gray Souls.

However, talents evolved to fill one purpose inevitably spill over into other areas, and the intelligence of the Children of the Voice did begin to express itself in other ways than the simple business of keeping them alive in a difficult environment and a tachytelic evolutionary régime.

Camlak's predilection for doubt might be regarded as one

of the painful steps in the evolution of a new perspective. It is one of the earliest steps, and in some ways it is one of the most difficult. A hundred doubters may die before one makes a beginning at the task of breaking down the barriers to doubt in his fellow men. Camlak was something of an enigma to his contemporaries, but the influence which he gained the power to exert when he became Old Man might have been crucial to their development as a community. Circumstance was eventually to rob him of that opportunity, but that does not detract from the fact that Camlak was a significant individual.

Yami was disappointed in Camlak. The elder man could have wished for a stronger, more successful son. Camlak did, it is true, win the right to adopt the Sun role in the Communion of Souls, and thus to replace his father as the man on the throne-stone, but Yami could still have wished for more fire and directness in his successor's manner. Camlak was unusually fond of his father.

Camlak's influence on his daughter, Nita, was considerable. If Camlak was an evolutionary step, Nita was an evolutionary adventure. She already had something of a new perspective relative to the rest of her people. She had the advantage of being female, and therefore less liable to fall prey to the hostile environment. The evolution of mind works, by necessity, more through the female line of descent than the male.

Nita loved her father in a fashion that was almost Heavenly. As a race, the Children of the Voice was far too confined to the fragile present in the living of their lives to project their emotions far into the unreal future, or to dredge up emotional jetsam from the dead past. The Shaira loved, but not in the same sense that the people of the Overworld loved. Their love was more momentary, less coherent, and discontinuous. Nita was different, at least in the instance of her relationship with her father.

Camlak was a strange man. Perhaps something of a tragic figure. Perhaps even something of a hero.

47

The Communion of Souls waited for Camlak.

The injuries he had sustained during the fight with the harrowhound were not serious, but they were painful, and needed a little time. One of the readers set the broken arm and bound up his ribs. He had lost very little blood and he was not so weak that he had to take to his bed.

While he rested, Ayria attended to him, but he preferred the company of the aliens. A few whispers began to circulate concerning unnatural lust, but such rumors moved slowly and quietly. There were few enough who dared trespass on Camlak's good nature at the present time.

Camlak was vaguely interested by Huldi, but he was absolutely fascinated by Joth. Initially, it had seemed to him to be a good idea to help Joth in order that the Children of the Voice might one day make use of him. Stalhelm had never had any direct supply of Heaven-sent goods, and it seemed obvious to Camlak that it never would have if Yami's attitude to strangers had been allowed to rule forever. Many of the villagers were suspicious of the tools which came from the Overworld, and even more so of the books and the learning which could be taken from them. There was always a reservoir of opinion which held that such things ought not to be touched and that the Shaira should live entirely by their own efforts and their own ways. But the usefulness of the implements and the quality of the learning which could be obtained only from Overworld sources ensured that this opinion never came to dominate the intellectual climate. Even so, the art of reading was a minority pursuit, and many of those who were taught to read learned only to enhance their status, and not to make any use of that which was written in the books.

Camlak, as the son of an Old Man, had been forced to read at an early age, and had passed the point at which he still needed to be forced. He became an enthusiastic reader, and he absorbed what he read, although much of it he could not understand. While the elders regarded reading as something of a mystic art—the extraction of useful and/ or meaningful details from a matrix which was largely cryptic and unfathomable—Camlak seemed to take it all more or less as it came. His attitude was one of pure inquiry, and he did not believe in the commonly held theory that books were constructed in order to conceal and protect knowledge by burying it in nonsense.

Joth confirmed Camlak's opinions about the books, and he was ready enough to take Joth's word, though many of the elders would have dismissed it out of hand. Among Huldi's people the printed word was regarded even more superstitiously than among Camlak's. The Men Without Souls had a separate sect of readers—and they most certainly did conceal and protect knowledge in order to maintain their monopoly in it. The readers of the True Men were fake magicians and false priests, and the fact that they were known by their more cynical brethren as charlatans did not alter the fact that they had possession and control of something real and valuable, and hence the power to maintain themselves as a mystic elite.

Joth wanted to inspect the books which were owned by the people of Stalhelm, but Camlak was reluctant. Eventually, Camlak brought him half a dozen, and let him touch them and inspect them. Joth found that they were real books, properly bound and printed on firm paper. He was more used to reading the disposable printouts from the cybernet. Bound books existed in the Overworld only as collector's items, prized as objects rather than as information. No one maintained a library for research purposes or for recreation —there was no need when any work was available on demand anywhere and at any time. Joth came to the conclusion that the books were prepared specifically for export to the Underworld, and again his mind struggled with the mystery of Burstone, failing to find an answer.

"What do the books tell you?" Joth asked Camlak. The question seemed particularly pertinent because the books he was permitted to examine seemed like a random selection from the cybernet's stores. They did not seem to have any relevance at all to the Underworld, nor any special significance of their own.

"A great deal," said Camlak. "I think there is always much to learn from the simplest book, although it is not easy to understand. When we find out how to make books like this ourselves, perhaps we will understand more clearly what is put into them. Our writings are very different, and the materials we have do not last, so that the readers must forever be copying and recopying. The books are products and pictures of another life, and it is a life very unlike our own. So much we cannot find because we do not know. But there is still much to be learned, if you are content to listen to the words and remember. I think there are books which are pictures of meaning rather than pictures of life."

"I don't know what you mean," said Joth.

"There are books which say what happens, and there are books which stay still, describing, thinking, looking. This is what the elders may think is put there only to clothe the truth and make it strange. I think it is truth itself, but truth of a different kind. It is a kind of teaching, because it is against the teaching we receive when we are shown how to read and what to read. There is more than one reality—this we know. There are two worlds, and perhaps more than two. But there is also more than one eye to look at reality, and the shape of a reality is in the eye as well as in the things the eye sees. This, it seems to me, is what is in the books. This is why it is so hard to see with the books, and so much easier to listen without understanding. If only we could see . . ."

"See what?" asked Joth.

"Your world. The sky. The people. The things. I would not want to live in your world, nor to stay for more than a moment. But I think I would like to see. A glimpse. I could understand so much more."

"Perhaps," said Joth. "But the sun would blind you. At night . . . perhaps I can show you the world, by night. If I can find a way home—a doorway to my world."

Camlak was silent for a while when Joth mentioned doorways. He knew of no way back for Joth, but he knew where to look for one.

Meanwhile, Joth wondered exactly how the Overworld *did* seem, in Camlak's imagination. Could Camlak tell the difference between fact and fantasy in the books? Could he tell the difference between representation and interpretation, between analogy and reality? Probably not. A glimpse of the world beneath the distant stars might well cause Camlak to reorder his ideas completely. Even a glimpse of the stars themselves . . . the sight of infinity and space . . . the Face of Heaven.

But Joth knew, as did Camlak, that a glimpse was all

that was possible. The Children of the Voice had their own world and their own life and their own reality, in which the stars were electric bulbs and the sky was a solid roof over their heads. To the people of the Underworld a different Heaven showed a very different face, but it was nonetheless the Face of Heaven. Joth knew that his father's crusade was meaningless and misled. One of the things which had come to worry him about the possibility of his return to the world above was the prospect of explaining to Carl Magner that his dreams had betrayed him.

48

The man that Joth became when he awoke from his long illness into the real world of the realms of Tartarus was somewhat different from the Joth who had run away from Heaven in pursuit of his brother's memory.

The new Joth dreamed, of course, and his dreams were plagued by the awakened images of instinct which had broken free of the i-minus effect now that Joth ate different food and drank different water. But the renaissance of instinct had come too late into Joth's life to change him drastically. The nightmares hurt him, in his head, but they did little more than hurt. It was not the nightmares that turned him into a different man.

The new Joth had new and strange perspectives. He looked out into a different reality, and as time went by, he looked into that new reality with new eyes, because—as Camlak had said—reality is in the eye as much as the things it sees. Joth had lost time—or, rather, he had replaced one consciousness of time with another. The whole idea of *change* which he embraced was different. Days and nights had gone, and with them had gone the metrication of time. He could no longer count time, and because he could no longer count it he no longer saw it as a thing to be counted. His temporal sensitivity shrank as the past and future lost their outlines and closed in toward the infinitesimal moment of the present. Events no longer took "a long time" or "happened suddenly." Things took the time they took. Things happened at their own speed.

Joth began to assess the contents of his temporal environment in their own temporal terms, not by comparison to the movement of the sun in the sky or the cycling hands of a clock which symbolize that movement.

Joth, awakened into the Underworld, wanted to go home. He wanted to go home very badly—it was his first priority. But the *urgency* of returning to the Overworld drained away from him because it could not hold tight to its meaning. From the moment he became conscious of his new reality, Joth was going home. But at the same time he lived in Camlak's house and talked to the people who used it, and answered their questions, and he waited for Camlak to show him a way home. He was not in a hurry, because going home would take the time it took, and that was all there was to it.

Camlak questioned Joth on a wide variety of matters, most of which were fairly trivial. He asked about words, about meanings, and about a whole host of irrelevant facts. Many of his questions did not have answers, because the questions themselves were meaningless, but Joth did the best he could to help the Old Man of Stalhelm understand the alternative reality which existed on the far side of the sky-that-was-not.

Camlak learned a great deal—perhaps a great deal more than Joth thought he was teaching.

Huldi, meanwhile, had a very different interest in Joth. Because the Shaira tended to lump her and Joth into a single category, and because Joth himself obviously thought that she was more like him than were the Children of the Voice, Huldi too came to think that she and Joth were of like kind. When she had come to Stalhelm she had come simply to escape, with no plans, no ambitions, no idea what might eventually become of her, beyond a few simple notions which added up to little more than a determination to survive. But Joth offered a different range of possibilities. Joth was a straw to be clutched.

Huldi, of course, was not a reader, and had no concept at all of alternative realities. She was a creature of moderate intellectual powers trapped in a single frame of reference and caged by a fragile, unextended form of time. To her, Joth was a supernatural being, but a being with some affinities with herself. Like, and yet unlike. Huldi quickly

came to love Joth, with a kind of love which was very unusual, if not unique.

Nita simply built the presence of Joth into the fabric of
her growing up. He was present at a time when she was
developing particularly quickly as a person, and her mind
was alert, alive and adaptable. She was learning from books,
from Camlak, and from her fellow-children. It was no
strain to add Joth and Huldi to her sources of perspective.
She loved to talk to the man with the metal face, and
though most of the talk went by her like water in a fast
stream, it had its effect on her, and in due course it would
be revealed to her as something important in her life—
something, perhaps, vital to the self she was to become.

Time—Tartaric time—bound together the people who
shared Camlak's house. It added a new facet to their collective identity. It made them kindred of a strange kind.

49

The people of Stalhelm were gathered before the long house
(all but ten warriors, who kept watch in the hills) making a
great half-circle whose center was the throne-stone.

Camlak knew that the festival of the Communion of Souls,
on this particular occasion, would bring him pain. He expected pain in the confrontation with his Gray Soul, because he was Old Man now, and the Gray Soul would be very
much more a part of him henceforth. In addition, there
would be pain in the ceremony—pain of a different kind but
no easier to bear—because he was to be the Sun to Yami's
Star King.

The drums were beating in a slow, steady rhythm. The
drummers crouched in the shadow of the long house. The
beat was muted, and when the horns blew, as they did in
turn, they gave forth long, low notes like the distant crying
of nightbirds.

The firelight was also muted. The flames burned red and
low, and the moths which danced in the smoke seemed to
have purple wings. They seemed to the villagers to represent
the ghosts of shadowed souls.

The circle was silent, though there were a thousand people, and nearly half of them were children, or at least unmated. The people were working at the pulp which each had taken into his or her mouth. Periodically they would add new leaves to the masticated fiber, and suck out new supplies of the bitter juice. They did not move with the rhythm of the drums, but took that rhythm *into* themselves, and united it with the tempo of their heartbeat. Deliberately, they slowed their own metabolism. Their eyes remained open, but took on a hard glaze, and though they saw still, it was not wholly with their eyes that they watched.

The elders, now in the role of priests, stood in a line behind the arc of the crowd. Their arms were raised so that their loose robes hung apart from their bodies in great voluminous folds. No breeze stirred the trailing cloth. The elders, as priests, needed no leaves to grind between their jaws. They reached for the inner sight using no more than the power of their minds.

Into the space which was clear around the base of the throne-stone came the Star King. He was covered by a vast robe of black which swirled about him as he moved, and his head was enclosed by a gigantic mask, also painted jet black. Both the mask and the robe were sewn with tiny sequins which caught the light as he came close to the fire. As the folds of the cloak swayed and swung, the sequins flashed in turn, fugitive, evasive stars in a cloth of absolute darkness. Inside the Star King was Yami, but Yami transfigured. He was no longer Old Man, but merely an old man, and his body had completely lost its straightness. Yami staggered and shambled around the throne-stone, and the billows of the sky which draped his tired limbs flickered with uncertain strength.

The Star King moved, hopping and swaying, very slowly, consumed by the tempo of the drumbeat. Inside him, the pathetic figure of Yami could be seen now and again as the curve of a shoulder or the bulge of a hand.

Yami: a dancing corpse in a black shroud studded with little glass stars.

The Children of the Voice steadily extracted the juice from the leaves in their mouth, and reached for inner sight.

Up in the hills, the lookouts closed their ears to the hypnotic rhythm of the drums. They ran their tongues round in dry mouths, tasting the bitterness of the juice that was not there, feeling cold and alone despite the cloying warmness of the Underworld. Their heads ached.

In Camlak's house, behind the trailing edge of the crowd to one side of the long house, the Sun waited. His head was aching too, and he felt slightly sick. Camlak was inside a costume which was colored brightly gold and silver. The mask which he wore was pure white and polished. It crouched on his shoulders like a great white eagle.

Time passed him by, flowing like molasses.

Beside him, waiting with him, were Joth and Huldi. They could see from the window slits, over the heads of the squatting people, what was happening in the circlet of bare ground. They watched Yami's bobbing mask, like a big black fruit dancing on a wind-shaken branch.

But Joth and Huldi could only see with their eyes. They had no real conception of what was happening and what was about to happen, and it could not have been explained to them. Camlak was already apart from them in that he was descending into the depths of his mind, guided by the seeing that was not done with eyes alone. The aliens could not participate in the Communion, not even as observers.

The pace of the drums grew slower and slower, and the long crying of the horns began to blend with it into a lethargic undulation of muted sound. The notes were tortured and sonorous, dragged into seemingly infinite extension, and the hollow, indefinite roar of the drums was like the waves of a turbid sea.

In the Star King's dance, Yami found that his feet would no longer carry him forward. The dance went on, in bizarre slow motion, but now Yami merely writhed, and the sky which he wore was anchored to the spot.

There was still movement in the circle, but it was the movement of another costumed figure. All that Joth and Huldi could see through their slit windows was that the new dancer wore green, and that the mask which topped the robe—a grotesque, huge headpiece shaped like the cap of a mushroom—was striped gray and green. The stripes were curved and uneven, and flowed around and around the mask.

The dance was smooth and graceful, and the cloak hung so sheerly about the body that it was obviously a girl—a slender girl—inside it. The girl slowed in her movements as she came closer to the Star King. By the time that she touched him, she was almost still, and she sank slowly to the earth, so that the outsiders could no longer see her.

The mask that was the face of the Star King dipped, and he too went down, out of sight.

Slowly, Camlak began the long walk of the Sun. In his hands he carried an axe, bladed with stone from the quarry of Stalhelm, honed to a perfect curved edge.

50

Yami was blind. Not only blind in his aged, whitening eyes (the mask, in any case, was eyeless) but blind in his inner vision. Yami was alone in that realm of Tartarus called the Underworld. As he went down on top of the girl he reached for his Gray Soul. He reached as far as he could, driven by desperation. He prayed. But he remained alone. He remained trapped in the cage which had closed upon his mind. He was isolated from the Communion of Souls.

He screamed, and listened to his scream echoing in the chasms of his being, but there came no answer. There was no sound at all. He was soulless. Abandoned.

Yami could remember that in the past he had played the part of the Sun, and played it to perfection. He tried to imagine that around him now was the *persona* of the gaudy, garish yellow sun. But he was imprisoned by the sky, and even his imagination could not set him free. He could not make a Gray Soul out of his wishes. It was beyond his power.

He was old. He had no control over his arms and legs. He had even lost control of his thoughts.

Yami was on his hands and knees, his hands placed in the dirt on either side of the girl's waist, his knees on either side of her thighs. She was absolutely still beneath him, absolutely quiescent.

He was forgetting who he was.

The Star King leaned forward, until his belly came to touch her breasts. The Star King was not breathing, not even alive. In the vacuum of his mind there was total peace.

Inside the gray-green mask the girl was waiting. Her heart was slow and her breath very faint and easy. She was alive, but lost. Without the juice, she had found her Gray Soul. She was with it now, though perhaps she was only marginally aware. It would be as though she was on the borderline of sleep.

She waited.

The body of the Star King was rigid, like petrified wood.

There was balance.

And the axe came down in a long loose arc, striking Yami's head from his shoulders.

51

The black mask rolled away like a big black ball, the loose earth sticking to it and blotting out the faintest of its stars. The head was still inside it. Blood—a torrent of it—*leaped* out to flood the stripes of the gray-green Earth-body and turn it deep red. The firelight was very close. The rushing stain turned black in the orange glow of the embers.

The Sun dragged the starlit Night from the clothes of the Earth, and thrust it aside. It slid away, rattling like charred paper crumpled in a fist. The Sun lowered his golden body, reaching to part the gray-green robes of the Earth, thrusting his light and his life into the parting.

The Sun made more life. More growth.

The Sun and the Earth were bound together, the Sun atop the Earth, their vast faces pressed to one another. The face of the Earth ran red with blood, and the polished white face of the Sun was stained, just a little. Smeared, as though by a careless hand. But it would not show until the Sun rose again.

Inside the Sun, Camlak was like ice. Physically cold, rigid.

He had achieved penetration—that was easy, because his penis was equipped with a bone—but as the Earth stirred against him with the oceanic swell of the drums he felt completely unmoved, as if nothing was happening, as if he were remote from himself. His penis felt hard and bone dry. Thin, and steely, like a knife from the upper world.

The Earth worked, and he moved on her, gently, in a rhythm which he only half felt, and hardly meant at all.

He was conscious that the Sun was acting out its role.

But he, inside the Sun, felt nothing like a fire, a source of energy, a bringer of life. He felt instead like a dead thing, trapped inside a womb.

He knew that his mask, on the outside, was white, and that his costume was brightly colored. But inside the Sun there was nothing save darkness. He was still seeing with his own eyes.

Seeing nothing.

His tongue was dry, his mouth gritty.

His spine was like a dry stick.

His ribs were running cold, like icicles.

His arm, splinted and set, was absolutely dead and without feeling. Likewise his heart, his belly and . . .

Seeing nothing.

And then the horns dragged him away from the unlit womb, dragged him down beneath the surface of an ocean of light. Hot, red-gold light. And through the flickering, radiant matrix the shadows moved.

Silver, called gray: the shadows.

A lighter gray than earth-gray. A softer gray. The gray, not of Earth at all, but of something and somewhere incalculably beyond Earth.

In an aureole of golden light, he came face to face with his Gray Soul.

52

Everything was still.

So far as Joth and Huldi could see, there was absolutely nothing happening. The sound of the drums and the horns had died away.

No one in the entranced crowd moved a muscle. Even the small children were silent and still. The priests, with their arms still upraised, seemed as if they had been turned to stone.

Joth felt constrained not to move, and he dared not make the slightest sound. Huldi stirred restlessly, but even she felt the pressure of the occasion. Each of them was alone.

They had no way by which they could take themselves into the presence of their souls—if, in fact, they had souls at all.

53

Camlak talked with his Gray Soul as an equal. He faced the being calmly, without the appearance of fear. He asked whether his way was not better than Yami's way, and the Gray Soul answered evasively. He asked many other questions, but he did not ask favors, nor did he ask advice. He spoke as a man might speak to another man (perhaps of a different race) and he listened as though he listened to the words of a man.

As well as words, they exchanged images, memories and emotional qualities. They conversed in many languages, of many different kinds, which contained many different varieties of meaning.

54

The Sun fed the Earth with fuel, and life began within the Earth.

55

Carl Magner was a self-haunted man. In a country of the bland he was a man with a very special sight. Not a king, but a victim.

In an age where a man born at his time might have expected to live a hundred and fifty years or more, he suffered sufficient psycho-physiological hardship to cut his expectancy of life to the ancient three score years and ten. Another man born the same day might have expected that his children would live to be two hundred. But Carl Magner had no such hopes of his own children.

Carl Magner was an emotionally isolated man, although it might be argued that the circumstances surrounding the death of his wife and the maiming of his younger son caused him to abandon the love of individuals in favor of a love for humanity in general which carried less immediate risk.

He was always a dedicated Euchronian, and became a fanatical Euchronian. Like any truly dedicated idealist he went far beyond the political boundaries of the doctrine and his beliefs lost their way in the wilderness of pure principle. The concept of Euchronianism which he eventually came to embrace was one which made many members of the Movement his enemy.

He honestly could not tell when his dreams began, or when the focus on a particular species of vision crowded out all other images. In the beginning, the dreams were only dreams, and were forgotten. The pattern, and the awareness of the pattern, took a considerable time to develop. It can be estimated that Carl Magner reached the point of obsession some five or six years before Ryan went into the Underworld in search of the truth. (It should be noted that Ryan's motives in venturing forth in search of that truth were founded on the hope that the truth would not resemble the dreams in any way, and that the obsessional hold of the dreams might be broken by virtue of that fact.) The dreams, as individual entities, probably began before the tragedies took place. Magner may well have been born with the seeds of conflict tainting his very earliest dreams.

Carl Magner was a big man, and a strong one, but over the years he lost the mental stature which went with his physique. He became increasingly brittle of temperament. One might almost say that in publishing *The Marriage of Heaven and Hell* he was preparing himself for another tragedy, making ready to meet it before its seeds were sown.

It was not Magner's wish that his son should go down into the Underworld, although at that particular time he did believe that it was important to verify the accuracy of his visions. When Ryan did not come back, Magner decided quite firmly that he would not be responsible for anyone's following in Ryan's footsteps. After all, by his visions, he *knew*. He was not the kind of man who would order another to descend into Hell. If anyone else was to go and discover the truth, it would have to be him, and before he went he had to deliver his message to the world.

His daughter might have told him about Burstone—about the fact that one man, at least, could confirm or deny his visions. But she did not, because she dared not. She was afraid of what might happen to him if he discovered that his visions were false. She was, perhaps, even more afraid of the opposite case.

After the publication of *The Marriage,* Magner was essentially a doomed man. The truth, whatever it might be, could only hurt him. He was a man at whom Fate had pointed the bone.

56

Carl Magner faced the cameras uneasily. He should not have been nervous about his arguments, which he had gone over a hundred times before, nor should he have been nervous about exposure to an audience, which was what he had always intended. But he was definitely uneasy.

Clea Aron was wondering faintly what she was doing in the studio. She had not been interested in the Magner affair and she had no strong opinions about it. It seemed to her that Heres or Ulicon should have been anxious to take her place in the ultimate confrontation, but they had been quite definite in leaving it to her. She had a fairly dogmatic party line ready to deliver—something patched up by Javan Sobol and Luel Dascon, under advice from several interested parties—but she knew that she was not committed enough to attack Magner with any real vehemence.

Yvon Emerich knew that too, but he had no intention of letting his broadcast lack fire. In a sense, the choice of Clea Aron to represent the Movement was a shrewd political move, because Emerich would be forced on to her side in order to add bite to her arguments. He knew that, too, but it did not annoy him. He was content to be used by the Movement tonight, in the confident knowledge that he could balance the account another time. Magner meant nothing to Emerich, one way or the other—if he was against the man it was only because the majority of the audience wanted to see him dissected. Emerich was only his usual clock-watching, super-organized self. It was all under his control: reason, sympathy, charity, morality. They were his to play with, because he was the eye of the people. And the mouth.

The cameras began to roll and Emerich introduced his "guests." He gave a rapid, inaccurate and rather insulting summary of *The Marriage of Heaven and Hell,* and then launched into Magner without further ado. As advised by Ballow he avoided the treacherous ground of how Magner came to write the book and whether the picture of life in the Underworld was factual or fanciful. He went straight to the moral meat of the argument.

"Supposing," said Emerich, "that there *are* people living in the old world, why should we let them into the new world which we have built?"

Magner, in closeup, seemed neither aggressive nor fanatical. His unease was under control. He simply said: "We have to recognize that there is only one world, and that we do not own it. We have no right to deny other men sunlight and clean air, and to force them to live in the excreta of our civilization."

"Isn't it true," said Emerich, hurrying along the obvious line which had been laid down for him, "that everyone in the ancient world had the option of remaking the world or dying with it? No man was forced to deny his children a share in the future of Euchronian man."

"That is what the Movement claims," said Magner, deliberately but indirectly challenging the truth of the statement, "but that was eleven thousand years ago. There is no justice in demanding that a man should bear the responsibility of his remote ancestors' decisions."

"So you believe," said Emerich, "that the descendants of the men who rejected the new world are just as entitled to enjoy the fruits of that new world as us, whose ancestors spent eleven thousand years in labor, hardship and deprivation."

"Of course," said Magner. "The eleven thousand years were years of Purgatory no less for their ancestors than for our own. There was hardship and deprivation for everyone. It is not just that we should inherit Heaven while they are condemned to Hell."

"You are familiar, are you not," said Emerich, "with the fable of the ant and the grasshopper? While the ant labored the grasshopper was idle. And when winter came the grasshopper asked to be sheltered in the ant's nest. The ant refused, and the grasshopper died. Wasn't that justice? Isn't the message of the fable the principle that those who provide for themselves are favored over those who do not? Isn't that the justice of nature? Isn't it the way things are?"

"It is not the justice of nature," said Magner. "Only the law. We can make and change laws. We need not be bound by unjust laws. That is what it means to be human."

Emerich was ready and waiting for the answer. It was all as expected. He turned to Clea Aron.

"You are a member of the Hegemony of the Movement," he said. "You make and change the laws. What do you say to the argument?"

Clea cleared her throat, preparing herself for the first broadside. She was easy in her mind and comfortable at this stage.

"We are alive today," she said, "because of the efforts of the Euchronian Movement. If there are men alive today on the old surface, then they too owe their survival to the Euchronian Movement. At the end of the second dark age, the Earth was dying. The human race was foundering in the wreckage of the biosphere. It faced extinction. The Movement was the one force which offered a method and—more important—a motivation for building a new world from the ashes of the old. The Movement made a Plan—a magnificent plan—to build a new biosphere, a new civilization and a new society. The new world was to be a good world, and the new society was to be a sane and stable society which would never again allow extinction to threaten. The goal of the Movement was not simply survival, but *responsible* survival, in harmony with the new world which we were to recover from the old.

"We live today in that society. We have sanity, and stability, and comfort, and culture, and peace. Above all else, we have harmony with our new world. We are living up to the responsibility our ancestors accepted. The new world will not be destroyed by an age of psychosis. We will protect it from that possibility.

"The Euchronian Plan has passed the test—it has been

fulfilled. We do not have Utopia, because we have not yet become Utopians. Perhaps we never will—that possibility we can accept, because we are human. But the fact that we may never have Utopia does not mean that we must sink to the level of our ancestors. We must accept the place in the scheme of things which we have strived long and hard to attain. We have a responsibility to ourselves, and to our ancestors—but most important of all, we have a responsibility to our unborn children—children born next year and *in the next eleven thousand years*. The one thing we must not do is abandon the responsibility we owe to our children because eleven thousand years ago the men who opposed Euchronia abandoned *theirs*.

"We tend to take for granted the countless generations of men who gave their lives so that we could enjoy a new world. The fact that we are here tonight is eloquent testimony to the extent to which we take it for granted. But we must not be allowed to forget that those generations of men worked for a *reason*—that they dedicated their lives to an ideal. They were building a world which they could not hope to see—for their remote descendants. The original Planners were not working for their children of eleven thousand years in the future, but for their children a hundred thousand years in the future. Thanks to the power and the determination of the Movement *we* have the world they wanted to build. We might just as easily be building it ourselves. And if we were building it ourselves, then I believe we would be content to do so. We would accept our responsibilities and we would accept them willingly.

The men who stayed on the ground were selfish men. They were interested only in their own lives, and in plundering what they could from a world which they knew to be dying by their parasitism. They acknowledged no responsibility toward their descendants. They did not believe that they would have descendants. We must remember that I am not talking about a single generation of men called upon to make a choice at a point in their lives. I am talking about a hundred generations of men who made their choice and stuck to it, and whose choice was reaffirmed by their children and their children's children. The men who stayed on the ground are an entirely different species. They are the children of greed and selfishness and destruction. If they live today then they live in exactly the way they have always lived—by plunder. They have stripped the old world to its bones, and now they are fighting desperately to consume as large a share as possible of the wastes of ours.

"These are the children betrayed by their millions of ancestors. We are the children who were not betrayed, and who must not betray our own children. Our ancestors accepted responsibility for building a world, and we must accept the responsibility along with the world. It would be the most terrible of crimes to open our world to the forces of greed and destruction that destroyed the old."

Emerich knew that she had gone on too long, but he had allowed her to do so because she was obviously in good form. She had begun to repeat herself in the end, but she had rounded out her argument quickly enough. If she had run over her time she had only taken time he had already won from Magner. The stage was set now, the arguments were arrayed. The issues were assembled—sins of the fathers . . . Euchronian responsibilities and principles . . . justice and humanity . . .

All Emerich had to do was keep the wheel spinning.

"Clea," he said, as the camera hesitated between the combatants, "used the term 'betrayal.' Don't you think, Carl, that your plan to open the way between the worlds is such a betrayal? Isn't it a betrayal, not only of everything your ancestors worked for, but of your own world, your own life, your own children?"

Magner was tempted to say "no" and leave it at that. It was as simple as that, to him. But he knew that he could not afford it. He was backed up to the wall now, he had to hit back.

"Clea spoke of men betraying their children and men betraying their ancestors," he said. "I think that such arguments are themselves betrayals. They are traitors to reason and to humanity. Perhaps the men who did not choose to participate in the Euchronian Plan were selfish. But you cannot simply declare a man 'selfish' and write him out of the human race. There is more to a man than his lack of Euchronian belief. These men had a choice, and they took it, and we must recognize that it was not an easy choice, that their motives were probably complex, and that the fact they chose to stay with the old world rather than with the new does not make them villains, let alone subhumans of 'an entirely different species.'

"We must recognize that our knowledge of the early years of the Plan is imperfect, and that our understanding is even more imperfect. We live now in entirely different circumstances. We do not have the means by which we might judge these men, and it is wrong that we should attempt to do so. We have a new world now, and a new way of life. We have a responsibility to the men who worked to give us this new life—but we must not make this responsibility into idolatry. We have a responsibility to *use* the gifts which they have given us, to adapt our thinking to our new life. We are failing our ancestors if we accept our new world but stick with fanatical rigidity to old prejudices, and ways of thought developed in old contexts. We are new men now—the human race has made a second beginning. Then let us find a new and proper humanity—let us aspire to the justice that our ancestors lacked as well as to the sanity and the hope for the future which they possessed.

"I say that we have no right whatsoever to condemn the men of the Underworld for the decisions made by their forefathers. But even if we had, would it not be just and reasonable to refuse to exercise that right? In the new world today we do not hate the men of the Underworld. Why do we ignore them? Why have we forgotten their world and their very existence? Is this not an attitude of *guilt?* You want me to speak about betrayal . . . well, then, I offer you this betrayal: the betrayal of the men on the ground by the men in the sky. The betrayal of our kindred, of our own humanity. Do we owe our loyalty to a cruel principle, or do we owe it to *people?*"

"We owe our loyalty to one another," said Clea, without waiting for Emerich. "Not to a principle of any kind, nor to an idea which is, in the final analysis, only a label. You say that we owe our loyalty to people, but what is 'people'? Who are 'people'? We cannot define a man by calling him a man. We must have an idea of humanity which is not simply a matter of shape or the ability to cross-breed. You yourself have talked of things which are 'truly human.' We all have some idea of the qualities which go to make up what we call 'humanity.' We cannot determine our loyalties as simply as you seem to think. You say that we condemn the people of the Underworld—I say that they stand condemned, and not through any of *our* doing. We can owe them nothing that we do not owe in greater measure to ourselves, and to our ancestors and descendants as far as the imagination can stretch. We must make a decision as to whom we might mean when we speak of 'people.' And we must also decide what we include in our concept of humanity.

"I owe my loyalty to the men and women of the Euchronian Millennium—to the men and women who made it possible and to the men and women who will enjoy its fruits. I owe my loyalty to the whole human world fashioned by those same men and women and provided for them. I will do my utmost to protect that world from those who attack or oppose it—whether from without or from within. The fact that those assailants may be 'people' does not exempt them from all judgment of their actions. Sometimes, in matters of loyalty, one must choose *between* people. I have made my choice and I have made it rationally and justly. The new world must be protected by and on behalf of Euchronia's citizens. The men in the Underworld, whether it is Hell or Heaven, must stay there. It is their world, to use as they will."

"And the sunlight?" said Magner. "Is the sunlight ours and ours alone? Do we own the Face of Heaven itself?"

"We do," said Clea Aron. "We have built a world upon which the Face of Heaven may smile. It is ours. The men of the Underworld chose the Face of their own Heaven. They chose darkness. It is theirs."

Magner drew breath. The camera was on him. Emerich made no move to intervene.

"All that I say," said Magner, "is that they should have that choice. They should be able to choose darkness, if they so wish. But they should also be able to choose light. As you have said, it was not one generation of men who were offered a choice by the Planners, but many. I say that we should still offer that choice to the men on the ground. Now, and to all future generations."

"But isn't the choice you want to offer a different choice altogether?" This time it was Emerich who took up the point. "The choice which was offered by the Planners was the choice between building a world and parasitizing a world. No one offered them Heaven, but only the opportunity of working towards a Heaven for their children. You want to offer them the reward without the labor. That's not the same choice at all, is it?"

"It's the choice that *we* face," said Magner. "There are men in Heaven and men in Hell. *We* have the choice of delivering the men of the Underworld from their life of torment, or of condemning them to suffer it for eternity. They have no choice unless we choose to give it to them. It is true that their choice is not the choice that was offered to their ancestors, but neither is ours."

"In that case," Emerich pointed out, "you can hardly argue that we should give the men on the ground the choice because the Planners did."

Magner shrugged. "I accept that entirely. We shouldn't be arguing on the basis of what the Planners did or didn't do. But it was by reference to the Planners that Clea was trying to justify her entire argument. My argument is based on the fact that in the Underworld there are men like ourselves, and that we should share what we have with them."

"There may be men," said Clea, "but there are certainly no men like ourselves. I have already said that you cannot simply call the inhabitants of the old world 'men' and leave it at that. What *kind* of men are they that live in the ruins of a murdered world, subsisting on the waste of another? If men live like rats in a sewer, are they not more rats than men?"

"You have a somewhat prettified concept of humanity," snapped Magner, his voice sounding slightly unsteady for the first time. "If the new world fell apart tomorrow and pitched us all into this Hell the Euchronian Plan has created do you imagine that none of us could survive? Don't you think that we would willingly take to dirt and decay and waste and the bare bones of a ruined world, if that were the price of survival? Don't you think that in a matter of days the environment of the Underworld could have transformed you, or I, or Rafael Heres, or even Yvon Emerich into a scavenger, living like 'a rat in a sewer?' Man is an adaptable animal, Clea. What is necessary, he will do. Whatever is necessary."

"Perhaps," said Clea, whose voice accepted the edge of hostility and magnified it in turning it back on Magner. "No doubt *some* of us might do perfectly well as citizens of the Underworld. You see the capacity for degeneration in all of us, and perhaps it is there, in all of us, to some degree. All the more reason, I would think, that we should not take these monster-men into our world. If the seeds of degeneracy are in us all, then the third dark age is not so distant from us as we might think. We must guard against it all the more watchfully."

"You say that man is an adaptable animal," said Emerich, taking up the thread artfully and concentrating the assault on Magner, "and we must remember that the Underworld has been closed for a very long time. The men of the Underworld, therefore, are presumably adapted to it. You call the Underworld Hell—but do they? Why is the Underworld a Hell if man is so adaptable? If the men of the Underworld have adapted to darkness, wouldn't it be cruelty to let the light shine into their dark world? Might not the sun be said to represent, from *their* viewpoint, the fires of Hell? In short, Carl, isn't it true that the men of the Underworld no more want a doorway into our world than we want a doorway into theirs?"

Emerich hammered out the questions in quick succession, with heavy emphasis on each one, and then just stopped, leaving Magner suspended in stiff silence. Magner, caught following the drift of Clea Aron's argument, was suddenly stranded by confrontation with Emerich's. The camera zoomed in on him and trapped him, caged his face in the well of sudden silence, closed in on his hesitation.

All of a sudden, his uneasiness flared into fear. His head, blown up to three times natural size, was cut off at the shoulders and held in a million holoviewers all over the world. He could feel the tightness of the frame, the claustrophobia.

"I said that man was adaptable," said Magner, arranging his thoughts while he spoke, and speaking slowly to steal time from the insistent cameras. "No doubt the men of the Underworld are adapted to their way of life. But they are adapted for survival. They survive, and of course they have adapted to the demands of survival under such circumstances . . . But that does not make the Underworld any less of a Hell. There is nothing in the Underworld *except* survival. They have life, but nothing more. We have so much more, so much more to offer, if we only would. We can offer them the opportunities of happiness, of creativity, of self-fulfillment—everything that was given to us by the endeavors of others."

"We can offer these things," said Clea, levelly. "But they could not take them. They could not even *want* them."

Magner wanted to shout. He wanted to shout: "You cannot possibly know what they want." But that was the one thing he dared not say. It was the one thing he had to avoid at all costs. Because it was true. Clea could not know, and nor could Emerich. And all they had to say was "Nor can you." They had deliberately stayed clear of that point. They had waited for him, waited until he would have to stray on to it himself, or concede them the battle. There was no way out.

Emerich came smoothly into the gap, once the point was established as theirs.

"Isn't it true," said Emerich, "that we *can't* offer these things? We live as we do because we are a stable society. Our needs are supplied because they are carefully balanced to *match* the supply. How could we conceive of absorbing millions of people into Euchronian society? There is no way. The population of the world stands only in the hundreds of millions. Less than half a billion. How many men are there in the world below? Ten million? Fifty? We could not absorb even five million, could we? Wouldn't opening the Underworld *destroy* the society designed by the Euchronian Plan?"

Magner went down before the sudden torrent, which was not so much question as accusation. There was no answer he could find. A simple "no" could not stand up against the odds. It would not even be true.

"We have no right," said Magner, "to deny the people of the Underworld the sight of the Face of Heaven."

"We must," said Clea Aron.

"You say that they are the descendants of a selfish and greedy people," said Magner, trying to salvage something of the debate, though the moment was already past. "But we are a selfish and greedy people. We are a people who will not see, who are willfully blind to the world which still exists beneath our feet. We are the guilty, not they."

"Must we give away the world," asked Emerich, "because *you* feel guilty?"

"They survive down there without a world," said Magner. "They would not destroy ours."

"Neither should we," said Emerich.

To that, Magner could say nothing. He had virtually nothing left to say. He could go back to the beginning, and try to plot a better course for the whole argument, but there was not the time for that. They had trapped him. They had beaten him.

He had known, of course—since the very beginning—that the Overworld never would be opened, that they never would permit the men of the Underworld to accept a place in Heaven. He had tried to remind them that the wrecked world was still beneath their feet, that they could never leave it behind them, that it would always be with them, and that the people in torment would always return, one way or another, to haunt them.

But he was not sure that he had done even that.

57

During the early years of the Euchronian Millennium there were six species extant in the Underworld which may be said to have been sentient and intelligent to some degree. Three of these races were descended from pre-Euchronian *Homo sapiens,* three were not. How many of these races might be called "human" is, however, a matter of definition. Also dependent on definition is the matter of *which* races might be called "human."

The so-called True Men (otherwise known as the "Men Without Souls") remained most similar to the parent stock, both genetically and culturally speaking. Physically, the True Men of the Underworld were not dissimilar to the men of the Overworld. It may be that interbreeding would still have been possible, and thus it could be argued that they remained the same species.

The True Men had, of course, abandoned all pretensions to the type of civilization characteristic of the age of psychosis. They had not begun to develop any kind of civilization based on an alternative pattern. They lived in walled towns, and though intercourse between towns was fairly well-developed there was virtually no political organization above that of the towns. The True Men were basically hunters and gatherers, with little agriculture or mining, but they retained the bare bones of a commercial system designed for a rather different way of life. The True Men tended to dominate those lands in which there existed substantial relics of the prehistoric second dark age, and the scavenging activities which they organized contrived to draw a certain amount of useful material from these areas even at this late date. This method of "production" served to keep the primitive activities of trade alive, but the source of supply was dwindling continuously.

The True Men retained literacy with the aid of material supplied by the Overworld, but the art fell under the complete control of a specialist sect, who thus became something of a power elite after the manner of priests or wizards.

Because of their relatively slow generation time the species was in slow decline under the prevailing environmental pressure. As a species, they were in no danger of extinction, but their way of life was being forced to undergo steady change, and ultimately they would have to look for an alternative.

A second species—or at least a subspecies—descended from prehistoric *Homo sapiens* was the Ahrima. Unlike the True Men the Ahrima had deliberately elected to remake their social organization and their way of life. The Ahrima may be regarded as an "artificial" species to some extent, because their genetic isolation from the True Men was a matter of rigid social ordinance. There is little doubt that fertile offspring would still have resulted from a cross, had such a cross been possible. However, the willful isolation of the Ahriman gene pool made it inevitable that they should diverge at a faster rate from the genetic heritage of the parent stock.

The Ahrima chose to become the predators *par excellence* of the Underworld. The founders of the species embraced a philosophy which declared that the only way to survive in such an ultimately rigorous environment was to give total loyalty to one well-defined group and none whatsoever to any other. The True Men and all other species of the Underworld thus became prey species for exploitation. The Ahrima were fighters, men and women alike, and they placed a very high priority on physical prowess, endurance, and the sheer power to survive. They did not practice specific rites of passage—such rituals were held to be false and ineffectual—but built into their whole way of life a rigor which ensured that the weak could not possibly survive. The total load on this species was socially increased, but it was also socially channeled to dispose of its random component. Owing to this socially promoted tachytely the Ahrima were slowly increasing fecundity and decreasing generation time. Simultaneously, however, they were putting such an intolerable pressure on the other major species of the Underworld that only two ultimate destinies were possible: either the remaining species would combine forces to obliterate the Ahrima entirely, or the Ahrima would wipe out their principal prey populations and have to reorder their own social organization.

The Ahrima fought without armor, unless one counts the masks which they wore. No doubt these masks did help to protect the head from injury, but their primary purpose was identification. The mask was the symbol of the Ahriman way of life, and no Ahriman would count a masked man his enemy, or a man without a mask as friend. The adoption of such an obvious and all-powerful symbol as the primary focus for social indoctrination led, eventually, to a strange form of pseudo-mimicry practiced by certain of the True Men. Occasionally, when a town of True Men was threatened by Ahrima they would put on masks of their own and join the marauders. In such an instance the Ahriman tribe would behave exactly as they would towards a second group of Ahrima which they encountered: the groups would move on together, and ultimately would fuse into one. *Ultimately*, however, could be quite a long time, and the simple fact is that the True Men were not equipped to cope with the Ahriman way of life. A whole town of True Men might join a band of Ahrima, and not one would survive the initial period of limited association. Undoubtedly, there was some introgression of genes from the True Men into the Ahriman species, but the process of selection involved in recruitment was such that the introgression was far from random. When a True Man donned the mask in order to save himself from death at the hands of the Ahrima he bought a stay of execution which would be served under difficult circumstances. His chance of getting away from the Ahrima at a later date was virtually nil. The Ahrima had a paramilitary organization and deserters were invariably killed.

The third species whose ancestors were prehistoric men were the Cuchumanates, whose divergence from the direct line was far more remarkable than that of the Ahrima. The Cuchumanates were almost certainly the product of genetic engineering, presumably deliberate and intraspecific. The Cuchumanates were parthenogenetic females, almost totally savage in their way of life, making no use of tools or artificial shelters. They moved in small groups or "families" (children were reared collectively) and were constantly migrating along established routes in order that their food supply should be allowed to regenerate constantly and maintain itself.

The Cuchumanates were not a warlike race, but would fight with great determination and courage if anyone attempted to displace them from their feeding grounds. As a species, they were in decline, but it seemed likely that they would survive for a long time as a rare and fugitive race. As conditions were perpetually changing it was not impossible that their ultimate fate might become more promising, but at the best their long-term chances of survival depended on factors outside their control.

The dominant species in the Underworld at the time the Euchronian Millennium was declared was the race which called itself "the Children of the Voice." Descended from prehistoric rats, the species may have been "aided" at some point in history by genetic engineering. In view of the fact that the species from which they evolved was the most highly developed semisentient of the old world, however, this conclusion must remain doubtful.

The Children of the Voice lived in walled villages rather similar to those of the True Men (probably imitative). However, while the village culture of the True Men appeared to be breaking up, that of the Children of the Voice was progressive and cohesive. Far more contact existed between villages, except when they were very isolated, and some semblance of national organization was in its infancy. The Children of the Voice were a quarrelsome race, but would work together consistently, if imperfectly. Their social organization was probably allowed to develop so quickly in spite of natural handicaps by virtue of the fact that their minds tended to dwell only briefly on emotional matters. Individual loves and hates were quickly forgotten, and behind those individual emotional reactions a more ordered conception of the world and its workings was allowed to develop. This manner of mental organization may have been correlated with the short generation time of the Children of the Voice, but undoubtedly their most important single difference from all other Earthly species was the symbiotic relationship which each individual had with a being he called his "Gray Soul."

The Children of the Voice regularly underwent certain forms of transcendental experience (drug-assisted, by sheer power of mind, or by pressure of extreme circumstance) which placed them in communication with these beings. Whether the Gray Souls existed in "another space" which merely came into contact with theirs, or whether the symbiotes were located wholly in the minds of the Children of the Voice themselves (but as totally independent entities) is not known.

The Children of the Voice were well able to sustain the load placed upon them by their environment, but perhaps less adapted to cope with the extraordinary pressures resulting from contact with other species. The fact that their culture evolved largely through "cultural contamination"—the imitation of the True Men and the inheritance of literacy and tool-using methods from the human-descended species in general—undoubtedly slowed their development as a unique species fulfilling its own needs and potentials.

Time, however, was on their side.

The so-called Hellkin were descended from prehistoric cats. They were a nomadic species with a high degree of sentience but rather limited intelligence. They lived in small groups and followed a nomadic way of life not too dissimilar to the Cuchumanates, except that they tended to be far more sociable. The Hellkin were essentially peaceful, and maintained friendly relations with all species, except the Ahrima. The Hellkin were articulate, but had no real racial identity of their own, all their pretentions to culture having been derived by imitation of other species.

Their long-term future as a species was indeterminate. To a large extent they were culturally parasitic, but their parasitism was obviously facultative. They had untapped powers of survival. If the Ahrima were to become dominant in the Underworld the Hellkin might well become extinct or regress back to semisentience, but under all other circumstances they could probably be successful, integrating themselves into any social organization or primitive civilization without necessarily being absorbed by it.

The last of the six species which might be reckoned as intelligent at this particular time was the species descended from dogs—the harrowhounds.

At one time the harrowhounds were a successful predatory species. Like the Hellkin they ascended from semisentience to full sentience very quickly in the decay of civilization which took place in the second dark age. However, the harrowhounds found that their principal prey—the rats—were evolving faster and more effectively than themselves. By the time the Euchronian Millennium began the harrowhounds were nearing the bottom of a long and steady decline. Harrowhounds hunting in packs still showed a high degree of organization, and communicated very effectively despite the fact that they never adopted human language. But the solitary harrowhound was becoming ever more familiar. As a sentient species, the harrowhounds had no future, but regression might well permit them to discover a new line of development as a semisentient animal species. It is not impossible that their survival might have depended on their redomestication, perhaps by the Children of the Voice.

58

Afterwards, there was a noticeable relaxation. There was no real end to the stillness, because the people on the ground did not return to their houses. But there was an end to the Communion of Souls, and the people of Stalhelm passed comfortably from trance into sleep. The priests knelt, and finally lay down. The crowd sagged and collapsed into a disordered heap. It was all over.

When the Sun withdrew from the Earth Camlak drifted into the realm of dreams. There was no real break in continuity between the vision that was real and the vision that was not, but he knew the difference, and he would know it again when he was awake.

Up in the hills, the lookouts also knew that it was finished. They, too, relaxed. They maintained their watch, and it was now easier for them to do so.

In Camlak's house, Joth and Huldi knew that it was finished. They had not spoken while the ritual was in progress, because they had both felt something of what it was about. But now they felt free.

"Your people," said Joth. "Do they . . . ?"

"No," she said, quickly. Almost too quickly. He was not sure that she knew what he meant.

"Camlak killed his own father out there," said Joth. "His father is dead."

"He had to," said Huldi.

Joth shook his head. He did understand, but it was difficult for him to accept. "It's the way things are," he said. "But it's cruel. Your people—are they as cruel?"

She considered the question. It seemed to be meaningless, but she knew that he was looking for an answer. She decided, in the end, that the answer didn't much matter.

"No," she said. The trueness or falseness of the statement was irrelevant to her. She went away from the window, back into the room where she and Joth spent the greater part of their time. She had a sheet in the corner, beyond the crude bed where Joth slept.

Joth hadn't finished with questions and answers. He had read the symbolism of the ritual but he found it hard to believe. He could not see that it had any meaning for the people of this world. He could see no reason why the Children of the Voice acted out something which happened in another world—something meaningless to them. He knew that primitive peoples in distant prehistory practiced rites of similar nature, but they did so as magic. They did so in order to emphasize their identity with nature. This was not the purpose of the rite he had just witnessed. The identity assumed in the play was false—it was a pretense of an affinity with a world which had little in common with that of the Shaira.

Why? He wondered. What kind of magic was it? Was it magic at all?

"Huldi," he said, "what kind of gods do these people have?"

"They have no gods," she said.

"They have priests. They have religion."

"No gods," she said again. He knew that she would only repeat what she believed. She was incapable of discussion, of changing her mind. But did she know the truth? *Could* she know the truth?

"Do your people have gods?" he asked.

"No," she said.

"Do you have priests?"

"We need no priests. We have readers."

Joth saw, suddenly, that it might make a kind of sense. They needed no priests, the Men Without Souls. But that was not because they had no gods. It was because they had no rituals. The Children of the Voice did have rituals, and they had priests. But did they have gods? Did they *need* gods, any more than the Men Without Souls? Perhaps not.

What were gods for? he asked himself. They were the forces in action behind the visible forces of nature. They were the forces in control, the ultimate determinants of the way life should be—and had to be—lived.

The gods were the manifestations of another world, a world of which the experienced world was only a part, a world whose laws made sense of the wayward behavior of the experienced world. The gods were the determinants of the random and the inexplicable.

The Underworld needed no gods. The people of the Underworld did not need to imagine another world. They did not have to invent creative and determinant forces. Because there *was* another world. There *were* such forces. There was a world above them—a real, living world populated by men and not by gods. A world which, so far as the men of the Underworld were concerned, fulfilled all the functions of the supernatural world in a wholly natural fashion. The Overworld was Heaven, but it was not inhabited by gods. The peoples of the Underworld did not worship, nor did they offer sacrifices, nor did they beg for favors from chance. They had a much more stable and settled relationship with their other world than the primitives of prehistoric time.

The Children of the Voice were religious. They were not superstitious. The ritual which Joth had just seen was designed to fulfil their own purposes. It was an execution, and a communion. The symbols it used were the symbols of the other world—the *real* other world—and their symbolic function was wholly religious and not magical.

"You have no festivals," he said to Huldi. "No ceremonies."

"We dance," she said. "We like dancing."

"But you dance because you like it," he said. "Not because it brings the rain, or makes for better hunting, or for better crops. You don't dance to make you kill your enemies."

She didn't answer. She had no answer to offer.

Joth knew that the Children of the Voice did have beliefs, ideas which might be called superstitions. They did have customs which emphasized in various ways the identities of nature. Camlak had hunted the harrowhound with a spear whose head was made of the bone of a similar creature. But this was nothing more than an affinity with their world. They had no dominant, all-inclusive concept of the supernatural into which such small fragments of behavior could be collected.

No gods. No gods at all.

Joth realized then what the Face of Heaven really was, in

the terms of the Underworld. He realized the mistake that his father had made in using the phrase in a context which made sense to him.

He realized that his father was very wrong. Even though the images were real, even though the picture was not wholly inaccurate. Carl Magner was utterly wrong.

Joth was still beside Huldi. He was kneeling. His brain was racing.

Huldi, already half asleep, pulled at his sleeve. The rotted material ripped, and he looked down, confused. Neither one of them was wholly conscious of what was happening.

Joth lay down beside the girl, and then he rolled on top of her. He felt the torrent of his thoughts begin to break up as he struggled with his clothing and reached into the folds of hers. By the time his head was clear he had no wish to recoil or reconsider.

He hesitated. But he knew what he was doing, and he carried on.

59

Chemec was running down the slopes of Clauster Ridge as fast as his crippled leg would let him run. The other lookouts whose posts commanded a view of Livider Marches were also running. Signals were passed from man to man. One paused long enough to blow a long, loud blast on the horn which he carried.

They had been watching and waiting for the Men Without Souls.

But it was the Ahrima who were coming.

60

Huldi was fast asleep, but Joth lay awake, thinking how easy it would be to escape. There was no guard at the skull-gate. He could draw the wooden bolts by himself and be away into the night. No one would know. No one would care.

He was indulging himself in a fantasy. He had no real plan to escape. The need which he felt to flee back to the Overworld was under control. He had faith, of a kind, that the need would be filled, in time.

In truth, the idea of going once again into the alien wilderness of the Underworld, away from the warm walls of Camlak's house, was a frightening one. He did not want to find himself adrift in that malicious landscape.

The sound of the horn captured his mind, and his idle thoughts died away. He was seized by a sudden fear, because he sensed that the crisis was suddenly close at hand.

61

The foremost runner arrived back at the skull-gate, seized the stick from the wall, and began to beat the drum which hung beside the gate. His breath came in great ragged gouts and his limbs burned fiercely, but he swung the stick as hard and as fast as he could.

The village was roused within minutes. From the frozen sleep which the Communion had left in its wake sprang running men, shouting men, spreading the panic and the urgency like wildfire. Life was restored, and it found a furious tempo within seconds.

Camlak threw off the bloodstained mask and heard the cry of "Ah . . . rima!" almost instantly. He was still in the

gold and silver costume of the ritual when the runner was
brought to him.

"How many?" he asked, and "How soon?"

"A horde," said the runner, squeezing his words into the
breaths that he drew. "Crossing Cudal Canal. Too many,
too close."

"Walgo?" he asked.

"It has not burned. Ermold must have taken the mask."

Camlak cursed. That would be Ermold's way. Ermold
should have been born to the mask. There was no way that
Stalhelm could survive. With the fighting strength of Walgo
added to the Ahriman horde, however briefly, the masked
marauders would smash Stalhelm in a matter of hours. The
women and the children would have to be sent to Lehr, to
make the best of their way to safety while the warriors tried
to hold the town. The elders, the readers, the old women
. . . all these would have to stay too, to bear arms, if they
could . . . to take the place of the dead as they fell from
the wall.

Death was coming. Death for all, unless Shairn could be
awakened to the danger. Runners had to be sent to Lehr,
to Opilion, to Digen. Perhaps the warriors would come out
of the Heartland, to meet those of his people who could flee
farthest. Perhaps not.

Camlak did not need to gather and command the people. They knew what the coming of the Ahrima meant.
They knew what had to be done. Camlak ran back to his
house, and while he discarded the ceremonial robes for armor he talked to Joth.

"You must go," he said, "and go quickly. To the metal
wall in the north. If there is a way home for you, you will
find it there. Do not come back here. If you come back to
this world at all, go west, into Shairn. Ask for me in the
northern towns, or make your way south to Lehr. If you
do not hear from me in Lehr you will know that I am
dead. Take Nita—she knows the map that hangs in the
long house and she will show you the way. Take the other
too—Ermold has taken the mask and she cannot stay here.
The women would kill her."

There was no time to say anything more. There was no
time to talk about the future, no time for good wishes. There
was no time at all. Shairn was invaded and Stalhelm was under the spearhead of the invasion.

"Good-bye," said Joth, when he was ready. But Camlak did not even hear him.

62

Simkin Cinner was not an important man by anyone's standards. The actions which he performed were on the whole quite irrelevant to the main current of life in the Overworld. But he was an *individual,* and not a representative of a particular type, and as an individæul he had his own unique role to play in the scheme of things. He was a killer.

Despite the fact that he was a passionately patriotic Euchronian and fanatically loyal to the people of Euchronia's Millennium, Simkin Cinner was not a nice man. He was neither stupid nor ignorant, but ideas tended to come into his head from all kinds of peculiar angles, there to be associated into a loose webwork of opinions and motives which had no real relevance to his fanatical faith although they enjoyed its full motive power. He was self-deluded, it is true, but not because he was an idiot. Merely because he was superficial.

Cinner lived half in and half out of Millennial society. He spent a great deal of his time in the so-called Sanctuaries—the areas specifically designated as outside the organized society of the Overworld. The purpose of the Sanctuaries was to allow any citizen the ultimate freedom to opt right out. They also existed in order to give the Euchronians somewhere to put their criminals. The Sanctuaries were supplied, to some extent, with the raw materials of life by Euchronian Society—a gesture of goodwill and humanity.

Cinner, of course, had no need of Sanctuary as a retreat from society or a refuge from it, and he was not a criminal. He went into Sanctuary in order that he might appreciate Euchronia even more. He also went in to kill people. (Sometimes, it was expedient to have people removed altogether from the possibility of contact with society. Crime, in theory, was not punished, save by expulsion from society, but occasionally it was deemed convenient to follow up on that sentence. There were, of course, no laws applicable to Sanctuary. Freedom was freedom. Freedom to kill, freedom to be exterminated.)

Cinner liked violence, for its own sake, but he would never have dreamed of using violence against the Euchronian civilization. On the other hand, he hated to see the Euchronian civilization insulted or threatened in any way. That made him feel very bad. Full of violent feelings.

Usually someone told Cinner whom to kill. They gave him no direct orders, nor did they have to bribe him. It was sufficient just to indicate that it would be desirable if certain persons did not have the opportunity to "break out" of Sanctuary. The suggestions always came from people he admired and trusted.

Eventually, however, it was inevitable that Cinner would make a judgment of his own, and would discover his own reasons why a certain person should be removed from a society whose bountiful generosity he patently did not deserve. And it was inevitable, also, that the boundaries of Sanctuary would come to mean less to Cinner as time went by. Sanctuary, after all, is only a state of mind . . .

63

Abram Ravelvent drove along the westbound highway. It was night, and there were very few cars on the road. He could make a good one-seventy in perfect comfort and safety.

"It isn't far," he said to his passengers (without taking his eyes off the road). "At this rate we'll be there in a matter of minutes. There's definitely a way down. One of a good many, I should think. I found it for Harkanter and his people, but I don't think they're going down until after the weekend. They're still getting together. I'm not actually sure what the thing is *for,* but the platform wasn't built in a day, and it wasn't turned into the Garden of Eden in a day either. There must have been quite adequate provision made for the transport of material from the lower world on a grand scale. I think this is only a door. There are probably much more impressive outlets. Many of the machines are built from the ground up, of course, and we still take quite a lot from the surface—or below the surface, I suppose, would probably be more exact."

Carl Magner made no reply. He was in the back seat, leaning back into the soft plastic, staring out through the window into the night, watching the blazing lights which whipped past the car so swiftly that their light became a continuous streak in the sky. He was hardly listening to Ravelvent. Ravelvent was no longer important.

He was going down into the Underworld.

Why? he wondered. Do I even know why? Is there a real reason? Is there any real purpose to be served?

He had no idea what he was going to do when he got down to the door which separated the worlds. Unlock it, if he could. Throw it wide open. And then? And . . . then?

Magner knew that the descent into the Underworld had become something of a meaningless ritual. He wanted to know the truth, but he knew—in his heart—that it wasn't the truth which mattered. Not to him. Ravelvent cared about the truth, and to Ravelvent the truth was important. But Ravelvent wouldn't go down into the Underworld. He couldn't. He was a coward, and he just couldn't face the idea. Ravelvent was scared of the Underworld and what it might contain. Perhaps that was why the truth was important . . . to him.

What can a look into the Underworld tell me? Magner asked himself. I have seen the Underworld a thousand times. I know it intimately—far more intimately than any glimpse from a tiny door in the wall of a machine complex. I know its life and its ways. I know it all. So why the door? Why, all of a sudden, do I have to go in search of the door? Never before, never in all the years . . . not even when Ryan didn't come back . . .

I can only lose, Magner told himself. I can only prove myself a liar. But can even that be said to be meaningful? What *does* it mean if I am wrong? Is there any meaning in it any more? Haven't Yvon Emerich and Clea Aron and all their hungry audience proved my dreams, my hopes, my fears and my determination to be empty? All empty? Is there anything between the world above and the world below except a wall of ignorance and blindness? Can there ever be anything else? The Overworld exists because it rises above the dirt and the decay of the Underworld. The Underworld exists because the Overworld is above it. Is there anything more?

He could see some stars out of the car window, very faint because of the glare of the lights alongside the road. They were faint, silver points of light. They gave the impression of vast distance. Through the windows of the car, a glimpse of infinity. Beneath the spinning wheels, beneath the thin veneer that was a road and a world, a vision of Hell. In between, Magner. Alone.

For a moment, Carl Magner wondered what he had been doing, for the past weeks and months and years. But when he shut his eyes, he knew. The very threat of sleep was enough. He had thought his dreams a revelation. He had thought himself . . . he had to admit it now . . . privileged, granted a mission. He had seen himself as a kind of Messiah. Perhaps even more than that . . . perhaps a God. Hadn't his own sons, Ryan and Joth, gone into the Underworld in answer to *his* call? Christs, both of them. He had fallen prey to all kinds of vanity when he woke from his dreams. All kinds of blasphemy. He knew that now. He could see that clearly.

His dreams . . . even if they were true . . . *especially* if they were true . . . had been a kind of temptation, a temptation with a curse, a curse that had carried him to defeat, humiliation, and now to . . . what?

"You know," said Ravelvent, breaking up the silence with determined verbosity, "it's very strange. There must be so many ways into the Underworld. All I had to do was look, and they were there. So many. And yet no man of the Underworld has ever ventured up to the world above. Now why would that be? Why has there been no voyage of discovery? Why no invasion? Why no theft? Why have they never come to look at the sun which we took away from them?"

Magner had no answers. It was Julea who spoke.

"It isn't strange," she said. "They wouldn't touch the machines. They wouldn't trust them. They wouldn't come near them."

"That's possible," said Ravelvent. "There are so many possibilities, with so many different implications. You know . . ."

He carried on talking. He felt obliged to talk, to mask his own confusion and faint trepidation. He felt that there might be some sort of pressure on him—the pressure of conscience—to go down the staircase with Magner. He knew that he wasn't going to do that. He felt slight guilt about it. He knew that Julea wouldn't go down—wouldn't even think of going down—and that he wouldn't be left alone no matter what. But he could envisage the long wait, the hours ticking by, the matter of deciding. Magner wouldn't come back. He was sure of that much. So what could he do? How long should he wait with Julea? Would Julea think that he ought to go down after her father, to search for him?

Julea didn't listen to him. She didn't need to. She knew that Ravelvent wasn't saying anything she wanted to hear.

She still hadn't told anyone except the Eupsychian about the name Ryan had given into her safekeeping, and which she had given to Joth. She didn't know whether this was right. It was obviously a secret, because *nobody* knew it. But whose secret? And why? And what did it mean? It was a deadly secret. It had killed Ryan, and Joth, and perhaps it would kill Warnet. One by one, it was subtracting everyone she knew from the fabric of her life. Her father was about to subtract himself. Who was left? What was the remainder? What was the answer?

All minus. All dead.

Ravelvent had called their destination a plexus. A nerve center. A vast lattice of nervous metal fiber. A reservoir of functional control for the cybernet. Gleaming threads of neuronal wire. Cytoarchitecture in pressed steel. Synapses in etched microcircuits. Metal-veined glass. Mile on mile of coiled plastic. A tangled knot of metal microorganism. A tiny fraction of the living leviathan corpse that was the cybernet: the Atlas which held the Overworld on its shoulders.

Ravelvent would send her father down into that. As if he was a bacterium oozing deep into the carcase of a sick body. Down and down and down, into the metal mental wilderness, into the deepest recesses of the Overworld's subconsciousness: Euchronia's id.

She alone understood (and only vaguely, in an instant of vision) the Odyssey which her father was about to undertake. She alone could see *where* he was going. Ravelvent and Magner were both sidetracked into *why*.

"I find it so difficult to understand," Ravelvent was saying, "why the failure to come to terms with a world which is only just below one's feet and is so *total*. I'm a loyal and convinced Euchronian, you know that. I don't believe for a minute that a society like ours is sterile. It's free, it's full of life. It's active, it's progressive. We haven't lost the dynamism of the Euchronian Plan, not by any means.

"But I could almost believe that there's some kind of *narcotic* aspect to the way we live. I could almost believe that there's something forcing our eyes away from certain directions. I believe, of course, that we must all look to the *future,* but I think there's a danger of becoming slightly obsessive, that we may become blind, in some way, to our present and the true extent that it has. I mean, when all said and done, we can't actually get *away* from the Underworld . . ."

He paused for a breath, waited for an echo of approval, a suggestion of an answer, a murmur of life.

There was utter silence.

64

Cinner followed Ravelvent's car quite openly. He was not afraid that the other driver might realize he was being followed. Nobody would. There was no need to conceal a car on a road. Ravelvent would not even notice that there was another car behind him, and that it was always the same car at the same distance. Suspicious minds were extinct in the Overworld.

The blood was warm—an alcoholic warmness—as it drained through Cinner's heart. He felt warm throughout. His heart did not pound. He was not excited, not jittery. Just pleasantly anticipating. He was perfectly assured. He was balancing himself delicately.

65

Ravelvent pulled his car to a stop, and hesitated. His heart was thumping hard, there was a tightness in his throat. He opened the door, suddenly feeling constrained, and breathed in the cool night air.

The plexus was set back from the road, nestling between two shallow slopes. It looked very clean.

Julea got out of the near side rear door. Magner came out after her rather than getting out his own side. There was another car coming.

Ravelvent saw the other car when he turned to speak to his friends. Carl Magner and Julea were side by side, Julea was shutting the car door. He could see the other vehicle between their shoulders. It was dawdling, still slowing down. Ravelvent thought that it was going to stop.

For a moment Ravelvent wondered how he was going to explain what it was that the three of them were doing out here. What am I going to say? he asked himself.

Then Cinner leaned out of the window of the passing car, straightened his arm and shot Carl Magner in the back.

66

The trek through the wilderness seemed endless, but Nita would not let them rest.

There was no road, no suggestion of a trail. They had cleared the cultivated fields in less than a mile, and once past the land which was under human governance they were in country which was totally wild. They had to fight their way through knee-high vegetation, wade through stagnant swamp, and scramble up, down and across rocky slopes.

Always the stars shone upon their efforts with absolute steadiness.

Their way was made easier by the fact that they had nothing to carry. Joth and Huldi possessed nothing save for the ragged clothes in which they stood, and Nita had brought nothing with her except a small all-purpose knife. She knew well enough how to live off the land. She had not even burdened herself with the map from the long house. That was committed to her memory.

Nita moved faster than either of her charges, and seemed never to tire. Huldi, of course, proved much more enduring than Joth. Thus it was Joth who determined the pace. It was for his benefit that they rested periodically.

"What will happen at the village?" asked Joth, while they rested.

"Most of the men will be killed," said Nita. "They will not keep off the Ahrima for long. A few will run away. The Ahrima will burn the houses, but they will not stay. They will be angry because the women and children have all gone. The Ahrima prefer to take slaves if they stay for a time in any one place. They will take what they can from Stalhelm, and then go. The work will be all undone, but it can be done again. When the Ahrima are gone, people will begin to come back. The land will still be there."

"What will the Ahrima do?" said Joth.

"Attack. Perhaps Lehr, perhaps Opilion. The Shaira cannot run away from every town. Somewhere they will have to stand. The Ahrima might run through Shairn without taking a town and slaves, but it is more likely that they will capture some good land, use slaves to strip it, and stay until the Shaira have mustered an army large enough to force them out. Then they might run, or they might try to get behind the army, to prey upon the villages whose warriors have been taken away."

"Either way," said Joth, "the country will be desolated. Destroyed."

The girl shrugged. "Hurt. No more. Shairn cannot be destroyed. It will always be here."

"Will the women and children reach Lehr?" asked Joth.

Nita shrugged again, apparently caring little either way. "If the fight is long enough, and the road is short enough. If the warriors of Lehr come out to cover their flight. Perhaps. Perhaps not. If the Ahrima catch them they will scatter in Dossal Bog. Many will be killed. Some will not. There are always some who live, some who return. The Ahrima will not be in Shairn forever."

"The men who took the mask will die," said Huldi. "All of them. In time."

"Even Ermold?" asked Nita.

"Even Ermold," said Huldi. Her voice was flat and self-assured, but Joth could not tell whether she believed it or whether she only wanted to believe it.

"Ermold could have fought the Ahrima," said Joth. "The men of Walgo could have warned the Shaira that the horde was on its way. An army might have come to Stalhelm."

"Then the Ahrima would have turned back," said Nita. "They would have taken Walgo, and all its people for slaves."

"The women and children could have come to Stalhelm, as yours went to Lehr."

Nita shook her head.

"They would not," said Huldi.

They went on through the empty, derelict world. They ate insects and drank water which tasted filthy. Joth made no complaints, and did as the others did. He no longer payed much attention to what he would once have considered rank foulness of smell and taste, but even so the sickness which had plagued him for a long time in Camlak's house returned to him, in some measure, in the wilderness. Often, he had to force himself on against the pain and the fever. But it was a battle he was winning, by degrees.

Joth had lost all notion of time. He had ceased to pay attention to time while he was in the Underworld, and was beginning to acquire the attitude of the people. The three slept when they felt sleep was necessary, and when Nita would permit it.

For a time they encountered few animals which seemed dangerous. They were menaced by no large predators, and they avoided snakebite and serious parasitism. They were slightly lucky, even in the early stages. But as time and the miles went by, all but unheeded, they penetrated deeper into the heart of the Swithering Waste, and they moved into a world as hostile and deadly as any of the Realms of Tartarus.

They passed through forests of shiny fungus as hard as wood—mycelia which mimicked trees, fruiting bodies like bushes. The ground was always ridged and slick because the bloated rhizoids and subterranean hyphae lay just beneath the humus. In every crevice there were clusters of small basidiomycetes, usually brightly colored and—so Nita said—poisonous. This multitude of tiny plants filled the air with an inconstant miasma of sporedust, and they all three had to protect their breathing apparatus with masks of cloth. The masks were crude and could not exclude the dust wholly, and all three found their bronchial tubes perpetually choking with phlegm. All three—but particularly Joth—suffered more or less constantly from allergic reactions in their sinuses and other mucous membranes. Nita made them take large doses of an extremely bitter membraneous algoid, which had some antihistamine properties, but it served only to ameliorate the symptoms, not to prevent them.

The ground was often covered with cockroaches and small black beetles. The dendrites provided a perfect home for a vast host of starlings and other, unknown species of birds which were hardly ever seen in the human lands of the Underworld.

In between the forests were wet regions, where the ground was either sodden or completely submerged. Here there was a different kind of vegetation, dark green in color and predominantly filamentous, though everywhere that moderately stable mud was available the puffballs and chytrids clustered, climbing upon one another's backs, forming grotesque conglomerates of form and feature, bristling with the ascocarps and the hyrdroids of two or three dozen different species. The water here was acidic, and it burned their skin, as well as hastening the rot which had already set into Joth's clothes. There were no replacements, and as time passed he grew gradually more naked. Even the spore-free air of the wetlands was no relief to them, because it carried vitriolic vapors which irritated the tissues inflamed by the spores.

They never dared rest in the wetlands, even where the soil was matted into plate-like ridges by the dense algal filaments. They had to share such refuges with a large variety of inimical creatures which, though small, were not negligible. Crabs in particular abounded in such regions.

There were also large plants whose gigantic rubbery leaves lay atop the moist surface, offering a refuge of a kind, but if they stayed on such a leaf for more than a few moments it would begin to sink beneath their weight, and they would be flooded. From time to time, when they walked over such platforms, they would be tipped sideways into the morass, which was more like deep slime than mud.

The wetlands also sheltered flesh-eating plants like soft sea-anemones, with tentacles which never ceased to writhe through the air and through the mud. The plants never stopped consuming victims of one kind or another—they had to keep moving in order to catch prey, and they had to catch prey in order to keep moving.

In the swamps they were occasionally alarmed by the sight of large animals. But the animals were always equally alarmed, and often they would know of the presence of the larger beasts only by the loud splashing of a creature in full retreat.

More dangerous, and on one occasion all but deadly, were the four-foot flatworms which lurked invisibly in the fluid subsurface. One of these wrapped itself around Huldi's ankle and tripped her. She fell full length, but caught herself on her hands, and did not allow her head to go into the mud. The worm flopped up on to her back like a great wet blanket. Huldi tried to shrug it off, but was too firmly imbedded in the mud. Joth grabbed it but couldn't hold it. Its head was between her shoulder blades, and it seemed to spit at her, everting its whole gut. Glands in the gut were churning out digestive juices like bubbling fountains, and the villi of the blind intestine could be seen flapping like a thousand tiny flags.

Joth eventually managed to get a hold as Huldi writhed and screamed, and between them they tossed the creature sideways so that the flood of corrosive liquid was lost in the slime. There was an audible hiss as the acids sank into the algal soup. Huldi was burned about the neck, and had to abandon what was left of her jacket, but she escaped without any serious injury.

Joth stamped hard on the worm, but the ground was so slushy that it came to no real harm. It writhed and sucked its gut back into itself and oozed away into the glutinous subsurface.

Eventually, they came to the edge of a land which seemed to have rusted away. Joth guessed immediately that here were the partially unreclaimed ruins of a city, and he wanted to go into this land in search of relics of an older mankind. But Nita stopped him, saying that it was too dangerous, and that such lands were deadly. She pointed away to the west, and Joth saw a strip of darkness in the further sky. The stars, which were clustered less densely even in the roof directly above, petered out completely in that direction.

"The black land," she said. "Perpetual night."

"Not quite," said Joth, straining his metal eyes, and then adjusting them with his thumb to give him better vision. "I can see a thin line of light, like a road of stars. It goes straight out into the black land. Where does it lead? It can't be there without a reason. It points a way . . . somewhere."

"No one knows where it goes," said Nita. "We have come far to the west. We are away from our true direction. We must turn away from this country. We must not cross it, and we would die if we tried."

They went on, away from the region where echoes of an older civilization still lingered. On towards the metal wall. They all became tired and sick, and ultimately neither Nita nor Huldi enjoyed any kind of an advantage over Joth, nor the one over the other. Whereas in the early times it had been Nita and Huldi who gathered most of the food, now they all shared equally in the work. They slept in turn, fitfully and uneasily, and they were all troubled in some measure by the quality of their dreams. They questioned neither the purpose of the journey nor the distance which they covered. There was no suggestion, at any time, that Nita might prefer to turn back and search for her father, or that Huldi might want to go her own way. They were united, by a kind of love. And also by a kind of fear (though love itself has always a component of fear, no matter what kind it might be). But their fears were quiet fears, which they neither voiced nor faced.

67

In the end, they found the metal wall.

68

Carl Magner went down.
  Alone.
  Neither Abram Ravelvent, nor Julea, had come into the plexus after him. They had not tried to stop him, though perhaps they might have had they realized what was happening. They did not follow him. Julea had broken down into tears, and simply collapsed like a rag doll, as if it had all been inevitable from the very beginning, and now was finished. Ravelvent had been momentarily torn between them, but there had been no real choice to make. He had

stayed with Julea, and with the world that was his, and Magner had gone into the plexus alone, with a bullet lodged in his body.

Perhaps there was the faintest of possibilities that if it had not been for the bullet Magner would have turned back. But any impetus which he might have lacked the bullet had most certainly provided. It was the final settlement, the *coup de grâce*. It left nothing else for Carl Magner but a descent to the Hell he had named.

There was no more help now. There was no more reality except the world of sleep (perpetual sleep) and dreams (are there dreams in death?).

Carl Magner was running. Down.

He was coming face to face with Heaven and Hell. Running between the worlds, he was their marriage—the only marriage they would ever know.

He went down.

And down.

And down.

Crystal eyes winked at him. Plastic mesh ears caught the sound of his coughing, the rattle of his clattering feet, the slow slap, slap, slap of the tiny drops of blood on the stairs. The blood would have clotted if only he would have let it, but instead he went down, and tore himself apart a fraction farther with every step that he took, tore the corners of the wound again and again, until a tiny rounded bullet hole became an ugly gaping mouth. Blood drooled.

Slap, slap, slap.

Down, and down.

The plexus could feel him as well. It could feel his vibrations, his hurry, his urgency, his need. And his slowly draining life. The plexus was conscious of him. It knew him. Impassively, it crouched around him and watched him, studied his scurrying figure.

He was very tiny.

He was tasteless. The machine could not smell him. It could only see and hear and feel. It had no direct emotional/sensory links. Its organometallic synapses were geared to a functional régime of an altogether different character.

He was not thinking. Not really. He had nothing to think about, nothing to keep his mind active except the simple routine of operating his motor nerves. After the bullet, the future had disappeared. In a puff of smoke. The past was dwindling and fading. In a puff of blood.

The whole consciousness of time and its meaning (past/present/future) which Carl Magner had used to fuel his life recoiled into him like a snapped watchspring. The past was kneeling on the grass up above, Julea in Ravelvent's arms. The future . . .

He was caged in the present, caged and confined by bars which pressed on his being like the laces of a straightjacket. His meaninglessness meant nothing, here. He was only acting a part as he ran down the staircase to throw wide the door which opened the Underworld.

He hurled himself down, trying to outrun the running of the blood.

And down.

And down.

And down.

69

When Carl Magner reached the door to the Underworld he found that it was open. All he had to do was push it and it swung out. There was no lock, no apparent catch, and the hinges were not stiff. It required only the effort of his feeble fingers to push it open.

The door opened to reveal the land of his dreams.

There was silence and starlight.

Carl Magner realized that the door had been open for thousands of years.

70

Joth watched the door in the metal wall swing slowly outwards. They had been walking beside the wall for some miles. Joth did not know how many. He did not know—he literally had no idea—whether it had been three minutes or three hours or three weeks since they had first sighted the wall towering above the Swithering Waste and occluding the far stars.

Nita and Huldi paused, and then stayed still. But after momentary hesitation Joth went on. He did not know what hid behind the door, but he knew that it had come from above, from his own world, and he knew that there could be no reason to be afraid.

By the time Joth reached the door, Carl Magner was stretched out on the damp earth. His face was in the dirt. His feet were still on the steel sill of the final step.

Joth turned him over, and cradled his head in his own lap. Carl Magner's eyes were open, and he was looking up at the still, pearl-white stars. Joth could not be sure that his father could still see.

"Joth?" said Magner. Magner knew that he was not dreaming. There was no Joth in the dreams. There never had been. There never could be. Not even a dream of death could bring Joth into the world of frozen stars. This was reality, of a kind.

"It's me," said Joth. "I was coming back. I found the way. If you'd waited, I would have come. There was no need."

Joth did not know there was a bullet in his father's back. He could feel the slight wetness where his father's spine rested against his thigh, but he assumed that the dampness was in his own clothing. He did not know that his father was on the brink of death, even though he looked down into eyes which stared, and which would soon be quite sightless.

"I came . . ." said Carl Magner.

"It's all right," said Joth. "You can see. It's all right. Look at the stars. The world is real. The people . . . only the people . . ."

"I was wrong," said Magner.

"Yes," said Joth, "you were wrong."

They were talking about two very different kinds of wrongness. But neither of them knew. They thought that they understood.

Then Carl Magner died.

II. A VISION OF HELL

1

Camlak was not unduly sensitive to time. It passed by without dragging his consciousness. It flowed over him in an easy stream. The silence was profound. The Ahrima had gone, but the fires they had left burning were still filling the air with heavy smoke and the stark smell of ashes. There would be a while yet before the fire yielded to the gentle smell of decay and carrion that would bring the scavengers in from the fields, and from the wild land beyond Clauster Ridge.

The Old Man of Stalhelm was hurt, but not badly—at least, not so far as bone and flesh and blood were concerned. The arm which he had broken in the fight with the harrowhound had shattered for a second time, and he knew that this time there would be no mending it. From now on he was a three-limb. But that was little enough. It would not have taken him out of the fight, and saved his life. A blow on the head had done that, without inflicting any lasting damage. His clothing was covered in blood—dry by now—and no doubt he had looked dead enough to the marauders, lying as he was within the star-shadow of the earthen wall, with the mutilated bodies of the honest dead all around him. It was, of course, their blood. Blood they had spilled on to him, so that chance might rule in favor of his continued existence. The principal hurt which he had sustained was the pain of the question: *why?*

He was three times lucky.

First, he had fallen from a light, glancing blow, and sheer exhaustion had sucked him to the ground and hugged him into the crack between earth and earth-wall. Somehow, he had found the strength to suppress his courage. How? The Ahrima were already over the wall and involved in the simple business of slaughter. It was natural that he should have fought with indomitable fury, without any such self-control, or even self-awareness. He should have bounced back from the blow. But he had not. He had sagged, had contained his instincts, had vanished into the black clothes of unconsciousness.

Then, somehow the Ahrima had failed to find him. Or failed to find him alive. The one who had felled him must have been felled in his turn, at the right moment. At precisely the right moment. He must have died very swiftly, spilling his blood with such profligacy that he seemed to have exploded. A combination of chances: a neat riposte of fortune. Too neat.

Lastly, Ermold must have been already dead. The Men Without Souls from Walgo had taken the mask and joined the Ahrima in the assault on Stalhelm. A victory not so much for cowardice as for Ermold's hatred. He had come to kill instead of being slaughtered by the horde. He would die anyway, but he had come to kill first. Had he survived the storming of the wall, he would surely have come to take Camlak's head. A gesture to underline the purpose of it all. For old time's sake. Chance had forbidden him that satisfaction.

Why?

Camlak hurt inside his head. There was a fever in his brain. A fog. He tried to reach down into the depths where his Gray Soul lived, but the way was blocked. Honest pain would have cut through the miasma like a hot spear. No man was denied the company of his Gray Soul in the moment before death, or the moment of bodily crisis. So Camlak believed, with reason. But he was trapped in his glutinous consciousness. He was not going to die. He was alone.

He believed that there had to be an answer to the question: *why?*

But he did not even know what shape such an answer might possess.

2

The Ahrima had not lingered long once Stalhelm was taken and set afire. There was nothing to stay for. Everything which was truly valuable had been taken by the women who had left for Lehr the moment the Ahrima were sighted and the warning given. Camlak might have been counted lucky even a fourth time, in that the marauders had chosen to move on, but it was not chance which dictated the decision. The Ahrima wanted blood, and a great deal of blood. They had not spilled so much as a mouthful at Walgo, and fully three-fourths of the population of Stalhelm had fled before their advance. They wanted the blood of that three-fourths. They wanted to ride down the women and children who hastened along the road to Lehr. They wanted the plunder of Stalhelm far more than they wanted the rest or the food that was standing in the fields. It was not their way. Once the slaughter of the townspeople was completed . . . *then* they could think of rest and the licking of wounds and the filling of bellies. At Lehr, or perhaps Opilion, where they might not be expected so soon . . .

In any case, Camlak would not have claimed luck for the decision which would—almost inevitably—lead to the slaughter of his people. If the Ahrima caught the women and children on the road through Dossal Bog, then Stalhelm was obliterated. What the fire could not do, the sword would accomplish. It was the people that were Stalhelm, and once the people were dead . . . no Stalhelm. The name would remain, but names mean nothing.

Some of the people would survive. Perhaps some of the warriors had managed to escape the burning village to fight again on the road. In any case, in Dossal Bog there would be ample opportunity to run and to hide. Some of the women, and particularly the children, would escape the Ahrima in the marshland. Some of those would survive the perils of the bog. Some, perhaps, would ultimately return to the blackened ruin that had been their home. But all that counted for very little. Camlak's Stalhelm could not be recovered by a handful of children. Unless the warriors of Lehr came out to cover the retreat of the women, or something delayed the horde on the road, that Stalhelm would be strewn in a gigantic pool of blood all over the road through Dossal Bog.

After that . . . well, the news would reach Lehr, Opilion, and fly like a freak wind through the north and west of Shairn. If the Shaira could then allow their common fears and needs and causes to overcome their petty quarreling and disputes over land, all Shairn might combine to raise an army and meet the Ahrima in a battle that would cut the horde's strength so hard they would have to run. Even that would only be a beginning. With the heart of Shairn ripped open, its strength expended in a murderous encounter with the Ahrima, the Men Without Souls would move in, raiding the good lands, stealing Shairan land and taking Shairan slaves. After the war of extinction, the war of conquest . . . And then . . .

Harrowhounds would come. The vermin from the dark lands would spill over into the lighted lands of the Children of the Voice. Time and time and time would pass before Shairn became Shairn again. And if the Ahrima were *not* defeated, if no army was joined and the horde was not cut to such dimensions that the towns were safe . . . then Shairn might follow Stalhelm, and by the time the country lived again it would be something different. Something new.

When Camlak finally came to his feet again he discovered that he was angry with Ermold. He was angry because of Ermold's hate—the blind, unreasoning hate which had made him take the mask and join in the attack on Stalhelm. Camlak saw no reason for that hate, and because there was no reason he was angry. He considered Ermold's taking of the mask a betrayal. Not a betrayal of the Shaira, to whom he owed no loyalty, but a betrayal of reason and of human nature. Walgo should have stood and fought. That was the way. Perhaps there was no difference between the Men Without Souls and the Ahrima but masks, but the masks meant something. They were real. The Men Without Souls had no reason to be something that they were not. They should have fought. Perhaps . . . perhaps they should have fought *with* Stalhelm, *against* the Ahrima. Was that against nature, too? Camlak thought not. Not against *his* nature. Ermold's nature, on the other hand . . .

Camlak dismissed the argument from his maddened mind.

He could not think. The anger remained. He could still feel
—perhaps too much.

Camlak's house was burning. The bricks were crumbling
as the wooden framework and the roof were eaten away.
When the fire died there would be nothing left but ash and
rubble. In time, dust. Only dust. The smoke was foul, but
Camlak managed to suck enough oxygen into his lungs to
keep himself conscious and active. Foul air meant little
enough to him, or to any child of the Underworld.

Some of the other houses still stood, untouched. Something
to come back to, if anyone could come back. Or somewhere
for Hellkin to find refuge, somewhere for the Truemen who
came from beyond Cudal Canal to establish themselves. Ultimately, the houses would decay, or form the focus for a
new community. Either way, the real Stalhelm would be
buried, haunted by the living and the dead alike. Nowhere
and nowhen. Gone.

Camlak wandered around the dried-up streets, searching
out the bodies of the fallen, putting names to the faces
and the faceless. He had the vague idea that others might be
alive. But there was no one. It pained him to count how
few of the bodies were Ahriman. He plucked masks off a
few of the fallen, and shattered them by beating them
against the cornerstones of houses which remained intact.
He did not know why. He might have been searching for
Ermold, though there was no real reason. In any case, he
could not tell the Men Without Souls from the true Ahrima
until he removed the masks. Though there were too few to
give his counting satisfaction, there were too many to sort
into real and unreal, looking for one filthy face, for no good
reason.

He felt guilty because he—the Old Man—should have
been the only one singled out to survive (except, perhaps,
for those who had run). He was the custodian of the staff.
While the Ahrima were crossing the borders of Shairn, he
had been taking power from the Star King Yami. Against
the odds, against all the accusations, against the feeling of
the people, he had established himself. He had fought the
harrowhound to earn the right. And now he was Old Man
of nothing, but still Old Man. What he felt was a strange
kind of loneliness. He felt responsible for what had happened. He wanted to take the burden of guilt for the disaster on to himself. He was the Old Man, and he had earned
it. He had earned it the hardest way of all. He felt that he

had the right to feel betrayed by the chance which would not let him lie dead with the people—*his* people. They had never learned to trust him. They had never had the chance.

Eventually, he tired of looking at the dead, and he went into one of the untouched houses to change his clothes. The Ahrima had smashed up what they could, but their assault had been cursory—there was no real reward, material or emotional, in destroying inert objects—and he had no difficulty in finding what he needed, and then in preparing himself a meal. What the Ahrima had left was sufficient—in fact, the stripping of the village was more the work of the women than the invaders. The women had taken all that they could carry. Too much. Too much in the way of baubles and cloth. Along with the working tools and the books, the irresistible trivia would make too heavy a burden. The fleeing women might find themselves betrayed by their fondnesses. The road to Lehr would be strewn with things which, after all, had to be thrown away. Would the greed and the delight in possession deliver them into the hands of the Ahrima? Would sound common sense or sheer blind panic have delivered them? There was no way of knowing.

Even when he was rested and fed, clothed and armed, he still hesitated. He went back to wandering amid the dead, finding it impossible to believe that there was no life at all in Stalhelm. But by now there was. The starlings and the crabs were invading in force. Camlak began to kill, shattering the crabs with a stone axe. Against the starlings, he could do nothing. Eventually, he threw away the axe, because there were too many crabs. No matter how many he killed, it would make no difference. They would keep coming until the village could hold no more. No matter how many crabs were killed the Underworld was always as full of them as it could be. It made no sense. Killing them only made him feel worse.

In the end, he had to leave Stalhelm to the scavengers. It was theirs now, and if he stayed he would be one of them. The only question in his mind was the matter of which way to go. Where and why? There was a road to Lehr, a road which might run with blood, and which might take him to his death. For no real reason. On the other hand, there was the Swithering Waste. No road was there, but perhaps some kind of destination. Nita had gone that way, with the man who had no face. Beyond the Waste was the metal wall, and beyond that . . . if there *was* a beyond. But that way was clouded with doubt no less than the road to Lehr. Whatever choice he made, there would only be more choices, until he was interrupted by death. There was no known way, now that Stalhelm was gone.

Camlak felt the loneliness eating him from within.

He went to find the map which had hung on the wall in the long house. It had been torn down and slashed into three pieces by a sword. He put the pieces together on the long table and adjusted the edges.

Nita would have taken the man without a face and the girl Huldi over the hills called Anarek and Stiver, across the rocks at Scarmoon, and then into the Swithering Waste toward the Great Wall. Camlak tried to form an estimate of how far they would have gone, but the calculation defeated him. He had no way of measuring the time inside his head. If he could catch up with them while they were crossing Scarmoon, it would be easy enough to find them, but in the Waste it would need a miracle. The Waste was hundreds of miles across, and to the west it stretched to the dead cities and the very borders of the darklands—a vast expanse of poisoned shallows and jagged rock, completely overgrown and teeming with vermin—and worse. A death trap. No place to be wandering in search of other travelers. Once Nita was beyond Scarmoon, he would have virtually no chance of meeting her until the Wall. If that were so, then time now was not really of the essence.

In the emotional battle between the father of the child and the Old Man of Stalhelm, the father really had little chance. That was the way love worked in the Underworld, at least in Shairn. Camlak needed to know what had happened to the people. He could not turn his back on the leadership which he had fought so hard to win. He had to know what happened on the road to Lehr, and he had to know by seeing. There was no other way.

From the vantage on top of the skull-gate he could see as far as the canal ridge out toward Walgo but only as far as the hilltops in the southwest. The forested slopes cut off his view of Dossal Bog. The Ahrima and the rogue Truemen were well out of sight by now.

As he went through the skull-gate and turned toward Lehr he reflected that Stalhelm had stood a long time in the farthest reaches of Shairn. By the tally of the gate the people had done well. But he knew that the dead get no credit in the tally of survival, and the contribution of the knitted skulls to the future of the Children of the Voice was purely negative. It was a symbol, not a magical guarantee. Yami's head-taking ways had not, in the end, preserved Stalhelm forever, even if Yami had not lived to see its fall. Yami, as a good leader, had even known precisely when to die. If anyone remembered Stalhelm at all, they would remember Yami, and the brief hour in which Camlak had reigned would be forgotten as the blackest time in the town's history. So much for three times lucky.

Camlak left his home for the first and last time, and went into the Underworld.

3

The history of the Overworld began, according to the Euchronian Movement, at the close of the second dark age (which they also called the age of psychosis). Naturally enough, there was no one to disagree with them. In point of fact, however, an unbiased observer—Sisyr, perhaps—might have traced the Overworld *mentality* much further back than that. At least a thousand years, and probably two. A devout Euchronian might shrug his shoulders, and point out that an odd millennium or two was little enough compared with the eleven thousand years of the Euchronian Plan (let alone the half a million years the Euchronians were prepared to spend if that were necessary), but a historian would have recognized the flaw in such a comparison of duration. The velocity of history is not uniform. "Progress" (a mythical concept dating back to prehistoric time) is not constant.

However, it was certainly during the second dark age that the Movement was formed and the Plan was born. According to Euchronia, the Movement and the Plan saved the world. No one would disagree with that, either. By Euchronian standards, Euchronia had saved the world. It had discarded the old world and built a new one, on a platform which was mounted over every convenient acre of the old world's land surface.

In the beginning, the Plan had been ludicrous. The Euchronians had accepted that in those days (they denied it now), but they had pointed out with some justice that if ludicrous ambitions were all that were left, they were the only recourse of hope.

Work on the Plan had been underway for several centuries when Sisyr's starship arrived in the solar system. The Euchronians never actually found out *why* Sisyr came to Earth, although they did discover that his arrival at precisely the time when they needed him most was purely fortuitous. Whatever the reason, Sisyr was ready and willing to set it aside in order to provide Euchronia with the technical expertise and the scientific knowledge which they lacked. The margin between failure and success was undoubtedly filled by Sisyr. Without his intervention time would most definitely have run out for the dying Earth. As it was, the assistance of the alien and his home world, though slow to be provided (starships took centuries to cross the interstellar gulf between the two worlds) turned the tide.

Euchronia was suitably grateful to Sisyr, but it also found it very convenient to forget him. The Movement had its pride, and it needed the credit more than he did. Sisyr went into quiet retirement somewhere on Earth, atop one of the mountains which projected its peak into the Overworld. He asked nothing other than a home and a quiet life. The Euchronians presumed that he would die one day and could then be obliterated entirely from the history of the Earth. They were wrong. While thousands of years rolled by, Sisyr showed not the slightest sign of dying. Earthly memories, however, were short, and Sisyr's active contribution to the Plan ended long before the platform was complete and the world rebuilt upon it. The only real reminder of his existence was the fact that two or three times a century a starship would land, but the aliens were discreet, and they bothered no one except Sisyr.

The platform was completed in six thousand years. The world in which the Euchronians were destined to live was finally pronounced complete after eleven thousand. The cities were finished, the cybernet which would provide the needs of the community was complete—a gargantuan mechanical beast for the humans to parasitize. The Euchronian Millennium was declared and the people settled down to enjoy it.

They did not know how. They only knew why.

Hundreds of generations of Euchronians had spent their entire lives laboring toward an end they knew they would never see. Billions of lives had been given up absolutely to the ideal of the Plan. For eleven thousand years, the purpose of life in Euchronia had been labor, unselfish and unrewarded: the infinitely protracted process of giving birth to a new existence. And when the birth was achieved . . .

The purpose of life was lost.

The Planners had anticipated this. They knew that there would have to be a period of adjustment, and they knew that period would be measured in centuries rather than in years. The Utopian potential of Euchronia's Millennium would have to be carefully developed and brought to flower. It would take time and effort. The Planners, with the supreme optimism which had guided their forebears out of a ruined Earth and toward a promised land, led them to believe that it could and would be done. It had to be done—to justify the Plan. But when the Millennium came, they only knew what and why. They did not know how. This time, they could only rely on their own resources. They could not ask Sisyr for help.

The people of Euchronia's Millennium were living in a functionally designed Utopia, but they had problems. They were not Utopians. They were, in a sense, a society of misfits. Empirically maladjusted. The builders of a new world are *ipso facto* ill fitted to live in it. The mother cannot be expected to live the life of the child. Mothers who try destroy their children.

Among the methods adopted by the Planners to facilitate the Plan was the i-minus effect—the chemical control of dreams. I-minus was calculated to exorcize instincts, so that social conditioning—functional social conditioning— might be made one hundred percent effective. It worked. It continued to work after the Millennium, but no one could tell whether the fact that it worked was useful or not. No one could judge the situation well enough to decide whether the effect ought to be continued or not, or even how such a decision might be made. This exemplifies the confusion of the citizens of the Millennium. They were as helpless as newborn children. An infant society. Ignorant, yet not knowing of their ignorance; blind to the contexts of their existence, yet not knowing of their blindness.

The society of Euchronia's Millennium was vulnerable. Its vulnerability was exposed by Carl Magner, who rediscovered the Underworld in his nightmares. (How? There was no way of knowing.) Perhaps the rediscovery of the ruined Earth was the last thing the Euchronians needed. Perhaps, on the other hand, the rediscovery of the Hell which the Plan had left behind was the only way in which the people could come to terms with the Heaven it had built.

Perhaps it would help them to rediscover themselves.

4

Rafael Heres had to make a statement to the Euchronian Council. The pressure on him had grown, and he knew that the current of opinion which was flowing through the Council was set against him. But it had been so before, and he had survived. Usually he stirred up big enough waves to make countercurrents of his own to drown out the others. He had faith in himself now. He knew that the only significant opposition to him, in the past and the present, was Rypeck. He had always controlled Rypeck, and he was sure that he could hold him now.

He opened his address by telling them that Carl Magner was dead. Some of them already knew, but to most it came as something of a shock. That a man should die was not uncommon, but that a man like Magner should die by assassination beside a public road was a strange and upsetting thing. That fact alone stilled the currents of hostility. It changed the game completely. Almost, if such a thing was conceivable in this day and age, it made it look as if the Magner affair might not be a game at all. (But even in games, pieces lose their lives.)

Heres talked about Magner, who had somehow become so important that the Hegemon of the Euchronian Movement could deliver an obituary for him. Heres talked calmly about Magner's background, and the tone of his voice not only expressed his own sympathy but went out into the multilink to grab sympathy from the listeners. He gave little attention to the tragedies which had marred Magner's life, but simply by numbering them he made certain that everyone appreciated what a hard time the man had had.

A less subtle man might have used the statement to build

a case against Magner—to turn his public image into the effigy of a madman, preparatory to burying his memories and his ideas forever. But that was what many of them expected. That was what most of them already believed. Heres knew, as any leader knows, that it is dangerous to confirm what people already know. A leader should always be ahead, moving amid the ideas that people have not yet discovered. Magner's death had changed the game, and Heres wanted to be the one to work out the new rules.

It took Heres a little over an hour to make a martyr out of Magner. Instead of claiming that Magner's experiences had made him mad, the Hegemon suggested that the pain and the anguish had lent Magner a keener insight into life than was possessed by the majority of the carefully cushioned citizens of Euchronia's Millennium. He said, in fact, that Magner had become a visionary—a man who saw beyond the present and the legacies of the past to the realms of possibility and the legacies which ought to be put in hand for the future.

"Before he was killed," said Rafael Heres, "Carl Magner stood at the focus of a controversy which grew around him like a storm. Some of you may have seen the discussion which took place between Magner, Clea Aron and Yvon Emerich on the holographic network last night. The arguments there made only a beginning in searching out the implications of Magner's theories, but they will have served to familiarize many of you with the fundamentals of the problem.

"Carl Magner accused Euchronian society of a crime of omission in that the Movement has, at least since the Millennium, ignored and forgotten the world which still exists beneath us—the surface of the Earth from which our ancestors came. Magner wanted to remind us that the old world, from whose ashes the new one arose, was never totally consumed. He claimed that there are still men in the Underworld, living in the darkness because our world enjoys the sunlight that once was theirs. We know that the sunlight used to be ours too, and some of you would argue that we have merely preserved it while the men on the ground willfully forsook it. That may be, but as Carl Magner has tried to remind us, that was thousands of years ago. The men who live in the Underworld now are not responsible for the decisions of their forefathers.

"I do not think that there can be any possible question

about the actions of the Planners in the remote past. No one was denied the chance to make himself part of the Plan, from the moment that the Movement was founded to the moment when the last section of the platform cut off the last rays of sunlight from the last few acres of the derelict surface of the old world. No decision which we make today or in the future will reflect on the choices made in the past by the men of the past. But the situation today is different. Different circumstances call for new decisions—we cannot simply keep echoing the old ones. The Planners of the Euchronian Movement set out to build a world for *us*— their ultimate descendants. They did what they set out to do. We inherited that world, we have it now, and there can be no limit to our gratitude toward those who made it for us. We value this world very highly—it is our life and we guard it as we do our lives. We will continue to do so. We will continue to value and protect our own existence and the manner of that existence.

"Carl Magner asked us to open the doors of our world to the people of the Underworld. This we cannot do. To open our world is to threaten it. But this does not mean that Carl Magner's accusations were untrue.

"We *have* forgotten the Underworld. The people who live in the Underworld today, if people there are, are *not* the people who refused to join the Plan, who made a free choice and chose to live their lives as they would.

"We remember the men who stayed on the ground rather than work for a new world as cowards and traitors, and perhaps we have reason for this. But we must not judge too harshly. It was their right to choose, and it remained their right throughout the centuries when the two worlds were co-existent. How many of us are the descendants of late recruits, who joined the Movement a hundred, or a thousand years after the Plan was first put into operation? We do not know. It makes no difference. It does not matter whether our ancestors in the age of psychosis were committed Euchronians, or the grandfathers of converts. Why should it? How can it?

"I believe that Carl Magner was right to remind us of the world we left behind. I believe he was right to ask us whether there are men on the ground today, and if so, whether we owe them something because we have taken away their sunlight. The Marriage of Heaven and Hell which he suggested is not the right answer, but the question which Magner asked remains the right question.

"The Euchronian ideal—the ideal which built the new world, and which gave us everything that we are and everything that we have—is the principle of working together for the benefit of others. The Planners worked for their children, many generations hence, but how many Planners died childless? How many of the men who worked for our world have no descendants living here? Again, we do not know. Again, what does it matter? For those men, the ideal remained. They still gave their lives to the Plan, if not for their own children, then for the children of their neighbors, and the children of men who lived and worked on the other side of the world.

"The Euchronian Plan was declared complete two centuries ago. We live now in what we are pleased to call the Euchronian Millennium, the world which is our heritage. But can we really call ourselves Euchronians? We work, we live useful lives. But the people *for* whom we work, and to whom we offer our resources, are ourselves. If we are Euchronians, then perhaps we should look beyond ourselves. Perhaps we should look beyond our children and our children's children, whose future, we hope, is secure because of the efforts of the Planners. Perhaps we should remember the Underworld, and ask ourselves whether we might devote something of our effort and endeavor toward doing what even the Planners themselves could not do and did not try. Perhaps, now that we have our world secure in the sky, we should begin to make another new world—another good and safe world, where men can live secure and free lives—out of the surface which languishes beneath our feet.

"We cannot bring the people of the Underworld into our world. But we can help them to rebuild theirs. We can offer them knowledge and supply them with tools and power. We can give them everything that they need to set in motion their own Euchronian Plan, and we can help them to make it successful. We can give them everything . . . except the sunlight, the Face of Heaven which Carl Magner wanted to give them. But we can supply light instead of sunlight. We can help them to find a different face for *their* Heaven. We owe them that. We must owe them that, at least.

"Members of the Council, I propose that we give our attention, from this moment on, to the making of the *new* Euchronian Plan."

5

Heres believed that he had saved the world. Two worlds, in fact. That was—had to be—the perfect solution. The ideal game is the one which everybody wins. Heres, it will be remembered, was a brilliant Hoh player. The idea of a *second* Plan, to accomplish what even the initial Planners had assumed to be beyond their talents, was, in Heres' eyes, *the* masterstroke.

Eleven thousand years of history demanded of the people of Euchronia a commitment—a commitment that was clear, altruistic, and ambitious. The declaration of the Millennium had left not only the Movement but the entire civilization stranded on a spiritual desert island. The age of psychosis could never return, and the i-minus effect seemed to assure social adjustment, and therefore social sanity, but Euchronian culture was nevertheless dangerously full of danger signals. Rypeck had read those signals, and Rypeck had been on the borders of fear and anxiety for years. Heres had read the signals, too, but Heres had a cool head. Heres had faith. And he had found the answer—the political and intellectual *coup de grâce*. Barring all accidents, not only was his political future as Hegemon secured, but also the future of the Movement and the human race.

Barring all accidents.

What accidents? For one thing, of course, he had jumped the gun. There was, as yet, no report from Harkanter and his party regarding conditions in the Underworld. Politically, the right moment had come before he had all the facts at his command, and thus there was a risk—of some kind. But Heres knew what Rypeck had found out about the Underworld—that it lived, that it was lighted, and that the Overworld was geared to resist the invasion of its lifeforms. He also knew what Abram Ravelvent had discovered—that materials were constantly exported from the world above to the world below—materials like steel implements and books, which spoke conclusively of human life and some degree of human culture. Heres knew little enough about the Underworld, but it was enough to be *sure*. It mattered little how severe the conditions in the Underworld might be, or how savage the people. The *magnitude* of the task was, thanks to the Planners' precedent, quite irrelevant. Heres was quite confident that any accidents of circumstance could be overcome. He still had faith in himself. Rather more than that, in fact—he had ultimate faith in the essential nature of things, in the fact that the situation (*all* situations) not only provided an answer by which everybody could win, but were so structured as to *demand* such an answer. This faith did not arise from the fact that he was a devoted Hoh player—the reverse was actually the case. That was the way Heres conceived of the universe working. It was his understanding of existence. Hoh was only a model—a simulation—of reality.

Heres also knew that he had sidestepped the thorny questions which the Magner affair had initially asked. Those questions, framed by Enzo Ulicon, had seriously disturbed Rypeck (who was, of course, ripe for disturbance). In Heres' scheme, there were no answers to those questions. Instead, Heres was prepared to hope that he had rendered the questions irrelevant and immaterial.

Magner had had bad dreams. Terrible dreams. That meant that either the i-minus effect was *not* effective, in his case, or there was another input into his dreams—presumably telepathic. Ulicon had held the latter alternative to be the more likely. Heres had said nothing, but he had always preferred the former. He had already known—as everyone with eyes to see must have known—that the i-minus effect was not operating as per prescription in the Millennial society. No one knew how, or why, it was going wrong, but it was. Heres was inclined to attribute the deficit not to the i-minus agent but to the social psychology of the people. I-minus favored social adaptation, the establishment of social values as absolutes. If i-minus was failing, then it was for lack of social values rather than lack of adaptive capacity, so Heres thought. Given a plan—an ideal, a great social goal—then i-minus would work again. So Heres believed. He had seen Magner as the tip of an iceberg rather than a unique case of something new.

Heres was prepared to assume that the second Euchronian Plan would solve everything. His understanding of reality encouraged him to make this assumption. He was aware, however, that it remained an assumption. He was not blind to the possibility that some unforeseen, incalculable factor might yet be thrown into the equation. He was mentally ready for such a thing to happen.

It did.

6

Jervis Burstone, whose amusement in life was to play God rather than to play Hoh, was in the Underworld, waiting. Usually, Ermold was at the rendezvous before him, unable to control his eagerness to get hold of the gifts which Burstone brought and dispensed so magnificently. (They were not quite gifts, but neither Ermold nor Burstone knew why the pretense of trading was maintained. They both believed that what Burstone took in return for his goods was worthless.)

Burstone sighed. He knew that Ermold was not going to come. Late meant never, in the Underworld. It was a world which did not offer second chances to its people.

Ermold had been a good contact. He had been the nastiest, most vile of all the men that Burstone had had to deal with, and by virtue of that fact he had looked to have a good many years in him. But time seemed to move so quickly here. A man might pass from maturity to senility in a matter of weeks. The people of the Underworld seemed to live their lives inside a span of time which Burstone hardly noticed in passing. Burstone could remember the contact before Ermold as if it were yesterday. And the one before that. He would remember Ermold with crystal clarity when three more contacts had all fulfilled their purpose and rotted into the stinking, polluted dust from which they came. That was the way of things.

Burstone waited, unwillingly, glancing at his wristwatch every few moments, giving Ermold the time that was his due, but begrudging the filthy savage every second of it. Burstone did not like the stillness and the alienness and—more than anything—the cold, steady perpetual starlight. He sweated, and knew that he was slowly absorbing the stink and the foul taint of the Underworld. Once back on top he would have to slink home like a rat in the shadows, to bathe for an hour and plaster himself with the medicines which would save his skin from rotting away, and save his body from the vile diseases he inhaled with every breath. If only he could wear a mask—a proper mask rather than a wad of cotton wool and a piece of perforated plastic. But he had been warned against masks.

He was afraid, as well.

But the thrill of fear, and the rather less conscious thrill of pollution were almost life's blood to him. He needed them. They gave something to him which he could not hope to find in any other way. The tainting of his body and the washing clean, the scouring of his body with the hormonal cocktail that was fear—these meant something to him. They were real to him in a way that the diversions of the Over-world were not. The ritual descent into Hell, followed by the ascent into Heaven—this was the purpose of life. It was the focal point of his existence. It was the reason that he was *needed* by the worlds. It was his duty, his honor, and his . . . joy?

Burstone was a completely sane man. His dreams never troubled him.

While he waited, he drifted on an ocean of feeling. An emotional castaway.

The creatures of the underworld would not come close. The smell of him, in their senses, was just as alien to them as theirs was to him. His sharp, chemical cleanliness was an affront to them. No predator would dare to come close, and the small creatures engaged in the business of survival detoured in order to pass him by. He saw the great ghost moths fluttering between the squabs some yards away, and heard their high-pitched screaming at the very limits of his audible range, but there was not enough light for him to see anything else. He was virtually blind down here. He had a horror of darkness, too. On this, too, his soul fed.

When the time was up, he simply picked up the suitcase and began the walk back to the cage with which he could hoist himself back to the platform. He walked with an easy, measured stride, unhurried. It took courage—genuine, completely pure courage. It took strength of mind and of character. He never looked around. The thought of finding a new point of entry, of setting up a new contact, and the inevitable risks that would be involved in so doing, did not disturb him. He accepted that part of his role.

Up on top, clean and healthy, he would still feel good, even though he had not fulfilled his mission on this occasion. He would feel the satisfaction of knowing that his part was played.

He was only an ordinary man.

7

The Hell beneath Euchronia's Millennium had not been cut from the cloth of existence in a single piece, or in a single moment. It grew as a patchwork, very slowly. The several evolutions which took place beneath the slowly expanding sections of the Overworld platform had every chance to discover new ways of coping with the conditions of life. The adaptation of surface life to Tartarean circumstances took place according to several different patterns. Each pattern was a collaboration between chance and choice. When the platform was complete and the Underworld was sealed— several thousand years after the process was begun—the patterns came together, and a new collaboration begun. (Collaboration in the Underworld did not take the same form as collaboration among the Euchronians. It took more familiar forms, like war—the war of nature: natural selection.)

There was no section of the Underworld under which the ecosystem of the old world failed to adapt to new circumstances. The adaptation was costly—the mortality of species was over ninety percent, and the mortality of individuals within species that survived was often on the same sort of scale. Some surviving species, on the other hand, proliferated vastly and enjoyed altogether unprecedented success. All the surviving species were unstable, and remained so. By the time of the Euchronian Millennium, some kind of stability was just beginning to assert itself within many communities of organisms, but on the previous evolutionary scale several eons of progress toward balance had been lost. Curiously, almost half the loss had taken place *before* the Plan got under way.

Homo sapiens was the species which adapted most easily to the new regime, and by his active interference he encouraged and assisted many other species to do likewise. (He also discouraged and prevented one or two, but his positive success was much greater than the negative corollary.) The Euchronians had very unkind things to say about the men who stayed on the ground, but it was not the fact that they resented the work and the dedication involved in commitment that made most of them do so. In point of fact, the weak and the degenerate almost invariably joined the Euchronians, fearing the darkness and the wild world more than they hated the work and the regimentation. The Euchronians at least provided food and shelter for their people. On the surface, there were no guarantees. The people who stayed on the ground at the end—who actually went into the Underworld rather than join the Plan (as distinct from those who simply retreated from the encroaching platform) —did so because they preferred their own idea of freedom to that of the Euchronians. They wanted freedom *from* the Plan, and they were prepared to accept Hell instead of the promise of Heaven for their children's children, in defense of that idea of freedom.

There was, of course, a great deal of fighting between the Euchronians and the men on the ground while the platform was growing. The supplies which kept the Plan going came from the ground—from the land of the men who could still make the land provide. In return, that land was eaten up as was the derelict land. When the landowners would not supply the Euchronians, the Euchronians took what they needed. When they cooperated, the only gratitude they received was the offer to join the Plan when their land, in its turn, came to be covered over. The Euchronians won every fight. They had the numbers and they had the organization. There was no way the men on the ground could defend their world. They had to take one of the new environments which was offered to them—the proto-Heaven or the neo-Hell. From the Euchronian point of view, that was no choice at all. Not everyone saw it the Euchronian way.

Hell was not kind to the men who chose it. The old world had been past redemption in terms of the human civilization which had grown up in it. From the point of view of society in the second dark age the world was ended, doom had come. But a derelict world is not a dead world. Life continues, somehow. Always. The old order was finished, and chaos was come, but life went on. Even the imprisonment of the old world—its condemnation to perpetual darkness—

could not make life extinct within it. The old species had to die by the thousand, and those which survived did so at tremendous cost, but the cost of evolution in terms of necessary death is always less than the cost of not evolving. The genetic heritage of the survivor species was ruthlessly stripped and rebuilt, with selection operating at very high levels and evolution being forced at a tremendous rate, but they could take it. Just. Adapt, or perish, was the only law. It applied to *Homo sapiens* no less than to all the other species. The cost of human survival was a complete genetic overhaul of the species. The men who went to Hell wanted freedom. Freedom from Euchronia they won, but freedom from evolution they could not have.

Evolution in the Underworld was necessarily rapid. A characteristic tachytelic pattern developed: divergent evolution of forms, rapid speciation, a high rate of extinction and specific genesis. An evolutionary explosion. It had happened before, on the Earth before man, but the evolutionary change of gear which took place when the Underworld came into existence saw the greatest-ever increase in the rate of evolution—the biggest explosion of them all. It echoed through the ages which followed, and would echo for many more. The impact was only just *beginning* to die when the Euchronians, in the Heaven which they had built up above, completed their Plan.

Man—omnivorous, intelligent, at the very highest level of the biotic hierarchy—changed least of all the species in the Underworld. Even man became not one species, but several.

The greatest evolutionary boost was evident in the semi-sentient species which had cohabited with man in the concrete jungles of the age of psychosis. They had the capacity to adapt *if* they could make the leap to full sentience and change their physical form in order to cope with a complete reorientation of their survival strategies. Some of them made that leap. Some became extinct because their gene pools drained dry in the attempt.

At the lowest strata there was complete reorganization. Millions of years of plant evolution went to waste, and progress began again with the lowest forms—the algae and the fungi. The stratum of the primary consumers in the animal kingdom was likewise completely refurbished, but here there were already patterns of life and forms of being which were useful. The crabs of Tartarus were not the crabs of prehistoric ages, nor the moths, nor the cockroaches, nor even the multitudinous worms, but the names did as well for the new versions. There are only so many ways to design an animal, and most of the models had been ready in the prehistoric world.

The microbiotica, of course, were reorganized on the same scale as the plants and lower animals, but from the macrobiotic point of view the revision was quite invisible. There are even fewer ways to design a bacterium or a protozoan than there are to design an animal. Form and function survived despite the fact that genetic complements had to be given a complete overhaul. The bacteria had the least difficulty adapting. Bacteria always exist in extreme circumstances.

From the microbiotic point of view, the division of the world into Heaven and Hell was virtually immaterial. A trivial incident on the path of existence. As if an immortal were stung by a bee . . .

8

Camlak did not hurry along the road to Lehr. He walked steadily, at a pace which he could sustain for many miles. He was forced to import a rather mechanical quality into both his thoughts and his actions. It was necessary to the situation. He already knew, in his heart, what he was going to see when he finally looked out over Dossal Bog, but he advanced toward that moment nevertheless. He would have to meet it.

Once he was past the hill called Stiver he left the road proper, and bore slightly southwest, taking higher ground so that he could command a good view of what was ahead of him. He did not climb to the ridges but merely moved as a hunter might, close to the road but not too close, stalking its length, tracking its curves. The stars were less dense in the roof of the world over these dried-up, coarse lands, and the light they shed was not bright, but Camlak had good eyes, and there was light enough for him to see what he needed to see.

And eventually, his assumed mechanism brought him to the climactic vision. From the slopes of the hill called Solum he could see the road as it straightened out to cross Dossal Bog. He could almost see the shadowed walls of Lehr itself in the furthest distance—or he thought he could. Perhaps it was just a suggestion of shadows—an imaginary goal to draw travelers on ever faster, until they dropped from weariness with the vision no nearer.

The women fleeing from Shairn had gone a good way down the road. They were nearly a mile away from where he stood.

The Ahrima had come down on their backs. The bundles they had carried were scattered in a ragged line for a quarter mile behind the place where they had been caught. The crowd had scattered both ways into the bog. Only a handful had died on the road. Camlak knew that the women and the children would have run into a radioactive waste, into a living fire, rather than stand and wait for the Ahrima. And the marauders would have followed them to cut them down. And come back again to join the horde.

Camlak wished the bog was one vast quicksand, to have sucked the Ahrima down after their prey. But it was not. It was only a bog. The corpses were sprawled across the dark tussocks, half-swallowed by the mud, floating on the pools of stagnant water. The Ahrima had caught their prey, had enjoyed their massacre, and had gone on. Perhaps two or three Ahriman warriors had been trapped in the bog, or knifed by the women, but only two or three. No more. How many of the Children of the Voice had escaped? How many infants had found a hiding place? More than two or three, no doubt. Twelve. Or twenty. But how many of those would survive, in the long run? The same two or three. Maybe none. Wherever they went—forward, or back, or just on the road, there would be enemies enough for all of them.

Camlak could read the whole story written in the dim scene which extended before his eyes, illumined by starlight. It was no more and no less than he had expected. He had not expected the men of Lehr to come out and try to cover the retreat. But he had had to go on to the end of the story in any case.

As he stared out from his vantage, he felt very little emotion inside himself. He did not curse, and he certainly did not cry. He merely looked, and let the looking soak into his being. He let the sight imprint itself on his memory, becoming a part of him. That was enough. There was no need for fury or mourning. The time for those was past, left behind in Stalhelm, even before the battle and the burning.

He would follow Nita, now. And when he found her . . .

He knew no more. The alternatives which he would find then would have to be discovered. They were not ready in his mind. No such alternatives had ever been shown to him, except in his dreams. In his dreams, they were phantoms. He did not know what it took to clothe such phantoms with reality. He would live, but he did not know how, or why. Those answers were lost, lying amid the dead like the trampled, shattered bundles the women had carried out of Stalhelm in the vain attempt to wrap up their lives and steal them away from the Ahrima.

He could see the Ahrima. He could see their fires, at least. Whether the fires were at the walls of Lehr, or still some miles away, he could not tell. Perhaps it was Lehr, or the fields of Lehr, that was burning. The light was red and blurred, a smudge in the pit of darkness which closed off the world at the limits of his visual range.

He could imagine the Ahrima as shadows within the ruddy glow, shadow-monsters with their heads encapsulated by grotesquely huge horned masks. Men taking the form of beasts, accepting the role of the beasts, prideful of their bestiality. Black shadows in the light, clothed in smoke. The masks would shine, in the flamelight. The eyes would sparkle through the eyeholes.

The Truemen, thought Camlak, would have it that the Children of the Voice are animals. They claim that we pretend to manhood, that our selves are false. But the Truemen are masked now, their eyes glittering like the eyes of the Ahrima, fugitive within the masks, hiding from the fire and the blood. A worthless attempt to save their worthless lives. Who are the fake people?

Inside himself, Camlak asked the question of his Gray Soul. He did not expect an answer.

As he turned away, content not to know the fate of Lehr and, ultimately, of Shairn—at least for the time being—he sensed a movement on the slope above him. Someone was stalking him as he had stalked the road. They had not been behind him long, but they were there now.

Ahrima!

He carried a bow and a long knife—he had left behind the axes and the Ahriman swords, which were too big for him. He put the bow across his back and drew the knife. He moved toward the sound, extending the blade before him. A shape rose from the barbweed, coming out from the hiding of a shallow recess. Empty hands spread wide.

"No," said the shadow. "Friend, not enemy."

Camlak did not need the sight and the sound to know. The way the shape had risen had testified to its crookedness. It was Chemec, the warrior with the bent leg. Of all the warriors, Chemec had lived. Chemec and Camlak. Why?

Chemec knew. Chemec knew his bent leg, and knew that it had taught him all he needed to know about the art of survival. He had had to learn new ways to run, new ways to fight. It had to be Chemec that lived. No one else, save by luck.

Camlak sheathed his knife.

"It would be you," he said. "It had to be." There was naked bitterness in his voice.

"And you?" Chemec retaliated. "I could say the same. We are both alive instead of dead."

It was true enough. Chemec flinched as he spoke, ready to run if Camlak remembered any one of a dozen times that Chemec had cast doubts on his manhood. Chemec had been a warrior when Camlak was yet a child. But Camlak did not remember now, and he did not react to Chemec's words. It was all over.

After a brief silence, when Camlak would not look at Chemec, and Chemec would not look at Camlak, the crippled warrior asked: "What now?"

It was a plea for guidance—a warrior asking the decision of the Old Man, whose function was to decide. Chemec had been a warrior while Camlak was a child, but Camlak had killed the harrowhound and played the Sun in the communion of souls. Even so, Camlak was faintly surprised. He could not help but feel that perhaps Chemec was mocking him.

"Stalhelm is dead," said Camlak. "Do what you like. Anything."

Chemec shook his head. "I'll come with you," he said.

"No," said Camlak.

Chemec did not understand. This would not have been Yami's way. Yami would have welcomed him. It would have been Yami and Chemec, together.

"We might go east," said Chemec. "The Ahrima will turn south."

"North," said Camlak.

"We go north?" Chemec deliberately misunderstood.

"The Ahrima," said Camlak. "They will go north, into the heartland, to rip the bowels out of Shairn."

"We go north," suggested Chemec. "To fight."

"No," said Camlak again. "You go."

Chemec was silent.

"It's dead," said Camlak. "It's finished. Stalhelm is over. A memory, nothing more."

Chemec still said nothing. He could not accept it. It was beyond him. He was getting old.

Camlak looked at the man with the twisted leg, and remembered that this had been his enemy. This man might even hate him, and hate him still. But he was ruled by the way, by the rule of the ritual.

"I don't want you," he said.

Chemec waited. He could do nothing but wait.

When Camlak turned away, Chemec followed him. When Camlak half-turned, Chemec dropped back, but still followed.

Camlak went north, but not to the heartland—not to fight. The heartland was well to the west of north, bordered by the vast Swithering Waste. It was into the Waste that Camlak went, heading for the great metal wall.

Chemec followed, with infinite patience.

9

As Burstone turned to lock the door behind him they slipped out of the shadows, and when he turned, they were there, blocking his way and pushing close to back him up against the wall. The alley was quite dark—it existed only to hide away the door from which Burstone had come. For a moment, he thought that they might be technics, on legitimate business, wanting to go down to the distribution units and wondering what he was doing there. But that was a hopeless wish. They had been waiting. For him. They knew who he was and where he had been.

He didn't know whether he ought to be scared or not. No one had ever interfered before. He *was* scared.

One of them took the key from his hand. Gently. Then he put it back into the lock, and turned it. The door eased open when it was pushed. The dim light of the machine room filtered out, throwing vague shadows across the faces of the two men.

Burstone overcame his momentary paralysis.

"Do you want something?" he asked.

"The suitcase," said the man who held the key. He was a tall man, but that was all Burstone could be sure of. The glimmer of light wasn't enough to let him see any facial details. It was much darker here than in the Underworld. The *real* stars were so faint.

He could hear the keys being clicked back and forth in the tall man's hand.

"We just want to talk," said the other man. Burstone became conscious that he was being held by the arm. He wrenched slightly, and felt himself released. But they still stood in his way, pinning him in the corner of the blind corridor. The door oozed shut, and the darkness became total save for the pale silver sheen of the sky, high above.

"Who are you?" he asked.

"Suppose we were the police?" countered the tall man.

"Suppose you were?" said Burstone.

"That's right," said the other man. "You don't have anything to fear from the police. Nothing to hide. You're doing nothing illegal. Any man in the world is perfectly entitled to take cases full of . . . whatever . . . into the Underworld. The police wouldn't be interested. Surprised, but not interested. So who would? Who'd be insterested, Jervis? You tell us that."

The calmly threatening tone somehow eased Burstone's mind. This wasn't right. Of course it wasn't right. They had no right. They had nothing against him. He wasn't doing anything wrong. The way the man spoke restored Burstone's confidence in himself. The surprise was fading. The situation was becoming known, and therefore controllable.

"What do you want?" he asked, in a cool tone which said clearly that they weren't going to get it.

"You've been followed before," said the tall man quietly.

Burstone said nothing.

"We know about that," said the other. "He didn't come back, did he?"

"Suppose," the tall man said again, "we were the police."

"I didn't do a thing," said Burstone, once more on the defensive, once more crawling back into a shell of fear. "Nothing."

"He *didn't* come back."

"No," said Burstone.

"What did you do?" demanded the tall man.

"Nothing," repeated Burstone.

"Suppose we knew what happened to him," said the other. "We know his name. Joth Magner. Did you know who it was? You must have, of course. You could hardly miss him, could you?"

"I never heard of him," said Burstone.

"You heard of him."

Burstone pushed himself out of the corner. One man—the tall one—stepped back, to remain in front of him, barring his way. The other slipped in behind him. Burstone liked the new arrangement even less than the old. He had the ridiculous idea that at any moment the man behind might crouch, so that the tall one could push him back, make him fall over, like a small boy.

"What are you trying to say?" asked Burstone.

"Briefly," said the man behind him, speaking close to his ear, "and without all the veiled threats, that Joth Magner followed you through that door a while ago, and he didn't come back. We want to talk to you. Because we know about Joth Magner and the police don't, we think you want to talk to us. All right?"

"I didn't kill him," said Burstone.

"What's in the case?" asked the tall man, ignoring the protest. "And why?"

Burstone considered the situation. He hadn't killed Joth Magner. Not quite. But he had wound up the cage, knowing that someone had gone down, and that the someone would inevitably be trapped. He knew what the Underworld was like. He knew what would happen to him if *he* came back one day to find that the cage had gone, and that there was no way home. He knew.

The worst thing was, he hadn't an answer to his own question. He didn't know why he'd done it. He'd been scared. He knew he'd been followed and he knew he was being watched. He could have just gone away and left it, but he was too frightened even to do that. He'd wound up the cage and solved the problem by elimination. He hadn't known it was Joth Magner. He'd never seen the man who followed him. He hadn't known. It was a momentary decision—almost a crazy decision. He regretted it now as he'd regretted it for a long time. He'd almost been expecting it to catch up with him. He knew that he was responsible for Joth Magner's death. He felt it. He only wished that feeling it would tell him *why*.

"Who are you?" whispered Burstone.

"Does it matter?" asked the tall man.

"Does it have to be here?"

"No. You want to go home?"

"Yes."

"Okay," said the other man, still behind him, still mouthing into his ear. "Let's go."

Burstone moved forward. The tall man stopped him by jabbing a key gently into his chest. "I'll take the case," he said.

Burstone surrendered the case. Then they went back to the cars, and he led the way home.

10

"Can we forget about the game, now?" asked Burstone.

"I don't know," said the tall man. "I'm not sure that it's over."

Burstone felt better in the light. Now he could see the two men they did not seem so fearful. His feeling of guilt had faded, to some extent. At the back of his mind, behind even the guilt, was the conviction that whatever happened, it was all all right.

"It's only just beginning," commented the other man. He was the younger of the two, slighter in build and sharper in the features. The older, bulkier man had a sallow complexion and gray eyes, which made him look somehow faded. Maybe careworn.

As Burstone studied them, so they studied Burstone. He was small, very dark and apparently strong. Hard and compact. He also stank, but that didn't surprise them. They knew where he'd been.

"Who are you?" the tall man asked him.

"You know who I am," said Burstone, faintly surprised. "Who are *you?*"

"We know your name," said the man with the gray eyes, "but we don't know *you.* We don't understand you. We can't figure you. You work in secret, in back alleys and dingy passageways. You fetch and you carry back and forth from the sewers. You work hard at it, like a little brown ant. And for what? We can't even guess. Why are you invisible, Burstone? What makes you work so hard behind the scenes, carrying out your little jobs in utter silence, while the rest of us don't know what, or how, or why? That's the *you* we want to know. Not your name."

Burstone looked up at him. "I'll settle for the names," he said. "For now."

The younger man laughed briefly.

"I'm Joel Dayling," said the tall man. "This is Thorold Warnet."

Burstone knew that he knew at least one of the names, and he groped for the memory. He found nothing specific, but he discovered an association of ideas—a label.

"Eupsychians," he said. "What's it got to do with you?"

"That," said Dayling, "is what we want to find out."

"This has gone on long enough," said Warnet. "All right. You know who we are. You know what kind of a lever we hold. You can deduce why we want to know. The Underworld is suddenly a matter for concern. We need to know about it. You can tell us. We want to know what you know, and we want to know who else knows it. That's all. We just want the truth, for once."

Now that Burstone knew who he was dealing with, he quickly recovered the last vestiges of his composure. He no longer feared exposure—not by the Eupsychians. He would be protected against the likes of them. His work was important—theirs was subversive.

"I can't tell you," said Burstone.

"Why not?" demanded Dayling.

Burstone looked blank. It was a question he had not expected.

"It's nothing illegal," explained the tall man. "We accept that. If you like, we'll take your word that you had nothing to do with Joth Magner's disappearance. If you like, and provided that we have something else to occupy our minds. We accept that everything that you do is perfectly in order. You could do it in the broadest daylight on a holovision spectacular, and we wouldn't care. But you don't. You do it in secret. Why?"

"It's better that way," said Burstone.

His tone was flat, and it was obvious that he was repeating something he had been told—something that he accepted without question.

"Open the case," said Warnet. Burstone reached out for it reflexively, as if to stop them, but Dayling had it safe. The tall man fished out the keys which he had confiscated from Burstone, and began to compare each one with the lock on the case.

"*Somebody* knows why all this is happening," said Dayling reflectively, while he sorted through the leaves of metal. "It just isn't us. Maybe it isn't you, either, but maybe between us we can work it out. *Do* you know who you're working for?"

"Of course," said Burstone. Immediately afterwards, he wished that he hadn't said it.

"But are you right?" Warnet intervened. Burstone's eyes flicked back and forth from the hasp of the case, where Dayling's hands were working unhurriedly away, to the sharp, aggressive features of the young man.

"What do you mean?" asked Burstone.

"I mean," said Warnet calmly, "that you might be wrong. If this thing is so secret, maybe they tell *you* lies, too."

"Nobody tells any lies," Burstone contradicted him.

The lock on the case gave way, and Dayling laid it down on its side, then lifted the lid. Inside the lid, supported by a double row of clips, was an assortment of metal implements. Knives, compasses, zip fasteners—a completely crazy assortment. In the body of the case there were a few heavier, more complex pieces wrapped in transparent plastic film, heavily greased. Two drills, two axe-heads and the blade of a scythe. Dayling lifted these out, one by one. Beneath the worked metal was a layer of books—not flimsy printouts from a household deck, but sturdy things, printed on heavy paper, bound in black plastic. They had been put together, obviously, by some complex accessory to the usual deck facilities. The sort of thing a collector might have. The world was full of collectors, despite the fact that almost anything could be had on demand from the cybernet. Most people liked to set aside some small area of experience as "theirs" and pander to their pretensions of uniqueness. Some people still liked to use books as of old—the "real thing."

Dayling pulled out a few of the books. There were some boxes stacked among them—boxes which proved to contain sets of small things—scissors, needles, even surgical instruments. Dayling put them all carefully aside. When the case was empty he surveyed the displayed contents with a bewildered expression. He picked up one of the zip fasteners as if it was a snake, looked at it for a moment, and then dropped it with a gesture of annoyance.

"You didn't manage to deliver it, did you?" said Warnet quietly. "This is your end of the deal. You supply the Underworld with trade goods like the prehistoric Spaniards dealing with the Indians. Or is it more like the slavers, buying Africans with colored beads and mirrors? No colored beads, though. I bet you've taken down a mirror or two in your time, haven't you? Do you really think it's safe to give them all those sharp things? And what about the books? Aren't you afraid they might learn something?"

Dayling was looking at the books. "It's a peculiar selection," he said. "Not really *selected* at all. No pattern. History books, novels, elementary science. Memoirs of women of note . . . why on Earth . . . ?"

"I see," said Warnet. "It's all backwards, isn't it. The books are the *real* exports. The useful stuff is the sugar on the pill. You're *trying* to educate them, aren't you. Missionary service."

"But why?" said Dayling.

"More immediately," mused Warnet, "what for? What would you have brought back with you if you *had* managed to dispose of this little load? Come on, Jervis, what do they give you in return? What's in it for you?"

"Nothing," said Burstone. "I mean—nothing in it for me. What they give me isn't mine."

"Nor is this," said Dayling. "It's ours. It belongs to the world. Production capacity of the cybernet. Loss of materials. Energy budgets. This is work, and time, and money, And it's all waste. It's all going down into the sewers. For nothing. What do we get in return?"

"Books," said Burstone, capitulating with the inevitable. "Their books. Scratches on bits of cloth and paper made of fibrous fungus. Hardly anything. What they can scrape together. Sometimes *their* trade goods. Colored beads, ornaments, carvings."

"No mirrors?" said Warnet.

"No."

"What's it for?" said Dayling. "Collectors? Scientific studies? Art lovers?"

There was silence. It was slow and uneasy. Finally, Burstone broke it. He revealed what he had been holding back, not even knowing why he wouldn't say it.

"It's part of the Plan," he said.

For a moment, there was blank misunderstanding on the faces of the Eupsychians. They both jumped to the conclusion that he meant the Plan which Heres had proposed only hours before. That was uppermost in their minds. Then, belatedly, they realized that he meant *the* Plan. The first Plan.

"But it's finished," said Dayling.

"Some of it," said Burstone. "But there are some things that can't finish. Won't ever finish."

"Are you trying to tell us," said Warnet slowly, "that this has been going on throughout history? For thousands of years? For all the time that the Overworld has existed we've been exporting materials into the Underworld? Supporting it, sustaining it, helping it? Is that what you're saying?"

"Yes."

"And the *Council* is behind this?"

Burstone hesitated, and Warnet pounced on the hesitation.

"They don't know, do they?"

"They must," said Burstone. "Heres, at least . . ."

"Where does it all go?" demanded Dayling. "All the things you bring back. Where do you send them? Who keeps it all? One of the Institutes? The Museum? The Colleges?"

To all of the suggestions, Burstone shook his head.

"So who?" Dayling kept on. "Who's doing the research? Who's supplying the stuff? Who's behind it? And what do you mean by saying that it's part of the Plan? Who told you that?"

Burstone said nothing.

"We want the names," Warnet said, in a soft voice. "That's the one thing we must have. We need the names."

"There's only one," said Burstone.

They waited for him.

"Sisyr," he said.

11

From time to time, Iorga was forced to leave the fire in order to go foraging. The fire needed to be fed, Aelite needed to be fed, and so did he. It was no easy task to live off the Waste. Whatever was edible was being consumed even as it grew, by myriad consumers who were likewise eaten while they fed. In order to eat in the Waste, one had to compete with other eaters, and also with the eaten. It was not so bad, if one could move through the bad land, because few eaters roamed far in the foul swamps. Iorga had hoped to beat the Waste, to keep moving, but that was no longer possible. Aelite was still, now, and what was still was eaten in the Waste. He could protect her while he was with her, but while he was apart . . .

It was difficult to feed the fire, too. Food for fires was as difficult to find as food for stomachs. With things as they were Iorga needed a bright fire and good food. For Aelite's sake. She would not recover from the smoke-cloak which was eating her slowly if all she had to eat herself were white worms and bog weed. If they had been on the move, they could have sustained themselves on a diet like that, but while they were forced to wait in the heart of the festering wilderness, they needed far greater reserves of strength and health.

So Iorga searched for special plants—sweet ascocarps and bulbed roots—and he stalked what animals he found to hunt. There were always many crabs, which he pulled to pieces and shelled, but crabmeat was thin and sour, and insufficient in itself. He made every effort to catch birds and bats, but it was not easy. Every now and again a starling would settle on a glued perch, or he would discover a hanging bat whose reactions were a fraction slowed by trance, but he had to count such captures as pure luck.

Every so often, when Aelite was fed, Iorga would build up the fire and search her fur carefully. The smoke-cloak had got holds in her legs and on her back, and because the silky hair grew particularly rich in just those places it was difficult to comb out the spores. Always there would be one or more which would escape to grow mycelia under the skin, and ultimately send up fruiting bodies like tiny orange star-bulbs unless they were located and burned out. Iorga had to sort through Aelite's fur patiently, guided by her itches when she was conscious and could make sense out of her own feeling. It was easy enough to pinch off the fruiting bodies but that was useless, if the infective mycelia remained. It was not enough to prevent spore formation. The mycelia simply grew, if they were not allowed to fruit. They turned the skin gray, burst and blistered the surface, caused bad pain. So they had to be burned out. But that, too, burst and blistered the surface, and caused pain, and weakened the body. It was a hard fight.

Aelite had been courageous, in the beginning. She lay quite still while he sorted out the infected spots and fired them, and she only sighed when the pain became intolerable. But lately, she was past sighing, and the stillness of her body did not reflect courage, but lassitude and imminent defeat.

Iorga knew that he was trying to fight the disease under impossible conditions, and that he was virtually certain to lose, but he would not give up. It was not in his nature. He would not let the infection alone to claim her.

She could not be moved. The decaying mycelia under the skin, even burned out, became toxic, and the toxin would only stay in the epidermal tissues while she did not try to walk. The skin excreted the poison in time, given a chance, but it would spread if she became active.

The center of the infection was an old mycelium on her upper thigh which had been fired twice and yet still, somehow, managed to survive. Iorga dared not burn the flesh any more at that place, or the leg would die from the burning, and so he had to be content to shave off the fruiting bodies until the first burns had healed. He continually plastered the exposed skin with the pap of a red squab which he believed to be useful in healing the flesh and limiting the parasite. It may have been effective, to a degree, but without time on his side there was little enough reason to hope that it would be effective enough.

Iorga, of course, picked up the spores of the smoke-cloak himself whenever a fruiting body got the chance to distribute spores, but he had managed to prevent the infection getting a hold on his own body. It would not, provided that he was careful, scrupulous, and sensitive to the slightest risk, but he knew full well that he was running a risk.

He did not trouble to debate with himself the chances which would dictate whether Aelite lived or died. He did not think of the fight in terms of whether things got better or worse. He knew both hope and fear, but he would not let them occupy his mind or dictate to his body. He had switched himself out of the agonizing cycle of self-examination and repair. In order to cope with the situation he had deliberately relinquished what others might have called his "human" qualities. He needed to see the battle to the end, and he could not fight himself as well as the parasite.

Camlak found him while he was combing Aelite's fur. He did not look up to greet the newcomer, and Camlak did not interrupt him, but simply sat down beside the fire to wait and watch.

When it was time, and the combing was done, the hellkin looked at his visitor closely. Camlak stared back, examining the large green eyes which glowed luminous in the firelight, with the vertical slits half-closed.

Camlak displayed his empty hands. It was hardly necessary, but it was proper. Iorga matched the gesture, sealing the truce.

"I have food," said the Shairan. "You will share."

Iorga nodded, almost imperceptibly. Camlak took what he had from his pack and began to sort it out. Until they had eaten, he would not say more. The hellkin was involved in something of his own, something difficult. Camlak did not really want to invade his privacy at all, but he wanted to help. The hellkin would not be grateful, but he would hardly refuse.

Afterwards, Camlak asked: "Have others passed this way?"

Iorga was silent, but Camlak knew that the lack of an answer was honest.

"How far is the iron wall?" asked Camlak.

The hellkin shook his head, again very slightly.

Chemec came out of the shallow water behind Camlak, carrying a handful of dead things. Small things, but warm. No crabs. The cripple looked at Camlak, and then at the hellkin. He gave the fresh food to the Old Man, and displayed empty but bloodstained palms to Iorga before moving closer.

"Smoke-cloak?" he asked.

"Yes," said Iorga. Chemec drew back.

"Not here," said Camlak to the bent-leg. "We'll move on."

Chemec was obviously relieved. He had a healthy fear of disease. His relief was quickly contaminated with disgust when Camlak gave the small creatures which he had labored hard to catch and kill to the hellkin. Iorga seemed hardly to notice.

When the Children of the Voice passed on into the wilderness, Iorga followed them with his eyes. When Camlak looked back and saluted, he nodded in acknowledgment. When they had gone, he went back to staring into the fire. Not until they were well away did he begin to rip up the fresh meat with his teeth, tearing away the fur and ripping the meat from the tiny, thin bones before he pressed the pieces into Aelite's mouth and helped her to swallow.

12

"Why did you do that?" demanded Chemec.

"He needed it," said Camlak.

"So did we."

"Then we catch more."

"You're a fool."

Yami would have threatened to kill him if he'd said that. In fact, Chemec couldn't think of any man who would accept such an insult. But Camlak didn't touch his knife.

"If you follow me," he said, "you accept my way. Go back. Go into Shairn. You can live whatever way you want there."

Chemec asked himself why he hadn't gone into the northlands of Shairn, instead of following Camlak into the Waste. He could find no reasons, or none in words. The reasons existed, but Chemec simply could not articulate them. While he could not articulate them, he could not cope with them. They compelled him. The force was the power of collective identity—when Camlak had played the Sun to Yami's Star King he had taken into himself the greater self that was Stalhelm. Chemec was still linked to that greater self. Helplessly.

Camlak had the words to reason with, but he was not sure of himself. In his mind, he had buried Stalhelm. He did not want Chemec. But he knew that the only way to get rid of the cripple would be to kill him. That, he would not do. He genuinely did not wish to kill—not Chemec, not anyone. He knew that there were other ways and they were the ways that he wanted to find. He was certain that with the aid of his Gray Soul he could find them. In the meantime, he would put up with Chemec, if not Chemec's ways. They were bound together by a tie of some kind.

"Where do we go after the wall?" Chemec wanted to know. "If we find Nita, what then?"

"I don't know," said Camlak. "Across the darklands by the road of stars. North and further north into nowhere. Maybe to Heaven. Anywhere at all."

Chemec set his teeth tight about his tongue. The ideas themselves were enough to frighten him.

13

Elsewhere, Joth Magner was also having trouble with parasites. On his back, out of sight beneath his shirt, he had allowed a handful of bulbous growths to develop. The spores had probably slipped down the back of his neck and stuck in his sweat. He had taken no notice because they gave him no pain, even when they grew into him. Had Nita or Huldi been able to see them on his skin they would have known enough to cut out the growths at the earliest possible moment. When Joth finally paid some attention to them and asked questions, the parasitism was well under way. Nita told him that something had to be done, and that it would be far from pleasant.

"What are they?" Joth asked. He could not, even by craning his neck, see the growths, but he could feel them if he reached over his shoulder. They were hard and granular, hemispherical, about the size of the ball of his thumb.

"They have to come out," said the girl, who had no ready name for them, but who knew the kind of threat which they posed.

"I can hardly feel them," said Joth. "I'll surely not die of them." But he already knew enough of the Underworld not to take that for granted. Life in the Underworld required ceaseless vigilance in self-defense, and the taking of no chances.

"They have to come out," repeated Nita.

The daughter of Camlak knew that it would have to be done with a heated knife, and she also knew that she had not the strength to hold Joth down, with or without Huldi's help. She found some small globular fungi with flame-red caps and offered them to Joth.

"You told me not to eat them," he said. "Poison."

"That's right," said the girl.

"Die," said Huldi. "For a while. Better that way."

"They'll put me to sleep?"

"Sick sleep," Nita told him. "But you wake, in time."

Joth wanted to postpone the moment, but in the Underworld there were no schedules in time. What was done was done. There was no tomorrow.

He put one into his mouth, and it burned his tongue as he held it there, temporarily unable to swallow. In trying to get it down he squashed it, and the bitter fire washed all around his mouth. He gagged, and almost threw up, but he managed to get the fungal cap down. Tears streamed from his eyes. Nita gave him another, and another, waiting patiently each time for him to do battle with it. When he had swallowed four, his whole head felt like a volcano. It was as if his throat was cut. Instead of lapsing into a deep and peaceful sleep the fire reached out to clothe his mind completely, sucking it into a hot, flaming prison. Only a few moments passed, however, before the pain became only an illusion, and his burning eyes refused to see. His mind melted, and caved in. He did not black out, but ascended as though upon a curtain of flame into a sky like shattered glass.

Memory did not quite desert him, although he would gladly have abandoned it wholly. He was parted from the external world, and felt absolutely nothing of the work which Nita did with the knife, but he was still alive in a world of his own—a hideous phantasmagoria of images and distorted emotions. Not sleep, but sickness—sickness of the internal self.

Outside, Nita cut out the discoid growths, and then began to trace the extent of the adventitious subcutaneous haustoria that were digging their way slowly into the connective tissue outside the scapula. Capillary blood vessels had been destroyed and the nervous tissue had begun to decay, but the great muscle was relatively unharmed.

Huldi fetched a handful of maggots from a rotting gourd, and placed them on the wound. They would eat the dead tissue, including the haustoria, but would not touch the healthy, living cells which were no use to them. When they finished, there would be a vast wound, but the damage the parasite had done in closing the blood vessels would actually help in keeping the leakage of blood under control. The difficulty would be in protecting the wound from the rigors of the Underworld while it healed.

Inside, Joth was lost in a maze of sensation which whirled him round, taunting and tormenting him with touch and sound and color. At first the crazy whirl was simply hurtful, assaulting his mind like poison, tearing at his sense of order and organization, clutching at the fibers of his being. There came a time, however, when it almost began to make sense. He found stars in the sky of his skull, Underworld stars that were still and staring, no matter whether he soared on imagined winds or huddled into a blob of jelly in the mud that carpeted the foul earth. Perpetual stars. There were creatures swarming in his inner being like the maggots that wriggled in his absent flesh; monstrous creatures which wore beast-faces or beast-masks. They all seemed preternaturally vast, and were made grotesque by virtue of the fact that all the wrong features were accentuated. What should have been negligible became prominent, and what ought to have been obvious became hard to focus on, hard even to see as the entity which it ought to have been. All the colors were wrong, unbalanced and unintegrated. The creatures had names but the names were garbled, real but pronounced so strangely that the sounds were tangled and wrenched beyond all meaning—or all recognition of meaning

The experience was real.

It was *not* a dream.

Joth knew that. He knew that he knew it. When he woke, he would know it still. It was real. He knew because he had touched the reality of which it was a part. His body had entered into it, though his mind never had, never could. But he had seen enough, sensed enough, deduced enough to begin to understand. The dead, fetid air which groped into his lungs, the filthy water which leaped down his throat into his gullet, the steady stream of terror which ran in his veins—these things were still alien to him, but he had looked into the face of the unknown, and he had felt their touch before.

He knew.

When he woke, the first thing that he said was: "How long?"

Nita was asleep. Huldi did not answer, because it was a meaningless question and because he was not recovered enough to hear.

The second thing he said was: "Listen."

She listened. She could not promise to understand, or to remember, but she listened, as she watched. She was keeping vigil over Joth. He was dependent upon her, and she was responsive to his need. She did not know why, nor even how to ask.

She listened.

"The dreams," he said. "No dreams." He had difficulty forming the words, but he felt compelled to speak, to make real and permanent what he knew, in case it faded with the vision of hell which had come to him through the fire-mind fungus.

"Images," he said. "Through other eyes. Visions. From someone else. Sent into my mind. *His* mind. He didn't know. Something . . . made him receptive. He saw . . . with the eyes of the Children of the Voice. He dreamed their lives . . . He saw with their eyes . . . He couldn't understand . . . He never saw.

"He didn't know."

Huldi rested her hand on the back of his neck. He lay face downwards. His head slewed sideways, his jaw resting on the ground. He had difficulty moving his mouth to form the words.

What he was trying to say was that at last he had been able to share his father's dream—the dream which had led Carl Magner to his death. He knew it, though, for what it was. Not a dream, but a jumble of sense-impressions. Leakage from a million minds.

His attempt to communicate with Huldi faded away as the sickness left him, ebbing from his mind and allowing him to fall into real and natural sleep.

He dreamed. Normally.

14

"I presume that you have no intention whatsoever of trying to find out what went wrong with Magner's mind?" Rypeck asked of Heres.

"It's no longer important," said the Hegemon. "Magner is presumably dead, the body has not yet been recovered. If and when it is the risk of contamination may be too great to warrant doing anything with it but burning it, and even the most thorough autopsy might reveal absolutely nothing. As an individual case, it isn't worth making a big issue out of."

"You seem to have made a big enough issue out of his wretched book without very much encouragement."

"I thought you would have approved," lied Heres. "You complained about our ignorance of the Underworld. You brought to light the fact that measures were apparently taken by the Planners to secure the existence of human life in the Underworld even after the Overworld was sealed. You complain about the tentative nature of the contemporary Council's government and its lack of ideas. The second Plan is the answer to all your criticisms."

"I don't want to reclaim the Underworld," said Rypeck. "If you want to know, I'd rather see it dead. I don't believe that you want to reclaim the Underworld either. I don't think that your interest in and involvement with this crazy second Plan is serious. I think it's a political move, and twice as dangerous to us because it's not sincere.

"I can see the sense in a second Plan. You may be right in saying that it's exactly what we need. We need to rebuild the Movement to replace some real and literal movement. But not into the Underworld. Why couldn't you look outwards, to the planets and the stars?"

Rypeck knew why. First, because Magner and his book had given Heres a convenient launching pad for the second Plan. It had allowed him to get the timing right. Secondly, the alternative plan—the outward-looking plan—was a Eupsychian catch-phrase. The conquest of space. The

Eupsychians had laid claim to that idea and used it as if they alone had a right to it. Heres had let them take it. Heres had no use for space travel—he associated it with the age of psychosis. Heres' brand of Euchronianism recognized one Earth and one alone, the most precious of all things.

"We have been reminded of the Underworld," said Heres. "We have rediscovered it. We can't forget it again—not overnight. We mustn't forget it again. It *ought* to be the next thing on the list of our priorities. How can we lay claim to a new world with the ruins of the old one still beneath our feet. The Underworld may be a sewer but we owe it to ourselves—never mind the people who live down there—to make it a clean sewer, hygienic."

"Do you honestly see this as a real solution? To *our* problems?"

"Yes."

"I think you're lying," said Rypeck. "Or blind."

"You've no right to say that to me," Heres told him. "You're letting your bitterness run clean away with you. You're an old man, Eliot. If you continue this way you're going to make yourself look like a senile fool. Not only to me, but to the Council—to the whole Movement."

"I'm sorry, Rafael," said Rypeck. He was genuinely sorry. His head *had* run away with him. But he was seriously troubled by the course of events. He was sure that there was something in the pattern which was more serious than Heres had ever considered.

"Can't we hold back?" Rypeck continued. "Can't we wait for a while, until we have a chance to look at the situation from all sides? Do we have to commit ourselves now?"

"We're already committed," said Heres, positively.

"Rafael," said Rypeck, "I'm going to keep on looking for the truth in this matter. If I find that the i-minus effect is going wrong, I'll break the secret. I'll have to. Maybe you can survive that, now, and maybe I can't. I don't know. But I can't let it go on."

"If you broke the secret tomorrow," said Heres, with a confidence which he did not quite feel, "it wouldn't matter. I can justify it, now. You can't hurt me, Eliot."

Rypeck was tempted to say: "I can try." Instead, he made what seemed to be a gesture of defeat. He allowed Heres to end the interview. But in Rypeck's eyes, he could never really be defeated, because—unlike Heres—he was really not fighting for his own ends. Like Heres, he was trying to play the game the ideal way—with everybody winning—but while Heres wanted to be the architect of victory, Rypeck only wanted the answer to come out right. He needed help —not to provide the answers, but to arm him with the right questions. He needed to turn to someone outside the situation, who could see into it without necessarily being a part of it. There was one person who might be able to do that—to tell him whether Heres was steering Euchronia into disaster, and if so, why.

That person was the alien, Sisyr.

15

They tried to keep going, but it soon became clear that it was a losing battle. Joth had not the strength, and the demands which walking put upon his body detracted seriously from the slow healing processes working on his wound. In any case, they were not sure that they were going the right way, or that they were going anywhere at all.

Nita thought that they should have stayed with the wall, and gone east, rather than striking southeast into the Waste for a second time. It was quite unnecessary for them to retrace their steps—when they had come into the Waste they were in a hurry, and had accepted the need to take a direct route. There was no urgency now. In addition, there was no real reason why they should accept automatically that they were going back to Shairn. In many ways it might be a bad idea. The whole of Shairn might be in thrall to the Ahrima by now.

Huldi, on the other hand, had been all too ready to take the obvious path, and she was prepared to be obstinate in defense of the easy decision. The unknown held no attraction for Huldi—she had launched herself into it initially merely to escape from Ermold. She felt the need of a destination of some kind for the security which the idea offered. While she was going somewhere she knew where she was and why. The direct way was the only way she could really be sure of. She thought in straight lines. Once she arrived in Shairn, the problem would remake itself—the security of traveling disappears upon arrival—but that was not an immediate concern. She lived each moment as it came.

They did not know what Joth thought. He did not say. When he had encountered his father at the doorway to the upper world, the whole purpose of returning had seemed to drain away. Unlike Huldi, Joth felt his identity extended in time. He lived as much in remembrance of the past and in anticipation of things to come as in the present—perhaps far more. The death of Carl Magner had taken away both his past and his future insofar as he could perceive meaning therein. Such things are not uncommon among people who live strung out in time rather than day by day. A factor in their life is erased, and the whole integrity of life simply disappears. All the threads fall loose, no longer knitted together. The bottom falls out of the world. It is a temporary effect, in most cases—it merely requires time for the threads of existence to clot, to reintegrate into a whole. In the meantime, however, the sense of purposelessness can be overwhelming, leading to almost total loss of the sense of being in the world, of being a part of the course of events.

Joth had fallen out of his role in the pattern of life as he perceived it. He was cut adrift, and he was drifting.

There is an analogy to be drawn between Joth's situation and Nita's. She, too, had lost her father, and with him her whole life. Like him, she was drifting. Huldi, though, had cut *herself* out of the cloth of her existence. She had exempted herself by an act of will. Of the three, only Huldi really felt the compulsion to refabricate a pattern, to decide on a destination, to know what she was doing and why. Only she felt the need to rediscover a purpose in life. It was largely her instigation, therefore, which had provided the motive force to take them back into the Waste toward Shairn.

It was largely her motive force, also, which knitted them together as a group. There was no thought in her head, or in Nita's, of abandoning Joth, or each other. The three of them were bound together. The binding force might as well be called love as anything else, but it was integrative love rather than directional. Like the tension in a stretched string, it pulled in both directions—action and reaction equal and opposite. The generation of the bond of love was very largely a response to Huldi's need—she brought it into being.

16

Joth's wound had opened, and blood was leaking slowly from the surface of the damaged flesh.

"It won't heal," said Nita, trying to mop up the blood with a soft pad of matted fungus, with little success.

"Let it dry," said Huldi. She was spearing crabs which scuttled across the broad algal fronds dipping into the water. They were resting on a patch of raised ground, but though it was raised it was by no means dry. Ideally, they needed somewhere better to rest, but the swamp was completely inhospitable in this region.

"It'll never heal in the Waste," said the girl.

"Nothing but Waste for hundreds of miles," Huldi pointed out, unnecessarily. She speared another crab which came too close. As she looked out over the vast network of green strips resting on and just below the water surface, she saw that more crabs were visible, and that they all seemed to be working their way closer. They were small, blue-gray creatures with small, ineffectual pincers. They were not a common species but they seemed to be swarming in this particular area.

"Something's attracting them," said Nita.

"It's the blood," said the human girl. "Joth." As she spoke she kicked at a pair of the bolder crabs, and sent them flying through the air, to land in among the green fronds with a double splash.

"They won't bother us," said Nita, albeit slightly uneasily. "They're too small."

"But what comes after the crabs?"

Huldi had a valid point. Scavengers which converge on wounded prey are themselves a temptation to other predators, quite apart from the fact that where one carrion-eater leads, others tend to follow. The blue-gray crabs would not feed until their target was dead, but by seeking it out and pointing the way for stronger creatures they might get to eat all the sooner. Evolution favors collaboration as well as competition.

Neither Nita nor Huldi had a weapon likely to prove very effective against larger predators. Nita had a thin-bladed knife of Heaven-metal, Huldi a larger, heavier one, but made of poor iron, dull and rusted.

"We had no trouble coming the other way," said Nita, trying to use words as a shield against fear.

"We spread no smell of blood," said Huldi. "And we were much further to the west, almost on the fringes of the poisoned land. Here it is not so dead."

"Look around for stones," said Nita. "Smash the crabs and let them eat their own kind."

But the area was not the place where stones might be found. That there was solid ground here at all was due to the proliferating plant life, which had raised itself up out of the mud, binding it and making layers of humus as one generation followed another in chaotic confusion. They were on a hummock in between two dendritic monsters whose multihydral branches supported vast colonies of passenger-plants and whose long, spatulate leaves and creepers formed the basis for webs and mats of lacy leaf-creatures and carpets of clinging, jelly-like tissue that was almost the texture of raw protoplasm. Such a vast profusion of life-forms inevitably attracted a complex complement of insects, and no doubt sheltered numerous potentially dangerous creatures.

"We have to carry on," said Huldi.

"It's no use," Nita told her. "He's exhausted. He's barely conscious."

Joth was not even aware of the danger. He only wanted to lie down. Had he known that his life was threatened, he would have been unable to react. He would have simply waited for death to come to him.

"We can make him move," said Huldi. "Between us."

"He's too heavy." Huldi had already known that—her statement had been wishful thinking rather than a declaration of intent. Joth was not unduly large, but Huldi was shorter and lighter. Nita was less than four feet tall, and though not delicately built, could hardly support even a quarter of Joth's weight. Though she was near maturity, by the standards of her kind, she had the strength of a ten-year-old child by the standards of Joth's kind.

So they fought the crabs, as best they could, with hands and feet. It was not difficult. But in reality they were waiting, waiting to see whether crabs were all that they would have to deal with.

17

Huldi screamed as something surfaced thirty or forty feet away. It was a reptile of some kind, with an elongated crocodilean snout and two rows of tiny needle-like teeth spilling out of its mouth. Water streamed from its warty skin, splashing from its ridged back as it shivered deliberately.

Its forelegs were longer than the hinder pair, and armed with vicious claws. As it stood erect in the shallow water it measured five feet from hip to neck, ten or twelve from its snout to the tip of the coiling tail, still invisible beneath the frothing water. With a few quick strokes of its arms it brushed away the bulk of the weed that had clung to its body.

It moved forward.

Its large, black-slitted yellow eyes were set in the sides of its head, in raised orbits—again like those of a crocodile or a frog. It did not appear to be looking at Huldi. Instead, it followed the movements of the scattering crabs. In chasing them, however, it came closer to the two humans and the rat. It stooped forward, and its long snout went perpetually back and forth as the foremost teeth snapped up the crabs and the tongue threw them back to be crunched by the jaws. It came forward, looking grotesquely like a chicken pecking for corn. It retained its upright posture, its arms waving to maintain its balance.

It flopped forward, creating a massive splash and stirring the green water-borne carpet for yards around. In the water, it came on, with a snake-like twist and then a glide like an arrow. There was no doubt now that its attention had been caught by something larger than crabs. And yet its eyes still did not seem to look directly at Huldi or Nita. It seemed to be looking all ways at once. Its jaws half-opened in a macabre smile.

Neither Huldi nor Nita felt the urge to run. Instead, they reached for their knives.

There was a momentary flurry as the long head darted sideways to snap up another crab, and the long forelimbs surfaced to rip yet again at the clinging weed. The gliding motion ceased, and once again the great beast paused to haul itself up on to the triangle of its back legs and tail. It was slow in rearing up, and this time it had to reach out with one of its claws to grip, just for a moment, a high branch of one of the dendrite colonies.

As it steadied itself, the whole of its yellow underbelly gleamed wet in the pale starlight.

Almost without thinking, Nita threw the small knife with all her strength into the center of the yellow expanse. It penetrated, but not far enough. The hide, even there, was too thick.

The crocodilean snorted, spraying thin mucous from its nostrils. It looked down, seeming suddenly unsteady again. Its jaws yawned and one claw brushed the knife from its lodgment into the water. No blood flowed.

"Throw it!" Nita howled, as Huldi moved forward with iron dagger extended, as though she intended to engage the monster hand-to-hand. The human girl stopped, and moved back, but she did not throw the weapon. She could not bring herself to release it.

Nita went to her knees beside Joth's supine form, groping for his pack in search of something—anything hard or sharp —with which she could attack the creature.

It was moving forward again, and Huldi was moving back from it, but too slowly. It would have her within the swing of its arms in a matter of seconds.

Then an arrow smashed into the reptile's belly just above the point at which the knife had gone in. The velocity of impact was akin to that of a bullet, the momentum of the shaft somewhat greater. If the crocodilean had been a man it would have been hurled backwards. As it was, it simply lost balance and teetered. Its claws waved in the air, making circles as they searched for something to grip. One found the dendrite branch again, but it was not enough. The beast fell, twisting as it did so, coiling even as it hit the water. This time there *was* blood—the water where it fell roiled, and the foam which flew up was flecked with red.

It thrashed in the water, and another arrow hissed through the air. Nita and Huldi watched it plow uselessly into the water, and Nita screamed, very faintly, having little breath to spare.

But the second arrow was unnecessary. The crocodilean wanted no more. The pain of the one sound blow was enough.

It was off through the water, horizontally, its body snaking and its four limbs thrashing back and forth in a mad, uncoordinated attempt to add to its velocity. It hesitated once, and Nita gasped again, thinking that it was about to turn and attack, but it was only the arrow catching on a submerged root. The wrench had hurt the creature, but had only made it more determined to get away.

It might survive, but the odds were probably against it. The arrowhead would remain in its flesh, though the wooden shaft would be easy enough to tear away. The wound would prove troublesome and fester. Ultimately, in its own time, the poisons in the wound would spread to the whole system. In all likelihood, the beast would end up prey for the little blue crabs. In the meantime, it would be very hurt and very dangerous, but it would not be back.

Iorga had fired from no more than twenty feet. He had come from behind the larger dendrite. He, too, had smelled blood, but he had not come to claim his share.

"Come with me," said the hellkin. "There is better ground."

Huldi, seeing the cat emerge from the cloud of mist and flies which obscured the area beyond the dendrite, had crouched with her knife, ready to fight. But when the hellkin spoke she relaxed immediately.

Iorga came forward, shouldering his bow. "I'll help you with the boy," he said.

Nita, meanwhile, was recovering her knife.

18

Randal Harkanter came back from a short walk in the wilderness with his gun slung over his shoulder and a big sweat-stained scowl behind his face-mask.

His select company had set up camp less than a hundred yards away from the door set in the metal wall, through which Carl Magner had come to his death. They had not found his body, although a request had filtered down from somewhere in the hierarchy of authority that they should locate and recover it, if possible. They had found what appeared to be an unmarked grave, but there was no one among them willing to take it upon himself to investigate by digging. No one wanted to get his hands dirty. The Overworld was a clean world, and its citizens had clean habits. With the possible exception of Harkanter, who had, over the years, cultivated an uncaring obliviousness to his remarkable propensity for copious sweating, the delegated representatives of the Euchronian spirit of scientific adventure were anxious to be as tentative as possible in their dealings with the Underworld. An inquiring mind was one thing—a filthy body was another. The Euchronian scientists tended to believe in *mens sana in*—and *only* in—*corpore sano.*

Harkanter alone had been prepared to undertake a march into the wilderness, and he had been overruled by the prudent majority. Investigation was a slow process—one did not rush headlong into it. It was not an attitude that Harkanter had much sympathy with, but he was well-known for attitudes at odds with the spirit of the Euchronian Movement.

As Harkanter unstrapped his gun there were a few faintly polite murmurs of interest with regard to his observations.

"Filth," he said, fixing his stare on the most convenient listener, who happened to be Felipe Rath. "Filthy, disease-ridden, vermin-haunted swamp. What did you expect?"

"Filthy, disease-ridden, vermin-haunted swamp," said Rath calmly. "What else?" Rath was squatting on an extensive groundsheet, surrounded by a multitude of boxes, trying to assemble equipment. His progress was slow and unhurried.

"Quite so," said Harkanter. "I always believed the Underworld to be a worldwide sewer. Now that we're here we find it to be a worldwide sewer. Very good. So what?"

"It would be rather ambitious," Rath pointed out, "to decide on the whole nature of the Underworld on the basis of what we see from here. No doubt what we see is representative, in some way, but a world is a big place. It can include a wide range of environments. Our world above, remember, has been shaped and Planned. This one hasn't. We mustn't expect anything like the same level of comparability between geographically separated regions. On the platform there are no deserts, and even the forests don't run wild. Here it's all wild. The old world *you* know about never really existed even then. The slick myth always outlives any semblance of the reality. You thought of this trip in terms of a safari. You're the big black hunter and we're the white bearers. But that won't work here—not even as a portable fantasy.

You can act out your daydreams up above—the world is geared for it. But down here it's still real."

Harkanter turned away from the patiently working scientist. Rath had delivered his speech more or less absent-mindedly, with the bulk of his attention fixed on what he was doing. He was unaware of the poisonous expression on Harkanter's face, although the mask did not hide it.

"I was asked to lead this party," said Harkanter, half-turning in order to direct his comments back to Rath. "I was asked to come down here and find the people."

"We'll find them," said Rath. "We'll find them with *this*, if they're here to be found." He lifted up the assembly on which he was working. It looked like a toy, and in a sense it was —it would have been nonfunctional in the upper world except as an amusement. It was a robot bird armed with a camera. The idea was to send it out to map the region photographically. Its basic scheme of operation would be by remote control, but it carried enough electronic gear and programming capacity to allow it to fly around obstructions and avoid other flying creatures.

Harkanter retired to his tent to breathe some sterilized air and drink some water. When he came back out, some time later, Rath was still sitting in the same place, still working on the same device.

"Why don't you do that inside?" Harkanter growled.

"No room," said Rath. "Full up." His head gestured very slightly toward the cluster of hemispherical plastic tents, wherein other members of the expedition prepared their various endeavors. Rath was by no means the only one to have been forced to do his work in the open, but most of the others were working with rather more extensive apparatus.

"You could catch fever, sitting here in the open," said Harkanter, with dour relish. "You're not wearing gloves."

"I've heard of picking up diseases," said Rath, "but I don't think one does it in quite that way."

Harkanter gathered the moisture in his mouth, but remembered in time that he could not spit without lifting his mask. Privately, he looked forward to the wholly imaginary moment when Rath would be ravaged by all manner of Hell-born ailments because of exposing his bare flesh to the air, but he said nothing. There was no point—not now.

"You're taking your time with that," he commented.

"Time has to be taken," answered Rath philosophically.

"If you get into the habit of saving it, you get out of the habit of spending it. It needs the time. What's worrying you?"

Rath knew perfectly well what was worrying Harkanter. Of all the people in the encampment, he was the only one with nothing to do. For the moment, he was the spare man. In time, he would come into his own—his willingness and determination to act, and his ability to make and force decisions would be needed soon. The scientists would be only too ready to collect trivial data till the sky fell, if Harkanter were not there to make them follow up their initial findings with some action.

When Harkanter didn't answer the rhetorical question, Rath continued. "Why don't you take Vicente out into the bush? He's got no intricate equipment to fiddle with. He probably wants to get busy collecting. Better take him out now, before the enthusiasm wears off."

"Nobody's stopping him," said Harkanter.

"He won't go out alone."

"I'm not his nursemaid."

Rath shrugged.

"It'll never get off the ground," said Harkanter, meaning Rath's electronic bird.

Rath felt it better to ignore him. One of the others— Gregor Zuvara—observed that Harkanter was inconveniencing Rath, and came over to tap the tall Negro on the shoulder.

"I've been looking at the grave," he said.

"You're not going to dig him up!"

"It's not important," said Zuvara. "It might be Magner. It probably is. That's not what I wanted to point out. Never mind the identity of the corpse—what we ought to be wondering is the identity of the one who buried him."

The suggestion had the desired effect. It obviously had not occurred to Harkanter that it takes two to make a funeral.

"The grave is fresh," said Zuvara. "Whoever dug it can't be far away. Unless they've gone for good, they must know we're here. We haven't been very discreet. What do you think?"

"We'd better mount a guard," said Harkanter.

"That's your province," said the other man. "But take it easy. Don't start handing out hours of duty arbitrarily. Try to fit in with our work schedule, if you can."

Harkanter nodded. Satisfied that the big man now had something to occupy his time and his talents, Zuvara left him. Rath looked up and gave a brief nod of recognition. He only hoped that the mysterious gravediggers were themselves discreet. In a pitched battle, the Overworlders would win without much effort, and probably without loss, but it would be messy and unpleasant.

Rath preferred things neat and tidy.

19

Later in the day—or what would have been the day had Harkanter's expedition been in the Overworld—Vicente Soron did manage to extend his hunt for specimens beyond the bounds of the encampment. Harkanter, now convinced of the need for vigilance, and his sour mood behind him, agreed to accompany him. Soron was determined to clutter himself up with an embarrassment of equipment and containers, but at Harkanter's insistence he also managed to accommodate a gun somewhere about his person. This, too, was not without its purpose in terms of collecting equipment, however, as it was a small compressed-air device which fired anesthetic needles. Soron considered it only reasonable that anything which attacked them should thereby qualify for the specimen collection.

Harkanter led the way into the Waste, with a confident stride that seemed likely to scatter all the wildlife from his path before Soron even got a glimpse of it, but in the meantime the collector was content to stick to the obvious, leaving the fugitive for more subtle methods at another time. Nor did he try to make Harkanter slow down or pause—it would be less burdensome to do the collecting on the way back, and it was always sensible to use the eyes well before beginning to use the hands.

Harkanter was a man of direct personality, and he had no prejudice against getting his clothing wet. He therefore strode forward purposefully, ignoring the lie of the land, and stepping knee-deep in swamp water as often as not. None of the water could seep through to his skin—he was well-protected. Soron was much shorter, and the water came up proportionally higher so far as he was concerned. In addition, it was not simply his skin that he had to worry about

—his pockets were full and there were specimen bottles decked around his waist in a wide belt. Thus he was forced to pay rather more attention to precisely where he put his feet, and sometimes he walked around areas that Harkanter plunged straight into. Though he covered a greater distance, he was not noticeably slower and did not get particularly tired, precisely because he avoided the circumstances which would slow him down and sap his strength.

As time went by, Soron began to feel a certain impatience, considering that he had come quite far enough for his purposes. Harkanter, however, was unwilling to listen to his mild hints. It was not that the big man was particularly keen to make a meal of the walk in the wilderness, nor that he had anything in particular against Soron, but he could not quite help himself overdoing things, simply to make the little man suffer a little for his inconveniences.

When Soron's complaints became rather more insistent, however, Harkanter stopped for a rest, sitting down and resting his rifle in the cleft of a dendrite. He then showed no inclination to move for some length of time while Soron methodically sorted out whole plants and pieces of plants, marking the bottles and making notes in cryptic ultrashorthand on his sleeves.

"It's easier than notebooks," he explained, "and more convenient than voice records."

"Sure," said Harkanter. "If you run out of space you can use the back of my tunic."

Soron consented to smile, without making any remark of his own to cap the comment. He might find it convenient to take the big man at his word, but there was no need to say so.

"Can you bring down some of the animals when we get nearer to the camp?" Soron asked him. "Birds and bats? They won't be much use as specimens but I'd like to have a look at them quickly."

Harkanter hefted the rifle in one hand. "Wouldn't be much left of anything I hit with this," he said.

"What about the handgun?"

"You want me to hit birds with a pistol? In the *dark*?"

Soron smiled again. "I thought you could do it," he said. "I don't know anything about guns."

"I'll try," Harkanter promised, sounding less than confident.

"Thanks," said Soron.

Harkanter watched the little man working away, with

infinite patience and complete confidence. A typical Euchronian, he thought. All method and endurance. Like a machine. All action under complete control. He did not think of his own manner and methods as at all mechanical, but in his way, he was as much a Euchronian as the scientist. Their differences showed up clearly, but what they had in common was not so obvious to either of them. It was because they had so much in common and taken for granted that they were so aware of the differences. But method and patience were the Euchronian attributes—not because of Euchronian philosophy but because of eleven thousand years of the Euchronian Plan. What Harkanter thought of as his qualities of imagination and creativity were really only his uneasiness and dissatisfaction with the quality of his life. He did not feel at home in himself or in the world, but he embroidered the vague and incoherent feeling into a network of ideas and assumptions which made what was simply inconvenient into something very complex and enigmatic. The explanations which he invented to account for himself were involved and detailed, but not really relevant. His was a common enough problem, although it manifested itself in different ways in different people.

By the time that Soron was ready to make his way back to camp, Harkanter was also keen to get back. But Soron did not want to return at the same pace—this time he wanted to collect as he went. Thus, when Harkanter fell, as a matter of course, into his long, loping stride, he quickly outdistanced his companion, and had to stop to wait for him. Every time the scientist caught up, the same thing happened again within minutes. It did not take long for Harkanter's patience to wear thin. Instead of stopping to wait for his campanion he began to circle back on himself every time he got far enough ahead. His path therefore became a series of loops running alongside Soron's more or less straight line. The more impatient Harkanter got, the bigger the loops became and the more purposeful his stride.

Inevitably, he took one careless stride too many.

He sank waist-deep in a patch of glistening mud onto which he had walked without considering its implications. It was smooth and dead flat, flecked with algal growths but not covered. It *looked* like a semiliquid, if Harkanter had only paused to look. But he had not, and now he was in it, stuck firm. As he struggled, he sank further. It took him a few seconds to realize that he was in real trouble. He had placed altogether too much confidence in his protective clothing.

"Vicente!" he howled.

Soron was out of sight, but when he heard the cry he came running. Not too fast, however. When he saw what had happened to the big man he stopped running and became very careful indeed about the placement of his feet.

"Come on," said Harkanter. "Help me out."

"I'll help you out," said Soron, in a poor imitation of a soothing tone, "but let's make sure that you don't help me in."

He advanced with exaggerated caution.

"I'm sinking," said Harkanter. His voice was quite even, neither loud nor anxious. In fact, he felt somewhat at a loss. He just did not know how to react. He had had no practice.

Soron came as close as he dared. When he extended a toe to test the ground before him it gave slightly, and he lost confidence in it completely. Harkanter considered that he was being too conservative, but he realized fully enough that if they both got stuck there was no one else to come running.

The big man twisted his body, and reached out toward the nearest clump of vegetation, hoping to get a handhold. He could touch the soft green tissues of the fronds, but could not grip anything solid. Virtually all the plant life in the Waste was only facultatively photosynthetic, deriving most of its energy from alternative processes, and the highly specialized structural modifications associated with leaf-bearing were simply not basic to the Underworld way of life. Tough stems and branches existed, but they were by no means everywhere to hand. Soron also looked around for something long and tough, but there was nothing immediately apparent in the vicinity.

"Hold out the gun," said the scientist. "I'll try to pull you back this way."

"It's no use," said Harkanter, comparing his size with that of the little man. But he extended the barrel of the rifle nevertheless. Soron gripped the gunsight at the extremity of the barrel, and began to pull. It surprised neither man that he made very little impression.

"You're too heavy," complained Soron.

Harkanter perceived at this point that he had stopped sinking. The mudpool had a bottom. The problem was simply to make some progress toward extricating himself.

"I can't come backwards," said the big man. "Come around the other side of the patch and I'll try to come out forwards."

Soron picked his way carefully round the glistening spot of colored mud, and then began shedding some of the load which was inconveniencing his movements. He seemed —to Harkanter—to take a long time about it. Then Harkanter extended the rifle again, and began to haul his legs forward through the sticky fluid. Soron helped as much as he could by pulling. Harkanter flopped forward, scraping for a hand-hold to draw himself out more directly.

Slowly, they began to make progress. As Harkanter became more aware of the fact that he *was* able to move, he became more confident of the fact that he could get out, and this helped him to make more progress. The mud made tiny sucking noises, like smacking lips, but slowly it yielded its glutinous clutch.

Then Soron let go of the gun, and tumbled backwards, leaving Harkanter completely off balance and floundering. The big man cursed volubly, but as he splashed in the mud and twisted to save himself from falling horizontally, he saw what Soron had seen, behind him.

Something had emerged from a clump of high-stemmed growths a few yards away, and it stood looking at him with large pink eyes.

Harkanter fought to bring the gun to bear, but it was no use. It had flopped into the mud when Soron had released it, and the barrel was oozing the stuff. Even if the gun would fire, it was more likely to blow Harkanter's head off than kill the creature.

It came closer. Soron picked himself up off his back and stared at it, fearfully. He was startled by the *calmness* in the creature's bearing. It walked erect, like a man. It was looking at him without fear.

It was just about four feet tall. It was gray-furred. Its head was large, but somewhat bestial in formation. It was wearing clothes, and in its right hand—it had *hands*—it was carrying a long and rather wicked-looking knife.

Harkanter had his finger on the trigger of the rifle, ready to take the risk of firing if there was no other recourse. Was this one of the men of the Underworld? he wondered. It looked more like a giant rat. An obscene parody of a man.

The pink eyes shifted—together—from Harkanter to Soron. Harkanter was frozen still, Soron was groping at his belt.

The creature displayed an open palm. "I'll help . . ." it—or he—began, in what appeared to be slurred but perfectly comprehensible English.

Then Soron shot it. It collapsed, falling backwards. It was not dead, though the dart had taken it full in the chest at short range. Soron's weapon was designed not to kill. The creature tried once to rise from the ground, but it could not. It lapsed slowly into stillness.

Soron was shaking uncontrollably.

"Get up," hissed Harkanter. "Run. Back to the camp. I'll be all right. Get men. *Quickly.*"

Soron came unsteadily to his feet and set off, moving convulsively for the first few strides.

"Get that knife," Harkanter shouted after him.

Soron returned, hesitated, and then bent hurriedly to pluck the knife from the nerveless fingers of the felled creature.

"Which way?" he said, uncertainly.

"That way," said Harkanter, pointing. *"Run!"*

"Suppose more come?" said Soron. "There may be more."

Harkanter was shaking the gun, trying to get the mud out of the barrel. "That's what I'm afraid of," he said. "Get moving."

Soron nodded, turned, and ran. He was no longer careful of his ground. He had left most of his specimens behind. Impelled by a terror that was almost panic, he ran for the metal wall.

Harkanter looked after him, for a while, and then put the rifle butt under his armpit, waiting.

Secure in his hiding place, Chemec also watched. He knew better than to show himself. He had dealt with the Heaven-sent before. They were dangerous, but they were stupid. Smiling to himself, he remembered Yami's way . . . and he looked at the fallen Camlak.

20

"It's very kind of you to see me," said Warnet.

"I don't have many visitors," said Sisyr. "I wish there were more. Your world long ago lost interest in me. And why not? You are ephemeral beings. We have little enough in common."

"You don't make your existence very noticeable," commented the Eupsychian.

"No," said the alien. "I don't like to become obvious. There is a possibility of . . . embarrassment. Of course, this is my world now. I make my home here. But it is not my world in the sense that it is yours. Your people built this world . . . they have a fierce pride in it. Pride means a great deal to ephemerals. Do you mind my referring to you in that way, though? Perhaps I am careless?"

"It doesn't bother me," said Warnet. "I'm used to it. I've no wish to live forever." He stopped, and there was a dragging pause which suggested that he expected Sisyr to make some reply to the comment. But Sisyr said nothing, waiting for Warnet to fill in his own silence. Warnet looked at the alien speculatively, and then let his eyes move around the room as if he were inspecting it closely.

"I know so very little about you," said the human. "As . . . ephemerals . . . we seem to be very forgetful of our friends—and perhaps our debts."

"Your people owe me nothing," said Sisyr.

"Life itself," said the Earthman. He paused again, with the same suggestion of waiting, but again Sisyr did not reply.

Sisyr was taller than Warnet by a foot, but he did not seem to be a giant. There were a number of humans who topped Warnet by similar margins. The alien's skin was red-brown; his eyes were pale blue, round, and had no pupils. He had no nose, but there was an area of skin enfolded on his upper lip that was slightly darker than the rest of his skin, and which occasionally fluttered slightly. The mouth had no lower lip to speak of—the lower jaw tucked up neatly behind the upper ridge. No teeth were visible. The whole face was dominated by the eyes, which, though very little larger or more protrusive than their human analogues, stood out by virtue of the striking color difference and the reduced lower jaw. Warnet wondered idly what range of radiation Sisyr could perceive with these eyes, and with what molecular delicacy his chemotactical sense operated. What senses did the alien possess which he had not? And what did *he* have that the alien did not. The same world, thought Warnet, and yet we might live in quite different worlds, hardly able to perceive one another except as shadows. What do I look like in his eyes? Would I recognize myself. What kind of concept does he have of my identity, or I of his? And yet we sit in the same room, and drink the same wine. We may read the same books and listen to the same music. Two worlds in one, neatly slotted together. But what do we each understand by what we read and hear? Have we so little in common, or so much . . . ?

Sisyr's hands, too, were inhuman, although the rest of him, clothed as it was in a manner which concealed rather than exposed, seemed quite ordinary. Warnet considered the hands. Fingers, of a sort, but thin, looking like insect's legs compared to the short, squat, knuckleboned fingers which twined round his own glass. Webs extended between all the fingers and when the hands were at rest they were folded. The palms were pitted, and there were ridges of what looked like suckers round the pits. The thumb was opposable, and was much more sturdy than the other fingers—strangely jointed, with a hard, horny claw.

Warnet was particularly fascinated by the hands. They seemed so strange and complex. One could learn so much of a human by looking at the hands—what could one learn of an alien? For what was the hand functionally designed? Why had evolution favored such a grotesque shape? But this question could not be answered. The context in which it might be applied—if it was applicable at all—was something which Warnet knew absolutely nothing about. He did not even know the name of Sisyr's world.

The Earthman raised his glass slightly, looking at the clear red liquid within. "It doesn't come from some faraway world of another star," he said.

"Of course not," said Sisyr. "It is wine of my own world. This one."

"Other ships call here occasionally," Warnet pointed out.

"Don't they bring you gifts . . . small memories . . . of an older home?"

"No," said the alien, simply.

"And your own ship? Do you never go into space? Voyages of discovery? Perhaps visits—after all, they come to you . . . do you never go to them?"

"You don't understand," said the alien. "The voyages in space . . . they take hundreds of years. The ships are not as fast as light. We have the time . . . time means little enough to us . . . but we do not take distance so lightly. Spacefaring is not a matter of pleasure . . . the kind of . . . adventure . . . which you might imagine has no meaning for us. I cannot explain—it is a difference of thought, of nature-with-time. I'm sorry."

"Do you know who I am and why I came to see you?" asked Warnet. His voice was even, and there was a hint of humor in it.

"Yes," said Sisyr, and paused. His tiny mouth moved slightly, as if he were simulating an Earthly smile. He might almost have been joining in the game of words.

"How much do you know?" asked the visitor.

"Enough."

"You know that I'm a heretic?"

"Yes."

"You know how I might choose to use the information I have concerning your . . . activities?"

Sisyr nodded. A casual, totally human gesture. Implying that he understood politics . . . that he knew how badly Warnet wanted to break the people's faith in the Council, in the Movement itself.

Warnet nodded too. "I thought you would. There's not a lot that escapes your attention, is there? You know a great deal about what goes on in your . . . *our* . . . world."

"Yes."

"Well then," said Warnet. "Which of us will sum up what we both know so that we can stray into fresh pastures?"

The alien gestured with his incredible hand.

"Very well," said the human. "I'm a Eupsychian. I'd like to be a councillor. The odds are against it. The interest in the Underworld which is being stirred up at the moment interests me greatly. I think there's potential here for political moves. Heres is ahead of himself—I don't know why, but I know that he is. There almost seems to be a flutter of panic running through the Hegemony, for some reason that

I can't identify. That beautiful book of Carl Magner's has made them think. Why? It's a fine piece of work—a truly revolutionary work—but its face value is zero. It means nothing. Ergo, there must be something *beneath* the surface if you'll pardon the word-play. There is more than meets the eye.

"Burstone, for one thing, meets very few eyes. Magner knows nothing about him. An odd coincidence that two people with such dramatically common interests should be operating in complete ignorance of one another. Another . . . person . . . who meets very few eyes is yourself. This world owes its very existence to you, and yet you maintain an existence which is virtually invisible. There are, of course, any number of possible explanations for that. But how many of them also explain that Burstone works for you? He thinks he works for the Movement, but he doesn't. He thinks his work is part of the Plan . . . perhaps that *is* true. You, after all, know far more about the Plan than any of us.

"So, when the Underworld is suddenly drawn to the attention of people in high places—some low ones, too—it becomes apparent to thinking men that there is some mystery here. What is the whole content of the mystery? Who is involved? I don't know. I've no way of finding out what Heres thinks, or what really happened to Joth Magner, or what Harkanter is in the process of finding out this very moment. I don't know. But I do know *you* know. And so I come to you, in search of a solution.

"Is that a fair summary? Does that exhaust our common ground?"

Sisyr was still "smiling." Warnet wondered whether it was a smile at all. Perhaps a deliberate mockery. For a brief moment, he felt a wave of eeriness as he realized that Sisyr might be registering fierce anger or carnal lust, and he—Warnet—could never know. All that passed between them must be words. Outside the words, one could be sure of nothing. Implication and inference might be vastly different. This was an alien being.

"Were you surprised to discover that there were men in the Underworld?" asked Sisyr.

"At first," said the human. "But when I thought about it, why not? I was surprised when I first met the rumor that the Underworld was a living, starlit world, but it wasn't nonsense, by any means. We didn't all come up from the surface in a long line, like the animals into Noah's Ark. The platform was raised from below—it didn't fall from Heaven. Of course there are lights in the Underworld. And why not leave them on, when the Overworld was sealed? If there were men still on the ground, it would be a gesture of common humanity.

"While I thought about Magner's book it occurred to me that there was almost inevitably a living world on the old surface. We left it wrecked, because it could support civilization no longer, but once we were gone from it the situation was vastly different, was it not? A ruined world, from our point of view, would not have to be a dead world, or a destroyed world. We came out of it into our new Heaven not because we desperately wanted life, but because we desperately wanted our descendants to live the kind of life the Planners thought was appropriate to humanity.

"It suddenly occurred to me while I read Magner's book how utterly absurd it was that we—the Euchronians—should have taken it so readily for granted that what we left behind was dead and gone for all time. Absurd . . . but how predictable! How typical of the Euchronian way of thinking. The Planners built their wonderful new world—thanks to you. They fulfilled their ambition of making their children into parasites, completely helpless apart from their custom-designed host. That was their ideal mode of life—the parasitic. Mechanical, undemanding, comfortable, assured not by human effort but by the endeavor—the ceaseless, ultimately *reliable* endeavor—of the machine. That's the Overworld: a gigantic, living machine, upon which we humans are content to be parasitic. Of course we forget the world which we left behind—the harsh and hostile *real* world. What do we care where the monster rests its belly? What do we care how the host has to work to make its living, just so long as it lives well enough for us to supply our own needs from its excesses? That's why we don't look up into the sky, either. That's why there's been a spaceship and a starman on Earth for ten thousand years, and yet no human has ever been into interstellar space, and no human has ever tried to build his own spaceship.

"I'm sorry. You asked me whether I was surprised to discover that there were men in the Underworld. No. Not at all. It would be more surprising, if you like, to discover that there are men in the Overworld."

Sisyr completely ignored the content of Warnet's carefully calculated outburst. He had nothing to say about the image of man as a parasite within the metal monster which he had brought into being.

"Knowledge," said the alien, apparently speaking with some care, for he spoke slowly, "is always adapted to need. One learns what one needs to know. Forgetfulness is a useful talent, as you must know. You live ephemeral lives. It is necessary that you should have a world which is . . . to some extent . . . forgettable. It is simply not possible for you to live in a *whole* world. Because of what you are, you are less than what you want to be."

"And what about you?" demanded Warnet.

"It is the same."

"You're not ephemeral. You're immortal."

"There are other limits," said Sisyr.

"Let's return to simpler matters," said Warnet. "I seem to be reaching no better understanding this way. May I, perhaps, be permitted to recall some of the things that Euchronia has found it . . . necessary . . . to forget?"

"I will answer your questions."

"You supply the Underworld?"

"I do. It has been going on for so long . . . it is almost a ritual now, with us—certainly with them."

"You also study the Underworld?"

"Not closely. My agents bring me their books, their work. It helps me to understand. But there is no direct study. I do not know everything about the Underworld—perhaps very little more than you have already guessed."

Warnet came to his big question. "Does the Council know that you are doing these things?"

"No," said the alien.

"*Is* it part of the Plan?"

"Perhaps. As you say, some of the Planning was mine. It would not be unrealistic to say that my actions were in accordance with the Plan, that they helped to ensure its completion without too much strife and bloodshed."

"You know that I intend to exploit this information in trying to bring down the Council?"

"Yes."

"Then why give it to me? You don't favor the Euchronians, obviously. Are you against them? Do you disapprove of them?"

"No."

"Then why help me? Why tell me this?"

"I have no secrets. Had the Council wanted to know . . . knowledge is adapted to need."

Warnet had finished his wine some time ago. Now he took the time to put the glass down, pausing for thought. He reminded himself that he could not make assumptions about the alien. The understanding which he had was inevitably an illusion of his own senses, only real in a limited context.

"This is your world, too," said Warnet. "Have you no interest in how it is run?"

"This is my world," said Sisyr, "but it is your society. No, I have no interest in your politics. They are a purely ephemeral concern. I do not want that to sound critical . . . you understand that I am not decrying your motives and your actions. But I think you can see that what is important to you is virtually meaningless to me. The society which you live in will change . . . is changing. Perhaps you, as an individual, will play a part in that change. That would be good . . . for you. But the Euchronian Millennium will die, and whatever follows it will die. Ideas will change, the labels will change, humanity will change . . . and I will be here, as I am. I will not say that I have no interest in change—I am most interested—but it would be pointless for me to *involve* myself in any way with change. In a sense, I cannot. I am immune to it. I could never be a part of it."

"That's not true," said Warnet. "You involved yourself with the Plan. If it were not for your involvement, the Overworld would never have been built. Even now, you are involved in the determination of change in the Underworld."

"I'm sorry. You misunderstand. It is my use of the words. When I speak of involvement, I speak from my own standpoint—you, of course, speak from yours. I helped the Planners—because they asked me to help. I accepted a contract to supply the men on the ground—again, because they asked me for such an undertaking. Men have involved me in what they do. But I do not involve myself. Nor do I involve men in what *I* do."

"Suppose," said Warnet, "that you were asked to uninvolve yourself with the Underworld. To stop supplying the ground with materials. Would you do that?"

"If the men on the ground did not want any further aid."

"And the Council? Suppose *they* ordered you to stop?"

"The Council do not order me to do anything. I am not a part of your society."

"There may come a day when the Council does not see it that way."

"Then my actions will depend on the way that they see it then."

Warnet looked at the alien pensively. "The Euchronians have remembered the Underworld. They're going to remember you, too. You know that, of course. Maybe from your point of view you don't have any part to play in our near future. But from *our* standpoint . . . you see what I mean?"

"I understand."

"I wonder if you do."

The imitation of a smile played across Sisyr's face yet again. "I understand," he said, "according to my understanding."

"I can't keep your name out of it," said the Eupsychian. "I don't want to cause you any embarrassment. I don't want to involve you against your wishes. But there's no way you can stay buried here. Not now."

"I know," said the alien. "There is always change. Nothing lasts forever."

21

Iorga declared that it was finished.

Joth, for that moment, couldn't meet the cat's eyes, but Nita and Huldi took the information as calmly as it was offered.

The hellkin had been fighting for his mate's life for a time which he knew no way to measure. He would have been prepared to continue the contest for twice as long or ten times as long. He had no real consciousness of what elapsed time meant. There was only the present in his scheme of things, and the possibilities of the present. He did not involve himself with his memory, save when it was pertinent to the moment, and he had no ambitions or intentions beyond that moment.

Just as Nita and Huldi had helped in his fight, so he had helped in theirs. Had they come earlier, they might have turned the fight for him. As it was, he had turned the fight for them, and that was all. The wound in Joth's back had not healed, but it was not so dangerous now. There was no infection—all that kept him from recovery was the fact that his capacity for bodily self-repair was not quite adequate to the conditions which prevailed in the Swithering Waste.

Now that Aelite was dead Iorga naturally transferred his purpose from the dead to the living. He had united his aims and his efforts with those of the other travelers, and now there were only their aims and purposes remaining. They remained his. Iorga was simply bound into the unitary existence of Joth, Nita and Huldi. He was absorbed into their bond of love. They were four people of four different races, and the circumstances which had conspired to combine them were unusual, but the bond was no less strong for any of that. For man and his satellite species to have survived in the Underworld at all, evolution had been necessary. Natural selection operates two ways: it favors the effective as well as eliminating the ineffective. Love is a force which is favored by natural selection because it leads to unity of purpose, collaboration, and the effective protection of offspring from the rigors of the environment. Evolution in the Underworld had favored love—a kind of love that the people of the Overworld would not have recognized, but love nevertheless. Factors which evolve for one purpose may often serve others, and perhaps the capacity for love which the people of the Underworld had inherited was not evolved to create ties of the specific kind which held Nita and Huldi and Iorga together with the man from Heaven, but such ties could and did form, and such ties could and did *work*.

Joth felt obliged to speak, when Aelite died, although he knew that the others were possessed of a fatalism which would not allow them to grieve. The same feeling which would not let him meet Iorga's eyes made him try to exercize his emotion in words.

"The smoke-cloak didn't kill her," he said. "You held that in check. You stopped it spreading."

"She was weak," said Iorga. "Too weak. All her strength was gone. We could not put it back."

"It was time," said Huldi. "Time for her to die."

The hellkin said nothing.

"Time was against her," said Joth. "But it wasn't just time. It was entropy. She just couldn't hold on to the sense of unity that held her together. Iorga wouldn't let her die, the smoke-cloak wouldn't let her live. In the end, she just evaporated. When neither side in a contest will give way, the rope they're pulling simply breaks. That's what happened."

They didn't answer. For one thing, they didn't understand. On top of that, it didn't really matter to them what had killed her. They did not have to explain how and why she had died. It was not necessary to their understanding. But they let Joth talk, because he did need to understand, in his own way. Joth, condemned to confine much of his being to remembrance, belief and introspection, had been the battlefield in a fight for life before, and he could not help but associate this moment with that one. When his face had been destroyed in the explosion, Carl Magner had fought for days, with the only weapons he had—more words—to make them repair him instead of ending his life quietly and mercifully. That battle had ended in life. This one had not—not for Aelite.

"What now?" asked Joth.

"We wait for Camlak," said Nita.

Joth tried to estimate, in his mind, how long it must have been since Iorga met Camlak. But he could not even make a guess at how much time had elapsed since Iorga had saved them from the crocodilean. There was no standard for comparison, no way to make a yardstick. It might have been days or weeks. The vital question was: where was Camlak now? Where might he have gone? If he were to return here, when would he arrive? Or when should he have arrived?

"He may wait for us, at the wall," said Joth.

"No," said Nita. She knew. She was sure.

"He might not be able to find us. In the Waste, he might cross our way again, and never know. We can't know that he will ever return here."

"We should go to Shairn," said Huldi, who obviously had no faith in Camlak's imminent arrival either.

"We are at the place where he met Iorga," said Nita. "He will come here. When he discovers that we have come back this way. He will come to this place."

"Why?" Joth protested. But no one answered.

22

Camlak never came.

Even so, they did not wait in vain. What would have happened if no one had come, Joth could not tell. In time, perhaps, Huldi's conviction that no one would come would have outweighed Nita's dwindling assurance that Camlak would return. But how long might that have taken? Joth did not know. There was no way for anyone to know. Events in the Underworld took as long as it took them to happen. That was all.

But their waiting came to an end when Chemec came into their camp and asked if he might share their food.

They had taken Aelite away from the resting place and abandoned her to the scavengers at a safe distance. It did not matter that they should have her. Joth had buried his father, but that was his way. He said nothing about what Iorga did with Aelite. That was *his* way. Chemec came to them just as they returned. He was tired and hungry. He was glad to find them, because they had warmth and food. It could not be said that they were equally glad to see him.

"What happened?" demanded Nita.

"We reached the wall—almost. There were Heaven-born. Many of them. Camlak tried to speak to them. Then he fell. I stayed in hiding. I saw them come to take him. They tied his arms—he was still, but I don't think he was dead. They carried him away. I followed them to the wall. They live there in houses like mushroom caps. They have metal —much metal. Big machines. They took Camlak into a house. The men who took him in came out again, one by one, but there were always others who went in. There were too many. I came away."

"You were going back to Shairn," said Nita.

"Yes."

"You left him to die."

"Yes."

"I don't think they'll kill him," Joth intervened. "If they tied him before they took him . . . they must have come down after my father, looking for the truth. Perhaps it's the men who shot him. I don't know. But they won't kill Camlak if they took him alive. He can tell them the truth. Everything they want to know about the Underworld. With his help, they can make the people in the world above believe in the Underworld. But . . ." He trailed off. But they wouldn't understand. That was his thought. There was no point in saying it. They couldn't understand either. Not even Nita, who understood perhaps more fully than Camlak. How could anyone understand?

What would happen when Camlak talked to the men from Heaven? Would they think that the substance of Carl Magner's dream was true? Would they want to do what Carl Magner had demanded of them? What would happen to Camlak?

"I've got to go back," said Joth. "I've got to go back, this time."

"For Camlak?" said Nita.

"I'll try," he said. "I'll try to return Camlak to you. With all my heart, I promise you. I'll get Camlak back if I can. Perhaps I can do that first. If I go back instead of him, I can tell them. They won't want to release him, but perhaps I can make them let him go. I *will* make them let him go. I might need help. Will you help?"

"Yes," said Nita, immediately. But Joth wasn't looking at Nita. He was looking at Iorga. If it came to a fight, Nita would be little enough use. Joth was thinking, at that moment, of rescuing Camlak first and going back to the Overworld afterwards. He needed a fighting man to help him —someone who could take care of trouble. He needed Iorga, who was as big as any man, and as strong. Even Huldi was too small.

"I'll help you," said the hellkin.

"And you?" Joth stared at Chemec, who was avoiding his eyes carefully while eating steadily. The cripple looked at Joth, and then at Nita.

"Will you show us where he is?" said Joth. "That's all. You're no match for a full-grown man—I won't ask you to go into the camp. But you have to show us where Camlak was taken."

Chemec nodded. For a fleeting instant, he smiled—a smile of pure joy. He had killed a Heaven-man, once. Bent-legged as he was, he had taken the skull of a Heaven-born.

It had been a good moment. That was in the days of Yami's way.

The image in his mind faded almost as it was recalled. The smile was born and died, in a fraction of a second.

"I'll show you," he said. "But I sleep first."

"We all sleep," said Joth, suddenly taking it upon himself to assume leadership. "Then we go get Camlak back."

He felt a strange satisfaction at the making of the decision. Underworld ways were infecting him. It was good to have a destination and a purpose. It was good to be committed, to know where—and when—he was. The *why* of the matter tended to get lost, but he was not so committed to the Underworld as not to know. He did know why. He had any number of reasons. The simplest of all was that Camlak had been good to him. Camlak was his friend. He owed it to the Old Man of Stalhelm to deliver him from his enemies, from those who would inevitably abuse him.

23

The camp was sleeping. That included Gregor Zuvara, who was notionally on watch. The rotation of sentry duty was regarded as a nuisance by most members of the expedition, who felt that they had better—or at least more interesting —things to do with their time. Hardly anyone thought that it was necessary, anyhow. They had all seen the rat-man, who did not seem a fearsome creature at all: child-size and sleeping peacefully. Zuvara, who had been at least partly responsible for the establishment of the duty, was even more off-handed about it than most. His attempt to stay awake on the night watch had been distinctly half-hearted. (In Underworld terms, of course, they were *all* night watches. But the expedition was still keeping religiously to Overworld timing.) Zuvara was not expecting visitors.

The attitude of the Overworlders to the matter of security was mildly curious. It was not that they were not afraid —every one of them was fully conscious of being a stranger in an alien world. But their fear did not make them vigilant. They were unsure in their reaction to what they felt. The

instinctive alertness which should have been associated with
it was not quite gone, but their instincts were unrehearsed,
blocked out of their being by the i-minus effect. Their fear
was not constructive.

Joth Magner, though, had learned the meaning of fear.
The i-minus agent had been leached from his body, and he
had slept for very long periods after his initial introduction
into Stalhelm. He had dreamed, and his mind had learned.
Now he knew how to use his fear, how to accommodate
and respond to it. When he came from the edge of the
Swithering Waste into the camp of the Heaven-sent he moved
like a man of Hell. Silently, carefully, balanced on the adrena-
lin thread of his emotional tension. He led the way, and
Iorga followed. They went straight for the tent which Chemec had indicated to them, not even pausing to relieve the
sleeping lookout of his gun.

The tent to which they came was one of the largest—a
vast plastic inflatable supported on rigidified half-hoops. Its
door was inset, with a press-seal and an antechamber. Offset from the antechamber were shower baths connected to
giant steel cylinders containing a sterilizing agent. The heavy
suits for outdoor wear were gathered in a long series in a
second invagination of the inner chamber. Joth and Iorga
came through easily, leaving both seals undone and the flaps
caught back, in case a hasty exit became necessary. That
they were exposing the men in the tent to possible contamination did not worry Joth. Indeed, he found a certain
wry pleasure in the idea. He had been pitched into the
Underworld without protective clothing, with no face-mask
or gloves, and he had survived. If these men wanted to get to
know the Underworld, then they could get to know it *his*
way, and welcome.

Once inside, Joth searched the tent carefully with his
eyes. There was absolutely no sign of Camlak. Neither cage
nor coffin. There were four beds in the tent, but three were
empty. Joth found this ominous. The man outside might belong to one of the beds, but if two men were missing there
was only one place that they could logically be. They must
have gone back to the Overworld. Carrying their prize.

The deduction, however, was not enough. Joth needed to be
sure. The man who slept alone in the big tent was Felipe Rath.
He was sleeping deeply—the kind of slumber which once
had been called the sleep of the just. He had been working
hard. His bird had gone out and returned three times, each

time bringing back long series of film. He had transmitted
the pictures back to the cybernet by wireless telephone, and
signals had been coming back all day to the mapping deck
which he had brought out. The deck had been producing
photographs and numerical analyses and maps for several
hours. Most of the paper he had been content to pile up for
later reference, but he had been unable to resist the temptation to collate some of the maps and get some idea of the
kind of world into which he had come. A good deal of the
paper was still strewn on the floor beside the deck and
around the bunk, but Joth managed to avoid stepping on
it and rustling it. He put his hand to Rath's throat and
squeezed hard, letting the pain and the asphyxiation wake
the scientist.

Rath's eyes opened, the pupils recoiling and dilating as
they adjusted to the dim light of the single lamp. When he
saw Joth's face he was stricken by terror. It was not surprising. It had happened to many other people under much
kinder circumstances.

"Don't make any noise," said Joth softly. "I'm going to let
go of your throat. But if you shout I'll cut it." He showed
the terrorized Rath Nita's small knife. Iorga kept well back,
shadowed from the lamplight. It was bad enough for Rath
to wake up looking into Joth's steel face, without having
him see the cat as well.

Rath gasped as Joth released him, but did not cry out.
His eyes moved away from the metal face, traveling down
the length of Joth's crouching body. Joth knew what the
other was seeing. Not a man but a savage half-beast in
rotted clothing, covered with dirt, no doubt with a stink
that was bordering on the overpowering. But Joth could
smell Rath, too. He waited for the look of horror to die
from the face of flesh, and for the realization to dawn, if
it was going to.

It did.

"I know who you are," said Rath, in a coarse whisper
which was just too loud for Joth's liking.

"I'm Joth Magner."

"I . . ."

"Yes. You know. You never saw me before, but you
know."

"They think you're dead."

"I'm not."

"The grave! It was you. You dug it. It *was* your father. You met him. Here, at the doorway. He *did* know."

Joth put a hand to the other man's mouth. Rath flinched from the touch, an expression on his face which suggested that he had just tasted—or imagined—something extremely foul. His mouth closed like a trap.

"Shut up and listen," said Joth. "My father *didn't* know, but that's not for now. There'll be time. Later. Maybe much later. For now, I want to know what happened to Camlak. Did he tell you his name? No, never mind that. I don't suppose you gave him the chance. The man that you took in the wilderness. You know who I mean."

Rath looked at him as if he were mad. Then the Overworlder's pale eyes slipped past Joth for the first time, realizing that his assailant was not alone. Joth watched Rath's eyes widen again. He could not see Iorga's face, but he could see the silhouette, and he knew that it was not a human shape.

"What is this?" said Rath.

"Keep quiet. I meant what I said about your throat. Not for my sake. I have nothing against you. But if they see *him,* there's likely to be shooting. I don't want that. I want to know where you took the man you captured."

"It's not a man," said Rath, the strain making his voice taut and high. "It was a rat. You must know that."

Joth shook his head. "Never mind that. Where is he?"

"Harkanter took him."

"Up above?"

"Right."

"Good." Joth nodded, as though he was offering encouragement to a child. "Now tell me where. Exactly. The geographical location."

Rath's eyes flared. "I don't know! Harkanter . . . maybe his house, at least to start with . . . but I don't know."

"All right," said Joth, smoothly. "Don't panic. This Harkanter. His first name?"

"Randal."

"I can find him. That's fine. Now something else. Who killed my father?"

For a moment, Rath could find no words. It was completely unexpected. He didn't know what kind of a reply to give. From the midst of his confusion emerged the realization that Joth thought the expedition might be connected with the assassination.

"No," he said. "I mean . . . I don't know. Nobody knows. He was shot from a car. Ravelvent saw it. And your sister. But nobody knows who or why. We came down to find out—that as well as other things. He was murdered by a man in a car. None of us had anything to do with it. I swear it."

Joth nodded again, several times. He was thinking hard.

Rath's eyes were on the knife. "But you're a man," he said, in a voice that was even tinier than his whispers. "You're a man."

"I don't look it," said Joth, "do I?"

"You're with *them*."

Joth felt tempted to laugh. He had not laughed for a long time.

"My father's son," he said. "Champion of the Underworld."

"Why didn't you come back? Why didn't you come to tell us?"

"I *have* come back. I will tell you. But not yet. There's something I have to do first."

"The rat?"

"The man. Camlak."

Rath shook his head, trying to move himself away from the point of the knife. But it followed him, hovering only an inch from his adam's apple. "Harkanter," he murmured. "Taken him back."

"What for?" Joth demanded. "To show off? How did they take him. Walking? Or drugged, caged, tied?"

"He was still drugged," said Rath feebly. "In the cage."

Joth took the knife away. Rath sagged slightly. There was a moment's frozen silence.

"I don't understand," said Rath.

"I don't suppose you do," said Joth, now seeming a little weak himself. Rath scanned the metal visage, no longer quite so frightening, and then he looked at the shoulder, where the livid wound showed through the vast hole in the shirt.

"What's *happened* to you?" said Rath.

"I've found out the truth," Joth told him. "In a rather more direct manner than the way you have planned. I know what this world is like."

"Your father . . ."

" . . . was wrong. But not the way you think. There's more to it than that."

"I don't know. Not yet."

"No," said Joth. "You can't." Abruptly, he stood. But he did not move away. He simply looked down at Rath. Rath stared back, the fear coming back again in a sudden rush.

"Where are you going?" he said.

"I want you to go back to sleep," said Joth. "What I tell you now is true, and you had better believe it. If you don't, or if you go against what I say, then you'll end up dead. I mean that. There are more . . . men . . . waiting out in the Waste. Don't bother to try and trap them. You won't. They'll be watching. Don't rouse the camp. Don't raise any kind of alarm. Not now, not when you all wake up to go about your business. Forget what's happened. Above all else, don't contact the upper world. If this man Harkanter is alerted, I'll kill you. If I don't come back, someone else will kill you. That's a promise. Do you understand?"

"Where . . . ?"

"Do you understand?"

"Yes."

"You believe me?"

"Yes."

"No alarm?"

"No."

There was a pause. Joth was making every effort to scare the man into obeying him. He thought that he could do it. If not . . . then whatever would happen would happen. There was no way to make sure Rath kept his word, no way to exact retribution if he did not.

"What are you going to do?" breathed Rath.

Joth was searching the room with his eyes for the second time. He did not answer immediately. Before doing so, he picked up a rifle and a pistol from the table where they were ready to be picked up by anyone who wanted to go out into the Waste.

"I'm going up," he said, finally. "To the Face of Heaven."

As they left the tent, Joth sealed the flaps. But the smell lingered behind him, and Rath suddenly felt utterly contaminated.

24

At the great metal door, he stopped.

"You must go back," he said to Iorga.

"I will come," said the cat.

"You don't know what it's like. You can have no idea. It's my world, not yours. I think I should go up alone."

"I will come with you," said the cat, again. He was not insistent. He was merely stating his decision. If Joth had ordered him to stay in the Underworld, he would probably have accepted the order. But in truth, Joth did not want to go back to his own world alone. He wanted Iorga's strength. It would be night in the Overworld now—he knew that because the camp was sleeping. If Iorga did not have to see the sun, why should the Overworld hold any particular terrors for him?

He said nothing. He opened the door, and they began to climb the stairs, together.

25

"I think that you can help us," said Rypeck.

"I hope that I can tell you what you want to know," purred Sisyr.

Rypeck was sitting exactly as Warnet had sat, in the same chair. The expression of controlled politeness on his face was precisely the same. The faint sensation which he felt, of being imminently engaged in some kind of conflict, was precisely the same. Of all this, Rypeck remained, of course, completely unaware. Sisyr did not smile at the thought—if, in fact, the comparison was in his thoughts. Sisyr only smiled at human thoughts.

"What do you think of this so-called Second Euchronian Plan?" asked Rypeck.

"In what way?"

"Do you think it's practical?"

"Anything can be done, given the requisite time and the requisite determination," said Sisyr.

"Do we have those?"

"That is for you to decide," Sisyr pointed out.

Rypeck paused for a moment, wondering how to phrase a question so as to extract the kind of answer which he wanted.

"Do you think that the Plan will be a good thing for our society?" he asked.

"That, also, is for you to decide," said the alien, again.

"Do you believe that it will actually come to pass?" Rypeck tried again. "Will we actually manage to reclaim the Underworld?"

Now Sisyr hesitated. Finally, he said: "No."

Rypeck felt a slight surge of excitement. This was what he wanted to hear. This was what he wanted to know. There was no empirical reason why he should be pleased to discover that—in the opinion of the one person qualified to offer an opinion—the scheme would not succeed, but there was an undeniable element of pleasure in the brief sensation.

"It's been argued," said Rypeck, "that we have desperate need of a Plan. The heart of the Euchronian philosophy is Planning. Some people say that we should have begun a second Plan before we even finished the first. The Movement exists to Plan, they say. Euchronia exists to Plan. Each Millennium, they say, should be a beginning as well as an end."

"And what do you say?" asked the alien.

"I say: why? Why is the point of ends which are only beginnings? If the purpose of the first Plan was only to create the opportunity for a second Plan, would it ever have worked? I believe that the first Plan was successful only because it promised to deliver something real, solid, worthwhile and permanent. I believe that we should secure what we have made. I believe that the Second Plan is an exercise calculated to divert our attention from the real area of concern—which is the Overworld and Euchronian society. Perhaps we do need a Plan, but not this one. We need a Plan which will work with what we already have—one which looks to the future. This Plan looks backwards in time. I don't like that."

Sisyr said nothing.

"Tell me," said Rypeck. "You were in very large measure responsible for the success of the first Euchronian Plan. Perhaps you had little enough to do with its ends, but you had everything to do with the means. Are you, then, a Euchronian? Did you believe in the Plan and what it was trying to accomplish?"

"In your terms," said the alien, "no."

Rypeck stared into the depths of his wineglass for a moment or so, while he digested the implications of that remark.

"I expected something exotic," he said, tilting the wineglass to show that he was referring to the wine. He was trying to fill in the gap before his next plunge into the esoteric realms of alien rationality.

"Wine from a distant star," said Sisyr, his voice deliberately conveying lightness and humor.

"Perhaps," said Rypeck. "Unusual, at any rate."

"Earth is my home," said Sisyr. "I live very much as you do."

"But you don't," countered Rypeck. "You don't live as we do. You live forever. You live outside our society, outside our terms of reference. Relative to Euchronia, you have objectivity. You can see what we do not in terms of our immediate future, or all the future we can reach in our imagination, but in terms of absolute time."

"There is no such thing," said the alien. "My view of your world is as subjective as your own. Mine is a different subjectivity, but is is formed in the same way: by experience. I have not lived through all of time. Even if I had, there is all of time still to come. I am not a man, but I am only an animal, just as a man is only an animal. I am sentient, as a man is sentient. I am not transient, but even a man is not ephemeral compared to those creatures which he has named the ephemerae. Are you objective enough to pronounce ultimate judgment on the destiny of the mayfly? Such a question is meaningless. What do you want to make of me? A god? Or simply the mouthpiece of a godly concept which you have, named Truth or Reason? There are no gods of the kind you want to make. There are realms beyond those you can perceive, beyond those you can imagine. But they are *real* realms, not quintessential dimensions superimposed upon your own. They are populated by real beings, living real lives, who are no less and no more relevant to your lives than you are to theirs.

"I do not know what kind of advice you want from me, my friend. I will tell you what I know in answer to any of your questions. But you must not try and make me into something I am not. You would not understand if I told you that I am only human, so I tell you that I am only animal. But I am forced to do so only because your concept of 'humanity' is so narrow."

Rypeck shook his head. "I'm sorry," he said, "but I can't think of you as 'only human.' I don't want to make you into a god, or a priest, or a seer, or a mouthpiece for some imaginary ultimate. But what you actually *are*—alien, immortal, enigmatic, knowing more than the whole human race knows—all this means that I cannot think of you as human."

Sisyr bowed his head. "I apologize," he said. "It is difficult. What you see in me, and what I see in you . . . there is little enough understanding between us. Forgive me. But please accept my answers to your questions. They are the answers I see, even though they are not answers as you see them. Please ask your questions."

Rypeck allowed a minute to drain past, emptying the air of confusion.

"Do you know what I mean by i-minus?" he asked.

"Yes."

"Please tell me. I . . . have to know that you know."

"It is the effect by which your Planners attempted to unify the Euchronian Movement when the Plan seemed endangered. By secret censorship of dreams and intensive propaganda in association they contrived to commit everyone involved in the movement to a single set of ideals and perspectives. The active propaganda became unnecessary very quickly—once it had 'taken' it was self-perpetuating. The agent to suppress what your scientists called the 'instinctive' input into dreams continued to be supplied. It still is. In order to control and monitor the administration of the drug the Planners laid down strict rules as to which persons and groups of persons were to know of its existence and purpose. As an executive body in charge of the secret itself they established a 'Close Council' to whom all those party to the secret would be responsible. You, I believe, were coopted into this Close Council on the death of one of its members shortly after you were elected to the Council sixty years ago."

"You seem to know more than I do," commented Rypeck.

"Probably," agreed Sisyr.

"I did not know that the Plan was endangered."

"It was never admitted. History is always subject to the most stringent censorship."

"You also seem less than certain about the operation of the agent. Are we wrong in believing that it controls the instinctive input into dreams, thereby short-circuiting the programming of instinctive behavior and response into the individual?"

"You are not wrong," said Sisyr. "But I do not see the process in quite those terms. What you understand as 'instinct' I understand in a rather different way. But it is merely a way of looking at things. Your conceptual model of the way that the brain works is no less real than mine."

Rypeck did not know quite how to interpret this statement.

"We believe," he said carefully, "that the i-minus agent secures social stability. I, personally, believe that its use should be discontinued because its presumed effects, as reflected in our everyday life, do not seem to me to be ultimately desirable. Heres, and others, argue that if it were not for the cohesive effect of the i-minus agent, our society might well begin to disintegrate entirely. I will not ask you whether you believe the agent to be beneficial, because you would not answer, but I ask you this: in your opinion, would the discontinuation of the i-minus project result in the destabilization of our society?"

"I will try to answer," said the alien, "but you must remember what I have already said. My answers are not necessarily yours. Your society is not stable. Change cannot be defeated, by any means whatsoever. In terms of the relative stability of your present situation, I would say that the i-minus effect is quite irrelevant. May I suggest—and this is merely a suggestion—that you consider the possibility that the apparent *need* for commitment to a new Plan is the legacy of the i-minus project."

Rypeck pondered that suggestion. It was not altogether new to him. But as an argumentative weapon, it was distinctly two-edged. As an argument against *both* the Second Plan and the i-minus project it was viable, but from the standpoint of someone committed to either, it would become an argument in favor of the other.

He began another line of inquiry.

"Suppose the Council were to approach you and ask for your help with respect to this Plan, just as they asked for you help with the old Plan. Would you give that help?"

"This time, my help is not needed," said Sisyr, ambiguously. "But I am always ready to help, in certain ways. There are kinds of help I cannot give, but my knowledge is always at the disposal of anyone who cares to ask."

Rypeck eyed the alien carefully. "Knowledge can be misused," he pointed out.

"Can it?" said Sisyr, blandly.

"If you favor one side in a conflict with knowledge which the other side does not possess, you give weight to that element of the conflict. However external you may be to the quarrel there remains an implicit judgment in your aid. You provide knowledge which supplements belief and morality. In a war, the side with your knowledge might win whereas under other circumstances it would have lost. Suppose the side which asked for your help were the aggressors? Suppose they used your knowledge to slaughter their enemies, or enslave them? Suppose both sides asked for your help, and you aided both, so that the result of the war, in terms of winning, was not altered, but that hundreds of thousands of people were killed, who need not have been had the warring parties not had access to the knowledge which made such slaughter possible?"

"For such help as I give," said Sisyr. "I accept the responsibility. The consequences of my actions have to be weighed—according to my standards and precepts. But what you describe as the possible consequences of action can, under other circumstances, be the consequences of inaction. My presence on Earth is a fact. When I am asked for help, I have to weigh the consequences of refusal as well as the consequences of agreement. According to my own morality. It is always possible—inevitable—that when some of you will judge me right, others will judge me wrong. In the end, only I can decide—but I cannot decide according to your criteria."

"I see," said Rypeck. "Then may I suggest—and this is only a suggestion—that you consider the following possibility. Neither Heres nor the Council will approach you for help with the Second Plan. They will see the Second Plan as an opportunity to accomplish something that is completely the work of the Euchronian Movement. They have claimed the credit for the first Plan, and perhaps that is right. They have excluded you from their history and their memory so far as is politic and practical. They do not want you in the Second Plan. They want to do without you, to prove to themselves that Euchronia is adequate.

"In this instance, therefore, we do not need to concern ourselves with the possibilities inherent in your action. What we do need to consider, however, are the possibilities inherent in your continued inaction. If you do nothing, then the i-minus project will continue, and the Second Plan will get under way. You have already said that you do not believe the Plan will succeed. The Underworld will not be reclaimed. We face failure, therefore. What would that do to our world? What is going to happen to both the Overworld and the Underworld if Heres' scheme marches forward to its failure? I offer these thoughts for your consideration. I do not ask you to intervene now, to further my aims or Euchronia's aims. I just ask you to think."

Sisyr nodded. Rypeck's suggestion was no more new to him than his had been to Rypeck.

"You know that the Underworld is lighted by electric stars?" said Rypeck, changing direction again.

"Yes," said Sisyr.

"You know that the Underworld is supplied with materials from the Overworld, somehow?"

"Yes."

"You know how?"

"Yes."

"No need to go into it now. I'll ask some other time. It's not important. Suppose that the Underworld doesn't want to be reclaimed. Suppose the Second Euchronian Plan becomes an all-out catastrophe. A conflict of motives. If Heres and the Council decide to reclaim the Underworld *in spite of* the Underworld, and it comes to war, who do you help? The Overworld, by inaction, or the Underworld, by intervention? What happens when Heres puts the stars out? Do you switch them on again, or do you let us destroy the Underworld before we can turn it into a garden? Just tell me that."

"I cannot see the future," said Sisyr, who appeared to be smiling. "And if I could, I am sure I would not see the kind of future that you see. I cannot decide on the kind of criteria by which you make your decisions. But I will say this. You think of two worlds, where I see only one. You have forgotten the Underworld, but it is still there, and whether you remember it or not, it is still a component of your past, your present, and your future. It is real. You have only rediscovered it in your imagination. Do not make the mistake of assuming that what you find *there* is real.

"I am not the only alien on Earth."

26

Iorga looked up at the stars. The real stars, unsteady in the sky. He watched the racing clouds, which dressed and un- dressed the pockmarked face of the moon. He breathed the fresh, clean, cold air.

And he shivered.

Joth stood by the roadside and watched him, impassive but keenly observant.

He isn't overcome with awe or fear, thought Joth. Does he feel fear? Of course. But he knows fear. He lives in con- stant company with it. It is under control. It's a healthy fear. There's no trace of superstitious terror in him. He knows this world is real. What he sees, he can name, even if he can't understand. This is a savage, and perhaps an ig- norant savage, but his mind isn't so limited. He knew this world was here, and he knew something of its nature. He isn't shocked. This is no challenge to his erstwhile under- standing of the universe.

And yet, Joth's thoughts continued, this is his Heaven. This is what supplies, for him, the image of the other world. This is his Valhalla, his Olympus. Only it's not populated by gods and the spirits of the departed. Men live here. Ordi- nary men . . . and one or two with metal faces. He accepts even that. His world is a complex place—inherently strange enough to include men with steel faces . . . friends with steel faces. This world is real to him. Strange, but not alien. In prehistoric times, when the farmers came to the city, when the poor invaded the land of the rich, or the rich the realms of the poor, they may have felt as he feels now.

Alone and afraid, but still entombed in reality. In a world unknown, but knowable. Genuine.

Joth's interpretation of Iorga's feelings was, perhaps, accurate enough. Iorga could not have discovered words to give an alternative account. But Joth could not really know. He could understand, but only according to his own way of seeing. In the final analysis, his analogies were limited, as all analogies are.

"We must hurry," said Joth. "There's not enough time left to do what we must tonight, so we have to find shelter for the day. A hiding place. If the people down below alert Harkanter, that's too bad. I hope they won't. Either way, if I can get to a public phone I'll requisition transport from the net. We'll go home. You can lie up in a dark room, and I can get a doctor for my back. After nightfall, we go find Camlak."

Iorga signaled his agreement without speaking.

"If the sun comes up," said Joth, "shield your eyes. If you look at it you'll be blinded."

Iorga nodded again.

Joth balanced the two guns which he had stolen from Rath in his two hands.

"You take the pistol," he said. "You know how it works?"

"No."

"That's a catch to stop it firing. Keep it sealed until you want to use the gun. Then release it, point the barrel, and press the trigger. Be careful. Don't shoot unless someone points one at you. It shouldn't be necessary to kill anyone. I don't want anyone to get hurt. All right?"

They moved off together, away from the plexus and into the night.

27

Randal Harkanter shook hands all around. There were a lot of hands to shake. He had invited a lot of people to his little surprise.

Vicente Soron fluttered round like a butterfly, nervous and excited. No one in the crowd knew who he was. Nobody cared. All eyes were on Harkanter, the man with charisma.

Among the guests, it was Yvon Emerich who naturally assumed the lead. Of all the people there he was the only one used to real crowds. For gathering in this fashion was not customary. People who lived their lives by courtesy of machines gradually become . . . sensitive . . . to the proximity of large quantities of flesh. It seems unnatural. But Emerich knew the small skills of organizing crowds in order to keep uneasiness at bay. His aide, Alwyn Ballow, was a tower of strength in his support.

There was one member of the Council present—Javan Sobol—but the Euchronian Movement was conspicuously underrepresented relative to prominent anti-Euchronians. Sobol had observed this discrepancy within minutes, but he read nothing into it. Harkanter was not popular with the average Hoh-playing, propriety-observing Euchronians. Sobol had no idea what Harkanter planned to show them, but it did not occur to him for a moment that it might be a revelation which intimately concerned Council decisions. Joel Dayling, who considered himself the leader of the Eupsychian opposition to the Council, was equally unaware of the nature and magnitude of the planned surprise. Harkanter, who slotted naturally and comfortably into the role of showman, had given out no hints, except perhaps to Ballow, who needed some leverage in order to make sure that Yvon Emerich would be sufficiently interested to turn up.

"You didn't stay long downstairs," said Emerich to his host, loud enough for anyone interested to hear. "What brought you back? Or sent you back? Have you had a revelation like Magner's?"

"In a manner of speaking," Harkanter answered.

"Then you've come to propose marriage," said Emerich. "Tell us, please, whether Euchronia is to be the bride or the groom?" Emerich was being deliberately trivial and inane. He liked to appear something of the eccentric, something of the clown, in his private *persona*. He believed it necessary to retain what he saw as his real self (incisive, brilliant and destructive) for "his" public, who met him only through the medium of their holovisual pseudoreality. He was their idol and their champion—his facade was theirs, packaged and distributed by the machine.

"If what you have to say concerns the Underworld," said Sobol, "I'm not sure that we'd rather not hear it. We've heard far too much of late, and we'd have been perfectly pleased if your little party down there had gone on for a year or two before coming back to bore us with all the latest news from Tartarus."

"That will be heresy this time next week," Dayling intervened. "Now we have a Second Euchronian Plan any negative thought regarding the Underworld will be anti-Euchronian. If I were you, Javan, I'd be careful what I said. You might end up driving a tractor instead of running the world."

"It will all be done by remote control," said Sobol. "This isn't the age of psychosis. We have the resources of the cybernet behind us. The machines will roll out of the factories and into the Underworld, and they'll all be controlled by a handful of men in a handful of control rooms. There will have to be a few men to go down to ground level, but I assure you that no one will need to get their hands dirty. It will all go very smoothly. It won't take ten thousand years, either. I wouldn't be at all surprised if some of us live to see the job nearly done."

For the most part, the speech fell on deaf ears. Most of the audience deserted him before he closed, and independent conversation sprang up in two or three places. One man, however, could not resist pointing out to Sobol the error of his assumptions. That was Vicente Soron. Ironically, he was one of the few people in the gathering who were actually more dedicated to Euchronia than the councillor himself.

"Javan," said Soron, in a low voice, "there isn't going to be a Second Euchronian Plan. You don't understand."

"Nonsense," said Sobol, whose faith in Heres was implicit.

"It's all a terrible mistake," said Soron, the intensity of his voice making little impact on his listener's conviction. "A terrible mistake. You'll see . . ."

He drifted off, carried away by a current of movement which began as Harkanter ended the preliminaries and led the group into another room. Here there was room for them to sit, while Harkanter explained. They did so, arranging themselves most carefully. Emerich sat off to one side, and Sobol was content to stay back. Lesser individuals were permitted to gather at the big man's feet. Dayling sat in the center, staring Harkanter full in the face. He wondered what it was all about. Harkanter seemed to be building up to a trick of some kind—a big joke. He could practically see the laugh poised in Harkanter's throat. Knowing the big man as he did, Dayling wondered who that laugh was going to hurt.

Harkanter began to tell them about his experiences in the Underworld. He was by no means an orator, and his descriptive powers were decidedly poor, but he rushed at his story with evident enthusiasm, and those present were prepared to bear with him for a while.

He was vague about the results of Rath's work in surveying the territory, principally because he had not waited for the results to turn up anything worthwhile. He left out the matter of the mysterious grave altogether. He concentrated on his own viewpoint and his own actions, and he succeeded in giving the impression that the whole Underworld was a gigantic polluted swamp teeming with crabs and less pleasant life-forms of lowly and loathsome nature.

He set out on a description of his walk with Soron, which Soron found to be somewhat embarrassing, and then he gave a wordy account of his own lack of good sense in getting himself stuck in the mud.

Then he paused. Knowing it was for effect, the crowd waited politely.

"It was then," concluded Harkanter, "that we found what we were really looking for."

There was no doubt in anyone's mind that he was referring to the much-discussed people of the Underworld.

"He came out of the bushes," said Harkanter, "with a dagger the length of my forearm. I was helpless—the gun was in the mud with me and if I fired it I was as likely to get killed as he was. But Vicente was magnificent. Up like a cat, with his gun in hand. One shot—all it took. Full in the chest. Went down all in a heap and never raised a finger again. Then Vicente went off like a hare to get the men out of camp to drag me out of the mudhole and cart the carrion home. Only it's not carrion. It's alive. And it's here."

The silence did not last long.

"Here?" said Emerich. "You mean, in the house."

"I brought him back," said Harkanter. "I thought you all ought to get a look at him. A good, long look. It will tell you better than I, or any man, could tell you the truth about the Underworld."

"Now wait a minute," said Sobol. "You can't . . ."

But Harkanter was already leading the way down to the cellars of his house.

28

Camlak was in a cage surrounded by screens. He had been shot full of sedatives half a dozen times since Soron had first knocked him out. Soron had been unable to estimate the dosage with much accuracy, and had been prepared to overdo things rather than run any risks. Camlak felt that he was not quite wearing his body. His mind was so sluggish that the hands on the clock on the wall, which he could just see over the top of the screens, and which was the only feature of the room accessible to his eyes, seemed to be moving very quickly indeed. He felt as if he were wholly immersed in a viscous liquid, and stretched out over a large area, yet not drawn taut. His mouth was bone dry and he felt infinitely heavy. He had been given neither food nor water since he had first been taken.

His eyes were open but they seemed to be stuck that way. He could see, but he was unable to focus his attention or withdraw his stare. The hands of the clock held his gaze absolutely.

That was *time*. Time passing. He knew.

He felt an odd echo somewhere inside himself, as though the knowledge was highly significant.

He heard the clatter of many pairs of feet coming down the stairway, but it seemed like a distant rumble, unimportant and irrelevant. In many parts of the Underworld, he knew, one could hear an omnipresent whisper which indicated the working of machinery above the sky. It was one of those things that had to be blotted out of consciousness. Real, but without meaning.

Then the screens were snatched away dramatically, and he was exposed, naked and only half alive, to the shocked stare of the people of the Overworld.

The suddenness of it was a dull jerk in his mind, to which he tried very hard to react, but he could neither move nor alter the direction of his stare. He tried to speak, but he was quite incapable of it. Only a hollow rattle passed his lips as the breath oozed out of his throat.

"I have to tell you," Randal Harkanter was saying to his guests, in a loud and commanding voice, "that the 'people' of the Underworld—the only *people* of the Underworld—are *giant rats!*"

29

The sun was rising just as Joth came home.

He indicated that Iorga should follow closely, and they went upstairs, quietly and carefully. No stealth was necessary, and he could not have explained why it came so naturally to him. But at present, even within his own home, the Overworld seemed to be a strange and unfamiliar place. He had entered it an invader, covertly.

He found his own room empty and he told Iorga to stay there. The windows were screened and only thin lines of light filtered through. Iorga would find it safe enough, if not exactly comfortable. The cat's eyes continually moved around the room, as if they felt the solidity of the walls and the perfect angularity of its construction. Unlike the Men Without Souls and the Children of the Voice, the Hellkin were not town-dwellers but nomads, who found natural shelter preferable to the crude brick and chitinous lath which provided basic material for virtually all Underworld builders.

The eyes were the only betrayal of Iorga's unease. He still moved with perfect balance and grace, he still said nothing. But inside himself, he had never felt more alone. That was particularly bad for him, because he belonged to a race which did not court loneliness, like the Cuchumanates, and possessed no foil against it, as did the Children of the Voice. A rat could never be alone while he held inside himself the access to the being which he called his Gray Soul. But if the cats had such souls, they had found no way to reach and commune with them.

Joth went into his sister's room. She was there, asleep, alone in the house. Her face on the pillow was not peaceful. How could it be? For her, this house must now be filled with ghosts. Her long-dead mother she would not remember, but Ryan and Joth, and finally her father, had all been taken from her, one after the other, in relentless succession. She had been the agent of Joth's disappearance—at least in her own mind, and the witness to her father's murder. She did not need instinct to be frightened by what she found in her dreams. She was haunted.

Joth would not have been surprised to find the house empty and deserted, with Julea gone. Why had she stayed? What was there here to hold her except memory and misery?

It was an easy answer. She was waiting. Waiting, perhaps without hope, because she had to wait. Because she did not know, for sure, that all the ghosts were the ghosts of the dead.

The ghost reached out to switch on the lamp beside the bed, turning down its intensity so that it became a dull yellow glow. He did not need to adjust his own eyes, once he had reduced the intensity. He had not yet seen the sun.

Julea awoke, her eyes flying to the light switch, and she saw Joth. Though his body and his clothing were beyond recognition his metal face stood out starkly clear as his one most meaningful feature. She knew him immediately, but she did not scream. Perhaps she had seen him hours, or even minutes, before, while she slept. The shock seemed to come slowly, but it struck deep into her, and paralyzed her body. Tears came to the corners of her eyes, but they did not fall. There was a brief period of silence, which seemed to both of them to be very long.

In the end of the silence, deep in the well of her emotions, there was utter turmoil. She did not know what to feel or to believe.

"I'm all right," said Joth, in a whisper. "I wasn't killed. I found my way back. Just take it easy."

He waited for her reply. He could have said more, but he wanted to hear her voice before he went on. The sight of her, haloed by the reflected gleam of the dim light, had reminded him that he had come back to his beginning, that this was his world, and that this was where he belonged, if he belonged anywhere.

"I thought you were dead," she said.

"Ryan's dead," he told her. "Our father died, too. I saw him die."

"So did I," she whispered.

He accepted the statement without surprise. He knew what she meant.

"But we were in different worlds," he said. Then, after a pause: "It isn't Hell. Sometimes we can come back. It's only another world."

"You're hurt," she said. Her voice was strangely cold and metallic. But she was no longer whispering, and the tautness was leaving her body.

"That's right," he said. "I want you to call a doctor. But don't tell him why. Just tell him to come."

"Why?"

"I don't want any record of my return to go into the cybernet. I requisitioned transport by remote. No voice. No one can know I'm here, yet. I want it to stay that way."

"The doctor . . ."

"He won't tell anyone. If I ask him not to. It doesn't matter so much about people—it's the net that I'm worried about. Once the net has the information, it's there for anyone to recall."

She said nothing, but she was searching his face with her eyes. She thought—she had always thought—that even the metal and the false flesh could contain meaning. But she could find nothing, and her face was clouded with uncertainty.

"It's all right," he said, gently. "There's something that I have to do, first. I'm not going back, I promise you. When I've done what I came to do, I'll declare myself. But for now, for today and tonight, I don't want anyone to know I'm here.

"If anyone asks," he added, remembering Rath, "then deny that you've seen me. I'll keep out of range of the decks and the holographic units."

She didn't understand.

"Just call the doctor," said Joth. "The quicker he gets to me, the sooner I can get my back patched up."

Julea got out of bed and dressed slowly. Then they went downstairs together, and Joth waited while his sister put a call through from the central unit to the doctor. Julea only had to ask him to come. He was ready enough to jump to the conclusion that she was in need of attention. He knew that she had been alone in the house for some time, and the unfortunate circumstances of her loneliness.

"I've got to clean myself up," said Joth. "I've been like this for so long I just don't get any dirtier. I must stink."

She followed him upstairs again, and into the bathroom. She helped him peel off the remnants of his clothing, and she

removed the makeshift bandage which concealed and protected the greater part of the vast open wound on his back.
She felt sickened by the ugliness of the tormented flesh, but
she tried hard not to react.

He could not lie down in the bath, and he could not
bear the direct impact of the hot water. She began to sponge
him with lukewarm water, without soap.

"What happened?" she asked, faintly, not knowing whether or not she wanted to know.

"I followed Burstone. I went down to take a look around.
He cut me off. Lifted the cage and left me stranded. I've
been there . . . how long have I been there?"

"Months," she said.

"Like years," he murmured. "I've aged years."

"How did you live?"

He laughed, quietly. The laughter was forced. "One lives,"
he said. "It's easy. You just go on. You start out alive and
you just carry straight on. They made me live . . . but how?
I don't know how. I ate dirt, I breathed foul air, I drank
foul water. And I just kept going, through all the fevers
and the pains. I don't know the way. I just kept on. They
brought me through."

"The people of the Underworld?"

"The people. The men in Hell."

"How did this happen?" She was referring to the wound.

"Never mind," he told her. "It doesn't matter."

"It must hurt terribly."

"It hurts," he told her, flatly. "But there comes a time
when things hurt and you just say 'so what.' Things hurt.
Life hurts, down there. You live with it."

"The book," she said. "It was all true. The dreams told
the truth."

"The dreams . . . yes, the dreams told the truth. The
dreams were real. But the book—that wasn't true. He
couldn't understand, you see. What he saw was just a confused mess of images, what he felt was just a boiling sea of
feeling. Everything all mixed up. He couldn't entangle it, because he didn't understand. He couldn't. There was no way.
The book is a mistake, Julea. It's their world. It *does* hurt,
but it's their world. We can't open it to the sun. We've
masked the Face of Heaven, just as he said, but the mask
has become the face. There's no other face, so far as they're
concerned. He didn't understand what's happened down
there in ten thousand years. They have a new world of

their own. They're new people. The men on the ground that *he* believed in don't exist. There are no people like us —just people *unlike* us. Whatever we do about the Underworld, it will be an invasion. There's nothing we *can* do, except keep to the world we have made for ourselves. That's what I'll have to make them understand . . . afterwards."

"After what?"

"Our father," he said, oblivious to her remark, following his own train of thought, "wanted to be a saint. He wanted to open up the old world as if it were the same as ever, entombed and waiting, ripe for resurrection. He wanted to go down there, a saint from Heaven to forgive and reclaim the condemned of Hell. Don't you see that the book is about *him,* not about them? They have no need of saints. The living can't be resurrected. There may be a hundred or a thousand doors to the Underworld, but it doesn't matter whether they're open or shut. Not to us, not to them. There are two worlds. Alive, different, touching. Nothing can change that. The doors can't be used. Not really."

"You used one," she said. "Burstone uses one. Back and forth, many times. Ryan said so."

"For nothing," Joth said. "It's all pointless. A thousand years ago . . . five thousand years ago . . . the job that Burstone does meant something. Not any more. The world is new. Burstone's a relic—a vestige of something that was once worthwhile but is now useless. I used a door, but it didn't make a difference. Not a meaningful difference. Camlak came through, too, but that won't mean anything either."

"Camlak?"

"A friend. My friend."

"A man from the Underworld?"

"That's right."

"I don't understand."

"Neither do I. No one can."

"Is that what you have to do? Find your friend?"

"And take him back. In the long run, it makes no difference, but for his sake. For the sake of his child. I have to undo all the trouble my father caused. I have to make sure the Underworld is left alone."

"They're going to reclaim it," she said.

"What!"

"The Hegemon announced a second Plan. We can't bring the people of the Underworld up here, so we're going to remake their world. Like ours."

"They don't know what they're doing," he whispered.

"No," she said.

There was silence. His skin was clean—relatively. He was drying himself gently, trying desperately not to tear the skin where it was scabbed and scratched.

Julea stood up. "I'll get you some clean clothes."

She was halfway into the corridor when he shouted "No!"

"What's the matter?" she asked.

"In my room . . ."

Her eyes opened wide. She was staring at him. From where she stood she could see all of his naked body, ravaged by the Underworld. It looked completely out of place in the clean, smooth environment which surrounded it. Everything was neat, everything shaped perfectly, surfaced brightly, angled precisely. Joth had brought into it the filth and the ugliness of elsewhere. For a fleeting instant, he seemed, himself, to be a kind of wound. A living scar.

"There's one of them here," she said. "A man from the Underworld."

Joth did not dare to nod or shake his head.

He said: "It's not *exactly* a man."

30

When Joachim Casorati arrived Joth was downstairs, lying full-length on a couch, face downwards. He was still unclothed, but his body was covered by a large towel.

The doctor stared at him for some moments.

"Joth," he said, finally. His tone was neutral. It was almost a formal greeting. He had defeated both his surprise and his curiosity, for the time being.

"Joachim," Joth returned the greeting. "I want you to dress some wounds. Some may need cleaning out, if there's danger of infection. I'll need some shots, but don't give me anything which will put me to sleep or slow me down. I can't wait to be put back together inch by inch. Patch me up so I work. That's all."

The doctor lifted up the towel to look at Joth's back, and then flipped back the edge to expose the big wound.

"What did this?" he asked.

"A surgeon with a knife," said Joth.

"A surgeon," repeated the doctor, blankly.

"An amateur," Joth told him. "It needed doing. I was growing something nasty and it had to be taken out. The operation was a success, the patient lived, but the healing was slow."

"I can't patch that up," said the doctor. "You need two weeks in a medical unit. How long have you been walking around in this condition? You could have died."

"You know where I've been," said Joth.

"The Underworld."

"I hadn't any choice but to walk around, just as I had no choice about the butchering."

"Did Harkanter find you?"

"No."

"Does anyone know you're back? Does anyone know where you've been?"

"No. And I don't want them to know. I'll explain it to you later. Not today, but someday soon. You'll have your chance to reassemble me. But I can't talk now. Patch me up so that I can keep going for a couple more days. Don't ask me any more questions now. All right?"

The doctor shook his head. "It's not all right," he said. He knelt to examine the wounds with his eyes and his fingers. Joth winced at every touch, but did not cry out. Casorati removed the towel altogether and looked at the abrasions on Joth's legs. Once or twice he looked more closely at specific injuries.

"I've had feelers out from the Council," commented the doctor. "About you. About your father. About your ancestry and every bug you've picked up in twenty years. They're very interested in you."

"The Council?"

"Somebody on the Council. I don't know what they wanted because I couldn't tell them."

"Don't tell them I'm back. Not yet."

Casorati shook his head again. "This is going to take time," he said. "If I do what you want I'll have to put plastic on your shoulder and back. If you wait, we can restore it. You'll lose some of the use of your left arm if I patch it. You've got enough plastic already, Joth. I don't want to put any more on if I can help it. You'll regret it later if I do. You'll have to live a hundred years with a bad arm, unless you let it heal properly."

"I want it patched."

"I'll have to requisition equipment."

"Just don't mention my name."

"What's it all for? The secrecy, the cloak-and-dagger game?"

"It's important. Requisition your equipment. How long will it take?"

"Could be hours. I'll have to give you antibiotics for some of these infections. If I dress all the wounds you'll have gel all over you."

"Just do it," said Joth. "Please."

31

"A rat?" said Warnet, incredulously.

"That's right," Dayling told him. "We all saw it. It was a rat all right. But what a rat! More than four feet long. With *hands*—tiny, but real. And Harkanter showed us the knife. Some weapon! Emerich was there, and ten or fifteen others. The only councillor was Sobol, but by now the news will be all through the Movement. Heres must be sweating. This has ruined him. His precious speech making Magner a martyr has made an absolute fool of him. When Emerich gets on the air tonight Heres will be dead and buried, politically. If we petition for an election now we're made. The platform is already cut and dried."

"Exterminate the vermin," said Warnet, drily.

"Of course."

"Don't."

Dayling reached out and grasped the younger man by the arm. Warnet recoiled slightly from the violation, but did not shake off the grip.

"This is it," he insisted. "There's going to be a wave of hysteria rippling all round the world tonight. Into every home in the world. Emerich is recording right now. He took film of the specimen while we were there last night, and he was interviewing Harkanter in the early hours. All day he'll be putting together a broadcast that will rock Euchronia on its stilts. This is our chance."

"No, Joel," said Warnet. "You don't understand. You've missed the point. Harkanter has made a mistake. You want to rush headlong after Heres. Don't you see? Heres jumped the gun, and you want to do exactly the same. We *don't know* about the Underworld. A rumor here, a specimen there, a compendium of chopped logic and uninspired guesses . . . can't you see how inadequate it all is? What sort of conclusions can we draw? If someone came up here and kidnapped a street cleaner would they conclude that nothing exists here except machines? Think about what you're doing, Joel. We need more information."

"We need to hit Heres," Dayling retorted. "Someone has to be prepared to go up against him now and make him out a fool and a traitor to the whole human race. He has to be obliterated. If we sit back and wait for more information, he'll regroup. He'll revise all his ideas and come out with more talk by the mile, and while time drags by he'll get himself out of it. Even if his head rolls do you think the Movement can't afford to lose him? *We* have to act now. *We* have to lead the attack. It's the best chance we'll ever have. Maybe the only chance. We'd be fools to lose it."

Warnet would not agree. "We'd be fools to commit ourselves. We already know better than that. We know full well that Harkanter has his facts cockeyed. Burstone wasn't trading with any rats. Sisyr was talking about humans. They *know*. Harkanter doesn't. If we start howling for the sealing of the Underworld we could run right into a trap. Heres will shift his ground. We know that. All right, where to? I'll tell you where—he'll say that Harkanter's find makes our intervention in the Underworld all the more necessary. He'll say that it is our duty to save the people of the Underworld from the menace of the rats."

"But that's just it," said Dayling. "Emerich is going on the air tonight to show that the so-called people of the Underworld *are* rats. That's Harkanter's claim!"

"Joel, he's *wrong*."

"The world doesn't know that."

"It soon will. Once Harkanter's through with his big show, what then? Do you think Burstone and others like him will sit still while this stupid lie is broadcast? What about the scientists down below? The ones who are *really* trying to find out what the Underworld is like?"

"*Then* will be later," Dayling persisted. "We can smash the Movement—the Council, at least—right *now*."

"For the sheer pleasure of breaking it? Do you think you'd last a day longer than the man you displaced when the truth finally comes out?"

"What do *you* propose?"

"That we adopt the course no one else can. We criticize Heres for rushing his fences. We criticize Harkanter for rushing *his*. We plead for sweet reason and time. We place ourselves in the right. In the long term, that will be far better for us than any panic-buying we can do now."

"Half the Euchronians will take exactly the same stance. What advantage is there in doing exactly what they do?"

Warnet paused for a moment. He took time out to dislodge Dayling's hand from his forearm. "I'm not sure that they will," he said. "Heres is in deep. He can't play for time now. He's spent all his. And the others . . . it seems to me they're far more likely to take Harkanter's evaluation of the situation at face value than we are. Most of them will *want* to believe it—they never wanted the Underworld to be resurrected at all. I think the Council might well go over like a pendulum and vote to seal it up forever. I think they may fight more bitterly between themselves than we ever thought possible."

"But if you're wrong . . ." said Dayling.

32

"We're getting deeper into trouble every minute," said Rypeck. "We've got to start pulling ourselves out now. This situation has complicated itself far too rapidly, thanks to Rafael's supposed masterstroke. I've tried to call him and he's just not available."

"We can ride out this ridiculous affair," said Acheron Spiro confidently. "Who listens to Emerich?"

"About half the world."

"Yes, but not the *Movement*. You've got to remember, Eliot, that the Movement is much bigger than this kind of scare-mongering. We work on a much vaster scale. We've had these waves of hysteria before, on a smaller scale, and none of them has amounted to anything. They pass, Eliot, they pass."

Rypeck swore silently. He felt like screaming at the other man's complacency.

"In the wider context, the problem is just the same," said Spiro, attempting to explain. "What we are facing is a loss of faith. This rumor about the rats is simply another symptom of it. The people have no *direction*. This is what Rafael's trying to give them. He's trying to give them a goal—a new vision."

"It's the vision of a blind man," said Rypeck. "I've tried to convey to all of you that we are abysmally ignorant as regards the true state of affairs, not only in the Underworld but in *our* world. The *real* reason that Rafael has embarked upon this idiot crusade on behalf of the Underworlders is purely and simply to evade the question of the i-minus agent."

"It's *irrelevant*, Eliot."

"It's not dead simply because Magner has been removed from the arena of decision. He may not have been the only one. There may be ten or ten thousand. We have to find out."

"This is an old argument, Eliot. I've heard it all before. Why did you call me?"

"I called you to suggest to you that it's time to pull out. It's time to leave Heres on his own and go our separate way."

"Who is *we?*"

"To begin with, the members of the Close Council. Enzo will be willing, and so—I think—will Clea. Dascon we don't need—he'd go down with Heres in any case. Sobol is already creating chaos outside the Close Council, and if we provide him with a base he'll come to us, and drag two-thirds of the Council with him."

"And what is this action supposed to achieve?" said Spiro, obviously unsympathetic.

"We call for a referendum on the Underworld question. We disassociate ourselves from Heres' statement in Council. We reject his Second Plan completely."

"And do . . . we . . . have any ideas of our own to propose as an alternative?"

"The cure of our own society. Isn't that our real aim? The abandonment of i-minus. A reexamination of the status quo. We don't need a second Euchronian Plan, because the *first* one hasn't yet been brought to its conclusion. That's our platform."

"You can't. It would be tantamount to undeclaring the Millennium. That's ridiculous."

"No, Acheron. It's necessary. It's vital. The Millennium, as we have called it, is a failure. It's a setback to the Plan. We must reinterpret and rethink. The *real* Millennium is not yet come. We have to face that. Rafael never could and never will."

"What makes you think that I could be persuaded to have anything to do with such a platform?" said Spiro. "If it comes to a struggle for power and support between you and Rafael, you can't win. Surely you must see that. No matter what sort of a tremor Emerich starts tonight you can't think that Rafael will be beaten. He has loyal support, Eliot, and you can count me in with that loyal support. What's more, I don't believe that Enzo and Clea will support you, either. There's no way you can get a majority of the Close Council. No way."

"That's the way you feel now, Acheron. All right. But you tune in to Emerich tonight and you watch the wind blowing. It'll blow a scare into you, Achéron. You can be sure of that. And one more thing . . ."

"Well?"

"If Heres goes . . . and go he will . . . we'll be needing a new Hegemon. He'd have to come from the Close Council, Acheron. I don't want the job. You bear that in mind, Acheron . . . Enzo and Clea aren't yet sixty, and *I don't want the job.*"

33

They had to take Julea with them. She did not want to go, and Joth would have liked to leave her behind, but it was imperative that they should be admitted to Harkanter's house. Julea could identify herself at the door and it would be opened to her. Joth could not be sure that the same would hold true for him. Even if Harkanter had not been warned by Rath, he would recognize the metal face, and he would want to know why Joth was alive and well, in the Overworld, and knocking at his door.

Julea was frightened. Paradoxically, she was frightened not so much by Iorga as by Joth. Iorga she took more or less at face value—he was strange, but in no way hostile. He was not loathsome to look at, and he said and did nothing to inspire fear in her. But Joth was different. She feared the new Joth because he did not match her image of the old. Joth had gone into the Underworld a man of Euchronia, her brother—despite his mental face he had been the least alien of beings. But the Joth who had returned was measurably distant from her. Though he assumed sufficient familiarity to stand naked before her, he did not show that familiarity in his speech or his actions. There was no *rapport* between them as they talked. The things he said, and the way which he said them, were strange to her, and he made no apparent effort to draw her into his understanding. He spoke to her as he might speak to a stranger, or someone more than strange. They had lost their point of contact. Their mutual understanding counted for nothing, now. The life they had shared had withered inside him, and the life he was living now was something apart. For the first time in her life, Julea thought of the steel face as a mask, and wondered what might lie behind it.

The long drive through the night reminded her, inevitably, of the night when Abram Ravelvent had taken her father and herself to the lonely plexus through which the staircase to the Underworld descended. The parallel between the memories added to her inner disturbance. She was glad when the destination was finally reached, but her gladness came mixed with a rush of new anxieties as she wondered what might happen now.

She identified herself at the door, and gave as her reason for presenting herself the eminently credible story that she had come to see if Harkanter knew anything about her father, who had gone into the Underworld by the same door. The intensely personal nature of the inquiry offered some sort of excuse for her presenting herself in the flesh rather than making contact *via* the cybernet.

Harkanter unsealed the door for her without question. Joth and Iorga had kept well back from the range of the door's eye, but when the eye blinked and the door yielded, they hurried forward to pass through with the girl.

Joth felt good, for the first time in a virtual eternity. His flesh had been repaired with plastic, he was clean and properly clothed, and the possible depressant effect of the antibiotics he had taken were offset by a metabolic stimulator. He felt fast, and alert, and fully alive.

Iorga was wearing black eyeshades which Joth had modified for him. Outside, in the night, he did not need them, but Harkanter's house would be full of blazing light, and the cat needed protection from that.

The room into which they came was large and furnished according to a rather bizarre conglomeration of tastes. There was a great staircase and a balcony. The curtains which decked the windows instead of screens were lush and heavy, colored wine-red. The walls were lavishly decorated with artificially aged designs in metal and smoked glass. The atmosphere of the place was anachronistic, but the release from present time was confused and ill made. It was not a scene from the prehistoric past, but a montage of ideas reflecting wholly imaginary pasts in jigsawed association.

Harkanter chose to make his appearance on the balcony. On coming through the door, Joth and Iorga had stepped sideways into an alcove in the vestibule, and were not visible from the place where Harkanter stood. Julea, however, went forward into the room. She was nervous, and her steps were tentative.

Harkanter was puzzled by her apparent trepidation, and when she caught sight of him and looked up he knew that something was wrong. But he was still thinking of the grave and wondering what—and how—to tell her what he believed. He moved to the head of the stairs, useless phrases flowing through his mind.

"I'm very sorry," he said. "I had not expected . . ." He left the sentence hanging, deliberately, but he could see that she was not going to answer. She was not going to say anything. She was waiting, with incipient terror in her eyes. The big man had begun to come down the stairs, but he stopped, suddenly. He curled the fingers of his left hand so that the tips scraped sweat from the palm.

Joth stepped out of the alcove. He was not carrying the rifle, and the pistol was not visible. There was nothing about his appearance, save for his face, which seemed immediately strange, but Harkanter could almost feel his hostility.

"Who are you?" the big man demanded.

"Joth Magner."

There was a moment's silence. Harkanter showed no evidence of surprise.

"I didn't know," said the Negro, finally. "I heard that you were dead. I didn't see you at the door."

"No."

Harkanter continued his descent. "You want to know about your father?" he said.

"I know about my father," Joth told him. "I buried him."

Harkanter continued coming down the stairs. When he reached the bottom he came forward three or four paces to stand facing Joth. They were ten or twelve feet apart.

"Then what do you want from me?" he asked, quietly.

"Why did you bring him back?" asked Joth.

"Your father?"

"No. You know who I mean. The man you captured in the Underworld."

"That wasn't a man," said Harkanter. "It was a rat. I brought it back to show the people what the inhabitants of the Underworld are really like."

"And you showed them. A rat. Did you let him speak?"

"I don't know what you mean."

"I don't know what you told Emerich," said Joth, "but it wasn't true. We've been keeping in touch with the holovisual network. They've released nothing yet, except hints. But I know that whatever you've told them is a handful of lies, and I think you know it too."

"I showed them the rat," said Harkanter blandly. "They were all free to draw their own conclusions."

"His name is Camlak," said Joth, "and he's a man."

"Vicente Soron and the science of biology say it's a rat," Harkanter insisted. "We have proof."

"So have I," said Joth. He motioned with his hand. Iorga came out of the alcove. The cat was carrying the rifle. He was quite relaxed, but he was holding the weapon in a manner which suggested unmistakably that he knew how to use it.

Harkanter stood very still for a long time. Iorga stood as tall as he, and the shaded eyes stared into his own with calm self-consciousness. But Harkanter did not see a man. He saw a caricature, a travesty. He saw a beast stood erect, clothed and armed. He read viciousness and bestiality in the face. He saw cunning, but not intellect. He saw a big cat, no more.

The last thing that Harkanter had envisaged was the Underworld extending its claws into the Overworld in order to take him to task for drugging and caging the rat. While he stood and stared, he still considered his world as inviolate —*the* world. He still considered the Underworld as a sewer, a dark hole filled with vermin. That was what he believed. His belief could not be shaken by what he saw. He could not react to Iorga's presence. There was no way that he could. Iorga and the rifle were beyond his conceptual boundaries.

"We want Camlak," said Joth.

There was no reply.

"The man you call a rat. We want him. We want to take him back."

Still no reply.

Julea, very faintly, said: "Please."

Harkanter looked at the girl. He was glad to have his attention distracted.

"It's a rat," said Harkanter, with all the force of Vicente Soron's word of scientific honor behind him.

"Just show us where you have him," said Joth. "That's all. Take us to him. We'll take care of him then."

Harkanter wanted to be stubborn, but when he turned the idea over in his mind he realized that he had no stake in the matter. The rat had fulfilled his purpose. He had played his game. He did not want the rat. Not now.

"Take him," said Harkanter. "And welcome."

He turned and led the way down to the cellars. Joth and Iorga followed. Julea, after a moment's hesitation, went after them.

Vicente Soron moved back from the door at which he had been eavesdropping, and called the police.

34

Camlak was drowning.

The oceanic swell of the drug was passing a gloved hand through his face, the fingers dragging at the mind behind the eyes, trying to claw him out of himself and spread him like a thin sliver of sunlit water on a pebble beach. It was trying to smear him into a thin sheet of egoic slime, and he felt inside himself that he was gradually melting into malleability. He was having difficulty holding himself together. The cohesive forces joining mind and brain were decaying and denaturing. He had already lost the sensations of gravity and heat to the counteractive gentleness of the drug. Soon, he knew, the force of identity would ebb away. The molecules of his mind would fly apart, their integrity ripped as if by a relentless tide, wrecked, disintegrating like a loose bundle of cotton threads. His being was no longer a knot, merely a tangle.

"Am I going to die?" he asked his Gray Soul.

The Soul was a shadow, a patch of darkness on the sunspun sheen of his slithering thoughts. It was shaped like a dart or a moth at rest. It was steady, but it appeared to waver and ripple because of the pressure that was rippling his consciousness.

"No," replied the Soul. "You won't die."

"Must I keep fighting?" asked Camlak.

"Yes."

Camlak did as he was advised. He kept fighting. But he still felt that he was losing the fight. He still felt that he was being dissolved into the thin, shallow waves, diffusing into the liquid layers of the drug which reached for him from the well of his bloodstream.

He trusted the Soul. He could see the Soul, and while he knew the Soul was there he knew that there was a chance for him to reverse the process of disintegration that was extinguishing him.

But he did not quite know how.

He struggled alone, in the abyss, for an eternity, while the molecules shuddered like windblown flags, their structures tottering and their edges crumbling and shattering, undermining him and reshaping him. The clock on the wall was lost to his eyes. The passage of time was no longer a factor in the battle.

As the pressure upon him grew, so did his own desperation, so did his own reason, and so did his need for faith in himself and in the silhouette of his Soul.

"Help me," said Camlak to the moth-shadow.

"Help yourself," said the Soul, coaxing him, asking him for an effort.

"Heal me," pleaded Camlak, who felt himself torn across.

"Heal yourself," demanded the Soul.

Camlak's mind made hands in nowhere, and extended them

outwards from the thin film of glistering light which spread
him over the surface of sucking death. The hands reached
into the naked, cold sky beyond his brain. They were reaching into *space*—a space he had never found before and
known only by implication. It was real space, with volume
and containment, but it was enfolded inside him, inside his
body and his being. He was wrapped around a whole cosmos.

Soul space.

He formed hands and his hands formed claws, and the
claws formed clutches and they reached up and up, and every
shattering, shimmering, thread-held fragment of him cried:
"Help me!"

And the Soul said: "Help yourself."

The hands continued to ascend into the empty, wasted,
derelict sky, feeling the cold and the needles of icelike fire
beating into their palms, fraying and cracking the fingers
and the claws.

Blood spilled.

But the hands did not matter.

The false flesh peeled off the unreal bones and the whited
wreckage of the fingers still reached out into the sky, hauling at false arms and clutching with the *rigor* of death at
the boundaries of the invaginated universe.

The thin strand of slime burst as the false shoulders
erupted, and then, with a single convulsive movement, the
real being grew, through the wall between the spaces, through
the shattered puppet self, free from its existential womb.

Camlak opened his mouth to drag in air, gulping and
swallowing and sucking. In the cage, the air flooded into the
lungs. In the soul-space the ultimate coldness chilled the na-
scent self.

The head opened its eyes and felt them burn in the bright-
ness, while the other felt pain and shock.

In the instant, Camlak was suspended, in transit, caught in
the process of metamorphosis, turning himself outside-in like
a snake swallowing its tail.

The mouth screamed: "Help me!"

And shadows clustered about the eyes, and claws reached
out to grip his dead hands and his shoulders. Fingers twined
in his hair and a million moth-shapes fluttered round and
round his face in black cascades, casting a kaleidoscopic
chaos of shadows on the darkening face of the carpet-mist
which had been eating Camlak's mind.

Camlak was free.

Reborn, by the power of his will and his need.
He burst into nowhere and he screamed in exultation.

35

As Joth reached out to unfasten the door to Camlak's cage he saw the torpid rat's eyes whip open. Inside the eyes he watched a sudden flare of light.

Then Camlak's scream struck him down.

Iorga, behind him, suddenly lost control of his body and collapsed to the floor like a puppet with snapped strings.

Julea folded up without a sound.

Vicente Soron, who was coming through the door, pitched forward, the momentum of his movement throwing him against the banister of the cellar steps. The gun which he had found flew from his hand, released by limp fingers, and clattered on the tiled floor of the room.

Only Harkanter had been standing quite still at the instant of the scream. He, too, felt his mind suddenly disconnected from his body, imploded into utter blackness. But he was balanced, and he did not immediately fall. His body stood, held erect and still by muscles that were momentarily frozen.

Moments later, the muscles relaxed of their own accord, and Harkanter swayed, then rolled over with exaggerated slowness to meet the ground with a solid thump.

Joth's eyes did not close immediately. He fell, but he could still see what happened while he fell. He was the only one staring full at the prisoner at the instant of the scream.

He alone saw the instant of Camlak's disappearance.

The shape of the rat seemed to become completely fluid. The body flowed into a hole that opened a core of cold light somewhere within the space that the body had occupied. Very quickly, but in finite, measurable time, Camlak's body was collected into that hold and delivered *through* it.

The release which Joth had brought came an instant too late.

36

The velocity of the shock wave was rather less than the speed of light. No electromagnetic radiation or sonic vibration was involved. The most sensitive instrumentation in the cybernet recorded only secondary phenomena—secondary, that is, relative to the Earthly continuum. Relative to the other space the wave itself was only an echo.

But it was an echo that woke a response.

The intensity of the reaction obeyed the inverse square law. Everyone within a mile or so of the location of the scream was affected in much the same way as those actually in the cellar. The reaction to the wave was the decoupling of all motor responses in the body—the effective isolation of the brain. The mechanism which permits such decoupling is located in the body known as the pons situated beneath the hind brain, and it may be assumed that it was within this body that the signal was received. Many of those affected within this range blacked out completely, and thus experienced nothing in the aftermath of the response. In other cases, however, the brain continued to operate although notionally cut off from all sensory input. The people so affected "dreamed," but the content of the dreams was only partly the issue of their own (subconscious) minds. A complex series of images transmitted by the modification of the shock wave itself were recorded, transcribed and reechoed within the program store of the subconscious mind. Engrammatic patterns were disturbed, destroyed and created. Almost all were to prove inviable, in the long term, and were broken up and erased by the mind's own defensive systems and faculties of self-repair. But that process would take time. In the meantime, the whole process of subconscious activity within the brain was disturbed. In no case was the disturbance so great as to cause permanent insanity.

Outside the critical radius at which the decoupling reaction was triggered there was no less of consciousness. By the same token, however, there was no immunity to the inflow of images. The extent to which the induced "dreams" interfered with the normal processes of brain activity varied according to the sensitivity of the individual, the type of activity on-going in the particular brain at that moment, and—of course —the intensity of the stimulus as defined by the inverse-square law. The experiential blackout which defended many minds within the critical zone operated in a very few cases outside that zone, the strength of the signal being insufficiently strong, in most cases, to activate such a response even where available. Even so, a rather large number of individuals remained unaware that their brains had, in fact, been affected by the wave. Until these people began, in the near future, to suffer from "bad dreams" there would be no manifestation of the consequences of the event available to the conscious memory. Outside a radius of approximately twelve hundred miles, virtually all affected people fell into this category.

37

Clea Aron, who was preparing for sleep, lying still in the darkness, allowing her thoughts to wander, actually felt the invasion of her mind like the blow of a fist to the back of her head. As the blow rocked her the blaze of confused images flooded her senses, causing her to gasp with pain.

She sat up and clutched her head in both hands. Following the initial shock there was a period of recoil, and then the images flooded her senses for a second time, more slowly, expanding and fragmenting. The experience was still too fast, and too complex, for her to sort out the imprints which were being stamped on the molecules which programmed her being, but she felt a few moments of utter strangeness that were beyond understanding. During those few moments she lived as an alien being with a wholly new identity.

She burst into tears and cried out aloud for someone to help her. Her own self reasserted itself, quickly and strongly, but the effects of the shock were absorbed.

That night, and every other night for many months, she would dream, and the dreams would belong only partly to herself.

38

Enzo Ulicon was sitting in a chair examining printout from the supply unit at his deck when the wave hit. He felt it as a stabbing sensation at the base of his skull. His hands shook, briefly but violently, and the thin paper of the printout crumpled and ripped.

His eyes closed, reflexively, isolating him with the pain, so that he could concentrate his control. A series of patterns blossomed on the closed eyelids, and rushed back into his mind. The patterns swirled into pictures and for several minutes he became delirious, hurtled through a sequence of visionary instants which flared and were gone. It was barely possible to extract any sense from the flickering confusion, but Ulicon was calm and undisturbed. He identified the sensation, initially, as an ordinary headache—it did not occur to him that it was anything unfamiliar. He saw, therefore—and *knew* that he saw—the burning town, the firelit masks, the long, straight, corpse-littered road through the dark wilderness. He saw the fire-illumined cat face, and the multimillion-colored cankers, sills, dendrites, drapes and frills that comprised the life-system of the Swithering Waste. There was no sense in the sequence—no causality, no logic. It was simply an imaginative mosaic.

But Ulicon knew that he had looked into Hell.

He felt very frightened for a few moments, afterwards. But it was gone, and—so far as he knew—finished. The fear drained away. His hands were still unsteady, but they trembled very slightly, and he found that he could make them still by an effort of will.

Later in the night, he attempted to recall some of the images, reaching back into his memory. They rushed at him from the caverns of his mind, and once again he became the focus of the display. It was then that he realized that it was not finished, and perhaps never would be. Hell had been revealed, and he could not unlearn the revelation.

He, of all people, should have been able to cope with this discovery. It was he that had insisted so strongly that Rafael

Heres and the others should become aware that there were two worlds of Earth, and not one.

Nevertheless, he doubted his sanity and he was suddenly possessed with the curious feeling that the floor beneath his feet was not secure, that at any moment it might begin to fracture, and precipitate him down, into darkness . . .

39

Eliot Rypeck was already asleep, already dreaming. He was quiescent, save for his eyes, which moved beneath closed lids while his mind ran through its sequence of programs, its patterns of life, rehearsing them subconsciously and modifying them slightly by correlation with lately gained experience.

When the wave came he felt neither shock nor pain, but the mechanical process which occupied his brain was completely disrupted. The dream which was playing through his gray cells was shattered, the cytoarchitectural limitation of the process was lost, the neuronal messages were scrambled. He was ripped back into wakefulness by a sensory hurricane.

Within his dream, Rypeck howled in anguish. There was a momentary sensation of flight which quickly became one of falling, falling into a black vortex while the whirling world closed in and reached out a multitude of claws. As consciousness returned to flush out the aborted program, wipe the circuits clean, sweat stood out on his face and he felt the compulsion to *move*. He sat up in bed, as if jerked erect by strings.

He rocked slowly back and forth as he felt the whole garbled mess ebbing from his mind. He felt his body coming back to him, his sense of being swelling like a balloon to occupy every inch of his living frame.

The realization came to him that he had had a nightmare. That realization was infinitely more frightful than the thing itself. The connective routes in his thought processes were already well established. Nightmare . . . i-minus . . . Carl Magner.

The moment had come.

For a few seconds, the images returned, dancing at the threshold of consciousness. They flew all around him like fluttering moths, striking at his eyes from within.

Ulicon was right, he said, silently, chasing away the fugitive ideas with cold, vocalized thought. They came from outside. They came from outside into his mind.

One word swelled to the forefront of his mind, and would not die, dragging itself out and finally yielding only to an endless chain of echoes.

. . . invasion . . .

He lay back, and tried to force sleep to return. He was struck by the silly illusion that his whole awakening had been a fake, that he had merely reentered the macabre theater of his nightmare, enfolding himself within. But if this was a nightmare, it was real. He knew full well as he fought against wakefulness that he was not asleep, not dreaming, not hallucinating.

He was covered with sweat, and the sheets felt unbearably, glutinously warm against his body. After a few minues, he sat up again and mopped his face. He sat still, staring out into the darkness, at the thin sliver of the night sky which filtered in through the screened window. While he waited, his heartbeat began to settle.

But he could not get rid of the obsessive word which still ran faint echoes tumbling round the inside of his skull.

It turned out to be a very long night . . .

40

The Ahrima were encamped to the south and west of Sagum, though parties of warriors covered north and east as well. The people of Sagum, forewarned by runners from Lehr, had elected to defend their town rather than desert it. They had stripped what they could from the fields, and strengthened the wall wherever significant improvement could be made in the time available. Even while the Ahrima rested before the assault the Children of the Voice worked ceaselessly, determined to hold the Ahrima and divert the horde if it were possible.

So far as they knew, no army was gathering in Shairn. The men of the towns were looking to their own and placing their faith in chance or destiny. The people of Sagum knew, however, that if they held the Ahrima for any length of time, warriors would come to them, in small groups, to harry the invaders from without, killing one or two at a time, destroying their supplies and poisoning their animals. If Sagum could hold, the Ahriman strength would be whittled away. The heartland of Shairn would grow relatively stronger. Stalhelm and Lehr had already taken some toll of the enemy's numbers.

On the other hand, if Sagum fell, the Ahrima would stay there, growing strong again on the produce of Shairan land, until they broke out to go whichever way they cared, with no town that would dare to stand against them. They would ravage the heartland and destroy the nation.

The fate of Sagum, therefore, seemed likely to determine the fate of Shairn.

Until the wave came.

The visions struck at the Ahrima, in sleep and in wakefulness. They saw what happened not as individual experience, but as collective experience. Every man knew that the visitation had come to all men, because not one warrior of the Ahrima was alone when the visions came.

There was not one among the Ahrima who could make sense of the "package" of images. To them, it was simply something that struck at the core of their being, something hostile and alien. It panicked them.

They turned away from Sagum, south to burned Lehr, and further south still, passing beyond the boundaries of Shairn into the lands of the Cuchumanate migration paths, and the isolated strongholds of the Men Without Souls.

Within the walls, however, the reaction was very different. The wave was no less a revelation to the Children of the Voice than to the Ahrima, but to them it was a revelation of an entirely different kind. They *could* see the images for what they were: the tangled memory web of one of their own kind. And more than that, they knew what had happened.

They knew it inside themselves, because they too had Gray Souls. When the impact of the wave turned their consciousness in upon itself, they did not find themselves isolated with confusion and fear. The Gray Souls were there. Even the warriors and the little children achieved communion of a sort, without the aid of music or trance or the mind-smoothing juice of the weepweed. Those who knew how to use the communion, who already had the most effective rapport with the symbiotic Souls, discovered the whole truth. They learned that Camlak had broken the barrier, had everted himself into Soul space.

It was a miracle. Of course it was a miracle. Shairn was saved from the Ahrima, Camlak was free from a cage in Heaven, and a wave of force was traveling across and through the world and out into space announcing that Camlak and the Souls, together, had transcended the tyranny of space.

For the Children of the Voice, it was the advance warning of a new threshold in evolution, which was there to be crossed.

The realms of Tartarus were no longer imprisoned by the rotten Earth and the sky of steel.

41

Rafael Heres was duelling with his doubts. He was alone, his mind was racing. He had advance warning of the various forces gathering about him. He knew that he had to face a revolt in his own ranks as well as the Eupsychian assault. He knew that the gloss had been taken off his Second Euchronian Plan in no uncertain terms by Harkanter's showmanship. He knew that he was deep in trouble, and that it might well take a miracle to save his political future.

The images came to him softly and quietly. There was no violence in the way they seeped into his mind. For a few moments, he lived within a mental environment where two realities conflicted for his attention. The safe, sane structures of his knowledge and his ego were forced to compete, for a few seconds, with the ghost of another being, the fragments of whose identity were strewn across the regions of Heres' inner world. It was neither startling nor particularly disturbing. Merely strange. Only shadows, in his mind.

He was awake, rational and quick to realize that something had happened—something utterly new, for which he had no name and no explanation. He relaxed, and waited, observing himself closely to see if anything more was to come. Minutes passed, but he could find no further trace of strangeness.

He was prepared to forget the moment of weirdness. There seemed so little to it, and there was so much that he needed to think about.

Then the telephone began to ring.

Urgently.

42

Thorold Warnet experienced little more than a momentary tiredness and a slight sensation of dullness in the back of his head, which lasted less than a minute.

He set down his pen, and sat back in his chair, allowing himself to relax.

When he closed his eyes, pictures seemed to form in his mind, but they flitted so quickly through his thoughts that he could not focus on them. He was, however, moved to put his hand to his head and exert gentle pressure on his eyeballs with the thumb and forefinger.

It never occurred to him that anything dramatic had happened. But within minutes he, too, was called to his main deck and coopted into the worldwide scare.

43

Sisyr was too far away for the wave to hit him with much force, but he picked it up faintly, and reacted immediately.

He was unable to recall the signal in detail, but when he exerted the full power of his faculties he was able to achieve playback of a kind. The images were blurred, and quite unidentifiable individually, but from the incomplete information he was able to gain a general impression of the sort of mind from which the message came, and the sort of sensory impressions which it contained.

He was, in any case, not really interested in the images carried by the wave—his principal concern was the fact that the wave had been broadcast at all.

He knew that this broadcast was intrinsically different from the kind of infiltration which had made Carl Magner's dreams into chaos. That, he felt sure, had been the leakage of images from a multitude of minds, which had at first irritated Magner's mind and gradually made it more and more sensitive as time went on. How Magner would have experienced the telepathic scream Sisyr did not know. Perhaps it would have destroyed his mind altogether.

The alien was certain that the wave had been generated by a single mind, amplified tremendously. How? Sisyr dismissed the idea that there had been supplementary augmentation. The sheer intensity of the experience which had torn the scream from the sender must have boosted the power of the broadcast.

Using the facilities of the cybernet it took Sisyr only a few moments to discover the focal point of the disturbance. The signal which he had picked up had traveled two thousand miles. He tried to estimate the power of the impulse at source, but could not make anything like an accurate guess. Obviously, however, the event which had been responsible for the generation of the wave was highly unusual.

Sisyr had not expected the manifestation to take this form. Nor had he expected it quite so soon, although the Magner phenomenon had been encouraging. He could not estimate the effect that the all-too-sudden revelation might have on the people of Earth. Not merely the Children of the Voice, but the humans. The people of the Overworld must have received a shock which could revise their whole attitude to life. No doubt they would get over the shock itself, but once the barrier was breached . . .

Once started, these processes did not stop.

Sisyr felt no excitement as he compiled the message which he would transmit to the stars. It was not a time for congratulations. Not yet. It was a delicate time, for close observation, for patience and for careful action.

The message which he transmitted would not reach the outpost for forty years or more. It would take even longer for the answer to come back—they would bring it in person.

The contents of the message were simple enough. It was simply to say that the gateway was there, and that it had opened for the first time.

He wasted no time in sending it, but there was no hurry. It was not an urgent message. Sisyr had all the time in the world. *This* world.

His world.

44

Randal Harkanter was a strong man. He was a brave man and a determined one. But these are relative terms. Among the listless citizenry of the Overworld he was virtually a man alone, an altogether exceptional case. By other standards, perhaps he was only a man with some kind of drive.

Of those in the cellar, however, he was the first to begin to recover from the effects of the mental explosion. He regained consciousness before Joth, and before Iorga (who was, by any human standards, tough and strong). The distance between them may have played some part. Joth, a mere arm's length away from Camlak, had taken the full intensity. Iorga was a pace or two behind Joth. Harkanter had been hanging back, and to the side—perhaps twice as far away as the cat. While Harkanter was beginning to rediscover his arms and legs, the hellkin's brain and body were still at odds, the brain in turmoil and the motor nerves switched off.

Harkanter was quick to realize his advantage. He looked both forward and back, and could see no sign of life anywhere. Apparently, neither Julea nor Soron were making any attempt to recover themselves, but Soron might have been knocked out when he fell on the steps.

The big man tried to raise his body, but the moment he lifted his head there was a wave of dizziness which threatened to black him out. Instead, he began to crawl, hauling himself slowly and painfully across the tiles. His arms and legs would not work as he commanded them, but he moved by virtue of a series of convulsive jerks. He found himself breathing very heavily, sweating cold, with faintness ebbing up within him every time he made any sort of real effort. His body did not want to obey his mind, and the instructions were somehow garbled in between thought and action, but he moved, gradually.

He moved toward the gun which had flown from Vicente Soron's hand to land on the floor of the cellar.

It was a small handgun, but it was a genuine weapon, not the anesthetic dart-gun which the naturalist had carried in the Underworld. It was not one of Harkanter's guns—Soron had apparently been sufficiently frightened by his experiences in the Underworld to obtain one of his own.

Harkanter was actually reaching for the gun when the backlash came. His mind had absorbed the energy of the discharge completely—Harkanter was not aware that his brain had been working during the period of unconsciousness. So far as he was concerned, it was completely black time. But now, as the normal patterns of thought and the cohesiveness of self began to reassert themselves, the way was clear for the images to display themselves. The energy which had flooded into the mind now flooded out again, as though a coiled spring were released.

From Harkanter's point of view, it was sheer insanity. His hand was snatched back from the gun before his fingers touched the butt, and he writhed like a wounded worm. The images flashed inside his brain like a firework display. Real pain racked his body.

It lasted only a few seconds, but it reduced him once again to near helplessness. He failed to collect himself; his muscles worked of their own accord. His fingers clenched and unclenched with such fierceness that his fingernails tore into his palms. He soiled himself.

In the meantime, Iorga became conscious. He watched Harkanter's agonies for a time, quite dispassionately. But then he saw the big man begin to reassert his will, and he saw the gun on the floor. He realized what was happening. He too began to reach for his weapon.

It was a strange and desperate race. Subjectively speaking, it was also a long race, although by the hands on the clock it took place within the span of a few seconds. The complexity of the actions involved made it a long race, in terms of mental coordination and control. Harkanter had to reach the handgun, take it into his fist, steady himself enough to aim it, get his forefinger round the trigger and . . . if necessary, or desirable . . . fire it. Iorga already had the gun which Joth had asked him to carry—the rifle. It was underneath his fallen body. But he, too, had a struggle before him. He had to lift himself, roll clear of the gun, grip the weapon, and then lift it into position. Then . . . it depended on Harkanter. Iorga had no intention of firing unless fired at.

Beyond the moment of firing—or not firing, as the case might be—neither man had any thought. They were both concentrating on the immediate task. Had they stopped to think about the future, they would have condemned themselves to failure in the present. To do what they were trying to do they needed all their strength and complete commitment.

Harkanter's groping fingers finally touched the pistol.

Iorga found his body moving, found himself coming clear of the rifle. But the mechanism of the gun caught in his clothing, and the gun began to drag along the floor with him as he moved.

Harkanter pecked at the gun with fingers that would no longer close. Blood running from his palms dripped on to the tiles. The gun rocked on its chamber, and the butt spun away from him.

Joth was beginning the long journey back from oblivion.

Iorga planted both hands on the rifle, one on the stock and the other half way along the barrel. He grappled it free of the entanglement. He lost balance and rolled backwards, but the gun was free. He was laid out flat on one side, the barrel was pointed the wrong way. He began to turn it, trying to bring it to bear on the crawling Harkanter before trying to come to grips with the trigger mechanism.

Harkanter dabbed at the pistol, uselessly.

Time dragged by, and nothing happened. Vicente Soron sat up on the staircase and looked through the guardrail, trying to understand what was happening.

Joth opened his eyes.

Julea, now conscious, kept hers closed tight. She did not want to know. She hardly knew whether she wanted to be alive.

Harkanter got his hand round the butt of the gun and picked it up. He rocked back on to his haunches and tried with his other hand to force his finger round the trigger. Somehow, his groping released the safety catch. He heard it click and knew that all he had to do was press. A burst of elation helped sensibility to return. He got his finger inside the trigger guard.

Iorga was picking up the rifle. It seemed incredibly heavy and cumbersome. He heaved at it, almost like a weightlifter trying to press a dumbbell. He heaved again, at himself rather than the apparent dead weight of the gun. His body was working again, the gun came up, and slotted naturally into his grip.

Joth tried desperately to clear his head, and in trying to speak he managed a groan.

Julea heard the groan.

Soron remembered something, and tried to shout, but no sound came.

Harkanter leveled the pistol and fired.

Iorga watched the dark finger tighten on the trigger. He reacted immediately, without conscious decision. Sheer inertia carried him through to the endpoint of his action, just as it carried Harkanter through to the endpoint of his.

The hammer of the pistol clicked harmlessly. The chamber was empty.

Iorga had already returned the fire. There was no way to hold the action.

The rifle bullet blew Harkanter's head off.

45

All over the continent, the holovisual network was carrying an interview which featured Abram Ravelvent and Vicente Soron. Other time zones were scheduled to see the recording at the same relative time, as they moved into night. They never actually got to see it at all.

While Soron, in the flesh, was trying to drag himself back through the cellar door, desperate to escape from the threat of Iorga's gun (an imaginary threat, as the recoil had thrown the hellkin back, and ripped the rifle from his hands) his image was in closeup in a million homes, ten times life-size, telling the world what the Underworld was like.

The world was not listening. It had other things on its mind. But the broadcast continued.

There was a certain irony in its contents.

After Soron had finished, Yvon Emerich turned to Ravelvent and said: "What do you think of the idea that the rats might be the dominant species in the Underworld?"

"I think it's absurd," said Ravelvent.

"But the evidence . . ."

". . . is virtually worthless. We have, apparently, one specimen. I haven't seen it, but I can't doubt Vicente's word that it is what he claims. Once having accepted that, however, it is by no means logical that one should proceed to say that the Underworld is full of beings like this. We still know virtually nothing. We can make no reasonable guess at all as to what might be the dominant species in the Underworld. We have no justification, in fact, for thinking in terms of 'Dominant species' at all."

"But suppose," said Emerich, "that it was confirmed that the rats *are* the dominant species down there. What then?"

"I refuse to suppose any such thing," said Ravelvent stubbornly.

"You are a scientist," said Emerich. "Very well, let us adopt as a scientific *hypothesis* the assumption that the Underworld is primarily inhabited by creatures of the rather fearsome type which Vicente has described . . ."

"Fearsome?" queried Ravelvent, determined to stop Emerich from loading his questions, if possible.

"It is fearsome," said Emerich, definitely. "I can assure you of that. In the photographs we have, it is quiescent, but let us look at the figures. It is rather more than four feet long—or perhaps I should say four feet *high*, as it walks on two feet rather than four. It has hands and a considerable cranial cavity, big enough—Vicente suggests—to hold a brain of near-human complexity and capability. And we *do* have, here, the knife with which it was threatening to murder Randal Harkanter when Vicente shot it with an anesthetic dart."

Emerich pressed the knife into Ravelvent's hand, making him inspect it in front of the cameras.

"You'll notice," intervened Soron, "that it testifies to a far higher degree of tehnology extant in the Underworld than any of us could have dared to suggest might exist down there. Are we to believe that this weapon came into the hands of the rat from somewhere else, or is it remotely possible that there exists in the world below a society of rats which is advanced enough to pose a definite threat to human life?"

Ravelvent was temporarily defeated by the way that Soron

had phrased his question, which suggested all kinds of horrific but tentative possibilities.

"I don't know how the rat got his hands on the knife," said Ravelvent, "but he didn't make it. I don't believe this was made in the Underworld at all. I think it was made up here."

"Are you suggesting . . . ?" Soron began.

"No," said Ravelvent, quickly, "I'm not suggesting that you planted it, or that any member of your expedition took it down there. I'm suggesting that there has, for many centuries—probably dating back to the early days of the Plan —been clandestine dealing between the Overworld and the surface. I don't know who is involved or why, but I do know that it happens. If you trace the flow of materials as recorded in the cybernet you'll find that there has been a steady drain. The missing materials must go to the Underworld because there is nowhere else for them to go. *That's* what your knife proves. It says nothing at all about the possibilities of rat civilizations. *Nothing.*"

Ravelvent settled back in his chair, satisfied that he had turned the entire course of the argument with his revelation. He believed that he had stamped hard on Emerich's scare story. Emerich, however, was not a man to give up easily.

"The rat had the knife," he said, "and was prepared to use it. Whether the object itself came from the Overworld or not does not alter the fact that the rat was possessed of it. If there has, as you say, been a steady supply of materials to the Underworld—a fact of which I was aware, but hesitant to confirm—there can be no doubt that some of these materials are adopted and used by the rats. Does that not suggest that the rats have evolved to the point at which they pose a danger to human beings?"

"We can't assume any such thing," said Ravelvent.

"But we cannot neglect the possibility?" persisted Emerich. There was no answer.

"In that case," said Emerich, "isn't the idea of opening the Underworld—*for any purpose whatsoever*—a very dangerous one indeed?"

Ravelvent opened his mouth to reply.

When the recording had been made, Ravelvent *had* replied, but at this point the tape was cut short.

Yvon Emerich appeared, in different clothes, broadcasting live. He explained the program had been cut off because of the strange and terrible event which had swept the world while it was in progress. He assured the people that every effort was being made to find out what had happened and why.

As soon as it was possible, Emerich assured the world, the explanation would be discovered and a full account of the happening released. In the meantime, live broadcasting would continue, as the anatomy of the phenomenon was explored, and as information came in.

Emerich himself would not be fronting the broadcast—he wanted to be behind the scenes, sifting the information and deciding how and when it was to be released. Before he handed over to someone else he announced that no deaths or serious injuries had—as yet—been recorded as a result of the phenomenon.

46

"You were warned," said Ulicon.

"I was warned," Heres admitted. "Never mind that now. There's no time for an orgy of recrimination. You told me it wasn't finished but I tried to bury it anyway. Eliot's been trying to stab me in the back ever since. Now it's blown up. You can go ahead with the back-stabbing if you think that's what's called for. But this is serious. It's no time for petty quarreling."

"I accept that," said Ulicon.

"All right. Now—you were the one who warned us all that the Magner affair might blow up. Give me an explanation of what happened tonight."

"An explanation! How can I? Rafe, I don't *know* what happened. What you describe as having happened to you is *not* what happened to me. You experienced something utterly strange . . . I had visions that were starkly clear and quite terrifying. Right now the holo is throwing out all sorts of garbage—people knocked unconscious, mental explosions . . . There's no way of knowing whether there was one event or half a million. How can I possibly give you an explanation until we have some clear idea of how the thing maps out?"

"We can't wait," said Heres. "When we discussed the Magner affair in Close Council, you were the only one ready with some guesses. You were the one with ideas. We need those ideas now. Why do you think I called you? This is a sealed circuit, Enzo, and half the world is at my back. I've got to find answers of some kind. Give me something to play with, please! Because if I can't quell this panic, Heaven only knows where we'll be come the morning."

"All right," said Ulicon, trying to halt Heres' flow of words with a gesture. "I'll tell you what I think. But this is sheer fantasy. It could be nothing like the truth.

"When I investigated Magner I made the point that the visions only came to him during sleep, but that they weren't ordinary dreams. I guessed that there was some kind of telepathic link tied in with the sleep process, possibly involving the pons. I guessed that Magner was picking up some kind of leakage from minds in the Underworld. I stand by those guesses.

"What happened tonight was related, but by no means similar. The visions came to *me* while I was awake. They not only came, but they stayed. They've come into my head and they've *stuck*. That isn't leakage—this . . . message . . . has been driven into my mind with real power behind it. And into yours, and—so far as we know—into every other human mind on the planet. To some, the message was meaningless, to others the impact of receiving it was like a physical blow —just as bright light or loud noise can *hurt* physically.

"First point of advice—find someone who got the *whole* message and got it clear. What I got was a mess of fragments. Maybe that's what was sent out, but we can't afford to overlook the possibility that someone is walking around with a complete understanding of what's going on because he got the content of the broadcast loud and clear. Maybe the word *message* is all wrong, and what hit us wasn't a deliberate attempt to communicate. If that's the case, we have a real problem, because like it or not we have communication. Mind to mind. Imagination to imagination. Whether the human race likes it or not, it has just been awarded telepathy. We might not be able to transmit to one another, or to read one another's minds, but *our minds can be invaded* from without. That's the crucial fact.

"At the very least, we need a method of defense. We need to be able to screen out anything like this that happens in the future. Because it is *going* to happen in the future. Magner showed us the writing on the wall and we let it go. Now it's here. Tomorrow morning, or tomorrow night, it can happen again. It will—if not tomorrow then the day after, or the day after that. This *could* be the beginning of the greatest thing that ever happened to us—but unless we can understand and control it, then it could be one of the worst.

"Find out what happened, at all costs. Find some singular event at the focal point of this phenomenon which we can correlate with the mental transmission. Find out the entire contents of the transmission. Find out who, or what, sent that message. Find out how, but above all else find out *why*. Until you know that there's no way you can promise the people that it isn't going to happen again every day from now until doomsday. Perhaps you'll never be able to make that promise, because perhaps it *will* happen again, and again, every night from now until doomsday."

"What did you see?" demanded Heres, after a momentary pause. "Exactly."

"It wasn't exact," said Ulicon. "I don't know even a fraction of what I saw. I don't want to know. All I can give you are the pieces of the jigsaw. I saw the Underworld. I'm sure of that. Not one part of it but many. Not a panoramic view from above but a vast series of images, like still photographs, of many different places. I saw . . . creatures . . . people . . . things. I saw faces that were covered, in fur, but not beast faces. I wish I'd seen that rat of Harkanter's, because it might allow me to be more sure. I saw many things which were like animals, but also like men. I saw one, in particular, that was not like the others—but it, too, was part-animal, part-man. I saw real men, I think, but their images were confused with painted masks. They seemed too large and utterly savage. The whole thing was somehow out of focus. Not blurred, but *wrong*. There wasn't much color, because all the images were dim, but the colors that there were seemed out of balance. All the signals were mixed—it was like looking at an optical illusion . . . one of those drawings which show impossible things, like staircases going round in a circle, upwards all the way. There was nothing like that in the images, but they gave the same sense of wrongness . . . wrongness that I couldn't pin down. It might be the effect of —as it were—seeing with someone else's eyes, experiencing the world *via* a different balance of sensory information. It might well be . . . but I don't know. I can't be sure. I don't know what I was seeing, but I'll tell you this . . . it was a vision of Hell . . . the Hell that Magner put into his book. I can imagine now what that man went through. I understand what he wrote. But if that was a cry for help, then it was the fiercest and most frightening cry imaginable. I don't believe it was, I think it was Magner who made it into one. That was his interpretation—his way of making sense of it all."

"And your way?" prompted Heres. "How do you make sense of it all?"

"I can't," said Ulicon. "Perhaps I never shall. All I'm sure of is the central fact. My mind has been invaded. Someone or something down there in the Underworld can make me hear him inside my head, see as he sees."

"Suppose," said Heres, "that he can hear you. See as you see."

"How would I know?" replied Ulicon. "How could I ever know?"

"Enzo," said Heres, suddenly becoming the Hegemon again. "I want you to take charge of things within the Movement. Recruit what help you need. The first thing to do is to keep the Councillors calm and silent. I'll put Luel on to handling Emerich and his crew. Get busy, and get as many people as possible busy. Make out that the entire Movement is a hive of activity, and for Heaven's sake try to preserve an illusion of competence. Whether we know what we're doing or not let's pretend that we have it all under control. Never mind the public—make sure the Council and the Movement believe it. Delegate whatever authority you can. Put everybody in charge of something, even if it's only putting other people in charge of other things. Create some work, and make sure it's hard work. Get the real schedule under way, but don't leave anyone idle, whether they have anything to contribute or not. All right?"

"I'm with you," said Ulicon.

The link was broken.

Ulicon wondered whether he had done the right thing. Maybe he was a fool to stay with Heres. Maybe Heres would steer the Movement straight into the heart of the trouble. He had been wrong once. Perhaps twice. But in this extreme situation, one had to have stability of command . . . someone had to hold things together . . . there had to be someone who could take the load of responsibility . . . off one's own back.

Mechanically, Ulicon began obeying his orders.

Meanwhile, Heres was sitting alone with just one thought. We have been *invaded*.

47

Alwyn Ballow was at the very heart of the massive operation to find out what had happened, how, and why. He was surrounded by screens and lineprinters, keyboards and microphones. Information flowed around him in a never-ceasing stream. He was in the seat of judgment, sorting out the flow, picking from it the significant morsels, allowing the rest to disappear into mute electronic storage. He was the brain coordinating the central nervous system of the cybernet. He was God monitoring the puppet strings on which the human race was dancing. (Or, from an alternative viewpoint, he was the maggot at the very core of Euchronian's apple.)

Yvon Emerich was at a much smaller deck, behind Ballow. He too was the brain, or God (or the maggot). That which Ballow sorted out was fed through to Emerich. Emerich collated it, reorganized it, shaped it for release. Ballow judged, Emerich commanded. Between them, they controlled Euchronia's knowledge and—far more important—Euchronia's belief. While Heres was forming the broadcast of Camlak's scream into an invasion, Emerich and Ballow were making it into a spectacle.

"Crash on seven," Ballow recited. "Car spun off highway. No injuries."

Screen seven continued to testify with regard to the accident, but neither Ballow nor Emerich gave it any further attention.

"On nine," chanted Ballow. "Car ran on uncontrolled ... police ... here's something! ... En route for Harkanter's address ... get this! Harkanter's house is in the middle of the black area ... whatever happened is inside there. Find out who made that call! Call Harkanter! Get an eye over Harkanter's place immediately ... track any vehicles, including that police car ..."

"What's that on five?" (Emerich)

"Crash ... coming in now ... two dead ... Makes five so far, Yvon. Safeties failed, manual interference ... third time that's happened ... can't have been a clean knockout ...

Hold on for the printer . . . reports from fringes of the dead spot. Here's one claims he saw a massacre . . . a burning town . . . we already have that . . . check against Magner's stuff . . . More people claiming they saw people in the Underworld . . . Reports of recurrence by the score . . . medical still blank . . ."

"Forget all the what-I-saw business. It's getting us nowhere. Those medic teams *must* be in the no-answer area by now."

"One of the car crashes caused a minor blackout . . . some faculties out of op . . . fail-safes in, no communication . . . east side of black area. Other homes should be unaffected . . . Police have reached Harkanter's place . . . report says call made by Vicente Soron—illicit invasion of privacy—no details . . . says Soron was in a flat panic . . . hey! . . . eye nine has something. Check nine. Close up . . . give us more detail nine . . ."

"Hell, it's only a car!"

"It's going the *wrong* way. It's come *out* of the dead area . . . sure it's had time to cross it . . . plenty of time . . . but we didn't spot it going in . . . get closer . . . no, I know you can't show me who's driving . . . find out who owns . . . oh, it's public . . . okay, keep on it . . . Keep calling Harkanter . . . the police are there now . . . they'll answer as soon as it suits them . . . just keep running the bell . . .

". . . Yvon, there's a suicide here . . . ties in. They have a note but they say it makes no sense . . . put it on the screen . . . makes no sense to me . . . I can't quite make out the writing . . . man's name Simkin Cinner . . . something about ghosts and revenge . . . must have taken the visions pretty hard . . .

". . . we have a trace of the log of that car coming out of the dead area . . . it's public, its journey was tracked automatically . . . it was driven out earlier . . . is that Harkanter's house? Check with the map . . . Yvon, that car is coming from Harkanter's house . . . must be connected with the i. o. p. call . . ."

"Stop the car!"

"Can't . . . don't have authority to override . . ."

"Get it."

"We're trying . . . take time, though . . ."

"Hell, it'll take an age to work through the police hierarchy . . . they'll get to where they're going long before. Keep that eye in close. Any chance of getting a vehicle to intercept?"

"The police have what we have, Yvon . . . if they won't override they won't intercept . . . they have their own chain of command tangled . . . something's wrong here, Yvon. They shouldn't be fouled up this way."

"Policemen have brains too," Emerich pointed out. "They got this thing between the eyes just the same as we did. Maybe worse. We got off light, to judge by some of these scare stories."

". . . they've completed the scan of the area . . . no further crashes. Death toll stands at five, probably five only . . . six including the suicide . . . maybe more inside the houses . . . accidents, maybe shock . . . call to Harkanter's place is through . . ."

"I'll take it," snapped Emerich, and moved forward to the switches on his own phone. Ballow's attention was momentarily diverted to the printout, and when he turned again to Emerich the news had already broken.

"Alwyn! Get Soron. In here. I don't care how, but move Heaven and Earth if you have to. Get Soron here."

"What happened?"

"Harkanter's been killed. Soron saw the whole thing. If the police want to keep him get someone in with him. Get a link of some kind—I want to talk to him as soon as humanly possible . . ."

Emerich's attention returned to the screen. Someone was still trying to tell him something.

"Gone?" he said. "Gone where?"

Ballow sent a quick stream of instructions into one of the microphones.

"Get a scan from one of the eyes," said Emerich. "Low down, round Harkanter's house. High resolution. The rat's loose. You probably won't pick it up, but try."

". . . Heres continues unavailable," reported Ballow. "Who else can we try? They don't think Heres will say anything at all. Not tonight . . ."

"Get that woman," said Emerich. "The one they put on in the Magner debate. *Her* thoughts ought to be worth a penny or two right now. Clea Aron . . . get her. And get that friend of Magner's . . . the one who was with him when he was shot. Abram Ravelvent. I was talking to him on screen last night —it was his recording that we had to chop. He's full of ideas about the Underworld—find out what *he* has to say about this . . ."

". . . More in on Harkanter," said Ballow. "He was shot

dead. Nothing more. They won't let us near Soron . . . not the police—the Movement . . . they've claimed him . . . Yvon! They're trying to close us down!"

"Have you got Aron?"

"She's not available."

"Ravelvent?"

"Just left home . . . That car! It's stopped . . . get that eye in closer . . . that building is the plexus where Harkanter's expedition went down to the Underworld. It's where the door is . . . I can't see them clearly in this light. Two, maybe three . . . they must be going down . . . you think the rat might be with them?"

Emerich was staring at his screen again.

"You can't close down," he was saying. "You can't just black out the holovisuals all over the world."

Ballow switched into the call. The man at the other end was Luel Dascon—Rafael Heres' chief satellite.

"We have the authority," said Dascon. "A state of emergency was declared a few moments ago. We are taking over all media. We will continue to broadcast, but your people may not interfere in any way whatsoever."

"You can't do that!" said Emerich, loudly.

"Please hand over all facilities to the authorized representatives of the Council," said Dascon smoothly. "They should be with you now."

"They are," put in Ballow.

"I'm telling you," said Emerich, his face white with anger, "that if Heres has any ideas of winning the petitioned election he can forget them! I'll kill his chances stone dead for this."

"There isn't going to be an election," said Dascon. "The state of emergency overrules the petition. We're all in this together, Yvon. All the quarreling is over. We have to unite now . . . against a common enemy."

48

When Ravelvent arrived at the plexus, Julea was still in the car. The camera eye was hovering in the sky, shining with the reflection of the silver dawn light, but with that exception she was alone. The car's microphone was still in her hand. She was not crying, but her face was flushed and the look in her eyes suggested that she simply could not find the tears.

"What happened?" said Ravelvent.

It was the wrong question. She gave him a look that was angry, almost hateful. He led the car door open while he took her arm and guided her gently out on to the verge at the side of the road. Her eyes were drawn to the door to the mechanical nerve complex—the door which gave access to a staircase into the world below. It stood ajar. They had stood here before, the two of them, not daring to pass beyond the doorway themselves. They had waited, and nothing had happened.

"He's not coming back," said Ravelvent, gently. He meant her father, Carl Magner.

"He is," she said. "He said so. He said that he would come back, but he had to go." She was not talking about her father but about Joth.

"It's all right now," said Ravelvent. "It's all over."

"No," she said. "It won't ever be over. He killed him. That won't ever end."

Ravelvent looked around for something to put over her shoulders, because she was obviously cold. But there was nothing in either of the cars. He put his arms round her instead, and hugged her close.

"Let's go home," he said. "My home. Not your father's empty house. Come home with me. It'll be all right."

She shook her head, and squirmed out of his grasp. He withdrew his hands and stood still, feeling rather lonely.

"Joth's coming back," she said. "It's Joth who went down there. He brought me here. I couldn't drive back. I had to call you. But we must wait. For Joth."

Ravelvent was at a loss.

"Before you called," he said, half turning away so that he did not seem to be talking to her at all, "the strangest thing happened. I was doing some work . . . some programming, for the educational facilities . . . I was deliberately not watching the holovision, because I knew that I was on and I didn't want to see, when . . . it was like a bomb going off in my head . . . and now, I have the crazy feeling that I can see . . . visions . . . as your father saw them. I can see the Underworld, Julea. I *know* it was true. It's not a game any more."

"It's not a game," she said, soberly. "He's dead."

"Who?"

"Randal Harkanter."

"Who?"

"The Underworlder shot him. It was . . . like a bomb going off in his head . . ."

"What *happened?*" demanded Ravelvent, for the second time. He was facing her again now, and his voice was raised.

She wouldn't say anything. She wanted to cry but she couldn't. He tried to take hold of her again, but she stepped backwards.

"It's all right," he tried to insist. "Whatever it was, it's over now. It was only a bad dream. It's over now. You must come home with me. It'll be all right, there. It's *over* now."

"No," she replied. "Not now. It won't ever be over."

Then she let him lead her to his car, and drive her away. The other car, which Joth had requisitioned from the omnibenevolent machine which served all life in the Overworld, remained.

Waiting.

49

"Eliot," said Heres, "I'm asking for your help. What happened yesterday and the day before simply doesn't matter now. We wake up this morning to a new world. We have to face that. There's no point in dragging all the old, tired arguments behind us now. Eleven thousand years of Euchronian history ended last night. This morning, the Millennium is meaningless. The argument about the relevance of the i-minus agent is shifted into an entirely new dimension. If you continue to push your petition for an election you could destroy the Movement. I'm asking you for your sake, and my sake, and for the sake of the whole world, to forget our differences and help me."

"Do I have a choice?" said Rypeck, bitterly.

"Would I be asking you if you hadn't?"

"The petition falls in any case. You're the Hegemon and

you've taken a tight hold on your Hegemony. The disaster which you may have caused with your willful blindness has come, and you've taken advantage of it to confirm your power. You have a frightened world, Rafael, and they turn to you because you've forbidden them to turn anywhere else. You're riding high, Rafael. But where to? I've been trying to call you for hours and getting nothing but a blank wall. Now you call me, and you ask for my help. Why, Rafael? Are you sure, now, of everyone else? Everyone but the Eupsychians? Are you trying to close the ranks completely?"

"If that's the way you want to put it," said Heres, "that's what I'm trying to do. We can't afford to have the Council divided now. I need your loyalty and I'm asking for it. Euchronia faces danger and tragedy, and we need Euchronian unity—singleness of mind and singleness of purpose. We have been invaded, Eliot. The invasion has struck into our very minds. You were right when you said that we are ignorant. We are worse than ignorant—we are vulnerable. We've all made mistakes—the whole Movement has left itself unready to cope with what struck at us last night. But now we have to cover for those mistakes. We have to unmake them. We have to deal with the threat which Euchronian society faces. If this thing gets loose, we will be destroyed. Now I ask you, Eliot, do you want to try to apportion blame—to waste your efforts in bitterness and recrimination—or do you want to help. Are you with me, or against me?"

And Rypeck realized, inevitably, that he didn't have a choice.

"Yes, Rafe," he said, "I'm with you. Let's save the world. How do you propose to go about it?"

50

Joth half-expected that they would be waiting at the bottom of the stairway. He was ready, if it proved necessary, to fight his way back into the Underworld. And yet he did not intend to stay. He only wanted to tell Nita what had happened—to explain why he had not returned her father to his world.

But the scientists in the camp were far too preoccupied to be guarding the door with guns. They, too, had been invaded during the night, first torn from their sleep and then kept back from it by the nightmares which threatened to engulf them whenever their eyes closed and their mind relaxed from conscious ratiocination. They had assumed, in the beginning, that the experience was theirs alone: that the Underworld had reached out to punish them for *their* invasion, that the dreams came because they were strangers in an alien world. They came together, to talk, because they felt the need for company, and for some collaborative exercise to occupy their thoughts and senses. They were afraid —desperately afraid.

By the time that dawn broke in the world above, and Joth and Iorga returned to the world of the fixed stars, the expeditionary force had learned that what they had experienced had also swept the upper world like a great tidal wave. It had changed the current of their argument, in frantic search of an explanation, but it had not alleviated their fear or their need to huddle together, cowering from the perpetual night. The man with the metal face and the hellkin escaped into the Swithering Waste unnoticed.

There they met Chemec, who had waited patiently for their return for many hours whose passage he had no way to measure.

He, too, had dreamed. He, of all people, should have known what was happening, but in fact he, alone, remained completely unmoved and undisturbed by the images which had flooded his mind. He had not been aware that they came from elsewhere. The scenes that were plucked from Camlak's ego might just as well have come from his own. He believed that he had seen only things which came from within himself, woven into the distorted, tattered cloth of a commonplace nightmare. Such things did not worry Chemec, who was used to nightmares. Had he kept closer company, within himself, of his Gray Soul, perhaps he would have known that something new and strange had happened to him, but Chemec was not a man who made much use of his Soul.

Possession of a Soul is no guarantee of understanding.

But Chemec led Joth and Iorga back to one who did know, and who was even beginning to understand. Nita, like the cripple, might have confused Camlak's mindblast with something echoing out of the inwardness of her own being, but her mind was younger than Chemec's, and she slept much closer to her Soul. She had heard Camlak's scream of anguish and pain as he had torn himself free from external space, and she had sensed the ripple which had been created in the fabric of space by that tearing, and which had acted as a carrier wave for the image-charged emotion which had been generated within his mind by the scream.

She knew, therefore, some time before Joth came back, that Camlak was no longer in the Overworld—no longer in the world at all.

"I think your father destroyed himself," Joth told her.

She shook her head.

"He was in the cage, and then he was gone. Absolutely. The force hit us, took our bodies away from our minds, left us fallen and helpless. It wasn't the force of an explosion. It didn't hurt us, but Camlak just disappeared."

"We felt it too," said Huldi.

"Camlak didn't die," Nita explained. "He found something the priests have always told us about. No one ever found it before. The priests couldn't know. But they were right. It was there."

"What did he find?" asked Joth.

"A way between the worlds," she said. "Not your world and mine. Another world."

"Where?"

"Nowhere. Enclosed within us. Deep. We can look into it sometimes, at the Communion of Souls. You remember. You saw."

Joth stared at her, uncomprehending. He had seen the Communion of Souls. He had interpreted it, to his own satisfaction. And he had been right—he was sure of that. Now he realized that he had not been right enough. He had seen only the tiniest fraction of the reality. He wondered where he could find the help which he needed in order to begin to know the truth. Huldi knew nothing—hers was only an animal mind whose sentience served animal purposes. She never asked herself questions, let alone created answers. Iorga, too, had little or no use for words except as signals. If he used them within himself, to try to come to terms with the reality in which he was a prisoner, he showed no outward sign of it. Chemec might some day come to understand what Nita knew now, but it would mean nothing to him. His way of life was Yami's way—the way that answered all challenges with the will to kill. And the people of the Overworld . . . how could they ever *begin* to understand, while they had made of themselves what they were?

Joth abandoned the tangled web of thought, without surrendering to the insidious despair.

"What will you do now?" he asked Nita.

"I don't know," she said.

"Will you do something for me?" he asked.

"Yes."

"I'm going back, now. I want to put right all the lies and the mistakes. I don't know what will happen to me, but I don't think they'll blame me for what Iorga did. I want to find out all they know, and why they know so little when men like Burstone must know so much more. But there's something else I want to know—something else I think is important. I want to know why there is a road of stars which leads from the edge of the Waste into the black lands. A road must lead somewhere, and it's a road that was left for you to follow, not for me. I can track it, from above—I think. If not, I'll come back and follow you down here, if I can. Either way, I'll try to find you at the other end."

They did not ask him for a reason. They lived their lives, for the most part, without reasons. Because they lived almost without time, they did not need to make plans out of their lives. Only Chemec had enough fear of the black lands to refuse what Joth had asked.

Chemec did not go. He went, alone, back to the country called Shairn. Nita, Huldi and Iorga took the Road of Stars. They all loved one another.

Joth, whom they also loved, went home.

51

The head of Rafael Heres hung like a bloated balloon in every home in Euchronia. Somewhere in the world it was midnight, somewhere else it was noon. It made no difference. The head was there, and the whole world was listening, watching the bloodless lips move. No one was missing out on sleep to listen. Wherever it was night, in Euchronia, it was a sleepless night.

"The purpose of the Euchronian Movement and the Euchronian Plan," Heres was saying, "was to build a world for men to live in peace. From the wreckage of a dying world the Euchronians made a new world grow. They designed that world for mankind, because they wanted their children —their ultimate children—to be able to live the kind of lives *they* wanted to live, but could not. They wanted to build a paradise for their children, and they did.

"We are those children. We live in the world that they made for us. We have used it as well as we could, and perhaps we have not used it as well as they would have wanted us to. But this is a new world, and there is time yet. There is time for us to become the children that the Euchronian Planners would have wished to inherit the new Earth.

"Our fathers wanted to give us a world which was not merely ideal for the purposes of mankind, but a world which was secure—whose own future was guaranteed. They designed our world to be stable—in a state of balance. They never claimed—they were never arrogant enough to claim —that ours would be a perfect world, but they wanted it to be a world where we could live our lives completely safe from the tragedies which they suffered as a matter of course. They wanted it to be a world where men could be free, and free forever.

"Our freedom is threatened now.

"Our stability is threatened now.

"Our world is threatened now.

"The Planners gave to us all that we have, to hold for all time. They never envisaged—they never could have envisaged—that a terrible threat to our way of life might emerge, not from within our society, nor from the infinite reaches of space in which our Earth is only a mote of dust, but from the old world—the world they interred as a failure, a disaster, and a ruin. The Euchronians left the past behind them, thinking that it was obliterated, cut off forever from the light of the sun and the face of Heaven.

"But that past has caught up with Euchronia.

"Our minds are no longer completely our own. We have been invaded, not merely by alien beings from an alien world coming into our world, but by an alien state of being which has come into our very selves, into our minds. Can we, at this moment, say that we have sovereignty over our own being? Do we have the power of self-determination, the power to shape our own identity? Perhaps we do . . . for the moment. But while our minds are threatened by the kind of invasion which we have already suffered once, we cannot be sure. We can never be sure, until we have removed that threat.

"The course of action which is forced upon us is not one that we would take lightly. What we have to do now is cause for regret, and sadness, and guilt, and shame. I do not seek to avoid these truths. But we have no choice. In order that we may preserve our selves against destruction —individually and collectively—we must take steps to assure that no such invasion of our being can ever take place again.

"Not long ago, I proposed the establishment of a Second Euchronian Plan, directed toward the reclamation of the Underworld. That Plan has been changed. We now know that there exists in the Underworld a menace to everything that we have, and everything that we are. That menace must be destroyed, and we can take no chances whatsoever in the matter of its destruction.

"I must tell you now that the Euchronian Council has already decided, and plans have already been put in progress, to take the necessary steps, with all attendant precautions.

"All life in the Underworld is to be extirpated. The surface of the ancient Earth is to be absolutely and completely sterilized. This will be accomplished with all possible speed."

52

The camp was ablaze with light, while the technical staff who had spent so many patient hours setting up the tents and the complex equipment now dismantled and disassembled them again. This time, there was not so much patience about the way they worked, and rather more unseemly haste.

There was little enough opportunity to talk to one another. When they stopped for food and rest they did so in small groups and they took their breaks seriously. For the most part, they had little to say to one another. They had talked themselves to a standstill in the fearful hours following the wave. They were tired men, now, moving like machines, with a permanent haze behind their eyes that was compounded of exhaustion and anxiety.

The exception was Felipe Rath. He wanted to talk. He was no less tired and no less distracted than his companions, but he had something niggling at his mind that he wanted to let out—that he felt compelled to set free. He chose to tell Zuvara, because he felt that Zuvara was likely to understand—and also because Zuvara was peripherally involved, *via* a small sin of omission.

"Harkanter's dead," said Rath.

"I know," said Zuvara. "We all know."

"But I'm partly responsible, in a way. In a way, you are too."

Zuvara stared at him. There was no emotion in his eyes, but with the mask obscuring his features and the strangeness of his manner due to fatigue, Rath fancied that he could see loathing in the stare.

"The other night," Rath explained, hesitantly. "You were ... on guard. You must have fallen asleep."

"What has that to do with Harkanter? I don't remember falling asleep."

"You must have. They came into the camp. Joth Magner and ... the one that killed him. It was my gun—the one that shot Harkanter. They came right into the camp and took it. You let them in. I let them out. That's what I mean when I say that we helped to kill him. If you hadn't fallen asleep, or let them through behind your back, or whatever ... and if I hadn't let them go ..."

"They stole your gun," said Zuvara. His voice was faint and monotonous, as though it came from a long distance. "So what? I didn't know that someone was going to steal a gun to kill Harkanter. Neither did you."

"But I did."

"You knew they were going to kill Harkanter?"

"No. But I let them take the gun. I knew they were going after Harkanter, because they wanted to rescue the rat. I could have warned him, but I didn't. I just let them go. I didn't tell anyone. Of course, I didn't know they'd kill Harkanter. How could I? But I didn't warn him. If I had, he wouldn't be dead."

Zuvara felt completely at a loss.

"Why tell me now?" he asked. "What difference does it make?"

"I just wanted to explain," said Rath. "I wanted to explain why I didn't warn him. Magner threatened me, but it wasn't that. He couldn't carry out any threats. But I still didn't warn Harkanter."

"Why?" Zuvara felt compelled to ask.

"Because he didn't have any right. Harkanter. He didn't have any right to go back like that, with the rat, to shout out loud to the whole world that he knew it all. He *didn't* know it all—my pictures proved that. He didn't know anything. So I let them go, to steal his prize specimen, because he didn't have any right.

"But I didn't know they'd kill him."

Rath looked into Zuvara's eyes, to see what he could read there now. But he couldn't read anything. Zuvara wasn't looking at him. In fact, he seemed not to have been listening to Rath at all. He was looking at something over Rath's shoulder—something in the wilderness.

For one brief moment, Rath felt angry. Then the anger died, and the scientist reasserted his will over the tired, self-pitying man.

"I'm sorry," he said. Then he turned.

Joth Magner was walking into the camp. His pace was measured. He was unarmed. His metal eyes—steel globes with horizontal slits, behind which ranged the artificial retinae and the circuitry which filtered and coded the information—searched the masked faces of the men who watched him.

The camp was suspended in a moment of stillness and silence. It was a moment carved right out of time: an encounter utterly strange because it did not involve a meeting of alien worlds or alien minds.

Joth's eyes found Rath, despite the mask, and it was to him that Joth came.

"I'm coming back with you," he said. "It's all done now. All finished."

Rath had to turn away from the stare of the steel eyes.

"It's finished," he agreed.

III. A GLIMPSE OF INFINITY

1

In Euchronia, arrest was only a state of mind. There were no prisons. Limitation by confinement was quite unnecessary, because there was nowhere in the world that a man might hide. There was no way to keep secrets within the machine that was host to mankind. There was, of course, escape, but not within the world—only without. In Sanctuary, or in the Underworld, there was no arrest. But in Euchronia, once a man was labeled "arrested," arrested he was.

Joth Magner accepted his arrest, signifying that he wanted to cooperate to the full with those who had so designated him. He took up temporary residence in the headquarters of the Euchronian Movement, in order to make himself available for consultation and interrogation, face to face. There was no real need, because he would have been available anywhere in the world *via* the screens, but that was the way he wanted it. He wanted to force his physical presence upon the Councillors who wanted his information. He wanted to be free to use all the power of his personality in his arguments.

Eliot Rypeck and Enzo Ulicon, who became his interrogators primarily because they were interested in hearing what he had to say, unlike the majority of their colleagues, were opposed to direct confrontation. They had adapted themselves, mind and body, to the mediation of machines.

In addition, they found Joth physically repellent by virtue of the fact that his face was half-metal. Nevertheless, they concurred. They felt that what Joth knew was important, and they wanted to know.

2

"Why did you decide to follow Burstone in the first place?" asked Rypeck.

"I wanted to find out what happened to my brother. He knew about Burstone. When he went into the Underworld it was by the route that Burstone used."

"And what happened?"

"I followed him down into the lowest levels. He used a cage attached to winding gear in order to go down from the floor of the Overworld to the surface. I waited for him to come back. When he left, I went down myself. I had to see. I hadn't expected the lights—the stars—beneath the platform. But someone—maybe Burstone—wound the cage back up. I was trapped." Joth fired these sentences quickly, wanting to race ahead, to get to the arguments he wanted to put, the information that was vital. But he knew that the whole story had to be told, in order to provide a context for his arguments. These people were not merely ignorant, but misled. They had to be guided to understanding. It could not be thrust upon them.

"You don't know what Burstone was doing in the Underworld?" put in Ulicon.

"I know," said Joth. "I didn't see him, but I know. He was taking knives and tools and books, to give to the Underworlders."

"Why?"

"Ask him."

"Carry on," said Rypeck. "What happened next?"

"I panicked. I was suddenly completely afraid. Drowning in fear. Not logical. It was like stepping straight into a drug experience. Everything twisted in my mind. I couldn't think, couldn't even use my senses. I ran. Anywhere . . . nowhere.

I ran. I fell, and when I got up I ran again. I lost contact with time. And then I ran straight into a man."

"Wait," said Rypeck. "This is one thing that we *must* have clear. A man, you say. A *human* being."

"So far as I could tell," said Joth, "he was as human as you or I. He was a savage, but he was a man. But there were others—chasing him, I think. He picked me up, and he made sure that they saw me. They were terrified, because of my face. He got away from them. But he wasn't terrified—*he knew what I was*. That's important. He knew that I was a man despite the face. He knew I came from the Overworld. You must realize that although he was a savage he wasn't ignorant. He knew what he was doing when he used me as a scarecrow to buy him time."

"And the others?" prompted Rypeck.

"This is the hard part," said Joth. "They were men, too. But they weren't like you or me. They were small and strange. Randal Harkanter had one in a cage, but that was wrong. What Harkanter had wasn't an animal, it was a man."

"Soron said that it was a rat," said Ulicon—not making an assertion, but putting the idea forward so that Joth had to react.

"What's a rat?" said Joth. "Have you ever seen one? Maybe they still exist—more likely they don't. Soron has nothing on which to base his identification except information from the prehistoric past. His opinion means nothing."

"He's an expert in his field," said Ulicon mildly.

"That's nonsense," Joth told him. "He's an expert in a field that's ten thousand years out of date. He knows *nothing* about life in the Underworld as it really is. Do you really think that a man can walk into a new world, armed with knowledge which pertains to circumstances as they were ten millennia ago, and make meaningful judgments about the nature of that world? Do you think that there is any way that Soron possibly *could* know anything?"

"We take the point," said Rypeck. "But what do *you* know? How can you contradict what Soron said?"

"I lived with these people," said Joth. "The warriors who picked me up took me back to their village. One of them took me into his house. They looked after me while I was convinced that I was dying. They talked to me. The man, Camlak, and his daughter Nita. There was a human girl there, too—Huldi."

"You are drawing a distinction between men and humans," said Rypeck. "How?"

"There's no other way," said Joth. "There's no word we can apply to these people except men, even though they aren't truly human. They aren't animals. To call them 'rats' is to make a gross and dangerous error. They call themselves the Children of the Voice. They claim to have souls, and to be able to communicate with those souls on occasion. They speak English, although they call it Ingling. That is to say, it's a form of English. It's a language with many new words, and some words we're familiar with have been abandoned. But they read books from the Overworld. They read them, and they make some use of what they read—when they can. What else can you call someone who reads the same books that you read, speaks the same language as you do, and cares for you when you're sick? What else but a *man.* And yet they have gray fur. Their skulls are a strange and grotesque shape. Why should those things make a difference?"

Rypeck coughed, and hesitated before speaking. "In your father's book," he said, tentatively, "there are references to the people of the Underworld. Which people did he mean?"

Joth waved his hand—a brief, angry gesture. *"He didn't know.* He had no possible way of knowing. If some of what he said was true, then it was inspiration or accident. But he didn't know. You *must* understand that this has nothing to do with my father. He's dead. He may have been the trigger which began all this, but now it's something different. If you confuse what I have to say with what my father said, then we can't possibly reach any kind of an understanding."

"I'm sorry," said Ulicon, "but from our point of view what happened to your father *is* important. It could be vital. We need to know how your father knew what he did and why he thought what he did. You have no real idea of what happened when the rat or the man or whatever disappeared from Harkanter's cage. You were there and you saw it, but it knocked you out. You were too close to the blast. That fearful burst of mental energy rocked half the world, and it *must,* in some way, be related to what your father experienced as a matter of course, in his dreams. We have to fit *all* the pieces of this jigsaw together, Joth—not just the ones you want to play."

Joth shook his head doubtfully.

"Carry on with the account of what happened to you," suggested Rypeck. "We can return to these points later."

Joth shrugged. "I don't know how long I was ill," he said, "or how long I stayed in the village afterwards. Without night and day, time became meaningless. The Underworld runs on subjective time—there are no clocks. From seconds to seasons, all intervals of time are the same to them. The only duration which means anything to them is the time it takes to get tired, or the time it takes to get hungry. Even the length of a man's life is unimportant, because no one dies of old age—there's no such thing as a lifespan. Everybody dies, when the time comes, by disease or violence.

"We—that is, the girl Huldi and I—watched one of their religious festivals—a communion of souls. I can't pretend to understand it. I wish I did. At the time, I thought I had a certain insight. Now, I'm not sure.

"There was a ritual, in which Camlak played the part of the sun, while his father—who had been the leader of his people—personified night. Camlak killed his father—executed him according to ritual—and so became the king. But the strange thing is that the ritual mimicked a different world. In their world, there is no sun, and no night. They were acting out a *mystery,* something which had meaning only within *another* world—a world which, for them, fulfills all the functions of the supernatural.

"To the Children of the Voice, the Overworld is both Heaven and Hell. It is the universe outside their own, within which their lives are sealed, and whose forces give structure and purpose and meaning to their own lives. This is completely beyond the scope of my father's book and its message. If my father, in his dreams, found some way of seeing into the Underworld, perhaps even into the minds of the people who live there, then he could not make use of what he saw. He could not understand. This makes nonsense of his ideas. We could not bring the people of the Underworld out into the light, because everything they are is identified with the darkness—it is not only their bodies which have adapted, but also their *minds*.

"You must realize that the inhabitants of the Underworld are *not like us*. They are *alien*. And yet they are men. In the Overworld we tend to have a very narrow view of humanity, and of life. We have learned to hate the men on the ground—the men who stayed on the ground in the dis-

tant past—because they did not think like Euchronians. Our
history makes us hate, despite the hypocritical voice of our
reason. But our history is out of date. Our attitudes are
out of date. There is another world beneath our feet—and
it is not the one we think it is. It is not the one my father
wanted to save, *and it is not the one Heres wants to destroy.*"

Ulicon and Rypeck exchanged glances. Each suspected
that Joth Magner was deranged—that his mind had been
somehow twisted by his experiences. But each man was
afraid of his own suspicion. Of the ten or twelve men close
enough to Heres to influence the Hegemon's thinking, only
these two wanted to believe that the present course of action was wrong. Joth Magner was their one hope of finding a
reason which could turn Euchronia aside.

The plain fact was that from top to bottom, the entire
Euchronian Movement—the authentic voice of Euchronian
society—was frightened. From the moment when rediscovery of the Underworld had been forced upon them by the
publicity given to Carl Magner's *Marriage of Heaven and
Hell*, fear had been building up in virtually every citizen of
the new world. At first, the fear had been a source of
stimulation, excitement in a world which lacked excitation.
Magner's absurd proposal to open the Overworld in order
to allow the inhabitants of the surface to emerge into the
daylight had been a fashionable distraction. But once revealed, the Underworld could not be forgotten. Magner had
died for what he believed, and his death had underlined
effectively the fact that something real was at stake—that
the issue, once raised, could not be put away again. The
rediscovery of the Underworld put all the old arguments
into a new context.

Rafael Heres, with his position as Hegemon of the Movement under threat, had tried to make political capital out
of Magner by making the Underworld a matter of Euchronian concern. Events had turned against him. He had
tried to quell the fear by drawing its source into a second
Euchronian plan, but the fear had run wild, and could not be
contained. Deliberately fed by certain dissatisfied and de-
linquent elements in the Overworld, the Underworld had
become such a bugbear that Heres had been forced to meet
it head-on. Instead of recruiting it, he was committed to destroying it. To soothe the troubled mind of Euchronian
society, he had undertaken to destroy a world. And Euchronia would accept nothing less. The people of the Over-

world knew no way to live with uncertainty—ten thousand years of Euchronian history had made certain of that. If Heres and the Movement had no final answer, then the Movement was finished—and so, perhaps, was the Overworld. Euchronia had always claimed to be the ultimate answer. Now it had to defend its claim. Heres and the vast majority of his followers saw one answer and one only: the Underworld must be destroyed.

Rypeck and Ulicon, however, believed that there was no such simple answer. But if they were to find an alternative—or even a reason why the obvious answer was no answer at all—they had to know more about the world below the platform. Only Joth Magner could tell them. If anyone could.

3

The convoy came to a halt at midnight. Midnight meant nothing on the road of stars, but Germont, inevitably, had carried the habits and the circadian rhythms of the Overworld with him into the realms of Tartarus.

He spoke into the microphone which connected him to the other vehicles. "We rest here for the night," he said. "No one goes outside, for any reason. Alpha-three, Beta-seven and Delta-five will maintain all-night watch using searchlights. Note anything moving, report anything dangerous, keep the lights circling. Do not open fire without orders. That's all."

The driver of the vehicle turned to look down over his shoulder at the commander of the expeditionary force. "Shall I switch off the headlights?" he asked.

"Yes," said Germont. "And douse the interior lighting as well. I'm coming up to take a look around with the searchlight." He left the communications network and hauled himself up into the cockpit of the armored car, to take the seat beside the driver.

High above—he could not estimate *how* high—the single line of electric stars ran back and forth across the solid sky, becoming a yellow blur in the distance as it faded toward the horizon.

"It really was a road," said the driver, quietly. "Ten thousand years ago. A long, straight highway running hundreds of miles. It's covered now, but it hasn't been wholly obliterated. It's an easy ride—the wheels go through this stuff like a knife. We're so heavy we must be running on the old surface itself."

"It was a road," confirmed Germont. "It's a road in the Overworld, too. When the platform was Planned, certain basic patterns were retained. This was an important road. That must be why the Planners left it lighted—after a fashion. It must have been a major access right up to the sealing of the platform."

They watched the white beam of the searchlight in the third vehicle back as it played across the terrain to the righthand side of the column. The Underworld had not reclaimed the road, but it had reclaimed the city. Even the flat, impermeable apron of the highway had been overgrown, but it had offered little enough encouragement to the fungoid life-forms which predominated here. It had been carpeted, and nothing more. But the old buildings had offered support and framework to an ecosystem which was not replete with self-supporting structures. The new life of the Underworld had found a use for cities, and it had taken over despite the poisons which often built up there. In time, even the atomic and chemical waste would be co-opted, somehow, into the cycles of life which were adapting to the corpses of civilization. The process was going on, even now. Poison is a temporary thing. It kills, but out of the death it causes there comes new life, ultimately.

This city had become a forest, its concrete bones substituting for the xylem skeletons which had been lost when the old world was condemned to darkness. All the trees were gone, but the forests simply moved into the cities. Life is never defeated—evolution simply changes gear, and the process of adaptation begins, and continues forever.

"It's all so still," said the driver. "Nothing moves at all."

"There's no wind," said Germont. "Not here. There must be air currents down here, and fierce ones where the situation is right. But here the air's quite dead. Stale."

"There are no animals," said the driver. "None at all."

Germont shrugged. "They won't wait for the light. They must have been able to hear the convoy for miles."

"But why would they run?" asked the driver. "They sure as hell haven't learned to be afraid of armored trucks."

"They'd be afraid of the noise," said Germont.

The driver shook his head. "I don't like it," he said. "That line of lights in the sky, these great hulking masses of sponge on either side. It feels as though there's something different about just *here*. It's as if that stuff out there was *full* of things just sitting on either side of the road but staying clear. Watching us."

For a few moments, Germont didn't reply. His eyes followed the cone of light swinging across the face of the forest. Then he said: "Get some sleep."

As the driver clambered down from the cockpit and moved back to the belly of the vehicle, where eight other men were waiting—resting, talking, peeping through the portholes, and trying to hold down the unease in their stomachs, Germont continued to follow the progress of the light.

All the plant flesh was gray. There were all shades, but no colors. This was a color-blind world. Even in the lands where the stars were clustered in the sky, Germont thought, the light would be dim enough to rob ordinary human vision of color perception and depth perception. But what about the men who lived here? Perhaps they could see colors. Perhaps not the same colors as the men of the Overworld.

The most noticeable feature of the plant masses which dressed each of the broken hulks that had once been human habitations was their corporateness. Every one consisted of thousands—perhaps millions—of individuals, and the range of specific types was considerable. And yet all the grays and whites and blacks were *blurred*. The whole structure was amorphous. All the individual cups and caps, bulbs and wracks, squabs and sacs, were *integrated*, making use of one another, intertwining with one another, almost blending with one another. Germont knew that the apparent corporate identity was an illusion—that there must be fierce competition, interspecific and intraspecific, for every inch of support and space—but he was not sure that the illusion might not be more real than the reality. The competition *was* collaboration, of a kind. The vast tangle of shapes, crinose and petinated, aciform and orbicular, *was*—in some way—a unit. Out of the internal balance of the struggle for existence there was made some kind of entity. The whole forest, which might stretch for ten or fifty miles back on either side of the road, was a colossal life-system, a superorganism. The city had come to life. And the convoy—forty-five vehicles in single file carrying five hundred men to inoculate a whole world with death—was just a worm in its gut. A dangerous invader inside it, waiting to bite.

Germont's vehicle was air-tight and armored. Its six huge wheels could cope with virtually any terrain. It carried a flame-thrower and a machine gun in the turret where the searchlight was mounted. It was a sealed package containing a fragment of the Overworld. Nothing could possibly harm him, or any of his men. They could spew out poison to eat up the life of the Underworld's cities, but the Underworld could do nothing to them.

And yet Germont was afraid.

He came down from the cockpit, seated himself in front of the miniature holoscreen at his communications console, and activated it. Some minutes passed before his call was answered. He did not know the woman who answered, and he did not ask her name. She represented the Movement, and that was identity enough so far as Germont was concerned.

He gave exact details of the convoy's position and confirmed that he was exactly on schedule.

"The Delta contingent will remain in this locale," he said. "They will make preliminary investigations in the morning. Preparations for experimental seeding will take place as per schedule. We have encountered no difficulties. The other three contingents will proceed to the rendezvous with Zuvára at nine A.M. We have seen no sign of any animal lifeform. All equipment is functioning, and air filtration is one hundred percent effective. Water purification apparatus has not yet been tested in the field, but contingent Delta will report tomorrow."

The woman acknowledged the information, and Germont switched off. There was no conversation. The woman's presence had been a formality—a concession to the principle of human involvement. The cybernet had recorded his report, and would have acted on it had any action been necessary. It would also have relayed any new instructions. The illusion of human communication was in some ways similar to the illusion of unity in the forest life-system. At the most basic level, no such communication was taking place. But the purpose of human communication was what gave the perfect arbitration of the cybernet a meaning.

He went back into the belly of the vehicle, and lay on his bunk waiting for sleep. He found difficulty in relinquishing his tight hold on consciousness, and when he finally slept, he dreamed.

More than once, during the long night, he awoke into his dreams. And what he found there frightened him.

4

"Why didn't you come back to the Overworld when you had the opportunity?" asked Rypeck.

Joth put the tips of his fingers to his mouth and pressed his palms together while he contemplated the question.

"The reasons are complicated," he said, finally. "They didn't seem so at the time, but I didn't think about it much. I just did what I felt I ought to do. I suppose I worked out the reasons subconsciously—or perhaps I invented them later to explain myself. When I found the door in the metal wall, I found my father. He'd finally been compelled to look outside his nightmares, into the substance of his visions. He'd found a way into the world he wanted to save, just as I'd found a way out. We collided. It wasn't really that much of a coincidence—the same things which moved him moved me, factors external to both of us.

"He wasn't quite dead when I found him, but he couldn't do or say anything. He was still bleeding from a wound—a bullet wound. Finding him there just knocked the bottom out of the world. I was running home, and suddenly there was no home to run to. By then I had other priorities. Nita and Huldi were cut adrift, just as I was. When I buried my father I felt myself thrown back into their predicament. Drifting in the world, with no purpose—cut right out of the cloth of existence. Whether I came back or stayed, I'd have had to start all over again. I stayed, because that's where I was. I stayed with them.

"I fell ill again. I just didn't have the constitution to live down there. They had to cut some parasites out of my back and the wound wouldn't heal. I got worse. Then we met the hellkin. He joined us. His name was . . . is . . . Iorga."

Joth paused, expecting some reaction.

"This is the . . . man . . . who killed Harkanter?" asked Ulicon, filling the pause.

"He had to," said Joth.

"Let's not leap forward now," said Rypeck, with a hint of impatience in his voice. "We'll leave the matter of judgment until the proper time. Tell us what happened."

"Iorga had seen Camlak, with another man from the village. We went back toward the wall. We found the other, but not Camlak. Camlak had been shot, by the man called Soron. He had come out into the open because Harkanter was trapped in a mudhole. He wanted to help. The other—Chemec—had been more cautious, and had stayed hidden. But Camlak didn't think there was anything to be afraid of. That was my fault. It was because of me that Camlak wasn't afraid. But they shot him."

"Harkanter claimed that he was attacked—that the rat had a knife." This interjection came from Ulicon.

Joth shook his head.

"There was a misunderstanding," said Rypeck.

"I had to get him back," said Joth, ignoring the remark. "It was up to me. He kept me alive in the village. But for him I'd be dead. If not for me, he wouldn't have been at the wall. He wouldn't have tried to help Harkanter. I came up to the Overworld to bring him back. I brought Iorga with me to help."

"Why come back in secret?" demanded Rypeck. "Why come to steal the rat? Why break into Harkanter's house with guns?"

"Do you honestly think," said Joth, "that anyone would have listened to me? Was there any other way? The one thing I wanted to do, at that time, was free Camlak. I had no other purpose. I set about doing it in the only way it could be done—by stealth. We didn't intend to kill anyone—we just wanted to take Camlak off Harkanter and back to the Underworld. When that was done, I intended to come back for the explanations. I had myself patched up by a doctor, and then Julea got Harkanter to open his door to us. It would have gone according to plan. We went down into the cellars. Camlak was in a cage. I saw him there. And then there was an explosion inside my head."

There was a brief silence. This was the climactic point. They all knew that this was the fulcrum of the whole matter, but none of them knew how to approach it.

Eventually, it was Ulicon who spoke.

"I was sitting in an armchair," he said. "I was reading some printouts. It was as if I'd been stabbed in the back of my neck, the blade traveling upwards into my brain. I couldn't hold the pages—I just lost control of my hands and they shook like leaves in a high wind. My eyes were closed, but I was *seeing*. The light—or the illusion of light —was almost unbearably bright. Images flashed in an incoherent sequence. It was all too bright and too fast for me to make sense of it, but some of the images I could almost focus, and recall. What I saw was a confused conglomerate of visual memories. I looked—through someone or something else's eyes—into the Underworld. I saw what your father saw. It took time, but I came to realize that what had happened to me—and hundreds of thousands of others—was no more than what had already happened to your father. With him, it took years; with us, less than a second. He, perhaps, saw through many pairs of eyes, had access to millions of memories. We saw through one pair of eyes one set of visual images.

"For a while, when I found that these alien memories were imprinted in my mind, I feared that I would go mad. Perhaps, by the standards which were mine a few days ago, I am no longer sane. If so, that is true of fully half the members of our society. Our minds have been invaded. We have memories that are not our own. When we wake, we are constantly aware, but at least we are in control. When we sleep . . ."

"The citizens of Euchronia have no nightmares. That is the way it was intended to be. Euchronia was intended to be the answer to intellectual unrest. But that is no longer true. We now know that our minds are open. Perhaps we have opened them ourselves—we do not know. But in any case, our inner being can no longer be entirely our own. Our inner space is no longer delimited by the confines of our physical being. We wonder, now, if any one of us can speak of *my* self, *my* mind.

"We now understand *The Marriage of Heaven and Hell*, and why your father wrote it. We think that we understand how the alien ideas coming into his mind comingled and integrated with his own. We now have nightmares, as he did. Some of us—I don't know how many—now catch, as he did, the leakage of other minds while we sleep. The mindblast has ripped away the shielding around our selves, and we are no longer secure.

"We know that the focus of the blast was Harkanter's house. We know that the being in the cage disappeared, and we can only believe that its disappearance was the cause of the blast. We live in desperate fear of this incessant pollution of ourselves which is coming from the Underworld. Our reflex action is to destroy—to obliterate the minds which are invading our personal space. What Eliot and I fear is that the destruction of the Underworld is not a real solution to the problem. We fear that the clock cannot be turned back, and that our minds are permanently altered. What we fear is that in destroying the Underworld we may destroy our chance to find a *real* answer. There are only two people in the world who might help us find such an answer. You are one. You must tell me *everything* that you know or suspect about what happened in Harkanter's cellar."

"I thought that he'd destroyed himself," said Joth, slowly. "I saw him—my eyes were actually upon him in the moment he disappeared. But Nita believes that he is alive. Elsewhere. She spoke about her soul—the festival I saw in the village was called the Communion of Souls. She said that during such a communion she had looked into other worlds, and that her father had gone into one. But the festival was just a ritual—it was a mime. Nothing happened that I was aware of. There must have been so much more—so much that I couldn't begin to know.

"Camlak's memories came into their minds too, but they just accepted it. They weren't even surprised. Perhaps it happens all the time, to them. But I don't think so. I think there's something about the way they live and think that we can never understand—something that is utterly different from us. And yet there's so much that is the same . . .

"I don't know what happened. What you've said may all be true. It seems reasonable. But all I know is what you know—that Camlak's memories have been blasted into my mind and your mind and many other minds. It could happen again. It probably will. Everything that you and the whole Movement fears could come true. Our minds might be dissolved inside our heads. But there's one thing that you must consider. Nita and Chemec weren't surprised. They *knew* what had happened. And if they, and the Children of the Voice as a whole, really know and understand what happened, then they can do it again. If you try to exterminate the Children of the Voice, then they may react as Camlak reacted when Harkanter put him in a cage. If you start a

war with the people of the Underworld, you might lose. They can destroy you."

5

Abram Ravelvent was tired. Since he had become tangled in this affair through acquaintance with Carl Magner, it had taken years off his life. His initial interest had been mere curiosity—a typical fascination for the unusual. He had once found intellectual puzzles a source of delight. Now he was lost inside one. What had been a game had become a prison. Once, he had been able to choose where he would stand in the argument. He had committed his belief on the instruction of a whim. Now, he was completely bound up. He no longer dared to believe, or even to guess. But still people came to him with questions and arguments. He was still an "expert" to be consulted. People still looked to him for confirmation and correction. They asked nothing of him but certainty, because they so desperately wanted to know that someone, somewhere, had answers in his pocket.

Even now, he kept up the sham. He would not, could not, bring himself to relinquish the pretense that had sustained him through so many years.

But the persistent answering, when he knew no answers, made him very tired indeed.

He stared at the image of Joel Dayling which hovered above his desk. Dayling looked equally tired. His expression was grim.

"It's no longer a matter of politics," he was saying. "I no longer *have* to defeat Euchronia, because Euchronia is dead. It died when its basic premise was overturned. There is no stable future. There is no secure present. It's no longer a matter of Eupsychians and Euchronians, trying to topple Heres from his pedestal. We're all in the same boat now, and the Movement is falling apart. Everyone has a voice now, not just the Movement. I'm not interested in getting Heres out of office now—I'm interested in saving the world, if it can be saved. What I want from you is an opinion, that's all. Not your vote or your endorsement. I just want to *know*—can Heres destroy the Underworld? Is it possible?"

Ravelvent didn't know. He didn't want to answer. But even while he hesitated and looked for an evasion, the rhetoric was trying to surface inside his skull. He fought, trying to keep perspective.

"Not the way the world thinks," he said. "Maybe *this* world could be destroyed with a snap of the fingers, but not the world down there. The people are used to thinking of the Overworld as one vast unit—one great big machine-wrapped family. That's their idea of what a world is. But the Underworld is very different. With our resources, perhaps we could destroy it—destroy all the higher life-forms, at any rate. But not in years, or decades, or perhaps centuries. They don't have a machine-host which can just be switched off. We'll have to go into that world and spread our poisons and our diseases mile by mile. No one in Euchronia has any idea of the true *size* of the world. We have instant electronic presence—we can go anywhere in the world by sitting in front of a screen and pressing a switch. You and I are thousands of miles apart, and yet we're face-to-face. No one understands how big the Underworld is. Not even Heres. He may destroy the Underworld, but I doubt it. You just can't conceive of the magnitude of the task that he's set himself."

"If what I've heard is true," said Dayling, "Heres' chief weapon—perhaps the only one that matters—is a virus. Rumor has it that this thing will lay waste the Underworld's plant life utterly, and that it will spread like wildfire."

"I don't know that I can comment on that," said Ravelvent.

"I'm not asking you to give away any secrets," said the Eupsychian, slightly scornfully. "Even if you know any. I'm not fishing for information I can use in a whispering campaign. I want to know just what kind of a chance Heres' present policy has of success. Treat the question hypothetically. What would be the limitations of such a virus? Can it be made, and if so, will it do what it has to?"

Ravelvent hesitated, but then carried on. He saw no point at all in concealing the truth as he saw it.

"What we know so far," he said, "suggests that the Underworld life-system is, at primary production level, almost totally derived from fungal and algal forms native to the pre-Euchronian era. If these can be successfully attacked, the bottom is knocked out of virtually every food-chain that exists down there. If the fungoids and algoids can be destroyed, animal life will cease to be possible. What Heres' scientists are trying to do is tailor a family of viruses to attack chemical structures unique to the kinds of cell which are found in the Underworld life-system, but not our own, which is derived from very different kinds of plant. This is not difficult. Fungi and algae survive in the Overworld as pests, and research to weed out such parasites using tailored viruses was going on as far back as the prehistoric ages. It was one of the first fields of research which the Movement reinstituted on the platform.

"The problems involved are twofold. In the first instance, we have no idea as to the possible reactivity of the Underworld's life-system, or its capacity for self-repair. We don't know what degree of immunity to expect, and we don't know how quickly the organisms in the Underworld will discover immunity. There is reason to believe that the Underworld's entire ecosystem is in the tachytelic evolutionary phase, which means that its capacity to absorb and withstand attack of this kind could be high.

"The second problem is transmission of the diseases. This will happen naturally, to some extent. In a given locale, the viruses will—as you put it—spread like wildfire. But introducing a disease into a life-system isn't like lighting a fuse and waiting for an explosion. Tailored diseases have difficulty in spreading simply because there's no reservoir of infection within the system as a whole. There is no such thing as an unlimited epidemic. These viruses are going to have to be assisted in their conquest by constant seeding over very wide areas. That will take a great deal of time and a tremendous level of production. A great deal of effort goes into the isolation of one gram of a crystalline virus. When we talk of destroying worlds, we talk in tons rather than grams.

"The viruses may do what Heres thinks is necessary, but it won't be done overnight, and the amount of resistance within the life-system may be far greater than we hope. And in the meantime—while Heres' grand plan is in progress —new factors may enter the situation. Anything might happen. Heres may have picked the simple answer, but it isn't an easy one. There are no easy ones."

"Thanks," said Dayling. "That's what we needed to know."

"We?" queried Ravelvent.

"Don't worry. We aren't a revolutionary movement. Not any more. We don't have to be. The revolution started without us. Now, we're the government-in-reserve. When Heres reaches the end of his rope, the Council will have to turn to someone. We intend to be the only people with ideas. If you want a job, Abram, you only have to ask."

Ravelvent laughed shortly.

"You always wanted to be dictator," he said, with a hint of bitterness.

"Not at all," said Dayling. "I always wanted to be messiah."

6

"Did you see *anything* which suggested that the rats are telepathic?" demanded Rypeck.

"They're not rats," said Joth.

"Do they use telepathy?" persisted Rypeck.

Joth shook his head. "Camlak said nothing to suggest that they could. But afterwards . . . Nita knew what had happened. Maybe they have telepathy but don't use it. I don't know."

"They have it," said Ulicon, quickly. "We *know* that. Memory images can be transmitted and implanted. What Joth's evidence suggests is that they can't control it. In all probability, they're not even aware of it. They take for granted the fact that their minds *spill over* from their selves, that there's some kind of unitary organization within the species —perhaps like a hive of bees. This property of their minds is completely bound up with ritual and religion—to them, it's natural. They personify the collective as their souls. The communion of souls is a social thing, where the whole social unit shares some experience through invoking this group identity."

Rypeck waved a hand angrily. "It doesn't even *begin* to look like an explanation," he said. "Enzo, we must do better than this. You can't use this garbled nonsense to explain the fact that the rat—or man, or whatever—*disappeared* from that cage. Where did it go? Did it dissipate itself into your hypothetical superorganism? What happened to its *body*? We mustn't lose sight of the fact that we're dealing with a *physical event*. The blast of energy was the result of the *physical* phenomenon. The mental side effect was just that—a *side effect*. We mustn't fall into the trap of thinking that the transmission of memories from the rat to everyone within receiving distance was the purpose of what happened. It wasn't. It was, in all likelihood, quite accidental. The wave which carried the information is what we should be interested in, and that wave was generated by what we would previously have considered to be an impossible event. The very fact that the intensity of what we *felt* seems to have depended more or less on the inverse square of the distance between ourselves and the focal point surely suggests that we are dealing with a physical phenomenon whose psychical effects are really secondary."

"That kind of division doesn't make sense," said Ulicon.

"Enzo, we communicate *via* electromagnetic radiation. We speak into a microphone, and at the other end, someone hears our words. The information is in one brain, which translates thought into sound. The microphone translates sound into electricity. The electricity is translated into modified radio waves, which are translated back into electricity, back into sound, and then back into informaiton in another brain. We can't try to understand such a process by what goes on in the brains, and *only* what goes on in the brains. Is that telepathy? Of course it is—information is transmitted from brain to brain. But in order to understand it we must understand the physics of it. We can't consider it simply as a psychic phenomenon. To do so makes nonsense of it."

"All right," said Ulicon. "So it's a problem in physics. So what?"

"We've already established," said Rypeck, "that the Children of the Voice don't *use* telepathy. What does that mean? It means that they aren't normally able to translate ideas into a form which can be carried by the kind of energy which is involved in the event we're trying to understand. It's as though they were mute—unable to translate ideas into sounds so that they can be transmitted from one brain to another. This failure could be at one of several levels. They might lack the physical apparatus for so doing—as if they had no tongues. Or they might lack the coding capacity—that is to say, they have the tongues but not the language. Or they might lack the power—as if they couldn't expel the breath through the throat in order to vibrate the vocal cords. Any of these might be true. But what we must do is abandon the notion that there is something magical or supernatural about what happened, or about the kind of thing we have to deal with. We may have to introduce a whole new physics into our scientific understanding, but what we must not do is try to make do with a whole new metaphysics."

"All that may be true," complained Joth, "but it doesn't help. You both seem obsessed with trying to find words to describe what happened. But that isn't going to stop Heres destroying the Children of the Voice. He must be prevented from committing genocide. Isn't that what we're here for? Isn't *that* what we're trying to do. It's what *I'm* trying to do."

"It's not so simple," said Rypeck.

"It's simple enough," said Joth. "It's saving millions of people from being wiped out because Heres and the Euchronians are scared. If they had been reasonable in the first place—if they'd only been prepared to recognize the fact that there *are* people in the Underworld who should be dealt with as people—then this whole thing wouldn't have happened."

"We cannot simply wait," said Rypeck. "As Heres and millions of others see it—as Enzo and I see it, even—our minds and our identities are threatened with destruction. We know that it could be done. We want to see that it isn't. If the threat is not to be faced in Heres' way—a way which we and others consider to be extremely dangerous—then we must find another way to face it. If we are not to attack the threat at its source, then we must find a defense. That logic may be hard, but it is more appropriate than the ethical logic which you are trying to apply. If Enzo and myself are prepared to hear your case and support you, it is because we are afraid that Heres' plan may precipitate the destruction it attempts to forestall, not because we want to save the Children of the Voice."

Joth felt stricken. "When I was injured," he said, in a very low voice, "my father fought for my life. He defended me against a medical committee which wanted to put me out of my supposed misery. My father won, and I have a face of steel and plastic. I was allowed to live. Sometimes, it has occurred to me to doubt whether or not my father did the right thing. I believed that the whole argument was one of ethics. After all, this is the Euchronian Millennium—the end-point of human ambition. And when my father wrote his book—I thought the argument then was a matter of ethics.

It occurs to me to wonder now—who *did* shoot my father? Who ordered it done?"

"Your father was killed by a man named Simkin Cinner," said Ulicon, gently. "No one ordered it done. And you must see that whether you approve of our motives or not, the only way of getting what you want is our way. The only way that the people of the Underworld will be allowed to live is by our proving that the Overworld has nothing to fear from them."

Joth looked him in the face, deliberately staring with his cold, metallic eyes. Ulicon could not meet the stare. No one could.

"I don't think you can prove that," said Joth. "Because you'll always be afraid. The Euchronians have always thought that the world was theirs, because of the platform and the Plan. But now we know that it's not true. The world belongs to the people of the Underworld. The Underworld *is* the world. Euchronia is a gigantic castle in the air. A dream. I think that if the Movement tries to destroy the Underworld, the Underworld will destroy the Movement, and the Overworld with it."

"That," said Rypeck, "is exactly what we fear."

7

The driver screamed, and the armored truck swerved to the left. There was a soft sound as the nearside wing sheared fungus, and then a harsher grating noise as the metal met something more solid. The vehicle came back off the wall into the road, its nose swinging as the driver jerked the wheel.

Germont was into the cockpit in a matter of seconds. By the glare of the headlights he could see something—someone —trying desperately to get out of the path of the vehicle. The driver had not hit the brakes.

It was too late. The truck hit the running figure and ran over the crushed body. Germont grabbed the wheel and held it steady, holding the vehicle on course. Finally, belatedly, the driver found the brake pedal with his foot, and the truck slowed to a halt.

"What the hell do you think you're doing?" demanded Germont.

"He threw something!" gasped the driver, who was shaking like a leaf. "The lights just picked him up, and he threw a rock. It hit the canopy just in front of me—I thought it was coming through. I couldn't help it."

The transparent plastic had taken the blow comfortably —there was no mark. The driver had been startled rather than scared. But the shock had been considerable.

"Cut the engine," said Germont curtly, and then turned to call to the men in the back: "Get on that searchlight! And the gun."

He dropped back to snatch up the microphone by which he could broadcast to the convoy.

"Hold your positions," he said. "Alpha-two, do you see what we ran over?"

"I see it," came the reply. "I can't make it out. Could be human. Do you want me to send someone out a for a closer look?"

"No! No one gets out. Can you maneuver to get the body into the light from your headlights? I want all searchlights on. Scan the forest."

"Jacob," said the driver, speaking with unnatural quietness now that he was past the shock. "The road ahead. There used to be a cutting. The land's slipped. It's blocked. We'll have to go back and around."

Germont, with the microphone still in his hand, climbed up to a position from which he could look out of the cockpit. The light of the many searchlights showed that the forest was banked unnaturally high on either side of them. The road ran through a long, shallow canyon. The obstruction in front was steep, but it did not seem impassable.

"We can climb that," said Germont. "We don't need a road. This thing is built to hold a slope."

Somewhere back along the line, a machine gun came to life. Almost immediately, searchlight beams converged, and Germont looked back to where tiny white figures were moving on the ridge, while the bullets tore fungal tissue to pieces all around them. The soft, pulpy flesh *splashed* as the bullets hit, and sections of leathery algal frondescence fluttered in the air and writhed as they slid down the slope, robbed of their support. One of the figures was hurled back, and another. Dead and alive alike, they disappeared as great clouds of spore dust poured from the afflicted area.

There was a series of dull thuds as rocks hit the plating of Germont's vehicle. He looked up, trying to locate the throwers, while the searchlight veered back and forth.

"Stop firing!" he commanded. "They can't hurt us!"

Then the land somewhere in the rear began to slide. It was the spot where the firing had been concentrated—the bullets had weakened the ancient structure which supported the forest, and it was tumbling, sliding down into the road.

Realizing the danger, the trucks which were in the path of the slide came forward in a hurry. The first two or three managed to get far enough. One or two didn't, and the loose rock, moving with fluid smoothness, washed into them, turned them, shoved them and began to bury them. One was turned over on its side.

When the slide was over, six vehicles were trapped. Two were breached, and all had some degree of internal damage.

Angrily, Germont ordered men out of the other trucks to begin digging out the trapped men and freeing the vehicles. They came out in closed-environment suits, and for every two or three men to dig, there had to be one with a rifle. The searchlights continued to scan the slopes for signs of the attackers.

Germont went out himself, to look at the corpse which lay in the roadway between his vehicle and the second in line. He waited while one of the doctors inspected the body.

"Is it human?" he asked, when the examination was over.

"Near enough," said the doctor.

"He must have been crazy," said Germont. "Coming at the truck like that."

"It's not a he," said the doctor. "It's a she." Then the arrow hit him. It went through the plastic suit like paper, between his ribs and deep into his chest. He died instantly.

8

Elsewhere in the Underworld, the men from Euchronia were building a city: a city of hemispherical domes and cylindrical tunnels. The encampment beneath the plexus which had been established by Randal Harkanter and the party which he had led into the Underworld had been packed up and removed to the surface, only to be replaced by a much larger and much better equipped invasion force, whose purpose was to begin seeding the Swithering Waste with the Overworld's various biological agents of destruction, and to observe the effects thereof. It was one of several such stations—Germont's convoy was intended to establish three more—set up in a number of rather different habitats.

The seeding was done from the air, the viruses being laid out along long lines radiating like spokes from the circular metal wall which was the base of the plexus. The "electronic bats" which dispersed the viruses also carried cameras to assist in observation, but small ground-cars were also made available to the observers. This group was headed by Gregor Zuvara, who had become an expert on the Underworld by virtue of having spent a few more days there than most of those called in to assist him.

As the miniature city grew, Zuvara was forced to make ever-more-plaintive complaints about the inadequacy of his labor force. As soon as the news concerning the attack on Germont's force and the several deaths among his personnel was made public, the number of volunteers for work in the Underworld fell rapidly.

Within a matter of days it became obvious both above and below that some form of conscription would have to become effective. The subjugation of the individuals in the society of the Euchronian Millennium to necessity, as defined by the Hegemony of the Movement, became absolute. The clock had been turned right back. For the second time, the Euchronian Movement demanded total loyalty in order that the world might be saved, not for the present generation, but for generations to come.

Almost everyone expected this mobilization of Euchronia's manpower to go quite smoothly. This, after all, was the principle on which the world had been made. It had worked once—it had to work again. But Zuvara found his recruits resentful and discontent. The Euchronian spirit—the determination and selflessness that had build a world on the roof of a ruined Earth—was lacking.

Slowly, Zuvara realized that everything had changed. The Euchronian ideal was not enough. Not this time. Something within society had shattered.

While he watched the blight he had brought spreading throughout the world, stripping the vast marshland of everything living, reducing all plant tissue to a sort of protoplasmic tar, Zuvara could not help thinking: "We are destroying the world. The whole world. We are doing this to *ourselves*. *Everything* will die. There will be nothing left."

He told himself over and over that this was merely a nightmare, but he could not rid himself of it.

9

Chemec the cripple had left Shairn with Camlak because the way his mind worked left him little option but to follow his leader. Camlak had been Old Man of Stalhelm—virtually all that was left of Stalhelm. He had been all that was left of Chemec's life.

Now Camlak was gone, and there was virtually nothing left of Chemec's existence. Nothing but his cunning and his failing strength, and his meager identity: Chemec the crab, Chemec the bent-leg. But Chemec hardly felt a sense of loss. Certainly he did not grieve for Camlak. Chemec took life as it came, and accepted events as they happened. He lived neither in his memories nor in his hopes, but stayed always within the moment of the ephemeral present, carried along by the current of life. It was the way of his kind, and Chemec was very much one of his kind. More so than Camlak or Nita, or even Old Man Yami.

It was because of what he was rather than in spite of it that Chemec became a prophet. He had never been a man at odds with his soul. He coexisted with the Gray Soul inside his mind, in the simplest possible way. It was there, he let it be. He had never tried to be a psychic parasite with regard to his Gray Soul, nor had he attempted any kind of exchange. At Communion, he merely looked his Soul in the face. Nothing more. It was perfect commensalism—Chemec and the Soul shared the body and the mind, and neither troubled the other.

And because of this, when the Soul began placing motives in his mind, Chemec did not realize what was happening. He accepted the motives as his own, and he obeyed their commands as if they came from his own self.

He needed the motives. With Camlak gone, he had nothing left to him but to drift back into Shairn, to find a new community or to live alone, existing until he died. The motives made something of him. They repaired the aspect of function in his life. They made him a man again, whereas he might otherwise have contented himself as a rat.

From the Swithering Waste he went southwest, and came to the townships of northern Shairn: to Isthomi and Escar, to Rocoral and Zeid. In each town, he persuaded the priests to look into their soul-space, and he caused Communions to be called. At the Communions, he preached, and because of the Gray Souls his words were heard and engraved into the minds of his hearers.

All had heard Camlak's scream and knew intuitively that something of moment had happened at that moment. They were ready to hear—and so were the Gray Souls.

Chemec warned of the coming of the men from Heaven —of the impending destruction of the world. This was prophecy. He described things which he had seen, and things which were yet to be seen. What he said was true.

He did no more than this—his function was to spread the word, and no more. His function was to alert the Children of the Voice in Shairn. Others took his warnings beyond Shairn, into other parts of the world. While Chemec prepared for the uniting of a nation, others made way for the uniting of a race.

And in all parts of the world, while the warning was carried, the priesthood of the Children of the Voice, in rapport with their Gray Souls, attempted to decide and define what role the Children of the Voice were to play in the coming climax of their world.

10

Everyone in Euchronia was familiar with the game called Hoh. It was played everywhere. Passionate believers in Euchronian ideology tended to be passionate Hoh players as well. Rafael Heres and Eliot Rypeck were both expert players. Perhaps strangely, some of the most dedicated opponents of political Euchronianism were also devoted to the game. Thorold Warnet was one. There was, however, a sharp difference between the kinds of strategy that the opposing groups favored.

If it could be said that there was a single key to Euchronian civilization—one social institution which could help one to understand the way that the Overworld society worked—then that key had to be Hoh.

All games are, to some extent, analogues of life situations. One can learn a great deal about relationships within a society from a study of the way popular games are staged and used by the members of the society, and from the kind of encounter mimicked by the rules of such games. The simplest games are redistribution-of-capital games, usually governed by sheer chance. Such games become complicated by the addition of player-options rather than by the introduction of manipulative skill. Other games which usually exist alongside these are war games, in which chance is minimized and skill becomes paramount. All games of this class are zero-sum games, in which one player's gain is another's loss. There are other kinds of games—accumulation or construction games—which are not zero-sum. In a society dominated by zero-sum concerns, this class is primarily represented by one-player games rather than group-competitive games.

The game of Hoh was a complex derivation of a much older game which consisted of locating dots on a matrix, and establishing rules determining conditions under which they "die," "survive," or "reproduce." As these rules are followed, the population of dots passes through a number of "generations" and—ultimately—one of several results is obtained. All the dots may be removed from the board; a pattern may form which reproduces itself exactly at each generation; a stable cycle of patterns may result; or a pattern may be formed which reproduces itself and simultaneously changes location so that it "migrates" across the matrix. This game is an elementary simulation of a population attempting to become viable. The rate of success or failure depends on two things: the rules governing death, survival and reproduction; and the initial pattern established on the matrix. Player participation is introduced if the player is permitted to "move" dots at each generation, according to options regulated by further rules. In its basic form, this is a one-player game. It becomes a multiple-player game when more than one population is introduced into the matrix, "competing" for available space. Again, new rules have to be introduced to govern *inter*specific interaction as well as *intra*specific. All the original outcomes are preserved with respect to either population. Several different "target situations" are possible: players may attempt to stabilize their own population and exterminate all others, or the players may collaborate so that *all* the populations become stable and viable. If "winning" is defined as stabilizing the particular population under a player's control, then the game may have only one winner, or no winners at all, or all the players might win.

In Hoh, the factor of evolution is added to the competition situation, providing for populations to change their properties as defined by the rules. The ability to do so, like the ability of the population to redeploy itself at each generation, is controlled by player-options.

The Hoh player, therefore, has a number of options open to him strategically. He may direct his efforts toward the situation in which his population alone survives, or toward a situation in which more than one—perhaps all—the populations survive. In so doing, he may endeavor to alter the properties of his own pieces with respect to one another and to other pieces in order to make them more efficient at survival or reproduction, or "killing" pieces of other species. The rules are complex, and if the matrix on which the game is played is large, a computer is required to alter the pattern at each generation.

The Euchronian Movement was founded in order to stabilize the human population of Earth and to provide a social pattern for the resultant society. The Euchronian Movement, in effect, played a game analogous to Hoh in reality, and the Euchronian Plan by which a platform was built to cover the entire land surface of the planet, was a sequence of moves—a strategy—for such a game. The fact that a game like Hoh should have developed within Euchronian society to the preeminence which it eventually acquired was an eloquent testimony to the success of Euchronian ideology as a socially cohesive force. It was highly significant that political polarization in Euchronian society, during and after the completion of the Plan, should be correlated with different approaches to the game rather than with the evolution of alternative classes of game.

The dedicated Euchronians always played Hoh by strategies which would allow the maximum possible number of players to succeed in stabilization: they aimed toward the situation in which all populations became viable. This is not any easy way to play. Even if *all* the players work toward this end, the element of competition is not removed from the game, because it is built into the rules governing interactions. On a small matrix, it may be almost impossible to discover a situation in which four or five populations may collaborate in a stable situation, and even if one such situation exists, it may be impossible for any sequence of moves to bring that situation into being. In the eventuality of one or more players adopting a different strategy, the problems become complex indeed, as such players must be forced to conform, or be eliminated—problems of this type become inordinately complicated.

The Eupsychians who played Hoh almost invariably attempted to win outright—that is, to be the *only* winner. When Eupsychians played one another, the game was usually straightforward, and when Euchronians played together it was moderately so. The most interesting games, however, were played by Euchronians *and* Eupsychians. These games were the most difficult and the most challenging. Strangely, however, they took place rarely, even among the most expert players. Certainly Rafael Heres would never have sat down to play Hoh with anyone who was liable to employ Eupsychian strategies—not because he was afraid of the competition, but because he felt such strategies were contrary to the *spirit* in which the game ought to be played. Eupsychians used the same logic.

A Eupsychian would argue that Euchronians played toward an end that was "unnatural." They would cite the biological principle known as Gause's axiom, which states that two species in competition cannot coexist—one must always drive out or eliminate the other. The Euchronians worked toward an end that was perfectly possible and perfectly legitimate under the rules of Hoh, but the Eupsychian would nevertheless feel that they were "cheating" with respect to some more abstract principle.

A Euchronian, on the other hand, would argue that Eupsychian players were both narrow-minded and simple-minded, and deliberately unintelligent. He would point out that if the moves were made at random, then Gause's axiom would probably hold up in virtually every instance. *But*, he would say, the whole point of having intelligent, calculating players was to rise above the random situation: to control the game, and to force the situations which would not otherwise be probable. In nature, he would claim, Gause's axiom might have some validity, but when applied analogically to the game of Hoh, it ought to exist in order to be broken. Hoh was a game played with the aid of computers—it was the game of a highly advanced technological society—and it hardly made sense, to a Euchronian, that it should be played according to the law of the jungle.

It was, however, noticeable that when Euchronians and Eupsychians did sit down to participate mutually in a game of Hoh, the Euchronians—unless they were vastly superior players—could not reach the ideal target situation. At best, they could usually eliminate the Eupsychians by collective action in violation of their own principles, and then reorder their affairs to assure that they themselves were collaborative winners. In most instances, the Euchronians had to outnumber the Eupsychians considerably in order to stay in the game.

Significantly, an inordinately high percentage of games in which both Euchronians and Eupsychians participated, regardless of relative numbers, ended in the situation where no population was able to become viable. Normally, therefore, when Euchronians and Eupsychians played together, everybody lost.

11

Yvon Emerich took pride in two things: his independence and his showmanship. Under normal circumstances, he had every opportunity to assert both these aspects of his character through his work in the holovisual media. Since the crisis, however, he had been removed utterly and totally from all assertive situations.

Formerly, he had been a kind of opposition that the Hegemony of the Euchronian Movement found advantageous to themselves. Emerich was anti-Council and anti-Heres, but he was also anti-everything else. He influenced opinion without controlling it in any way. He was a noncreative thinker, purely destructive in argument. He voiced perpetual objections to Council policy and behavior, but provided no alternatives. While he represented the voice of dissatisfaction, the Council was always secure, because there was never any pressure upon them to act differently, merely a perpetual challenge to justify the action which they took. Emerich gave resentment a focus, directing it away from channels where it might have become a threat to the power of the Movement. Though the society of the Euchronian Millennium was by no means the perfect world which had always been the Movement's promise, and though social unrest was evident in a hundred ways, the only real opposition to the Euchronian Movement—the Eupsychian party—had never gained a place on the Council in an election. Most people thought of Emerich as a Eupsychian, or at least a sympathizer, but he was by no means the kind of mouthpiece the party wanted or needed. From their point of view the association in the public mind was a handicap.

When the "invasion" of the Overworld had taken place, however, Emerich had become a luxury that the Council could no longer afford. They wanted no challenge to Heres' proposals—they did not even want it spoken aloud that the proposals (and the objectives) *could* be challenged. Heres wanted total control of the electronic media during the period of crisis, because after saving the world, he had to save Euchronia, and he knew full well that even if he succeeded in the former purpose, the latter might well be impossible. But in deposing Emerich from his position of preeminence he made himself a very determined enemy. From Emerich's point of view, necessity was no excuse for the injury and the insult which had been done to him.

The Eupsychians wasted no time whatsoever in taking advantage of this situation.

"The Movement," Thorold Warnet told him, "is finished. It's clinging to power now simply because there seems to be nothing to take its place. We must organize something to take its place. In order to do so, we need control of the cybernet, including communications."

"You want me to join the revolution?" said Emerich bluntly.

"Not quite," said Warnet. "We want you to stop the revolution—the revolution of the people against this crazy trap they find themselves in. At the moment, there's virtually nothing keeping the world running. Every citizen of Euchronia's Millennium is on the verge of insanity. Every one of us has been led to accept that Euchronia has absolute control. Education says so, and history says so. The Movement did the impossible, and built a new world out of the ruins of the old. We have all been taught that Euchronia is omnipotent, that society is stable and secure and completely ordered. That's all been wiped out in a single night. All it took was the revelation that something exists which Euchronia can't handle, can't control, can't bring under the aegis of its total order and stability. All that Euchronia can do is destroy—if it can even do that. But the destruction itself testifies to the redundancy of Euchronian belief. If Euchronia is omnipotent, it shouldn't have to react this way. The destruction of the Underworld may take care of the problem, but it's not an answer. There is no answer. The answer is for someone else to provide—not the Movement. We can provide one. What we need is someone to deliver it."

"Crap!" said Emerich. "As long as I can remember you people have been spouting garbage like that. It means nothing. If you want to talk to me, talk sense. You want Heres out, fine. But don't tell me why—tell me *how*. What are you going to do, and what the hell makes you think it might *work*?"

Warnet felt like laughing at the short, plump man who contrived to know everything by refusing to admit anything. But Emerich was right. Exquisite analyses of the philosophical complexion of the situation, correct or not, were meaningless. The important thing was to discover a program of action. Unfortunately, the argument between the Eupsychians and the Euchronian Movement had been so long confined to philosophical argument that prescriptions for social action were not easy to come by.

"We know what we want to achieve," said Warnet. "The trouble is coordinating our efforts. We know how and where to act in order to take control out of Heres' hands into our own. What we don't have is a way of keeping control—of preventing complete chaos. It's no good taking the reins of government if the people react by becoming ungovernable. Somehow, we have to make them trust us. You're the only man in the world who can do that, because you're the only one who knows how. If you collaborate with us, I think it can be done—I think we can find a way. If not, then I think the entire structure of society may break down, and we'll have no government at all. In a world like ours, that would be total disaster. If a mechanized society doesn't function as a unit, then it will stop functioning altogether."

"All very fine," said Emerich. "But what about the Underworld?"

"Perhaps we can destroy it," said Warnet. "But we may have to come to terms with it. We're not committed. Heres is. That's all the difference there can be."

12

When the last of the armored trucks had passed, the three came out of the forest and stood on the apron. The carpet of plants had been so badly cut and crushed by the tires that the ancient road surface was exposed here and there.

As the roar of the engines died away into the distance, the return of the silence seemed momentarily unnatural. The silence was real: nothing moved within the forest, no moths or birds called as they fluttered, even the whisper of the Overworld was still in this region.

"The road leads to Heaven," said Huldi, her eyes still fixed on the smear of light which marked the horizon where the trucks had gone.

"Perhaps," said Iorga.

Nita looked up, into the sky, to the roof of the world in which the stars were set. It seemed so very high above the world beneath. The dull gleam of the nearest pillars, set well back from the road yet still managing to catch a little of the starlight, seemed to stretch a long way. The pillars had always seemed to Nita to be as tall as anything could be, to set a limit to the tallness which anything could achieve. And yet the road *could* go to Heaven. Iorga had told her that he had seen mountains whose slopes went as far as the roof, and perhaps further. And in places the Overworld sagged, extending itself deep into the world beneath, at places like the metal wall. That the road went to Heaven even seemed to her to be some justification of the fact that it extended across hundreds of miles of blackland. It stood to reason that a road to Heaven would be a long road and a hard road, and one not easily followed. The blackland must be the borderland—the barrier-land—between the world which Shairn shared and the world from which Joth had come. That there was a road across the border, through the barrier, seemed to her to be significant. Everyone in Shairn knew of the road of stars, but no one, so far as she knew, was aware of where it went, or had ever attempted to follow it. It had been a challenge the Shaira had refused. But perhaps it was _for_ the Shaira, so that those with the curiosity and the courage might be able to gain the sight of Heaven that her father had always wanted. Perhaps the road had been waiting for the Shaira—waiting since the beginning of time.

The alternative possibility—that the road existed not to permit the Shaira access to Heaven, but to permit the men of the Overworld access to Hell—did not occur to her. In her view, the men from the world above must have many ways of descending into the Tartarean realms. Logically, it was passage in the other way which would be difficult and hazardous.

They continued on their way, without speaking. They talked more between themselves now than they had previously, but they talked mostly when they rested to eat and sleep. They spoke about themselves, told things that they knew, and recalled images from the past. They did it without questions, because none of them was habituated to questions. But they all remembered Joth, who had been saturated with them. It was really his questions that they were answering, still.

They did not know how far they had come into the blackland, nor how far they might have to go before they reached some kind of a destination. But they kept on going, and they would continue for as long as it took to get to wherever they were going. There was never any temptation to give up and go back, because they were never conscious of the time that was being absorbed by the journey. As they were now, they were in passage, and they might have set out a moment before or a hundred years. The end of the journey might be just outside the blur which limited their sight, or they might be traveling forever, until they died. Such possibilities never came into their minds. Once they had accepted a purpose, they continued until the situation changed and events deflected them from their course.

The trek along the road of stars had not been without incident—several times (they had not bothered to count how many) they had been forced to defend themselves against slinking predators which had come too close. Some they had killed and eaten. But the predators were relatively few, and they were not the most serious danger. The real threat to the success of their journey was poison. In the blacklands, there was poison everywhere. The land which the Overworlders had left, in and about their cities, had been poisoned ten thousand years before, and as the Underworld life-system had become viable in these areas, as it had everywhere else, it had simply adapted to the poisons. Now, while the Overworld still pumped such wastes that it would not or could not reclaim down to the blackland surface, the life of the Underworld thrived on a constant supply of chemical and radioactive substance which would have been deadly to organisms elsewhere. The Underworld's life-system was by no means homogeneous. The Overworld had provided itself with a stable biotic environment as well as a mechanical and sociocultural one, but the Underworld could not and had not. Adaptation had required adaptation to a vast range of habitats. Perhaps the blacklands posed less of a threat to the people of the Underworld than to the Overworlders, but its dangers were nonetheless considerable. There was food here that they could eat, and water to be found that they could drink, but it was not easy to find or identify sources of their needs. And the worst of the trouble was that if they were selective, the parasites were not. A hundred or a thousand kinds of worm and winged thing would find them perfect hosts, while they would find the parasites deadly companions simply because of the poisons to which the tiny creatures were so adapted that they carried them around inside them in concentrations which Iorga, Nita and Huldi would find fatally toxic.

Even in the Swithering Waste, which was a wilderness, but a wilderness of the lightlands, Iorga had failed in a long fight against parasites and lost his mate. Here, the danger was exaggerated and ever-present. That was the true hazard of the blacklands, and that was why no one came here by choice, except perhaps the Cuchumanates, who had used the road for so long that they were probably made of poison themselves.

A little further along the way, they found one of the Cuchumanates, where rocks had spilled out over the road. One of the trucks had run right over her, and her body was smashed.

One of the trucks also remained. It had been caught broadside by the full force of the slippage, and had been turned on its side and carried off the road to smack into the slope on the far side, ending up sandwiched between two faces of rock and soil. The tires had not burst, but the suspension of the wheels had been so badly twisted that there had been no possible hope of getting the vehicle going even had the men from Heaven been able to dig it out. The truck had been resealed at the back, and it had obviously defied the attempts of the Cuchumanates to break into it after the convoy had gone. There were scars where the locking mechanism had been attacked with rocks, but it had not yielded.

Iorga made a brief attempt to do what the Cuchumanates had been unable to do, but it was only a token gesture. The vehicle was built too solidly for his meager resources.

The proximity of the Cuchumanates—there might be ten or a dozen in the group—was an extra reason for alertness. The species was quite unpredictable, and there was every reason to suppose that having lost at least one of their number recently the group would be ready enough to attack anyone or anything they met. Their weapons would undoubtedly be inferior—Iorga still had a gun—but that would not necessarily be significant in determining the outcome of a pitched battle.

They had no option but to move on quickly to a place where the road was clear, and not so confined by the looming forest. They walked for many miles before they stopped once more to sleep.

13

Abram Ravelvent came to see Joth face to face, rather than using the cybernet, because he felt an intense personal involvement in the affairs of Joth's family. He had never met Joth, but had been caught up inextricably in the tangled web of associations which surrounded him. It was Ravelvent who had found for Carl Magner a staircase into the Underworld, and had taken him there, and had seen Simkin Cinner shoot Magner dead. Ravelvent had returned to that same spot, on a different occasion, to find Julea Magner waiting there—waiting for nothing.

Ravelvent half-hated Joth for what had been done to Julea, but reason would not let him blame the youth. He did not find Joth's metal face frightening or intimidating. He found it, if anything, more comfortable to face than most faces of flesh. It was a machine, and Ravelvent found the machineness of it easy to deal with. To Ravelvent, all faces were properties of a machine—the cybernet—and they were only difficult to understand when they pretended to be real: flesh and blood instead of image.

Ravelvent had never married, and had never lived with a woman until he took Julea Magner into his home following her abandonment outside the plexus.

"How is she?" asked Joth.

"Hurt."

"Why didn't she come? I tried to call, but the house was empty, and the net couldn't locate her. You must have done that."

"She thinks you're dead," said Ravelvent.

"Why?"

"You shouldn't have taken her with you. Why did you let her see what happened at Harkanter's house?"

"I didn't know it was going to happen."

"You let her see the one in the cage. And the other one —the cat-man."

"I let her see them," agreed Joth. "I wanted her to see them. I'd have liked the whole world to see them, not as they wanted to see them, but as they are. But the world won't believe in them. It believes in cats and rats and monsters instead. Is that what *she* believes too? That's not what I showed her. I showed her men."

"You left her in the car when you went back down."

"Should I have taken her with me?"

"You shouldn't have gone down. You should have stayed."

"I couldn't."

Ravelvent shook his head. "You don't realize what has happened to her. Her whole world has just been screwed up and thrown away. Everything she knew, everything she loved, everything that meant anything to her. It all dissolved, and left nothing but chaos. Ryan went into the Underworld, and never came back. Her father was shot in front of her, and he expended his dying breaths running down a staircase—into the Underworld. She sent you after Ryan, and she thought that you were dead, too. But you came back. You gave her some kind of hope. And what then? You brought the Underworld into her world along with you, and then you went back. You left her in the car and you went back. What had she left? Had she even some vestige of hope? I found her there, and she couldn't even talk to me. She could speak, and make words, but she had nothing to say. Once she'd told me what happened—some of it—she had no more to say. There's nothing left of her life, except the dreams which killed her father. You even brought her those."

"It wasn't my fault," said Joth, quietly.

"No? None of it?"

"I'm sorry," said Joth. "You have no idea how sorry I am. She's my sister. She didn't want any part of this—she was caught up in it, because she was Carl Magner's daughter, just as I was caught up in it because I am his son. And the whole world is caught up in it because it was Carl Magner's world. She was hurt, and I'm bitterly sorry that she's hurt. She's lost her world, you say. It's just been ripped away from her. But remember how easily the world tore, how simple it was to crumple it up and throw it away. Whose fault is that? Nobody's to blame. All that happened is that we discovered that the Underworld still exists, that the Euchronian Heaven isn't ten thousand years away from the Hell it ran away from. That's all. Julea was too close to that discovery. So was I. So were you. But there's no point in looking around for someone to blame, whether it's me or my father or Heres or the Children of the Voice or the founder of the Movement of God Almighty. What we have to do is put it *right*."

Ravelvent did not speak for several minutes. When he did, he said: "Why should *she* have to suffer?"

"I'm sorry," said Joth, again. "I'm sorry I had to use her to get into Harkanter's house. But what else could I do? Would he have opened the door to me? To Iorga? I was trying to put things right. It wasn't my fault that everything blew up in my face. I'm still trying to put things right. I'm trying to stop them destroying the Underworld. But they don't listen. They just won't *see*."

"They *can't*," said Ravelvent. "You must understand that."

"I don't. I don't understand it at all."

"You've been into the Underworld," said Ravelvent. "You've lived there. I don't know how, but somehow it's become real to you. It's not real to me. I *know* it's real, intellectually. I can consider it as a fact, I can think about it with complete rationality. People ask me questions, and I can give them answers. I can offer opinions, make predictions, analyze and theorize. But I can't make it real.

"I'm an old man, Joth. Most of us are old, because we can live a long time, and our birth rate isn't large. Maybe that's what makes the difference. The Underworld, to me, is just not real. It's a fantasy. There just is no place in my mind which can accept the reality of the things which you have revealed—or even the things which are happening in the world. Until the last few days I never had a bad dream in my life. Now all my dreams are nightmares. Even while I'm awake, things come into my mind that make me think I'm mad. I don't accept the reality of these things, because there's no way I can. To me, it seems that the world is becoming *unreal*.

"You don't understand why people can't accept what you tell them. I don't understand it either, but I know that it's so. The things which you talk about are beyond our conceptual horizons. It was the same with your father's book. Many of us found it fascinating, but in a purely speculative sense. It wouldn't have mattered if everything your father wrote had been true, and demonstrably true, because we simply aren't mentally constructed in order to accept it as true. We can talk about the Underworld, and appear to do so quite sensibly, but it's as though we were trying to solve a puzzle. What's worse is the fact that we know we're wrong—we know that we're failing to confront the problem, not even beginning to come to terms with it. And we're *frightened*. But our minds just aren't equipped to face up to what's happening. If it goes on, we'll *all* end up like Julea. Our worlds will simply dissolve."

For the first time, Joth realized how badly Ravelvent was disturbed. And not just Ravelvent. Rypeck and Ulicon too. Perhaps everyone who had been affected by Camlak's mindblast. He began to understand why he seemed to be on a totally different wavelength whenever he talked to Rypeck or Ulicon. He discovered a new dimension to the problem. This, he thought, is why they seem to struggle so desperately to understand, and yet never gain any real insight. Ravelvent's phrase *"beyond our conceptual horizons"* echoed in his mind.

"If that's so," he whispered, more to himself than to Ravelvent, *"what makes me different?"*

14

As Rypeck looked at Heres' image in the screen, he could almost sense the mental blockade which the Hegemon had built. The hostility and rancor which existed between them had supposedly been left behind when the crisis arose, but its legacy was still there. And there was more. It was not simply that Heres did not want to listen to Rypeck. Heres did not want to listen at all. He no longer wanted to hear anything. He had already made up his mind. He was entrenched so deeply and so firmly that no other assault upon his sense of reality could possibly succeed.

Perhaps he was insane. Or perhaps it was the world which was insane.

This time, though, it didn't seem to matter to Rypeck. He no longer wanted to steer Heres away from one course to another. It wouldn't really matter at all whether Heres listened to him or not.

"It's too late," he said. "We've already lost."

"If we can muster the powers at our disposal," said Heres definitely, "then we will be safe. All that we require is the level of commitment that our forefathers gave to the Euchronian Plan. If we can all come together and give our utmost to the project, then we must succeed. We will not fail."

"That speech is eleven thousand years out of date," said Rypeck. "And so are we."

"You're supposed to be reporting to me on what you found out from Joth Magner," said Heres. "Every time you speak to me you begin like this, with deliberately veiled comments which you hurl at me as if you were throwing stones. It's only your way, I know, but it's tiresome. What have you found out?"

"There are at least three, and probably more, intelligent species in the Underworld. There are humans, and animals which have evolved to mimic humans—rats and cats. All these races share cultural as well as biological similarities. There appears to be no genetic intercourse between the races—that's almost certainly impossible, because they aren't related enough to hybridize—but there's a good deal of intellectual intercourse. Ideas don't obey the principles of heredity, and cultural evolution isn't subject to Darwinian selection. So both the cats and the rats have absorbed human culture and habits, once having evolved physically to the point where their brains could take it. It is, therefore, just as meaningful to call Harkanter's specimen a man as it is to call it a rat. That's the first thing you should know.

"Secondly, we have every reason to believe that the mental blast, or invasion, or whatever you want to call it, was not a deliberate act in itself, but the side effect of whatever the rat did to remove itself from that cage. We suggest that what happened was that the rat wanted to escape from its predicament, and it twisted itself into another space parallel to our own. The energy of the translocation manifested itself in the way we experienced.

"There are several million of these creatures in the Underworld. It is possible that every single one is capable of doing what Harkanter's specimen did. If you attempt to destroy them, they might very probably do so. On the other hand, if we do nothing, it seems likely that it will happen again anyway. Even if it doesn't, the evidence is that many people have been sensitized by the experience, and are now in the same situation as Magner—while they sleep their minds can pick up images carried by energy waves of this type radiating from the Underworld—presumably from the brains of the rats.

"So, as I said, it's too late. It doesn't matter what you decide to do. Not any more. We're on borrowed time, Rafe."

"If what you say is true," said Heres, "then we must destroy these rats completely."

"I doubt whether you can," said Rypeck. "They received the broadcast from the rat's mind just as we did—except that they're in a much better position to make sense of it. They know the trick can be done, and they almost certainly know how to do it now, even if they didn't before."

"There has been no repetition."

"Not yet."

"So we must act quickly. Germont's force will move into the lighted area very soon now, and we should also have reports on the effect of the seeding by tonight. It will take some time to achieve the levels of production which we need, even if the seeding experiments are totally successful, but it can be done."

"All we have to do is keep mind and body together," said Rypeck drily.

"If we remain calm and self-disciplined," said Heres, "there should be no difficulty."

"You're wrong, Rafe. You're dead wrong. Our minds just can't stand up to any of this. We should have guessed earlier. Our fathers and our grandfathers should have guessed. But they only saw the useful aspects of i-minus. For thousands of years now, the i-minus agent has been censoring our dreams, tidying up our minds, making us utterly and completely children of the Euchronian way of life. Maybe i-minus saved the Plan, by shaping the workers so carefully to their purpose in life. But i-minus has made us all into mental cripples. It has bound us so closely to Euchronia that we are no longer capable of looking beyond Euchronia. We have adapted ourselves too closely, in mind rather than in body, to the Overworld. We've become parasites within the cybercomplex, and parasites always evolve to become totally dependent—they lose their adaptability. That's what's happened to us, Rafe. We have no mental adaptability. None whatsoever. We believed so utterly and completely in Euchronia and in nothing else that our minds were simply ready to shatter at the discovery of anything new.

"The disaster has already happened, and there's no way back. You can try to destroy the universe, Rafe, if you want to. But you can't remain calm and undisciplined. You can't face up to the situation. It's the simplest little things that are beyond you, even though you rule the world."

"Eliot," said Heres, "I think that you're cracking up. I think you may be going mad."

"I think you're right," said Rypeck. "For more than a hundred years, I knew nothing but Heaven. Now I have looked into Hell. How can the sanity I had then help me now? Carl Magner wrote a book about *The Marriage of Heaven and Hell*. That marriage has taken place, in my mind as in yours. There can't be any divorce. Not ever."

Heres never heard the end of that particular speech. He had switched off the cyberlink halfway through.

15

Gregor Zuvara and Felipe Rath, with half a dozen others, were in the largest of the plastic domes in their Underworld city. More than any of the others, this was obviously an extension of the mechanical organism which covered the continents of the world. It was packed with equipment as sophisticated as any in the upper world, and all of the electronic devices were in constant communication with the cybernet and all its facilities. Once inside the dome it was quite easy to imagine that one was on the platform rather than the surface. The only thing which testified clearly to the fact that these men were on an alien and hostile world was the fact that they were physically together, sharing the same space and the same air.

Vicente Soron entered through the complex doors, disrobing and submitting to sterilization procedure with angry impatience. As soon as those inside saw him it was obvious to them that something was very wrong.

He went to Zuvara and said: "We have to talk in private."

"Why?"

This question came from Rath, not from Zuvara. Soron looked around, and saw that every eye was upon him, and that every ear was listening. He licked his lips.

"It's important," he said.

"If it's important," said Rath, cutting in just as Zuvara was about to reply, "then I want to hear it. We all want to hear it." His voice was strained, and he seemed to be on edge.

"I think you'd better tell us all," said Zuvara, in a low voice.

Soron looked at Rath, then at Zuvara, and it struck him very suddenly and very strongly that they already knew what he had to say. Something had frightened them, and frightened them badly. The news which he had to impart had been thrusting at his throat, the words waiting to tumble out just as soon as he could get Zuvara alone. But his need to talk died away suddenly.

"What's the matter?" he asked.

"You tell us," said Rath.

Zuvara waved at him impatiently, trying to shut him up. "Something's wrong, Vicente. If that's what you've come to tell us, don't bother. We've lost contact with Germont's Delta contingent. We think that they're all dead."

For a few seconds, what Zuvara had said simply did not make sense to Soron. He repeated the words over in his mind, but still they evaded him. Then he realized what he had been told. They didn't know at all. This was different—something entirely unexpected.

"What happened?" he asked.

"We don't know," said Rath, again quick to interrupt. "We got no message. Nothing. Whatever it was must have killed them quickly, and without any warning. Now, if there's anything we should know, you'd better tell us, because if the same thing is going to happen to us, we want warning."

Soron shook his head slowly. "No," he said. "It's something entirely different."

"It's throwing quite some panic into you," observed Rath.

"I can't tell you," said Soron. "The Council has to know. It's for them to decide what's to be done. I daren't release the information to anyone except Gregor. Not until the Council knows."

"You'd better . . ." Zuvara began, but again Rath was ahead of him. Rath was almost shaking, and his face was white. Soron realized that the news about the lost vehicles must only just have come in. It must have had a profound effect upon the men in the encampment, who had been in the Underworld for some time now, and were beginning to hate every moment of it as it became obvious that the likelihood of an early return to the Overworld was out of the question. Rath, Zuvara and Soron had all come down with Harkanter's party—to look around, to see what the Underworld was like. It had been a game then. Now, it was no longer a game. Cut off from the world they knew, with the mechanical extensions of the cybernet more an accentuation of their removal than an amelioration of it, they had begun to sense imminent danger everywhere in the dead, decaying land that surrounded the dome city.

"The Council," said Rath, "are up there. We're here. Never mind relaying information to the Council so that they can alert us at their pleasure. We should be the first to know, not the last."

"This shouldn't be made public," insisted Soron.

"Let's *all* be the judge of that," said Rath. "We want to know. Are the plants withstanding the seeding? Don't the diseases work as well as they should? Is there an army marching from the south? What's wrong, man?"

Soron wiped his mouth, and turned away for a moment. Zuvara said nothing, now that he had the opportunity. He waited, with Rath and the others.

"I've been out in the southeast sector," he said. "Checking the progress of the viruses. Everything seems to be dying all right. Everywhere is covered in gray slime. Literally everywhere. Including the pillars which support the platform. You know how they have lichens and small prokaryot cells growing all over them. The encrustation on every pillar is dying, and you can just scrape the stuff away. That's what I did.

"Some of it must have been chemosynthetic. Some of the stuff has eaten its way back into the pillars half an inch or more. The surface under the crust is corroded and pitted."

He stopped and waited, but no one said a word.

"Don't you see?" he said. "The columns which support the Overworld are being steadily weakened. And we knew nothing about it. Sections of the platform may already be in danger. It may begin to collapse at any time. Tomorrow, or next year. We simply don't know."

16

"I come to you," said Heres, "as my ancestors came to you some thousands of years ago. I need your help. The world which you helped to build—your world—needs your help."

Sisyr's expression did not change, but he seemed suddenly very thoughtful. The alien was considerably taller than the Hegemon, but they were both seated, and the difference was not obvious. They were dressed in the same type of clothing.

But the alien's skin was red-brown. His eyes were round, and had no pupils, being uniformly pale blue in color. A darker area of soft tissue served as both nasal organ and upper lip. The lower jaw closed behind this flap of tissue. Nevertheless, the face gave the impression of being "mammalian." It was not horrifying. The hands were different. There was something about the hands which suggested insects. Their structure was complex—far more so than human hands. The hard, thin fingers looked as if they might snap like pencils if pressure were applied to them.

It struck Heres most forcefully that there was a certain *hardness* about Sisyr's whole frame and bearing. He looked strong, not simply because of his height, but because of the way he held himself. Heres, for some reason, always saw human beings as *soft* creatures. The sensation of wearing his own skin always exaggerated in his mind the delicacy and vulnerability of flesh. Heres hated to scratch himself, and he was hypersensitive to pain.

"How can I help you?" asked Sisyr.

"Exactly as you did before," Heres replied. "You will advise us, and give us the benefit of your scientific knowledge and technical skill."

"Toward what end?" asked the alien.

Heres pursed his lips slightly. The alien knew perfectly well what end Heres had in mind. Why was he asking for it to be spelled out?

"Ultimately," said the Hegemon, "the security of the people of the Overworld. We wish to exterminate all sources of danger or potential danger on the planet."

"You want to extirpate life in the Underworld," stated Sisyr.

"It may be necessary," said Heres, smoothly. "We may be able to save many species of potential usefulness and harmlessness. If, with your help, we can weed out the inimical varieties, we may have the means to begin the work of remaking the surface of the Earth into a habitable environment. I have not abandoned that possibility."

"The Underworld is habitable now," said Sisyr.

"By habitable," Heres said, his voice still smooth and his manner unruffled, "I mean suitable for habitation by the standards of the Overworld."

"What you want me to do," said the alien, "is—as I understand it—help you to wage a war of extermination against the people of the Underworld."

"We need not consider them people," said the Hegemon. "Even those of apparent human ancestry are now a genetically isolated species. They are not men, as we are men. They are evolutionary side branches. We are engaged in a struggle for existence. We cannot afford to handicap ourselves with philosophical niceties." While he delivered this speech, Heres recalled the very different ideas he had advanced while proclaiming to the world his Second Euchronian Plan for the reclamation of the Underworld. But circumstances had changed since then, and ideas had to be brought into line with circumstance.

"Why do you think that the Planners put lights in the Underworld?" asked Sisyr.

"Because they needed them," said Heres, "in the days when the platform was under construction, and there was constant intercourse between the two worlds."

"But the lights still burn."

"For now," said Heres, matching words unsaid with words unsaid.

"You know that I have been sending small quantities of material from the Overworld into the Underworld for thousands of years?" asked the alien. Without waiting for an answer, he continued: "Manufactured goods—mostly tools and books. All in the name of the Plan."

"It has been brought to my attention," said Heres.

"Do you know why?"

"If you say that it was provided for in the Plan," said the Hegemon, "then I cannot contradict you. But now the Plan has been changed. It is no longer required that you should distribute necessary materials in the Underworld, helping to keep its people alive and—to some degree—civilized. We have new priorities now."

Sisyr shook his head deliberately. The calm mimicry of the human gesture alarmed Heres. This creature had perfected a false humanity which existed alongside his real self. Heres, as a human, could confront only the human analogue, never the alien. There was no way to guess what Sisyr's priorities might be—what he thought and felt. There was no way to answer questions relating to the alien, like *why?* and *who?* As Heres watched the red-brown face, he tried to call to his own mind some appreciation of the fact that Sisyr was thousands of years old. He had lived on Earth for nearly ten thousand, and he might have been thousands, or millions of years old before his ship first came to Earth. Was he any nearer to death now? So far as Heres, or anyone else, was aware, the alien might outlast the Earth itself, and the sun, and the galaxy.

But Heres had no sense of the infinite. He could not begin to conceive of a span of time so vast that the things which Heres concerned himself with might be so evanescent as to be meaningless. And yet the alien lived second by second, hour by hour, just as Heres did. His past and his future might be infinitely extended, but his present moved at exactly the same pace from one to the other. Heres' affairs of the moment were Sisyr's too. And Sisyr had not been content to stand aside from the problem of the first Planners. He had involved himself. He had tried to become a part of Earth. He had made Earth his world.

"I cannot help you," said Sisyr.

Although he had expected this, Heres recoiled from the flat statement as if it were a physical blow.

"You must," he said . . .

Sisyr shook his head again.

"We have the power to compel you," said Heres. "You are subject to our laws."

"I have the right to refuse," said Sisyr. "I have the right to remain silent. You may pass judgment upon me, and I must accept the judgment. But you cannot compel me to do what I will not do."

Heres suppressed his anger with the ease of long practice. The anger was not insistent. It died at his command.

"Tell me why," he demanded.

"You know why," said the alien.

"You have a duty to us," said the Hegemon. "You helped us create this society. You have a responsibility toward it. You cannot stand by and see it destroyed. It is your fault that we are in such extreme danger now. Had you not continued to supply the Underworld, had you not provided them with light, they would not have survived. There would be no people of the Underworld. I am not accusing you or blaming you, I am simply stating the facts. No one will hold this against you. But the fact remains that you are responsible for the threat to the world which you helped to create. You cannot simply turn your back and deny involvement. You must take action now, along with the citizens of the Euchronian Millennium, to set aside the earlier actions which have led to this crisis. We demand your assistance. Without your knowledge we may very well fail to overcome the threat to our existence. But with your help we will be able to do what we have to as quickly and as cleanly as possible."

"I do not deny involvement," said Sisyr. "But I do deny commitment of the kind which you are trying to thrust upon me.

"I did not design and build the Overworld. That was the work of your Planners. What I did was to put within their reach the means by which they could bring their Plan into effect. I showed them how the platform could become an engineering possibility. I showed them how to make the best use of their raw materials. I showed them how to get the necessary power. But I did not create the Overworld. The world which *I* created was the Underworld.

"Your Planners were convinced that the surface was irrevocably ruined. They mistook the end of the environment to which they were adapted for the end of life, for the end of the world. They committed themselves entirely to the new world built above the old. That was their only hope—not for mankind, but for their particular image of man, for their particular human ambitions.

"I did for them what they wanted me to do. But at the same time, I took what steps I could to assure the future of the Underworld. Life there would have survived in any case, without any intervention on my part. What would have happened there if I had not done as I did is not very different from what *has* happened there. Rapid divergent evolution of those forms best equipped to survive would have brought into being much the kind of life-system which has established itself. What I did was to contribute just a little to epiphenomenal continuity. I made certain things happen more quickly. Where chance might have resulted in two or several outcomes I made sure of one particular outcome.

"Your Planners wanted to save the human race which existed in their own imagination. I wanted to save several human races—several potential routes for human evolution. You say that the people of the Underworld need not be considered as people. They might say the same of you. Neither your human race nor any of theirs is the same human race which existed in prehistoric times. Nor was that race static in an evolutionary sense. Indeed, the human race readapted itself throughout its history with remarkable speed. Humanity has always practiced self-change. And it has always been able to pass on this self-change, not by heredity, but by control of the environments which shape the individual.

"Your Euchronians always believed that the process of self-change was directional, and that there was an end-point to it all. I helped them reach that particular end-point. You have found, of course, that there is no such end. Time does not stop. Change does not stop. If you wipe out all life on Earth except yourselves, and make the environment totally unchangeable, and—with the aid of your i-minus drugs—shape every member of your society as completely as possible to the Euchronian ideal, you will still find that there is no end. That is what I believe. I would not be alive if I did not.

"You cannot destroy the Underworld. If you kill every living thing within it, it will return, in time. And even in the meantime it will not be lost, because it exists inside you all, as a potential, as an alternative. In the same way, the Underworld cannot destroy you, even if it kills you all. Euchronia exists, if only as a possibility. No matter who, or where, or what you are, there are always Heaven and Hell. You cannot divide infinity and eternity. Wherever you draw a line, there is always infinity and eternity to either side of it."

"I'm not concerned with infinity and eternity," said Heres. "I'm only concerned with now."

"The identity you have shaped for yourself may not recognize its concern with infinity and eternity," said the alien, "but it is nevertheless contained therein. I *am* concerned with infinity and eternity, because I am eternal, and have access to infinity."

"If this is the way you think," said Heres, "then why did you help us in the first place?"

"Because I am concerned with preserving real alternatives," said the alien. "I am concerned with eternity, but I am also concerned with now. The present is where the eternal happens. Everything may come to one who waits, but he need not wait. He may act, and thus control what comes.

"You say I have a duty to my world—a duty to save it from destruction. That is what I intend to do. But my world is Earth, not Euchronia. I cannot help you."

"Then I must place you under arrest," said Heres. "According to the law, you are guilty of treason. And I warn you that we may be forced to discover ways by which we can make you help us."

Sisyr stared the Hegemon in the face, and he seemed for a moment to be preternaturally still.

"I doubt it," he said, quietly. "I doubt it."

17

The three remaining contingents of Germont's force split up in the lightlands, and separated by some twenty or thirty miles, moving southeast into Shairn. Germont's own third of the force moved slightly ahead of the others, and it was this fraction which first came within sight of one of the villages of the Children of the Voice.

The column halted, and Germont asked for instructions from above.

The man to whom Germont was actually talking was Luel Dascon, who stood, in the present situation, second only to Heres. He was the only man whose loyalty Heres dared trust completely. Dascon could see what the village and its surrounds looked like by means of a camera eye mounted on Germont's vehicle.

What he saw was a wall of Earth, with the tops of tall conical roofs visible behind it. The land around the village had been divided up into rough squares thirty to a hundred yards in length, which were separated by footworn pathways. In these fields grew an assortment of plants, the most common of which was a dark gray thickset stalk with a paler bulb, rather like a foot-thick matchstick. In some of the fields compounds were divided out by walls of sod daubed with some white substance—apparently to stiffen the barriers. Within these compounds were animals: burly, pallid pigs.

There was no one working in the fields—in fact, there was no one visible outside the wall. A warning of the approach of the armored cars had been given some time previously, and the villagers had withdrawn. A few scattered heads were just visible at the wall.

A rough road—or, at least, a track rather wider than the

footpaths in the fields—led away to the east, but it was impossible to follow its course across the terrain for more than a quarter of a mile.

"Move forward slowly," said Dascon. "Pass the village on the west side, staying well clear of the walls. Try to follow the paths through the fields, and spray the crop with the virus as you pass. Don't open fire on the village or the villagers unless they come out to attack. Ignore anything they throw or shoot from the wall."

"We could raze the village in under an hour," said Germont.

"That's the last thing we want at the moment," said Dascon. "There's a whole nation to the south of you. We don't want open war. We just want to destroy their food supply, quietly and completely. No matter how superior your firepower, pitched battles mean losses. You already know that."

"I'd be happier with them dead," Germont replied. He was convinced—although there was no evidence—that the contingent left behind in the blacklands had been destroyed by some mysterious mindpower of which the Underworlders were possessed. He was very frightened by the idea of such an insidious threat. Dascon, too, was anxious about the potential power of the Children of the Voice, but his approach to the problem was different. Fear made Germont want to shoot, and keep shooting—to eject the fear with the bullets, to be conscious that he was fighting back, was killing. Dascon was concerned that the rats should not be frightened, that they should be convinced that they had nothing to fear from the Overworld invasion, and would therefore fail to make use of the extraordinary action to which Camlak had been driven. Heres had decided that they should work on the theory that the Children of the Voice would accept the blight of all plant life in their area as a natural occurrence —merely an extension of disasters which must have happened before—and that they would not thereby be prompted into any unusual action.

The column moved forward slowly. Germont's driver took what seemed to the commander to be elaborate detours in order not to cut across any of the fields, destroying the standing crops. Some of the matchstick plants inevitably got crushed by the great wheels, but the damage was done in a tidy, orderly fashion.

The man at the machine gun was visibly nervous. He was

above Germont's station, and his feet were not far away from Germont's face. The smell seemed very noticeable.

When they were closest to the village wall they were broadside-on, and the camera eye showed only empty land ahead. Germont moved to where he could see out of the cockpit, and relayed his impressions to Dascon.

"There are thirty or forty of them watching us over the wall," he said. "They seem patient and relaxed. I don't understand why there are no signs of fear or hostility. Trucks don't drive through their agricultural holdings every day —these things can never have seen a vehicle like this in their lives. They can't have got beyond the wheelbarrow themselves, without horses or cattle. I can't make out their eyes at this distance, and I presume the expressions on their faces wouldn't mean much to me anyhow, but the way they stand and watch suggests to me that they know—or think they know—exactly what we are and what we're doing. But they're making no move to stop us. It doesn't make sense to me."

"You're imagining things," Dascon told him. "They're probably scared to death."

"No," said Germont. "That's just not so." After a pause, he continued: "There's another gate on the south side, much larger than the ones to north and east. There's a road—a track of sorts—leading away south. Geographically, that should be the main road. The big gate is white, and looks for all the world to me as if it's made out of bones. Maybe that's so."

"Not necessarily sinister," said Dascon. "There's a shortage of woody tissue in the Underworld. They probably can't afford to waste bones—they have to use them for tools and frames. The supply of animal bones probably isn't enough."

"I don't care why they use bones," said Germont. "The fact that they do is enough for me. Mine are longer, and maybe tougher than theirs. They aren't going to lose any opportunities to kill us, once they're convinced they have a chance."

"You're safe enough," said Dascon drily.

"That's easy for you to say."

The column passed by the village without the slightest incident. Not a rock was thrown, nor a spear, nor an arrow loosed.

"I wish they'd come at us," said Germont. "I really do. That, I can understand. I can understand them coming out and attacking, and getting themselves shot to bits. I can understand them running or hiding. But the way they look says to me that they know something we don't. They have something all ready. It just looks to me as if they know we can't hurt them. I feel like a rat in a trap."

"Don't be a fool," said Dascon.

"Don't call me names," Germont snapped back. "If you want to pour scorn, you come down here and pour it. This is no picnic, Luel, and you know it. We've already lost more than a quarter of the force, and for what? Nothing. We don't even know how they died. We wouldn't know what killed them if it was inside with us now.

"And I'll tell you something else. When I look at the map and see what kind of distance we've covered these last few days, and what kind of area we *might* be infecting with these damned virus sprays, I begin to see how little impression we've made on this world. I tell you now that I'm not going to be here for years, and I don't think any of the men along with me are going to take it for much longer either."

"You won't need to be there much longer," said Dascon, soothingly. "Certainly not years. We don't need you to spread the virus—we need you to tell us what happens. You're observers. Once we know what to expect of the sprays, the seeding will be handled mechanically. Yours is just the test project. That's all. If you keep your eyes open, you won't die. Nothing can get at you inside the vehicles. Nothing at all. We'll know what happened to the Delta group in a matter of hours. Whatever mistake they made won't be repeated."

Germont found the calm voice extremely irritating. He had never liked Dascon. He *knew*, somewhere inside him, that Dascon was wrong. He was half-convinced that the team sent out to find out why the Delta contingent had disappeared or died would meet exactly the same fate, but he dared not make such a prediction out loud, in case it should be accurate.

He knew, also, by the same mysterious means, that the Children of the Voice could read his mind, and therefore anticipate his actions. It was the only explanation that made sense to him of the fact that the Underworlders were obviously not frightened of him.

He felt—to use the words of his own ironic simile—like a rat in a trap.

18

There was a single searchlight burning, its beam pointing diagonally upward, like a finger of light. Near to the ground the beam was clear-cut, sharply defined by virtue of the dust that floated in the air. Higher up, it became dissipated, and ultimately lost. The roof of the world was too far away for a circle of reflected light to show upon its dark face.

Iorga knew when he was still a good distance away that the men from Heaven were all dead. There was no sound at all—no clink of metal against metal. Nothing moved in or around the vehicles. Such stillness could only mean death.

There had been a dozen vehicles in the Delta contingent of Jacob Germont's invasion force. They were huddled together in two lines of six, nose to tail. All the lights were dead except for the one lonely beam.

"Stay here," said Iorga. "Something bad. Something evil."

Nita looked around, at the bones of the city, beslimed with what had once been the forest, now decaying and putrefying. She shivered. She had never before been in the presence of such death—such all-consuming blight. She assumed that the death of the Heaven-sent was part and parcel of the death of the forest, and she could find no rationality in it, no meaning.

While Iorga went forward, Huldi and Nita hung back, crouching close together in the star-shadow of a crumbling wall.

The hellkin moved slowly, with the gun in his hands. He had faith in the gun, which had come from Heaven and must therefore be an answer to all possible perils, but he was cautious nevertheless. He did not want to use the weapon.

As he came closer, he saw that the vehicles were no longer tightly sealed. The plastic windows in the front and in the side were gone—removed quite cleanly and totally. Then he noticed the tires. He recalled the truck which had been rendered useless by the landslip. It had had six wheels, all bearing massive black tires—gigantic things, four feet in diameter. The tires of these trucks had lost both shape and size—they had been partially dissolved and were still in the process of being dissolved. On the surface of the plastic mess was a thin silver sheen. Patches of the sheen were on the road, and on the blighted plant tissue which still decked the roadside structures.

When he came closer still, he could see that the interior of the lead vehicles was also covered with the thin slime. In the back of the cockpit of one of them there had been a man attending a gun. He was now a skeleton, but a skeleton which shone, glittering with soft reflected light, perhaps even giving out some light of its own: a bioluminescent glow.

They could not have noticed the invasion. It had come upon them while they rested, perhaps while most of them slept. A living fluid, it had eaten its way into the vehicles, unable to affect the metal but easily digesting the plastics. It had digested everything soft. Silently and painlessly, it had dissolved the men from Heaven.

Iorga realized that the blight which was laying waste the forest was not the agent which had brought death to the convoy. It occurred to him while he stood and looked that what had happened was reciprocal. The men from Heaven had brought the blight which destroyed the plants. The protoplasmic predator which lived on the plants had moved, instead, to the invaders and their vehicles. Poison—the strongest poison—had destroyed them in a matter of hours. Against a liquid life-form with such corrosive power they had no conceivable defense.

Iorga backed away, and returned to his companions.

"We must move," he said. "Quickly. We must escape the region of the blight, or we will die with the forest. We must not eat, or sleep, or be still."

"Everything is dying," said Huldi. The note of fatalism in her voice suggested that she had no faith in her ability to except herself from the condition.

"We must go quickly," said Iorga.

They went quickly, and carefully. As they passed by the stricken vehicles, they trod with great care, avoiding the silver gel wherever they could see it. They did not run, but they moved swiftly, and when they were tired they continued to move.

Eventually, they felt the pressure of time building up inside them. They needed rest, they needed food and water, but they dared not stop while everything around them was dead or dying. Their minds became confused, and the seconds slowed to become painful. Many hours passed—and, for once, they were *conscious* of their passing—before they began to outdistance the spread of the viruses that contingent Delta had seeded before meeting its death. But they did, eventually, come once again into land that was free of the blight.

They continued to follow the road of stars, and death followed them, at its own pace.

19

If the Euchronian Plan, in all its languid majesty, may be considered as a sequence of moves in a game of Hoh, then the i-minus project may be seen as a crucial ploy within the overall strategy: an attempt to "promote" the pieces with which the game was played, an attempt to force human evolution in a calculated manner.

Euchronian history, as represented to the citizens of the Millennium, depicted the Plan triumphant and the commitment of the people to it as absolute. The reality had been somewhat different. The builders had never been happy under the Plan. History admitted that—it was not the purpose of the builders to be happy, but to build so that their descendants should inherit the promised land. Where history evaded the truth was in its suggestion that the builders were always content to be unhappy, to suffer hardship, to give over their entire lives to the great work. They were not. Their willingness to devote themselves entirely to the Plan was perhaps never absent, but it was also never constant. The Movement had its overt rebels, and even within the most devout believers there sheltered doubts, and momentary revolts against the tyranny of the Plan. How could it have been otherwise?

In order that the Plan should not falter, that it should be certain of successful completion, the Euchronians had found themselves required to encourage commitment, and finally to compel it. They found human nature to be against them,

and they determined to change human nature. The world
which was to be the end-point of the Euchronian Plan had
to be worthy of its builders, but its builders also had to be
worthy of the world they were to create.

The aim of the Euchronian Movement was education. It
wanted to teach its people to be perfect Euchronians. But
somehow, the people always seemed to learn different priorities, different standards and different attitudes to stand beside those taught by Euchronia and conflict with them.

The Euchronian psychologists decided that the extra
educational input was somehow innate. They theorized that
the instinctive programming of the individual was against
them. They came to believe that while men were asleep and
dreaming, while the programs of the mind were being re
played, rehearsed and continually readjusted, the social conditioning which they sought to impose was being infected by
instinctive programming and weakened or subverted. To
combat this, they designed the i-minus agent—a selective
genetic inhibitor which prevented all innate input into
dreaming. The programs which were replayed in the dreams
of Euchronia's citizens were those supplied by Euchronia.
Theoretically, the psychologists decided, this should lead to
perfect social adjustment and effective education.

They were half-right. The instinctive input was muted.
But the external input could not be completely unified. The
undercurrents of dissatisfaction, of dissent, of rebellion, were
sustained—not by constant instinctive reinforcement but simply because of their presence in the social reality at the
commencement of the project. The plurality of opinions and
the multiplicity of ideas could not be destroyed by the i-
minus agent.

But the i-minus agent, administered in secret to all of
Euchronia's citizens, did what was required of it—it ensured the safety of the Plan and the Movement until the
completion of the platform and the declaration of the Millennium. The pieces in the game of Hoh *were* changed,
and their inner life was significantly affected. The children
of Euchronia did not become children of Reason, but they
were very much the children of Intellect. Perhaps for the
first time, civilized men broke free from their animal
origins, from the evolutionary legacy of mind. They freed
themselves from their nightmares.

Then the nightmares came back.

Joth Magner, by escaping into the Underworld where he ate

food and drank water which were both innocent of the
i-minus agent, recovered the old input—the instinctive input preserved genetically through the relatively few generations which had passed since the beginning of the project.
Other men, however, found a new input—a telepathic input receptive to radiation broadcast by the Children of the
Voice, or their Souls. Carl Magner was the first, but—at least
potentially—there had been many more. The blast of radiation accompanying Camlak's translocation from his own
space into the parallel space where the Gray Souls lived had
activated that input in thousands of brains, perhaps millions,
in both the Overworld and the Underworld.

The i-minus project was wrecked. The "promotion" of the
pieces in the game of Hoh was rendered meaningless. A
new evolution was taking place.

20

Heres could not help staring at Sisyr's fingers. He felt a
lump in his throat, and there seemed to be an incipient
tremor welling up inside him. He had to hold himself rigid,
and he knew that if his concentration relaxed for a moment
some part of him—perhaps his hands—would begin to shake
uncontrollably.

The room was featureless. No part of the cybernet extended herein, neither sensors nor receptors. The walls enclosed nothing but empty space. It was deep within the
plexus, but in a real sense it was "outside"—beyond the
host-machine, a hole in the artificial organism. There was a
heavy chair, to which Sisyr was secured by steel manacles.
There were men on either side of him. Confronting him
were Heres, Luel Dascon and Acheron Spiro. Heres was in
control. Only Heres knew what was happening.

Dascon had never seen the alien before. He had never
thought about him. He considered the alien a kind of semi-
mythical creature, in whose existence he had never quite
been able to bring himself to believe. He found Sisyr rather
repulsive.

Spiro found the alien frightening. The concept of an immortal creature was, to him, a rather frightening one in it-self. Spiro feared death and disease and injury, just as Heres did, and felt an overwhelming bitterness when forced to con-template the reality of a creature to whom these things meant nothing. Like Heres, Spiro was apprehensive, but not for the same reasons.

"I have considered the demands which we have to make," said Heres. "In the end, I decided that there are two—only two—which we must put to you. Firstly, you must tell us how to protect our minds against any further invasion of the kind which we have once experienced. Secondly, you must tell us how we can destroy the Underworld in the minimum possible time. We must have a date that we can publish, and a method we can be sure of. There must be no more deaths in the Underworld."

Sisyr remained silent. Not a muscle in his face moved in the slightest. A minute dragged by.

"Well?" said Heres.

"There is no way to protect your mind against invasion," said Sisyr, "and the Underworld cannot be destroyed."

"Your civilization is a good deal more advanced than ours," said Heres.

"Your concept of advance has no meaning," Sisyr stated flatly.

"Your technology, then," persisted the Hegemon. "You have the technology to achieve things we cannot."

"We are different," said the alien.

"You can do things we cannot."

"Yes. But we are not miracle-workers. We cannot do everything."

"I think you're lying," said Heres. "I think that you know the means to destroy the Underworld, but that you will not help us."

"There is no way," said Sisyr, "but I will not help you in the attempt."

"What would you have us do?" broke in Spiro. "You say that we cannot protect ourselves. What can we do but fight? We have no alternative."

Sisyr made no answer.

Heres began to speak again, but Dascon cut him off. "Wait," he said. "Let us try to be clear about one thing. When this . . . shall we call it a mental invasion? . . . oc-curred, did you experience anything?"

"Yes," said Sisyr.

"You were too far away," said Heres. "It can hardly have had any effect at all."

"Nevertheless," said Dascon, quickly, "you did experience something. A touch, perhaps, and no more—but something. Perhaps we can assume that what you experienced was not so very different from what some of us experienced. May I ask how you reacted to that experience? I ask this because it seems to me that we are talking at cross-purposes. What happened to us frightened us very badly. We feel the need to act quickly and definitely. But you, apparently, do not feel the same way. Why not? Perhaps you have known things like this before. Perhaps you simply do not understand the character of our reaction."

"Perhaps," said Sisyr. "Almost certainly. I cannot feel as you feel. But how can I begin to explain how I feel? There is no way."

"We have concepts in common," said Dascon. "You can use our language. Its words must have meaning for you. Tell us, in words, what the experience meant to you. Did it frighten you?"

"No."

"Surprise, then? Were you startled?"

"No."

"You were expecting something of the kind?"

"It was unexpected. But I was not surprised."

"Then you have felt something like it before. Before you came to Earth. Something similar has happened to you in the past?"

Sisyr paused before answering. Finally, he said: "Similar . . . perhaps. But not the same. The nature of the force involved was known to me. The precise nature of the manifestation was not."

Dascon rapped the table with his clenched fist. "At last," he said, "we begin to get somewhere. You know the nature of the force involved. Do you know how it was generated?"

"An aberration in space. Perhaps you would call it a knot, or a lesion. The physical nature of the event I am familiar with, even if I do not understand it as some of my race might. But what it means in terms of your minds—that I cannot know. I do not know how you can isolate yourselves from another such occurrence. I do not believe that there is any way that you could. How can you shield yourselves against the force of gravity? There is no way."

Dascon looked sideways at Heres, and shrugged.

"If what you say is true," said Heres, "then we have no alternative but to destroy the sources, or potential sources, of this force. We must destroy the Underworld. Can you see the logic of that?"

"Your logic, perhaps," said Sisyr. "Not mine."

"You ask us to do nothing. To hope that the thing will not occur again, or—if it does—to suffer it. To have our minds destroyed."

"Perhaps it is not destruction," said the alien.

"What does that mean?" demanded Spiro.

"I do not know what it means—to you. You cannot know what it means to me. If you wish, I will try to explain."

"There is no time," said Heres. "We do not want explanation. We want help. We demand help. You say the Underworld cannot be destroyed, but we know that is not so. In time, we could do it. But we do not have the time available to us. We need the aid of your technology to speed up the task. You must tell us how to make our methods more efficient, how to make equipment which will do the job more quickly. All we want from you now is the same help that you gave our ancestors. We want you to improve our means of production, refine our methods. Simply help us in the task we have set ourselves. You owe us this."

Sisyr shook his head deliberately. The mimicking of the human gesture seemed to Heres somehow profane.

"We can compel you!" he said, anger flooding his voice. To this, Sisyr said nothing.

Heres half-rose from his chair. "You don't die," he said, harshly. "But we can kill you. Are you immune to pain? We have the power to *force* you. You must see that."

Dascon had seen this coming, but Spiro, strangely enough, had not. It was Spiro who had become angry along with Heres, but as Heres threatened the alien it was Spiro who recoiled, who began suddenly to sweat. It was Spiro who was nauseated.

Sisyr's pale blue eyes stared steadily into Heres' gray ones.

"You could kill me," conceded the alien. "Though you would not find it easy. I am not immune to pain. But you cannot use either the threat of death or the administration of pain to force me to go against my will. It cannot be done."

"I don't believe you," said Heres.

"It is so," replied Sisyr. "I am immortal—at least potentially. I endure. I feel pain, but if necessary I can endure pain. Forever, if necessary. That is what immortality means. I can be killed, if every cell in my body is destroyed, but I am not afraid of being killed. One is only afraid of the inevitable. You must understand that I am not like you. You cannot force me to do anything. No matter what you may do."

Heres became suddenly conscious that his hands were trembling. He could not control them. He realized then that he *did* believe the alien: that he was convinced of his own helplessness.

21

The driver brought the truck to a halt some twenty feet short of the bridge. Germont raised himself to as high a vantage as the canopy would permit, and looked carefully all around. There was no sign of life.

There was, in fact, no apparent need for suspicion at all. Thus far, in moving into the heart of the inhabited country, Germont's expeditionary force had met with no hostility whatsoever. The crop-spraying had proceeded unhindered at five townships. There had been no outwardly aggressive action on either side. Now, for the first time, the rough road of the Children of the Voice had led them to a waterway too wide for the vehicles to cross. There was a bridge, but a bridge built by the Shaira for their own use. It did not look as if it would take the weight of one of the armored cars, and there was no reason to suppose that it would. Somewhere back in the convoy there was equipment capable of erecting a bridge from scratch, or—if it proved more convenient—strengthening the structure that was there already. But for the first time the party would be obliged to stop for a moderate period of time while its personnel were working outside, unprotected by armor plate, in what was theoretically enemy territory.

"If they've only been waiting their chance," said the driver dourly, "this is it."

Germont spared him a sour glance.

The river flowed at the bottom of a valley. It was not

deep, but it was deep enough for the slopes on either side
to be difficult ground on which to maneuver. Germont could
see no more than a mile in any direction—considerably less
in the direction they had come, where the slope was steepest
and the top of the hill closest. The slopes were covered with
matted vegetation rather like bracken, with occasional tall
clumps of quasi-dendrites. The whole aspect of the plant life
here seemed different from the weird conglomerate forests
of the darklands and the moist confusion of the Waste away
to the north. Here, the general appearance the vegetation was much closer to moorland and heath. Only on close
inspection were the basic structures of the environment revealed to be alien.

Germont sent one truck back to the crest of the hill, and
instructed its commander to keep scanning with the searchlight. Then he moved his own vehicle off the road while
those carrying the pontoons and hawsers came to the fore.
He sent men out to both left and right, telling them to hold
fixed positions and signal to one another at regular intervals.
A third party went across the bridge.

To demonstrate his faith in the invulnerability of his force
he got out himself—the first time he had done so since he
had seen the doctor shot on the road of stars—to supervise
the operation.

He walked out on to the wooden bridge, where the man in
charge of the pontoon team, Gunn Spurner, was already inspecting the possibilities. As he set foot—somewhat gingerly
—on the native structure, he heard Spurner giving orders to
his men, waving them off the bridge and away to the left.
He directed them primarily with gestures. They moved quickly—perhaps a little too quickly, keen to play out their parts
and put on a show of efficiency. As Germont drew level
with Spurner the noise of the drills was already beginning.

"No good?" said Germont, pointing down at the bridge.

Spurner shrugged. "Good enough," he said. "Not really
wide enough. It's easier to start from scratch. If we used this
one, we'd only smash it up. Wouldn't be much use the next
time."

"Next time?"

"When we come back."

Germont shook his head. "We'll go straight through to another exit," he said. "If necessary, they'll take the men up
and abandon the vehicles. We aren't going back."

There was a moment's silence, while they reflected on the meanings implicit in the statement.

"Do you know what happened to the Deltas?" asked Spurner, quietly. His voice was flat and apparently unconcerned.

"Not yet," said Germont.

Another silence inevitably followed this statement. Germont moved to the edge of the bridge, now convinced that the structure was secure, and looked down into the water. It was flowing so slowly that its movement was hardly detectable. The water was murky and carried a heavy, oily scum.

"Foul," he commented. "I wonder why."

"Effluent?" suggested Spurner.

"I don't think so. We don't expel waste in this area, or anywhere upriver."

"The water must be ours," Spurner pointed out. "It doesn't rain here. Not ever. If it weren't for our water management there wouldn't be any life here at all. If we only tipped it all straight back into the sea this place would have been desert thousands of years ago."

"It's not as easy as that," said Germont. "We can only exert a certain amount of control over the water flow. We don't rule the rainfall. And even if we could . . . enough would get through. There'd always be enough. We could poison a lot of the water as it passed through the ducts in the platform on its way down here . . . but there'd still be enough. Enough water, not enough poison. The blight is the best way. The quickest way."

As he spoke, Germont moved along the bridge, still looking down at the water. He was tempted to reach down and dangle his gloved hand in the turbid liquid, testing its texture, but he dared not. He wondered vaguely whether there was anything alive in there. Obviously, by the way the water flowed turgidly and glutinously, there was a great deal of weed, but were there fish? Or crocodiles? He breathed deeply, trying to suck the air through his filter-mask in larger, more satisfying drafts. It felt good to be walking again, unconfined by the steel walls, able to stand up straight. After the first moments had passed, he no longer felt exposed, fearful of what might happen at any moment. He no longer anticipated the whiplash movement of an arrow, the cry of shock and pain that had barely escaped the doctor's lips before he died. This was a different environment—starlit, and far less eerie.

He turned to look back, to look at Spurner, still standing some five or six yards away on the bridge, to watch the men working with enthusiastic patience to get hawsers slung across the river and the pontoon units strung out to provide a road for the armored cars. He looked up at the slopes, and waited for the occasional, unsteady winking of the lights by which the soldiers signaled to one another that all was well.

He was suddenly struck by the oddness of the protective garments which the men wore. Here, where the stars were clustered and the light well-scattered, the suits tended to glint and gleam as the men inside them moved. The plastic was not really shiny, but it was smooth enough to reflect, almost in the same way that the silvery scum on the river reflected as slow, tedious ripples wound their way away from the bank where the men were working. Once, Germont had seen film of men walking on the moon, in thick, shiny suits. His own men wore filters instead of vast domed helmets, and their suits hung slack because there was no excess pressure inside, but there was something of the same quality about their aspect and appearance.

We might as well be on the moon, he thought. Or Mars . . . or a world of another star. The air here is our air, and the water is the waste from our world. Nevertheless, we are aliens. We come wrapped up in our fragments of the real world—the world above. We dare not face this world on its own terms.

He had to back off to let men carrying the hawsers pass him, to begin work on the far bank. Spurner joined him again, and they stood together watching the work proceed.

"Looks like everything's all right," commented Spurner.

"Of course," agreed Germont, sounding and feeling anything but completely sure of himself.

"They seem to be scared to death of us," went on the other man. "They daren't come near. What do you think they see us as? Gods from the sky? A supernatural visitation? They're bound to blame us for the blight, but they may take it philosophically—an act of fate over which they have no possible control."

Germont felt suddenly angry. "Have you looked at them?" he demanded. "While we cut slowly through their fields, they stand on their walls and watch us. Have *you* watched *them?* Do they seem to you like people in the presence of heir gods or their demons? They look to *me* as if they know exactly what we are. They *know* what they're doing, and hey know why. And I'm scared because I think they can stop us any time they like. We have the fire-power and the armor, but if they wanted to they could stop us dead in our racks. I think they're going to kill us all."

Spurner recoiled. Not only did he make no reply, but he searched his mind assiduously for a way to change the subject. This was not something he cared to think about.

Germont did not wait for him to find something to say. Instead, he went back across the bridge to his own vehicle, and swung himself back inside.

"I want six men," he said. "You three will do for a start. Pick up three from Alpha-two. Follow the road beyond the bridge for a couple of miles. I want to know what's there. Get back here in an hour. You'll have to move fast, but be careful. Now!"

The three men he had addressed were already suited and their weapons were beside them. They were reluctant to move out, and rather surprised that they had been ordered to, but they put their masks on hurriedly.

Germont went forward to the cockpit. The driver looked at him critically.

"Sending men forward on foot is a bit dangerous, isn't it?" he asked.

"Once we're across that river," said Germont, "we'll take up the hawsers and the pontoons for the next time. That means we can't get back across in a hurry. If they're waiting for us, they'll be just beyond that hill. And they'll be waiting for us to cut off our own retreat."

"And suppose that they are?" said the driver. "What then? Do we stay this side and run?"

"I wish we could," said Germont, in a low voice. "I really wish we could."

22

Enzo Ulicon looked carefully at the image of Vicente Soron which presented itself to him on the screen.

"You look ill," he said.

"I am ill," said Soron. "It was the Underworld."

"Not an infection?"

"Oh, no. We can deal very easily with any infection picked up down there. It's not organic. It's just . . . general debility. Being down there for any period of time simply drains the life out of you. I just couldn't stand it any longer . . . not the second time. The doctor says that it's psychosomatic—that I'm thinking myself ill. But that doesn't make it any the less real. And when I found out about the corrosion . . . the shock."

"Yes," said Ulicon, feeling that further discussion of Soron's state of health was rather pointless. "That's not what I wanted to talk to you about. I thought that I'd take advantage of your recall to go over the matter of the creature' disappearance. We still can't piece together a reasonable account of what happened and why. I'm convinced that we've missed something and I'm trying to find out what it is."

"I've reported absolutely everything," Soron said. "I really don't want to discuss that any more. I'd rather be left alone I'm bitterly regretting that I was involved in that particular incident."

"Please, Vicente," said Ulicon. "This is important."

"What do you want to know?"

"I want to know exactly what was administered to the creature. Some circumstance arising as a result of your handling of it allowed it to perform that disappearing act So far as we know this is a unique event. It never happened before and it hasn't happened since. I must know *exactly* what you gave that creature."

"I made a list," said Soron, tiredly. "It's all there. I gave it a dose of the same anesthetic that was in the dart gun when it began to show signs of life, and I continued to shoot it full of the stuff as the dose continually wore off. The drug is a mixture, but all the constituents are fairly commonplace We had nothing to feed it, so I administered intravenous shots of glucose. I also gave it some shots of ferric tartrate and phenylalanine to compensate for some of the metabolic side effects of the sedatives."

"That's all here," said Ulicon, referring to a printout in front of him. "We wonder if any of these things may have had some effect on the creature quite apart from the purpose for which it was given. If that were the case, which of these might it be?"

"That's ridiculous," said Soron. "The only substance that it wouldn't meet in its own environment is the anesthetic cocktail. The effect *that* had was perfectly obvious. It worked as it should. Certainly, there might have been side effects that don't occur in humans, but they'd be organic, metabolic effects. How could an anesthetic give the thing the ability to teleport itself?"

"I don't know," said Ulicon, "but *something* did."

Soron shook his head.

"It may have been an innate ability that was simply triggered by the drug," persisted Ulicon. "If that's so we need to know what the trigger was. Now an anesthetic acts on the brain—it causes lack of consciousness. The drugs in the mixture act in slightly different ways—some suppress neural activity, others can have slight psychedelic properties. Our only method of trying to find a likely candidate is logic—this isn't something we can play about with. We must be sure at the outset that you didn't administer a different kind of sedative at some point, or any other kind of drug. Are you certain that your list is complete?"

"Absolutely," said Soron. "The only thing the rat had except for those drugs is water."

"Water?"

"We let it regain semi-consciousness a couple of times. It drank a lot of water—those sedatives can give you a burning thirst, you know."

Ulicon said nothing. A pause grew and extended.

"What's the matter?" said Soron.

"Nothing. Just a thought. Thanks, Vicente. That's all I wanted to know."

"It's a wild goose chase," said Soron. "Believe me. You're on the wrong track."

Ulicon switched off the circuit. He scratched his chin, and murmured: "Eureka."

23

While Nita slept, she dreamed. She had always dreamed, and each time she slept there had always been a time when the dreams were unnaturally deep, and unnaturally real. In these deep dreams the shadow of her Gray Soul was ever-present. Sometimes, it would talk to her, but on most occasions it was content to wait. There was something valuable, something inexpressively pleasant, in simply being together, in meeting and almost touching. They never could touch, because of the interface which lay between them, the surface of one mind within another.

The closeness of dreams was something which affected consciousness only transiently. To retain an awareness of the experience special measures had to be taken. The priests of the Children of the Voice were able to participate in the communion more or less at will, by the aid of mental discipline. The others generally needed drugs to heighten their awareness, to give them more freedom within their minds and in the inner space delimited by their minds. Without the pulp and the gum prepared by the priests and issued at the Communion of Souls, Nita and the common people among the Children of the Voice remained consciously unaware of the experience of Soul-nearness to a considerable extent. Nita was always aware that there was more to her inner life than she could remember or command, that there were worlds beyond the narrow fiction which she constructed and called her self. This mystical aspect of her inner life was continually reinforced by the fragments of experience which remained when her deep dreams dissipated and her mind returned to the surface of consciousness. Sometimes, one such fragment of memory would survive intact—a flake of secret reality, a rivet of insight—and would continue to haunt her waking mind thereafter, its meaning perpetually out of reach but its significance sharp and clear.

So it was when, without warning, Camlak came to her in her dream.

He was often present in her dreams, of course. He was always in her mind. But this time, while she slept very deeply, her body and mind exhausted by the long flight from the death that was devouring the blacklands, it was the real Camlak who came to her. He was with the Gray Soul, beyond the interface. She could not quite reach out and touch him, but she could see him, in a strangely shadowed way, and she heard his words.

When she woke again, committing herself totally to the external world, to the self she had created for facing that particular aspect of infinity, she could not remember his speech in full. The words he had used could not be seized and held by her waking mind—they ran through its crevices like quicksilver. But the meaning remained with her, unclear, but nevertheless tangible . . . memorable . . . real . . .

He had spoken to her not of a world, but of worlds. He had spoken of bodies becoming shadows, of minds becoming liquid creatures unconfined by *shape* and dimension, creatures into which time *dissolved* and *flowed*. He had spoken of clouded mountains holding everlasting sunset, of white oceans like liquid ashes, of darkness and light, of . . .

She lost the images even as she tried to recall them. In her world, they made no sense. In her words, they had no meaning. Only within the tissue of the dream had they been able to become real, just for a few moments. The concepts were beyond the boundaries of her own being, outside the horizons of her mind.

But what reality could not snatch away from her was the assurance that Camlak was alive, that the Overworld had not destroyed him, that somehow he had transcended even Heaven and Hell.

24

"I came as soon as I learned what had happened," said Rypeck. "I was shocked. Please believe me when I tell you that if it were only within my power . . . this is a terrible thing. They simply do not realize what they have done . . . what they are doing."

Sisyr did not react in any way to Rypeck's obvious distress. His hands were no longer manacled—that symbolic gesture had proved quite pointless, and Heres had directed that the offensive objects should be removed. But the alien was still held in the featureless room—an absolute captivity, in a world which relied so totally on its electrical senses, where life was conducted and mediated by mechanical extensions of the hand and brain.

As the silence lengthened, Rypeck added: "I'm sorry."

"The crisis will pass," said Sisyr. "This is a transient thing."

"They are lost," said Rypeck, sitting down. His body seemed to fold up as he relaxed himself—perhaps overre-laxed himself. He was tired. "They have no idea how to react or what to do next. They feel an unreasonable urgency which simply cannot be assuaged. I don't think they will harm you.

Sisyr said nothing.

"We talked about this," said Rypeck. "Such a short time ago. I asked you what would happen if the Movement asked your help again. We talked about the consequences of ac-tion and the consequences of inaction. Your answers seemed to me to be unclear."

"Within your contexts," said the alien, "they were unclear. They still are."

"But there was one thing that you said," Rypeck mused. "You said that while we saw two worlds, you only saw one. You saw Earth, Underworld and Overworld, as an integrated whole. What do you see now? A world tearing itself apart? That, I think, is how I am beginning to see it. A world involved in the single-minded business of self-destruc-tion."

"There is no self-destruction," said Sisyr softly. "Only self-repair."

"Repair?"

"Self-change, if you prefer."

Rypeck shook his head. He wore a bitter smile. "We have never preferred self-change. We preferred stability. Total order. The state of parasitism. That was our Utopian dream. We still cling to it. We *prefer* self-satisfaction, self-steriliza-tion . . . the homogeneity of life."

"Something," said the alien, "which can be all too easy to find."

The remark seemed to Rypeck to be unnaturally cryptic. He looked hard at Sisyr.

"What must you think of us?" he said. "As you look out upon us from your lofty heights of eternity. Are we ants sur-rendering everything to the greater glory of the anthill, un-aware that the land where our universe exists is about to be plowed up, drowned by a tidal wave, swallowed up by the Earth? Is that what you see? Is all our human vanity so utterly ridiculous?"

Sisyr shook his head.

"How do you see us?" demanded Rypeck. "You have seen us through eleven thousand years. You have seen us pour

our lives, our being, into the construction of this almighty metal anthill. You have helped us find and use the materials with which to make it fulfill our dreams. To me, Euchronia is everything. It is my universe—the past when Euchronia did not exist is to me unimaginable, composed of dreams. But you know how little that is. You have *dabbled* in the building of my world. It has been a mere pastime, the tiniest fraction of your life. To me, it means everything, to you, almost nothing. Tomorrow will be the end of our world, but *your* world is infinite, eternal. It faces no crises, no climacticon. Do we seem to you to be absurd?"

"No."

"I don't believe you."

"It is true. Believe me, I am far more involved in your world, in your affairs, than you imagine. This Earth is not my toy, not merely a momentary distraction. I am not a god, despite the fact that I will not die. You read too much into that simple fact. Perhaps your people mean no more to me than the Children of the Voice, but they mean no less. You are real, you are human. You are so like to me in so many respects, so unlike in others—but I see the like as well as the unlike. Please believe me when I say that I *care* about what is happening to you and to your world. But I cannot help in the way that Heres understands help. If there is any kind of salvation, you must find it yourselves. There is nothing I can do."

Rypeck's eyes played over a white wall, as if searching for some tiny crack to distort its smoothness, its emptiness.

"I believe you," he said.

"Thank you," replied the alien.

"*Is* there any possible salvation?" asked the human.

"I cannot know," said Sisyr. "In your terms, I simply do not know what salvation is."

"The survival of the Overworld," said Rypeck. "The peace, the stability, the safety of our lives."

"Perhaps that can happen," said the alien. "For now. But is that salvation? For your children's children, forever and ever, is that salvation?"

"It's what we believe in."

"Beliefs change," said Sisyr. "They can never be constant. Don't you find that there always has to be something new to believe in, and that the beliefs you have are steadily eroded away?"

"I don't know," said Rypeck. "Nobody does."

25

"There's a barrier across the road," reported the spokesman for the party Germont had sent on across the bridge. "It's just beyond the crest of the hill. Not half a mile. It extends to either side in a rough semicircle, and ends up in the dense vegetation on the slope itself, over there, and there. It doesn't look like a barricade from here, but I think they've dumped stuff in between the clump of vegetation. Once we're across the river, we're effectively hemmed in. Water behind us and the wall on all three sides. The barrier's all of a mile and a half long—it isn't something that was thrown up overnight. This is where they intend to stop us all right."

"How close did you get?" Germont demanded.

"Just close enough to see. We weren't about to go up and say hello."

"Did you see the rats?"

"No. But they were there. I could feel it. They're behind that barrier, I'll swear it."

"What's the barrier made of?"

"What passes for wood hereabouts, I think. The same sort of stuff that stands up straight on these slopes. It's high, but it can't be strong. The trucks would go through it like a knife. I guess."

"Then what's it for? If it's that soft it won't stop bullets?"

The spokesman shrugged. "To hide behind, I guess. Maybe it's the best they could do. Perhaps there's a ditch behind it—perhaps they hope we'll crash through and cripple the vehicles. What are we going to do?"

"Tell Dascon," snapped Germont. "Let's see if he has ideas."

He went back to the communications panel, and relayed to Dascon exactly what the scout had told him.

Dascon was unimpressed. "You have the fire-power," he said. "Tear the barricade apart. Blast it out of the way."

"You wouldn't like to come down here and do it yourself?" said Germont.

"You're making a fool of yourself," replied the Councillor. "There's no need to be frightened of a lot of half-animal savages. I know you've lost men already, but that has no bearing upon the present situation. Leave a truck to hold the bridge, if you want your rear protected and an escape route assured."

"Thanks," said Germont. "Just stay close to that screen. You can watch through the cameras. At least, if anything does go wrong, you'll know what it is."

"I'm watching," said Dascon, his voice smooth, showing no trace of irritation because of Germont's bitterness.

By means of the camera eye on the front of the truck, Dascon watched as Germont's truck ventured on to the makeshift bridge, and lumbered across the slow-moving river to the opposite bank. As it ascended the hill Germont ordered the searchlight and the machine gun manned, and Dascon watched the light pick out the crown of the hill as the truck rode up the slope. He heard Germont give instructions for Spurner to stay with the tail-end truck on the north side of the river.

In a matter of minutes the armored vehicle created the rise, and then Dascon saw the wall—just a loose assemblage of dead, dry vegetable matter piled up in a long, straggling line which arced away to present a concave arc to the lorries as they changed gear and sped forward. The lights from the other trucks joined Germont's searchlight, scanning the wall for sign of the enemy.

And then the wall became a wall of flame. At least a dozen lights, maybe more, were applied simultaneously. Either the material of the barricade had been soaked with some flammable liquid, or the dry stalks were very combustible indeed, because once started the flames sprang up with considerable eagerness.

The truck braked.

"Back off," commanded Germont. "Back off and let it burn itself out."

The vehicle was thrown into reverse, and the mechanical eye through which Dascon saw retreated steadily. The ribbon of flame extending across the viewfield seemed rather futile— a ridiculous gesture of defiance. But the eye was fixed. It looked forward, and it was locked into the frontal stare. As the truck pulled back to the crest of the hill, Dascon could see only the pall of thick, oily smoke that was already blotting out the electric stars beyond the barrier. But he heard

Germont's cry of anguish, and—though no words came to him—he guessed what had happened.

The Shaira had fired the river. The water was polluted, loaded with oil and alcohol. The scum on the surface was not vegetable, but mineral.

And Germont's trucks were trapped, ringed by fire. The fire could not burn for long—it would be a fast flare and little more. But the circle was tilted by the slope of the hill. As the air within the ring rose the hot gases from the surface of the river would be sucked inwards, up the slope. Inside the trucks, the men would have their own supply of oxygen, but the armored walls of the trucks would become red-hot in a matter of moments as the firestorm raged around them. If they got out, they would burn and choke. If they stayed in, they would be cooked.

All Dascon could see was the great cloud of smoke billowing over the crest of the hill. He was forced to cut out the sound that Germont's microphone was picking up. He simply could not stand to listen to it.

26

"There's no way to prove what you say," said Rypeck.

"No way at all," agreed Ulicon. "But it fits. It's an answer which fits the question, and it's the only one we have which does. The water which we drink is recycled—not because we're short of water, but in order to conserve the i-minus drug. The drug has to be constantly supplied because it is excreted so easily, and so the supply is—to all intents and purposes—a closed circuit. The i-minus drug is not expelled into the Underworld with our waste except in the most minute quantities, and it is so easily degraded by strong alkali that virtually none of it will have got into the Underworld life-system. The concentration in our water is quite high—on the order of several parts per million. Quite enough to affect the creature if it drank a pint or two of Overworld water."

"We have no way of knowing what effect it might have had."

"But we have. The drug acted on the creature exactly as it was designed to act. It cut out the instinctive input into his dreaming. And left what? The input from his conscious mind—the memories and visual images which were the content of the telepathic broadcast, plus the other input—the input from *elsewhere*, from the Gray Soul. By cutting the instinctive input into the dream state, the i-minus agent made possible a closer contact between the creature and the thing which it called a soul than ever before. That's what made it possible for the creature to disappear—to go wherever it went, into the space where the Soul is."

"You think this Gray Soul is a real being, not just a mental archetype?" queried Rypeck.

"I do. It fits. The rat people are in telepathic contact with other beings, but the contact is blurred by the fact that it takes place in the same bodies within the brain that are involved with dream-sleep—the focus of the whole thing is probably the pons. Harkanter and Soron, quite unknowingly, made it possible for the creature to make much better use of that telepathic linkage."

Rypeck nodded slowly. "It's all very speculative," he said.

"But if it's true," persisted Ulicon, "then we have grounds for thinking—at least for *hoping*—that there won't be a recurrence. Without the i-minus agent, the rat people might not be able to effect a similar contact. We might be *safe* —at least for a time. We have time to think, time to adjust, time even to adapt, if we must. Surely we can stop this mad panic!"

"I think it's gone too far."

"We must try."

"With this mass of conjecture? We need more than a chain of ideas to persuade people. Not Heres—we'll never persuade Heres—but the people who might be in a position to halt the panic if Heres can be removed. We need hard evidence, and there's no way to get it."

"There's one way," said Ulicon.

"Repeat the process?" said Rypeck, his lips forming a half-smile at the irony. "That's what we're trying to prevent."

"We could try to make a contact," said Ulicon. "We know that the potential exists in people as well as in rats. Carl Magner had that potential. And after the blast . . . I think there's a good many of us can now pick up the kind of leakage he did. Joth told us that in the village, they chewed plant pulp to help them communicate with their Gray Souls.

We have specimens of that plant, courtesy of Harkanter's expedition. I think we should try it on a man."

"Who?"

"If he's willing, the man most likely to succeed. Joth Magner."

27

Joth's first reaction, when they came to him with the proposition, was: "Why me?"

"Two reasons," Ulicon told him. "First, you are your father's son. We don't know that his ability or potential was heritable, but it seems at least possible that there was a genetic predisposition. Secondly, you were closest to Camlak when he disappeared. Whatever effect the event had on our minds, it will have been at a maximum in your case. The only other person with your qualifications is your sister. But you have extra advantages in that you know more than any of us about the kind of context into which any contact you do make is to be put. As well as being the most likely candidate to make the contact, you are the most likely one to make sense of it."

"And what will it prove if I do make contact?" asked Joth.

"What it may prove," Rypeck interposed, "depends very much on the nature of the contact itself. What we want is to convince ourselves that we are on the road to understanding—that we are beginning to come to terms with the events that have happened. But if we succeed in the experiment, there is no knowing what we may learn. Perhaps very little—I doubt that we are in a position to learn very much because we are so totally naive to the implications of what is going on—but perhaps something very important."

"I want to help," said Joth. "You know that."

"But you're afraid," added Ulicon. "That's understandable."

"Suppose," said Joth, "that what happened to Camlak happens to me. We don't know that what he did was voluntary."

"We assume that you will retain a degree of control over what happens," Ulicon told him. "We think that it's unlikely that the contact will harm you. By your own evidence, the Children of the Voice are convinced that the intimacy with the Souls is a good thing, that the Souls are benign."

"Exactly what do you want to do?" asked Joth.

"We will inject into your veins an extract from the plant which you have identified as the one used by the villagers to stimulate contact during their Communion. We have tested it, and it seems to be harmless. Then we will induce deep sleep by direct electrical stimulation to the brain. With the encephalographic cyborg we can control the incidence of dream-sleep—can maintain or break it. The i-minus agent is already present in your body, but we will monitor its level continuously, and perhaps boost its concentration. We cannot monitor your dreams, of course, but we can stimulate retention within your own mind. We will always be able to wake you if you show any sign of physiological distress, but we will not do so unless we fear that you will come to some harm. We expect that the experience will be stressful to a degree.

"Perhaps there is one more thing that you ought to know, and that is that the experiment will be conducted without the knowledge or consent of Rafael Heres. In order to make it meaningful we will have to break the secrecy of the i-minus project. We have already told you that the agent exists—we must also inform the medical and scientific observers we coopt into the experiment. We intend to inform Abram Ravelvent and your own doctor, Joachim Casorati. Clea Aron will also be present, as the only other member of the upper echelons of the Movement who seems likely to be sympathetic toward what we are doing. There may well be others in attendance. In a sense, what we are doing is betraying the system of the Close Council, and Heres may wish to construe this as treason against the Movement, *if* Heres is still in power when the experiment takes place."

"There's a chance he may be stopped?" asked Joth.

"A chance," said Ulicon.

"Welcome to the revolution," added Rypeck, drily.

"Well," said Joth, quietly. "I've already been on one journey through Hell. Wherever this one takes me . . . I'll survive.

"I'll do it."

28

Rafael Heres was a man devoted to—and committed to—the principle of a pattern in life. His mind saw Hoh as a perfect analogue of Euchronia, and Euchronia as a perfect analogue of Hoh. Winning, to him, meant the imposition of a pattern, the enforcement of stability, and his idea of fulfilment in life was control over the pattern of life.

He had a tremendous capacity for finding answers to problems of great complexity (or what appeared to be great complexity), but the basis of this ability was not really intellectual acuity so much as an unbreakable faith in the fact that all problems, no matter how complex, had a single answer which would impose the sacred conformity to pattern. He was not, in any sense, a precise analyst of problems, merely an accomplished solver. Like Alexander confronted with the Gordian knot, he was a great believer in pragmatic solutions: if a knot would not yield to logic, then it must yield to force, it must be severed, even if it could not be untied.

This insight into Heres' character goes a long way to explaining his utter helplessness in the face of the circumstances following the Overworld's vision of Hell. Here was a knot which would not yield to the sword. It could not be forced to comply with Heres' assumptions about Knots. There was no way that the Euchronian pattern to which Heres was committed could be reconstituted, but Heres was incapable of admitting this. And so the very source of his erstwhile success was the instrument of his total failure. The faith which had served so well in other circumstances now showed itself to be, in the ultimate analysis, inadequate, and even absurd.

When Luel Dascon came to him and reported that the expeditionary forces in the Underworld were meeting with failure on every front, and asked him to recall the remainder in order to save lives, Heres came face to face with his own fallibility. He saw the negative counterpart to the self-image which, according to the mirror of his mind, had always been the "fairest in the land."

"Zuvara's report," said Dascon, "indicates that the viruses are not one hundred percent effective, and that their spread is not so rapid as might be desired. The implications of his results, he claims, are ambiguous insofar as our declared program is concerned. Provided that the seeding is heavy enough, there is no way that the higher life-forms in the Underworld can survive the consequent disruption of their ecology. However, such a seeding would have to continue actively on a large scale for many years. The extinction of the people of the Underworld cannot be regarded as imminent, even in the limited areas where heavy seeding has so far taken place.

"The force now commanded by Gunn Spurner following Jacob Germont's death has been reunited, but over half the vehicles and men have been lost. The force is no longer proceeding south, but is retreating through the blighted country already seeded. The people of this region are migrating south, and we have evidence which suggests that the rat people are fighting the spread of the plague by burning the blighted areas. The spread of the viruses by wind, water and animal is being limited by this policy, though not completely stopped.

"The corrosion of the supporting structures of our own world discovered by Vicente Soron is, in some places, advanced enough to be a danger. The platform is not threatened by small-scale collapses, so far as we can tell, but stress and strain are building up in certain regions which may result in damage to systems. The conclusion here is that intercourse between Overworld and Underworld must be reinstituted on a worldwide basis. The repair of the platform's supporting structures must, from now on, be regarded as a priority. Bases like Zuvara's must be established on a permanent basis in many areas. To some extent, their continued existence must depend on their ability to withstand attack not simply from the subhuman inhabitants, but also from the kind of life-form which destroyed the Delta contingent of Germont's force. Identification of this organism is at present tentative, only mechanical devices having so far been sent to the scene of the disaster."

"Is that all?" whispered Heres.

"There's a great deal more," said Dascon. "But these are the most vital points."

"And what conclusions do *you* draw?"

"We must go back into the Underworld on a big scale," said Dascon. "That's vital. The idea we have been nursing that our own activities down there can be kept to a minimum no longer seems tenable. We must conclude that the Planners made a mistake when they sought to shut out all the problems posed by the surface by sealing it up and ignoring it. The Plan must be continued—perhaps on the kind of lines which you proposed in your program for a Second Plan. If we are to begin the reclamation of the surface with the extirpation of the life-system currently dominant there, then we will obviously have to make the extirpation a long-range objective rather than a short-range one. The question is: how can the people be reconciled to these ends. It won't be easy to persuade them to abandon their Millennium and go back to work. Not this kind of work—dangerous and dirty. Our citizens were born the children of a dream—the ultimately privileged. It isn't going to be easy to take that privilege away, especially in the current climate of stark terror. All over the world there are people barricading themselves into their houses, trying to requisition supplies for two years or twenty years from the cybernet, because they simply have no confidence that the cybernet is still going to be working next year or next month—no confidence that society will still be functioning next year or next month. All over the world, people are beginning to exempt themselves from Euchronia, trying to retreat into their own tiny corner of it, which they hope they can sustain by their own efforts forever. And in the meantime, we may lose our minds. Tomorrow, or the next day. Not one of us can claim control of his own sanity, his own inner being. Our quasi-Utopian order no longer means a thing.

"In order to survive at all, we of the Overworld have to rediscover commitment—a commitment far more difficult than that which the original Movement fought for. We cannot offer the same assurances they could. Perhaps we can no longer offer even the *hope* of Euchronia. We can only try. We must do what we can."

"Sisyr is to blame," said Heres. Dascon had not expected the remark. It seemed to him to be a non sequitur. He had expected an affirmation of determination, support for his own verbally expressed conviction of the need to carry on. Dascon had always looked to Heres for confirmation of his own Euchronian cant—for the ultimate faith which he, in the final analysis, did not have. But Heres' conviction had come to a dead end. Suddenly, it was no longer there. It is always the deepest faith of all which submits to instantaneous evaporation, when its weakness is finally admitted.

"Sisyr kept the Underworld alive," Heres went on, when Dascon failed to reply. "He nurtured it in order that it could become our enemy. While he pretended to help the Plan, he sowed the seeds of Euchronia's destruction. He never intended that the Plan should succeed. He is the destroyer. All this time, through hundreds and thousands of years, he has been playing a game with us. It was never his intention that we should attain our ends. He has cheated a whole world."

"It's not so," said Dascon. "It can't be. He only wanted to keep both worlds alive. Isn't that *right?* Isn't that the proper way? In a game of Hoh, the ideal is for everyone to win."

"No!" said Heres. "He *never* intended that both worlds should become viable. He never intended that the Overworld should succeed. He has said so. He has confessed that he always knew our aims to be unattainable. He knew, because he made it so."

For the first time, it was Heres that looked to Dascon for confirmation, for justification. He expected it, for in all the years that Heres had known Dascon, he had seen him as little more than an echo, a testament to his own ability to be unfailingly correct.

But now Dascon said nothing, because for the first time Heres had failed to stand full-square with Euchronian ideology. For the first time, Heres spoke as a Eupsychian, and there was nothing left to believe in. Nothing at all.

29

The stars stood still in the sky. Bright, clearly defined, pearl-white. The land they illuminated was likewise sharply defined, but somehow unreal and insubstantial, almost two-dimensional. The shapes were shadows, with the thinness of shadows. Bright illusions stood forth while realities hid, cloaked in darkness.

At one moment he experienced the world as though he were floating in midair, looking out and across the bleak panorama of the realms of Tartarus; and in another he felt himself huddled in the slime, with the touch of the cold, foul earth creeping into his flesh as though licking at him, dissolving him, consuming him. There was sweat on his body, perhaps in the external world as well as the microcosmic existence of the dream.

He sensed the presence of the Children of the Voice, not through hearing or seeing, but through some mystic sense of collective being: a transcendental sense, the property, perhaps, of the fourfold vision. He was aware of the Children *en masse,* as a quasi-hive organism, perpetually growing and dying by degrees, but he was also aware of stresses within the whole—tensions and repulsions, the ceaseless effort of exemption, of isolation. The identity of the species seemed, from Joth's Godlike viewpoint, to be in a state of constant flux, like a chemical reaction in virtual equilibrium, with associations constantly forming and breaking down. But, as well as being outside and above, Joth was also inside and below—if his seeing eye was Godlike, it was also wormlike—and in himself he felt the ebb and flow of their existence. Their fear was his fear, their dream was his dream.

As he drifted in space, so he began to drift in time. He felt himself caught, as though by a rapid current, and suddenly hurled into a dark corridor, as though falling—but falling *through,* not down.

The stars were whirled away with him—they did not leave him but they lost their roundness, like teardrops becoming streaks of silver. He moved as though through a sleeve of shooting stars.

He began to be overwhelmed by a black absence of any sense of direction, any sense of speed, any sense of distance or location.

He was not afraid. There was no conscious element in the psychophysiological reaction which entrapped him, and which was shuttling him through the chaos of his inner world —not the surface of consciousness, or even the underlying interface of dream and symbol, but the depths, the Tartarean realms. His movement, his senses and his being were in the grip of something more basic than essential self.

Joth ran, his heart pumping, his limbs sucking up energy from his physical core. His eyes reflected the whirligig gleam of the stars, but what he saw . . .

The Star King, dancing . . . night, decked with painted stars, the pace of the dance slowing as the rhythm of the drums grew turgid and the King himself could do no more than writhe, his dead legs unable to carry him, but still dancing, dancing . . . .

The moist hand, lingering on and near his lips, his face hot and dry but the hand moist, tasting of . . . the lingering echoes of another dream, making his back rigid, the touch of madness . . .

An empty, derelict world . . . forests of shiny fungus hardened like wood . . . ground ridged and slick with bloated rhizoids and thick, matted humus, covered with cockroaches and small black beetles, and fleshy, squashy insects for eating with dirty, foul-smelling water thickened by slime . . . mud and puffballs and chytrids, monstrous edifices of mutually supportive hydroids . . . acid burning skin and mucous membrane . . . soft tentacles waving blindly in the air, sting-cells charged and constantly consuming, constantly sucking, constantly oozing through the morass . . .

Broth spooned into his mouth, gulped down and then vomited back, a thin, gray stream running down his cheeks and into the straw . . . and water pouring, running through him, over him, in baptism . . . and rebirth . . . out of the sickness and the wasting, and from the margins of death, the retreat of the world within and the world without . . . then the healing, the growing anew, the rebuilding and the self-repair, and the finding of fear . . . and love . . . *One lamp burning on a bracket in the wall, bricks and square stones showing through the plaster, cracks in the ceiling* . . .

The Star King, leaning foward, his belly touching her breasts . . . not breathing, not even alive . . . rigid . . . and then the Sun, striking like a snake . . . the flash of the axe as the blade caught and threw the starlight . . . the black mask rolling like a great black ball . . .

A great flat worm flopping like a rubber blanket, spitting out its guts . . . bubbling fountains of digestive juices . . . the villi of the blind intestine flapping like tiny grasping fingers . . . the deadly hiss of the acid in the algal scum . . . the worm, soft underfoot, writhing and sucking back its gut, sinking away into the ooze . . .

Blood, flooding the gray-green colors of the Earth-body . . . a torrent . . . a red sheen in the firelight, turning black . . . sliding the Night from the body, the Sun descending . . . bound together . . .

Metal eyes . . . are the men of your world made of metal?

All men are flesh and blood. I was hurt. I have been re-paired . . .

A strip of darkness in the further sky . . . the black land . . . a thin line of light like a road of stars . . . echoes of an older civilization . . . the ruins of a city and the relics of an older mankind . . .

Torrents of thought, breaking in his mind . . . the Face of Heaven . . . the sound of the horn, the sudden face and the sudden fear . . .

The stars in the sky, pale and still . . . his whole body being eaten by pain while cockroaches moved over his body and he could not move . . . helpless and lost . . . mental continuity broken . . . tears in the corners of his eyes . . .

And then, quite suddenly, faces:

Huldi.

Nita.

Carl Magner.

Iorga.

Camlak.

Inside Camlak's eyes, a sudden flare of light. A scream, striking him down.

And . . .

In slow motion, Harkanter leveling the pistol and pulling the trigger. Harkanter's head, exploding . . .

Patterns blossoming on closed eyelids.

Firelit masks, bricks crumbling as a house burned, eaten away by flame, searching among the dead, the map, the road, the stillness and the death, and after that . . . nothing. No more.

Inside himself again, Joth as Joth, now still. The cone of stars no longer spinning, his world cut out in light and darkness, nothing more, the pattern nonsense but the shapes of darkness sharp and well defined.

His tongue felt suddenly very large. His mouth was grained, filled with grit and fur. His ribs felt like ice—a cage of ice around his heart. His bones, within him, felt cold. His belly was absolutely without feeling. There was a nearness about his body that made him aware of it, all save his gut, which was numb and void.

Then the light began to flicker, the radiance separating from the shadow. What had been a cocoon of two dimensions became a womb of three. There was a liquid cascade of light, and through the living matrix the shadows moved.

As though a curtain were drawn aside, to reveal to him a window ... and beyond the window a gray world like fog and smoke. And in the window, a face.

Camlak's face.

30

While Enzo Ulicon, Clea Aron, Abram Ravelvent and Joachim Casorati supervised the attempt to awaken Joth Magner's latent telepathic ability, Rafael Heres was once again confronting Sisyr. Luel Dascon was with him.

"We have come to a decision," said Heres.

The word "we" was, in fact, empty of meaning. The only mind involved in the decision was Heres' own. Even Dascon had been excluded, and Dascon did not know what had been decided. In fact, Dascon was almost afraid of what Heres might have decided to do.

"What have you decided?" asked Sisyr, responding smoothly to Heres' obvious expectation.

"You must leave Earth," said the Hegemon. "You must leave and never return. Whatever your interests here, they are at an end. I do not profess to understand your actions during the time you have spent here, but the outcome of what you have done is intolerable. In the beginning, our predecessors asked you for help, and for this reason only we do not regard what you have done as completely hostile. But you cannot stay."

Sisyr's blue eyes stared first at Heres, and then moved to Dascon. Dascon felt their pressure, and was compelled to speak.

"It is best," he said.

"I will go," said the alien. "I will need time to prepare."

"You have twenty-four hours," said Heres.

"I need more," replied Sisyr.

"Why?"

"I am a long way from my home. I will have to make preparations for the journey. Interstellar journeys are measured in centuries, not in days. My ship has to be supplied, fueled, tested. It has been a long time."

"Very well," said Heres. "But you will understand that this work must be supervised."

"I do not understand," said Sisyr, flatly.

"We must be certain that there is no further interference," said Heres. "Your house is being searched. All records you have kept and all property which you have accumulated is being confiscated. We are not yet acquainted with the full range of your activities here, nor are we certain of their purpose, but no further activity must take place. You must make such preparations as are necessary, and depart with all due speed."

Sisyr said nothing, but gave a slight bow. There was no way of knowing whether this signaled acquiescence, or whether some irony was intended.

"Call in the police guard," said Heres, this time to Dascon.

Dascon opened the door. There were four policemen waiting outside. With them were a captain of police and Thorold Warnet. Dascon's eyes met Warnet's, and the recognition struck him cold. He felt the shock in his heart, a sharp, small pain that died quickly as he realized how little it meant.

Dascon stepped aside, holding the door wide for Warnet to enter the room.

Heres was still facing Sisyr, and he did not turn instantly. It was only when the silence went on too long that he finally turned.

"Rafael Heres," said Warnet, almost lightly, "Luel Dascon. You're both under arrest."

The color drained from the Hegemon's face. He tried to speak, but the words simply would not come.

Warnet watched the effort which Heres put into trying to speak, and thought it very strange that there was real pain written in the other's face.

"We control the cybernet," said Warnet quietly. "We have the holovisual networks, and all the operative facilities. The takeover within the cerebral complex was orderly. There have been no casualties. We anticipate a good deal of intellectual dissent when we begin transmitting, but we have the machine, and the machine is the world. It will be a very quiet revolution."

"It's impossible," said Heres.

"It was inevitable." This whispered denial was Dascon's, not Warnet's.

"No one could get control of the cerebral complex," said Heres. "No one has the means. Only the Council could . . ."

"We have Council support," said Warnet quietly. "Not a majority, but enough. We have the police, and we have the technicians. It has been necessary to arrest perhaps ten or a dozen major councillors and technical supervisors. The rest either support us, or are prepared to stand by. Believe me, the structure of authority which supported you no longer exists. It dissolved, and it has been replaced."

"By whom?"

"That's not important. You must go to your home now, and you, Dascon, to yours."

"Rypeck," said Heres, slowly. "Ulicon . . . Sobol . . . they betrayed me. Even now . . ."

31

Afterwards, Warnet said to Sisyr: "We still need your help. In fact, we need your help now more than we have ever needed it before."

"What kind of help?" asked the alien. Warnet heard bitterness in the tone, but whether the bitterness was really there, he could not tell.

"To make new plans," said Warnet. "Not a Plan, but plans. There will be no destruction of the Underworld."

Sisyr turned away. "I am tired," he said.

"You'd better go home," said Warnet. "We can contact you later. But we'd like you to join us . . . not the revolution, that is, but the new executive authority . . . whatever we put in place of the Council."

"There are men at my house," said the alien. "Searching . . . for what, I don't know. Are they under your command, now?"

Warnet shook his head. "We hold the brain of Euchronia. Outside, we have no actual authority, except that which extends through the cybernet. There may well be isolated groups and individuals who would rather stage their own counterrevolution than capitulate with circumstances. Would you rather stay here?"

"No."

"Then I'll send men back with you. If the men at your house are police, there'll be no trouble. If they're employees of the Movement, there's a chance they'll stay loyal to Heres, but I don't think they'll be very difficult to handle. You'll come to no harm."

"It's not for myself I'm afraid," said Sisyr, "but the house and its contents . . ."

"I'll do what I can," promised Warnet.

"Thank you."

32

"What's happened?" asked Clea Aron.

"He's still dreaming," said Casorati. "His brain is still active. But his body is now fully relaxed. The pons—the organ responsible for decoupling brain and motor nerve network during dreaming seems to have become suddenly more effective. Normally, there are quite distinct physical signs of dreaming—although the grosser effects of the motor nerves are damped, there is usually some muscular activity, and the physical aspects of emotional involvement are usually detectable. But Joth is physically stable to a considerable degree."

"Are you sure he's still dreaming?" asked Ravelvent.

"The encephalographic register hasn't settled into black-out rhythm."

"This could be it," said Ulicon.

"We've no way of knowing that," said Casorati. "No way at all."

"Isn't this the dangerous phase?" asked Clea Aron. "If something . . . untoward happens, it will be now."

"Perhaps," said Ulicon.

They waited. Their eyes watched the trace on the oscillograph as it flickered, amplitude and frequency changing—apparently at random.

"Isn't there any way of ... de-coding ... that?" Again, the question came from the councillor.

"It's been tried," said Ulicon. "But there's no way. It tells us, in a vague sense, what's happening, but the signals aren't in any way a *language*. The patterns don't correspond to specific *thoughts*. We have some degree of control over what's happening, though. We can feed in signals of our own *via* the cyborg linkage. I can bring him back to dreamless sleep—shallow blackout or deep blackout—at any time. There is a state—the shallow state—in which we can communicate with him while he's still unconscious. It's rather like asking questions under hypnosis. He may be better equipped to tell us about the dreams in that state. The return of consciousness is bound to confuse him. The trouble is that we may not be able to make any sense out of what he says. If that's the case, we'll have to rely on conscious memory retention and reinterpretation."

"His heartbeat is slowing down," said Casorati.

"Markedly?"

"It's noticeable. It's a slow, steady decrease."

"Understandable," said Ravelvent. "He's no longer active."

"No," said the doctor. "There's more involved than that. I'm afraid he may be slipping into coma."

"Not with this kind of brain activity," said Ulicon.

"I think the pons may be working rather *too* well," Casorati said. "The decoupling is too effective. His body is losing the rhythm of its continuity. It's as though he were changing metabolic gear. I don't think we dare let this go on too long."

"I don't want to interfere unless I have to," said Ulicon. "It's bound to affect retention and the coherency of the experience if I try and break it up."

"That's a risk you'll have to take," replied Casorati. "I can give you a couple more minutes. That's all."

"It's all right," said Ulicon, quickly. "I think the decline is having a feedback effect. Look!"

The oscillograph trace changed its character rapidly, the ever-changing pulse giving way to a rhythmic, high-amplitude, low-frequency trace that gained stability very quickly.

"It's over," said Ulicon. "Now I'm going to stimulate him just a little, bring him out of the deep sleep, so that he'll hear what I'm saying, and be able to reply."

"Not so fast," said Casorati, reaching out a hand to make Ulicon pause. But Ulicon pushed the doctor's arm away.

"It has to be now," he said. "While the experience is still accessible."

On the oscillograph, the frequency of the wave increased, and the amplitude began to vary slightly.

Joth's mouth opened—as far as the complex web of apparatus around his head would permit it to open—and a thin sound between a moan and a sigh escaped from his lips.

"Joth," said Ulicon, careful to pronounce his words clearly, "can you hear me?"

They waited.

33

The voice filled Joth's internal cosmos. There was nothing else. Except for his hearing, his sensory apparatus was disengaged and disinterested. He was in the mental limbo which results from the complete relaxation of the higher faculties. The voice was an invasion. It came to him not *via* the vibration of the tympanum, but by electronic stimulation of the auditory receptors in the brain, *via* the artificial ears of the medical cyborg of which Joth was a part.

Joth did not respond.

But the voice came again, cutting into his state of relaxation, disturbing the limbo of his mind. It would not let his consciousness rest, but forced it into a state of minimum reactivity.

From the words, he read the meaning, and he organized an answer. The process by which he did so was largely automatic, involving no actual cogitation.

"I hear you," said his mind. The voice picked up the words, and they came out in a low murmur.

"Joth." The words came at him again. "Joth, did you make contact?"

He sorted the meaning from the words, but did not react.

("I'll have to ask more specific questions," said Ulicon to his companions, his hand covering the microphone. "I'll have to lead him. He can only answer literally—I can't leave too much unsaid, because he simply won't be able to supply the extra meaning.")

"Joth," said the voice, "you have been dreaming. When your dream was ending, you saw something, didn't you? What did you see?"

And Joth replied: "I saw Camlak."

A pause. Then the voice said: "Did you talk to Camlak?"

"I talked to Camlak," replied Joth.

"Where is Camlak?"

Joth hesitated. Words trembled on his lips, but all that finally formed was: "Camlak is ..."

"Is he in the Underworld?"

No answer. Ulicon amended the question: "Is Camlak in the Underworld?"

Still confusion. Still searching for words. Finally, Joth said: "Camlak is inside elsewhere."

"I want you to tell me what Camlak said to you," said the voice. "What did Camlak say to you?"

(Ulicon licked his lips. This was the crucial question. If Joth could answer this—and if his answer made sense—then here was the only possible direct access to what Joth might have learned. If this did not work, then he would have to rely on Joth's interpretative mind to try and recover the essence of the experience. If it could.)

Joth spoke:

"Soul space," he said. "Child two. One and one. Link chain. Change mind. All soul. Child shadow. Shape wall. Flow all. Soul through. Hillsunfireli ... shi ... see ... flo ... o ..."

Joth's voice died into an incoherent mumble, where the sounds crumbled together and would not make words.

("It's gibberish," said Clea Aron.

"No," said Ulicon. It's the vocal component of the communication—so far as it can be approximated. Where it breaks down it does so because that's where the vocal component of the exchange broke down. The substance of the contact must have been imagistic, with verbal support ... mind to mind, direct telepathic communication with a minimum of translatory mediation. What we have is the verbal core of the message. That's what we wanted. If only Joth can build on that. When he returns to full consciousness, his mind is going to try and integrate the message into his awareness of existence—it may fail or succeed incompletely. The ideas may become changed, or may even be erased. But we have the core as it is. We have something to work with."

"For what it's worth," added Ravelvent. "Some of those two-word units could mean any of a hundred different things."

"But Joth can help us," said Ulicon, "if only his mind can retain enough of the experience.")

The voice was still. Everything was still. Joth floated in limbo, inactive, unaware, for a timeless interval . . .

. . . And then began the coalescence of consciousness which would bring him back to the reified world, and secure him within the cage of solid reality.

34

The broadcast which was intended to capture the world and secure the new government required only three people. Plus, of course, the technology and the technical staff required to package the message and see it safely into every home in every continent. The three people were to play three archetypal roles, and between them, they were to define the synthetic product which, following the end of the broadcast would define the "way of life" in which the citizens of the Overworld were to be participants. The purpose of the broadcast was, quite simply, to redefine the entire context of life: to rationalize the change, not of circumstance, but of intellectual ecology, which had become necessary. The revolutionaries set out, in fact, to rewrite the entire mental environment of Euchronia's citizens, so that they would no longer *be* Euchronia's citizens.

The achievement of this purpose would be by no means easy, but it was a practical aim requiring a relatively simple method. The people of the Overworld were parasitic upon the machine complex which supplied them with all the necessities and luxuries of life. They had no option but to be defined by the machine. It is a principle of evolutionary inevitability that parasites, in becoming adapted to their hosts, lose their organs of locomotion, their sense organs, and everything which extends them beyond themselves: they cease to be whole organisms, and become part-organisms. When the host is redefined, so is the parasite. The people of the Overworld contained relatively little of their whole existence within their individual minds—most of it was contained by the cybernet. As the nature of the information carried by the cybernet changed therefore—as the holovisual network began to "think different thoughts"—so the nature of Euchronia's citizens was made to change. The people themselves began to think different thoughts. The change was not easy—there was confusion, emotional disturbance and insecurity—but it was inevitable.

The first of the three people involved in the renaissance of the Overworld was Yvon Emerich. He represented the people—he was their representative within the "thoughts" of the cybernet. (The reference here, of course, is to the projected image of Emerich rather than to the real individual—it was the image with which people were invited to identify.) It was Emerich's task to "present" the program, to organize it and provide the ideas which were to be contained in it with a human context, a human environment. He was to be aggressive, but not destructive, rhetorical but not informative.

The second of the three was Eliot Rypeck. His job was to define the problem. It was up to him to destroy the old patterns of thought, to expose ruthlessly the error and the hopelessness of the old regime. He represented the problem, building an edifice of fear and naked truth, defining a firebreathing dragon to threaten the world.

The third man required by the scheme was, of course, the hero—a new figurehead. He was not required to do anything at all, but simply to *be*. He (the image, not the man) would become the new focus of hope, the new organizing principle within the mechanical mind of the Overworld. His name, of course, was Joel Dayling.

35

"What happened to Camlak," said Joth, "wasn't simply a translocation. He ... twisted himself ... out of our space into another, but there was more to it than that. In a way, it was also a metamorphosis, a transfiguration. Camlak now is not the same kind of being that he was. He has *transcended* that whole mode of being, and now he is something new. He retains aspects of himself, and it is through these aspects that he was able to make contact with me, and to transfer ideas from his mind into mine. But there's more to it than that . . . more that is beyond our understanding. I can't explain because there is no explanation. It is outside what we know and understand."

"I want you to go over the things which you said while you were still unconscious," said Ulicon. "Expand on them any way you can. We don't want exact explanations—we simply want to know the contexts in which the words are to be set."

"All right," said Joth. "One by one. Give them to me."

"Soul space," said Ulicon.

"That's what I've just been trying to tell you about," said Joth. "There are other spaces, outside, or perhaps alongside, this one. But the space where Camlak is is not only apart from ours—it's intrinsically *different* from it. There seems to be less fixity in it, the reality is less *solid*, less unitary. It's as though several possibilities may exist simultaneously . . . except that there's no simultaneity . . . go on to the next."

Ravelvent obviously wanted to interrupt, to ask for clarification, but Ulicon signaled him to be still.

"Child two," he said.

"That's simple," said Joth. "It simply means that the Children of the Voice are two beings in one. They have a human-like aspect, but they also have a Gray Soul—they aren't individuals."

"One and one," read Ulicon.

"The same point. Meant to convey, I think, some kind of equality of the creature which we see and understand, and the Soul. We mustn't think of the Soul as being 'in' the person—there is simply a touching point between them: an interface, not in the brain, but in the mind."

"You're making a clear distinction between the two?" asked Ulicon.

"I think we have to."

"Very well. Link chain."

Joth considered for a moment. "I think this refers to the fact that the nature of the relationship between the Children of the Voice and their Gray Souls, the potential exists for the linking of minds in some kind of linear fashion. I can't quite see how."

"What about 'Change mind'?"

"Just what it says, I think. Minds can be changed—they have the power of metamorphosis, though I don't know how or why. The act itself seems rather self-evident, but I think that's all there is."

"All Soul."

This time, Joth paused for a long time before answering. "All I can make of that," he said, finally, "is that we can all become like the Souls. But that may simply be a rationalization of the statement itself. I don't remember anything in connection with the phrase."

"Child shadow."

Joth shook his head. "I think I'm losing it," he said. "These things must have meant something *then*—during the contact. But I've lost the meaning now. It seems to me to suggest that the Children of the Voice are in some sense shadows—perhaps from the viewpoint of the Souls. There's an old saying—something about our world, as we see it, being only the shadows of reality . . . perhaps that's the perspective the phrase is intended to convey."

Ulicon nodded. "I think you may be right. The next phrase is 'Shape wall', which seems to tie in."

"It may," said Joth. "We are merely the shapes on the wall—the shadows cast by the firelight. I think that's right —it's just an image, to help us think."

"There are two syllables in the final jumble of words," said Ulicon. "After 'hill' and 'sun' you said 'fireli.' That may be the beginning of 'firelight.' And at that point the verbal thinking seems to be giving way to visual imagery. 'Shi,' which came next, might be the beginning of 'shining.' But there are two more distinct phrases yet. The first is 'Flow all.' "

Joth rubbed his eyes, and tensed the muscles of his face as though to force reluctant ideas into his head. "It could mean so many things," he said. "I have no intuition . . . I honestly think that at this stage I'm no more competent to interpret than you are. It might mean that in the other space everything can flow . . . nothing is fixed. But it may mean something else entirely. It's just gone from my mind. There's nothing there to echo."

"Try the last," said Ulicon, kindly. "Soul through."

Joth was shaking his head even as the words were spoken.

"Nothing," he said. "It means nothing. The only thing I can think of is that the Souls can come through into our space just as Camlak went into theirs . . . no, I'm sure that's not it. It's something else. But something I can't reach . . ."

"Relax," said Ulicon. "There's no hurry. It may come to you some other time—it may even come back to you in your dreams. You've done magnificently—far better than we could have hoped. You established contact, and you brought something back from the contact. Perhaps we can't understand, but we know that we're on the way to understanding. We've brought this thing into the realm of things we can *study,* things we can work with. We may not know what we're doing, but we can begin to feel our way."

"It's dangerous," said Ravelvent, no longer able to contain his impatience. "You seem to have become so wrapped up in this that you've forgotten that we're playing with forces that could destroy the world."

"We already have those," retorted Ulicon, calmly. "We've been living with atomic power for millennia. To an extent, we run the world on forces which—if we couldn't control them—could destroy it. Such forces exist, and we can't pretend we live in a world without them." He paused to glance at his wristwatch. "And now, I think we must return to the real world. We've exempted ourselves for a considerable time, in order to conduct this experiment. If you, Joachim, would activate the holovid, I think we can listen to what Eliot has to say."

He looked round at the expressions of startled puzzlement.

"There's no need to be alarmed," he assured them. "The world simply has a new messiah. Like all the others, he's only going to promise to save us from ourselves."

36

"The objectives of the Euchronian Movement," Rypeck was saying, "were both clear and narrow. They were products of the age that we now call the age of psychosis, or the Second Dark Age. In earlier periods of history there had been no clear and narrow objectives adopted and accepted by any substantial and cosmopolitan body of men. This is not to say that individuals lacked any sense of purpose, but that the race as a whole lacked any unified concept of historical ambition. The Euchronian Movement set forth a system of priorities which, for the first time, provided a focus for the whole of mankind.

"We still live with the objectives and priorities of the Movement of eleven thousand years ago. We have the world that they designed. In order to build the world we now inhabit, the Movement changed mankind. The Movement *became* mankind, first of all, by so defining itself—the men who would not accept commitment to the Movement's ends were abandoned, and left to die on the surface, entombed by the platform.

"But that was not enough. Mankind had to be changed in order that the Movement's evaluation of itself should be justified. The Movement had defined the destiny of man—plotted his future history. It had designed the world he must live in, and prescribed total commitment to the Plan as the only means of achieving that world-vision. Having defined the Plan as the perfect statement of human need, it proceeded to adapt mankind to the Plan. Having defined clear and simple objectives, the Movement set out to manufacture a clear and simple human race.

"One of the instruments which the Movement found in order to further this end—to protect the Plan against human weakness—was a drug known as the i-minus agent. This drug was administered to the builders in both food and water. Its purpose was to eliminate the instinctive element in human nature, to make men more pliable, more easily indoctrinated—to make them, in fact, better servants of the Plan. This was done in secret, and the secret entrusted to a handful of men—not even to the whole Council of the Movement.

"That drug is still being administered today. The motives behind the i-minus project were good. The Movement saw the Plan as the only hope for humanity, and human nature as the only threat to the Plan. In attempting to enslave humanity to their particular set of ideals they were—by their own definition—'right.' And in some measure, they succeeded in enslaving mankind to their particular set of ideals. We still hold, for the most part, to the set of values established by the planners. Such dissent as there is among us is not due to the instinctive, animal qualities which the Movement sought to exorcise, but to variance in what we learn, what we think, and what we come to believe.

"But it is surely time, now, to ask questions about this drug, and what it has made of us. Such questions have always been asked, but they have been asked and answered in secret, debated by a handful of individuals. While this has been going on, our world has come to the brink of disaster. It is my conviction that part of the reason why we seem so completely helpless in the face of our present circumstances is the work of the i-minus agent. We have been fitted to the well-defined and narrow concept of what a human being should be, as decided by the Euchronian Movement. But the problems we face at this time are not problems which—according to Euchronian philosophy—human beings ought to face. In defining man as they did, the Euchronian Movement also defined the world in which he existed. We have discovered that the world is simply not like that.

"We live in the Overworld designed by the Planners. But the Planners saw the Overworld as the *whole* world, the limits of existence. Outside the walls of Utopia, there is supposedly nothing. If the vast universe of the stars exists, then it is somehow apart from human life: quintessential. If the world within—the Underworld—exists, then that, too, is apart from human life and completely irrelevant to it.

"We have found that this is not so. Outside the walls of Utopia, the world goes on. We have found that the Universe is real, that the stars have worlds and peoples. We have contrived to ignore that, despite the fact that had it not been for the people of another world the Plan could not have been brought to its conclusion in the manner that it was. We also contrived to ignore the Underworld, doubting its reality, for thousands of years. But now we can lo longer ignore it. We can no longer retain even the illusion of our total isolation from anything beyond the machine in which we live. We have been invaded—we *can* be invaded. We have reacted to the first of these, but it is really the second which concerns us.

"The fact is very simply that we have been wrong. The Movement defined humanity and human life too narrowly. In trying to shape man to the mould which it made for him, the Movement robbed him of an adaptability which may have prevented our ever reaching the predicament in which we now find ourselves. Of all the people on the platform, only one—the alien, Sisyr—remembered the Underworld. Had there been more—if the Planners, too, had remembered—then the terrible shock of confrontation which we have suffered could not have happened.

"The aims of the Movement were a response to the situation of the Second Dark Age. They were designed to end that Second Dark Age and prevent any such age of psychosis from recurring. Now, we need a new set of priorities—a new prescription for action—which is a response to our present circumstances. Rafael Heres reacted to what has happened in the manner of a man totally committed to the ideas which are now out of date. His only answer was to destroy—to fulfil the assumptions which had proved unjustified by destroying the proof. It was his belief that the Overworld was the *whole* world, and he attempted to confirm that belief by destroying everything else. At first, he wanted to make the Underworld an extension of the Overworld—to convert it into a human world for human beings. When he found that that was simply not possible, he found no other alternative but to exterminate all life within it, to render it inert.

"But even if that were possible, it would not be an answer. We know now what we ought to have known all the time—that the Overworld is not all that exists. It is not the whole Earth, and it is certainly not the whole Universe.

"It is we who must change. It is we who must adapt to what we know, rather than wasting ourselves in the futile attempt to adapt what really exists to our narrow concept of existence.

"We should be grateful for the fact that this revelation has been forced upon us now, and that we did not endure in our state of willful ignorance for a few centuries more. If we had continued as we were, the realization that the Overworld is not inviolable would have come to us in a manner even more frightening than the way in which it has.

"The pillars which support the platform—the structures which hold up our world—have been corroded and weakened. At the present, there seems to be little danger of imminent collapse, but it is clear that the supporting structure not only needs rapid repair, but constant attention thereafter. If we had not been forced to look into the world beneath our feet we would not have discovered this until it was too late.

"We must, therefore, in order to maintain our existence,

go back into the Underworld—not as invaders or exterminators of vermin, but as workers and builders. We will be forced to come to terms with the Underworld and its peoples, and those terms cannot and must not be the terms of total war, because our total war is a failure.

"The reactivity of the life-system in the Underworld is such that the viruses with which we sought to destroy it are by no means effective. If all that we had to do was kill, perhaps, in a very long time, we might succeed in wiping out the life of the Underworld. But we have much more to think about than killing. We have to think about repairing the pillars—*all* the pillars, in all quarters of the globe. The work that needs to be done is tremendous, and it will require a concerted effort on the part of our society. We cannot do this work if we are simultaneously to wage an all-out global war with the Underworld. Rather, we need to make peace with the people of the Underworld, to cooperate with them, and—if possible—to enlist their help. This will not be easy, and in some respects it may be as difficult as our attempt to wage war, but this is what needs to be done if we are to adapt ourselves to reality. We must come to understand the people of the Underworld, and find a means of coexisting with them. We must cease to think of them as 'the men on the ground'—Euchronia's enemies—because they are something different, something new. Carl Magner tried to tell us that we must show the Face of Heaven to the people of the Underworld, because we were wrong to deny them the sight of it. I think that we must also show *ourselves* the Face of Heaven, because we have been wrong to refuse to look at it."

37

It was not until Rypeck was replaced by Dayling that Ulicon's companions fully understood what had happened. Clea Aron had known what would happen, in an approximate sense, but she had not been involved in any way with the transfer of authority—she had merely agreed to remain passive. Ravelvent was not surprised by the turn taken by events, although he was somewhat startled by the apparent smoothness of the operation, which had happened virtually while his back was turned.

Casorati was the only one who expressed his surprise:

"You *knew* this was happening!" he said to Ulicon.

Ulicon nodded. "I think it was well done," he said. "Eliot was perfect. Long-winded and dry, but casual and rhetorical. Then Dayling, to repeat the same message in brief, emotional tones."

"And that's it?" asked Clea Aron. "That's going to change the world, overnight."

"Oh yes," said Ulicon. "You shouldn't assume that because the Movement held total control for thousands of years, and claimed absolute stability, that it can't be set aside. Its very constancy has led to its being taken wholly for granted. The people had simply become unconscious of government—so far as their everyday lives are concerned the machine rules, and the mind behind it is totally invisible. They'll accept the change. All, perhaps, except the hierarchy of the Movement, many of whom will find themselves out of a job. But it's only political positions that will be affected —the civil services will simply carry on. I doubt if there will be any more unrest in the world tonight than there was last night—perhaps less, now that the people have some new hope of order being recovered out of the confusion."

"But you just carried on with the experiment," said Casorati, as though he was almost unable to conceive of it.

"The experiment was important," said Ulicon. "More important, perhaps, than what was happening out there."

"It won't work," said Ravelvent. "The new program is as helpless as the old in dealing with the one thing which really matters—the fact that the people are desperately afraid of a recurrence of the mental invasion."

"There will be no recurrence," said Ulicon.

"Why not?"

"Because the i-minus project is finished. The i-minus agent which, we have reason to believe, enabled the event to take place and—perhaps more important—helped render people vulnerable to the event when it did. The cessation of the project will minimize the effect of the telepathic input, and may even stop it altogether."

"You don't know," said Ravelvent. "You don't know that at all. This experiment isn't proof of that theory, isn't even evidence for it."

"We will act upon the assumption that we are right," said Ulicon. "We will promise the people that there will be no recurrence of the blast. We won't tell them that everything will be wonderful—the recovery of the instinctive input into the psyche isn't going to be easy. But what we are doing—what we will say that we are doing—is readapting them to the world. They will accept what we say, unless there is another blast to prove us wrong."

"And if there is?"

"Then what can anyone do? What solution could there be? We can only act upon the assumption that we will survive. If there is another mindblast, if our minds are taken apart and destroyed, then that spells the end. Adapting to *that* would be far beyond the scope of political action. We must assume that we will win, and we will assure the people that we *know* we will win. And we will hope that we are telling the truth. Only time will tell."

Clea Aron pointed at the image of Joel Dayling on the screen.

"Do you honestly think that *he* is any better than Heres?" she asked.

They all turned to look at the new Hegemon. He was winding up his own version of what Rypeck had said, speaking in clipped sentences, with convinced sincerity and carefully practiced self-assurance.

"No," said Ulicon. "Not if you mean 'Do I think he is a better man.' In many ways, Rafe and he are alike. But that's not what matters. What matters is the fact that he can organize some kind of social action which will help to get us out of this mess, whereas Heres no longer could. Heres had worked himself into a blind corner. A trap. A new figurehead was desperately needed. Rypeck tried to persuade Acheron Spiro, before the emergency arose, but Spiro couldn't have taken Heres' place. Not as we are now. It needed someone new, someone from outside. Dayling is all we had."

"A Eupsychian."

Ulicon shrugged. "That doesn't matter either. The changes which will happen now will render the conflict between Euchronia and its Eupsychian rebels quite meaningless."

"I think you overestimate the power we have to change ourselves," said Ravelvent. "I don't think that Dayling and his party—whoever his party are—will be able to organize society along the lines you suggest. I think we may well see a breakup of central organization. I think you'll see other leaders emerging, and—more important—you'll see mass resignation from the social order. People will simply quit."

"We control the cybernet," said Ulicon. "And while we control the cybernet we control *everything*. Not only what people do, but what they think and what they are. Your thinking is thousands of years out of date, Abram. Certainly, they'll opt out. Tomorrow morning, they'll be flocking to the sanctuaries. But they won't stay there. How can they? The sanctuaries depend on the cybernet for their existence just as everything else does. In a matter of months, the sanctuaries will be back to their normal transient population, and the people will be working under the new regime, according to its ministrations."

"And anyone who objects, no doubt, will be working in the Underworld." This piece of sarcasm was contributed by Casorati. Ulicon did not favor him with a reply.

"At least," said Joth—the first words he had spoken since he had heard Rypeck tell the world that the Underworld had to be saved rather than destroyed—"we are returning to sanity."

"If we can find it," said Ravelvent.

38

Iorga knelt to drink water from the shallow pool surrounded by blocks of cracked cement. The blocks were encrusted with red and yellow lichenous growths, and the water was thick with monads and thin filaments of algae. Huldi threw herself full-length on the ground, leaning over the lip of the pool to splash water into her face.

The region was hot, and the air heavy and humid. Under his clothing, Iorga was sweating copiously, and both Huldi and Nita were flushed—almost feverish. They were in a clear area, relatively speaking. The buildings forming the framework of the forest were gigantic, but they were well-spaced. In between them, the plants clung to other structures, but none more than a man's height. Iorga felt very small as he contemplated the vast blocks which reached high into the sky—so high that their roofs seemed almost to touch the stars.

These reinforced concrete monsters had—in the old world —been faced with glass, but that was all gone now. Only the skeletons remained.

The life-system had moved into the buildings as well as dressing their exterior walls, and inside each of the structures there would be great communities of organisms on every floor. Every building was a multilayered concrete island.

Iorga's ears pricked, searching the damp air for any vestige of vibration. His eyes searched the mottled carpet of fungus. His nose told him that something was wrong, but he searched with his other senses for some kind of confirmation.

All he could see and hear were the great ghost-moths fluttering around the towers where they swarmed. The unsteady flickering of their vast white wings caught the light and reflected it with a curious stroboscopic effect which constantly drew his eyes only to mislead them. The thin screeching of the moths, in the highest register of his hearing, filled his ears, and any more subtle, lower pitched sounds were lost. Smaller insects, silent in flight, with jeweled, transparent wings, mingled with the ghost-moths in their aerial dance. Some of them were stinging wasps, but they did not seem alarmed by the presence of the three invaders.

Iorga climbed a low ridge of basidiomycetic fiber, attempting to command a better view of the surroundings, but it would not bear his weight. In supporting himself with his hand he found that the vegetable tissue was rotten inside, swarming with maggots. As he held up his hand to inspect the putrefying gel which stuck to it, flies began to gather around it. He shook off the gel and wiped the moistness from his palm.

Nita, seeing the suspicion in his attitude, sniffed the air carefully.

"Fire," she commented.

"Cuchumanates," said Iorga. "They came through the blight ahead of us. These lands are their lands if they are anyone's. They may attack."

The doubt in his mind was clear in his voice. The Cuchumanates were dangerously unpredictable. If they did attack, the fight would be savage—it would be no mere skirmish.

The safest thing by far was to keep well clear. But the heat did not make traveling easy.

Huldi caught a hopping insect with a swift movement of her hand, bit into the abdomen, and sucked out the soft part of the creature, then threw the chitinous shell away.

"Eat," she said. "While we can."

"There!" said Iorga, suddenly, pointing west—the direction they wanted to go. When Nita followed the direction of his arm, she could see nothing, but she knew that the hellkin had detected movement.

"This way," said Iorga, reaching down to haul Huldi to her feet. With his head, he indicated that they were to move to the right, into the shadow of one of the monstrous frameworks. Huldi gathered together the food and the weapon she had been carrying, and they all ran across the open space to the overgrown wall.

As they reached its shelter, an arrow struck the plant flesh above the hellkin's head, and sank into it with a dull, liquid sound.

Pushing the others before him, Iorga retreated along the wall. He saw one of the Cuchumanates coming forward at a run, then another. There was no longer any question of hiding—they must escape or kill.

They found an opening in the wall—what had once been a considerable doorway but which was now reduced to a narrow, oval aperture.

"Inside," said Iorga. Nita went through immediately, but Huldi was reluctant. To her, the interior seemed pitch-black, and she had a horror of closed, dark spaces which were certain to be full of biting insects. Her eyes were not so sharp as those possessed by Nita, let alone the cat-eyes of the hellkin. Iorga had to go ahead of her, and then pull her in after him.

Nita found the corridor within much wider and taller than the entrance had suggested, but strands of webbing were everywhere. She had to pull the thin, slightly sticky strands away from her face. She could see little save the broad dimensions of the place, but she could hear multifold rustling noises as the denizens of the hall retreated from the intrusion.

Iorga drew the gun—it was a pistol—that Joth had left with him on his return to the Overworld. Huldi also held a weapon at the ready—a long, stout knife of Heaven-sent metal, but Nita's best knife was made of bone. Iorga considered giving up his own metal knife, but decided against it.

He had only a limited quantity of ammunition for the pistol, and when it was empty . . . it made sense to let the biggest and strongest handle the most effective weaponry.

The hellkin crouched in the doorway, looking out. The Cuchumanates had decided that caution was required, and they were approaching slowly, hidden by the tangled maze of puffballs and toadstools.

While he waited, Huldi crouched by his side, crowding him, determined not to move back from the entrance and the weak light of the road of stars.

Another arrow scored the collar of fungus round the aperture, harmlessly dislodging a piece of rind and carrying it ten or twelve feet into the maw of the cave.

Then one of the attackers came to her feet and ran forward, bone-tipped spear clutched in both hands and extended before her. Iorga had time to look at the thin face, the skin stretched like tanned pigskin over the sharp cheekbones. He saw the crazy anger in the bloodshot eyes.

She was no more than five strides away when he fired.

She had been running forward at a good pace, and she was big and raw-boned, but the bullet nevertheless picked her up off her feet and threw her backwards. It struck below the rib cage, just above the navel, and its flat trajectory carried it clean through her body, blasting out half her gut through the exit hole. As she hit the ground she writhed, as if trying to bounce back to her feet, and though she could not, her arms continued to grope for support. Her convulsive movement broke the soft haft of the spear in two.

Had Iorga been facing the Men Without Souls or his own kind—perhaps even a pack of harrowhounds, that might have been the end of the battle. The others would have run. But the Cuchumanates, more even than the Ahrima, did not withdraw once they were committed.

Two arrows flew into the aperture, missing both Iorga and Huldi, who made as much use of the cover as possible. One nicked Nita's clothing as it went past, and drew blood from a scratch on her arm. Although she was not hurt, the shock of the impact made her draw back, moving sideways to the wall of the corridor, where she pressed her body up against the rusts and the masks. She felt something crawling in her hair, and picked it away with her fingernails, cracking its exoskeleton as she threw it aside.

Iorga fired again, and missed.

Two of the attackers were coming at him, and though he

was careful to let them come far enough so that he ought not to waste bullets, his aim was not good enough. The pistol was a little unsteady in his fist. As the point of a spear jabbed at his face, he recoiled from the doorway, cocking the gun again. The narrowness of the opening saved him, as the Cuchumanates got in one another's way trying to come through. Huldi thrust at one, and gashed her leg, while Iorga's third shot tore a black hole in the other's left eye. Again, the momentum of the bullet carried the body backwards, and the second attacker was bowled over. Because of the wound pouring blood from her leg she was slow to rise, and Iorga had no difficulty in putting a bullet into her.

Huldi expected more of the Cuchumanates to be crowding the doorway within seconds, but there were none. Iorga leaned forward to see better, but only one of the attackers was visible, half-hidden by a swollen dendrite. She was notching an arrow to the string of her bow. Iorga dared not fire, because she was too far away for him to be sure of hitting her.

Nita shouted a wordless warning, and he whirled, to see three or four shadows moving from a distant corner. He fired at them, and they parted as though to let the missile through. He heard it hit a wall behind them and whine as it ricocheted. Realizing that the Cuchumanates knew of—or had discovered—another way in, Iorga moved back, away from the dimly lit aperture.

"This way," he hissed, and moved off diagonally across the hallway, toward the darkness where there were other doors. As he heard the Cuchumanates coming at him he sprinted. Nita scuttled alongside him.

Huldi, meanwhile, could not simply launch out into the blackness. She could not see the darker shadows for which the others were headed. Instead of following directly, she moved along the wall, feeling her way with one hand while the other waved the metal knife in slow horizontal arcs. She felt blind terror, knowing that the Cuchumanates must be able to see her even though she could not see them. But nothing came near to her blade, and nothing ripped at her throat.

Iorga stumbled, and pitched forward out to a ridged slope —a staircase. He took the skin off the knuckles of his gun hand, but did not lose his grip on the weapon. He started up the stair, with Nita following. After ten or twelve steps he whirled round to look back. The Cuchumanates were well-nigh at the girl's heels. Steadying his right wrist with his left hand he fired over Nita's shoulder, once, twice and again. Then the gun was empty, but the Cuchumanates were gone. One was crumpled at the foot of the stairs, screaming in agony, the others had leapt backwards, retreating behind the corners of the opening at the foot of the stairs.

Iorga pushed Nita, indicating that she must go on upwards. He took advantage of the momentary respite to empty the spent cartridges from the gun and fit a fresh clip. Then he followed, backing up the steps one by one.

Meanwhile, Huldi had come to a corner and rounded it, and was still moving along, her hand guiding her by touching the wall. She heard a sound, and was sure that at least one of the Cuchumanates was now coming after her. She began to run.

Then the wall which half-supported her was suddenly no longer there. In reaching to find it she overbalanced, and fell into a yawning, invisible opening.

Vomit rose into her mouth as she fell, and there was just time to wonder if she would shatter her bones before she smashed into a concrete floor and lost consciousness.

39

The helicopter settled on the flat area at the western edge of the roof of Sisyr's house. The alien eased himself out of the safety harness and climbed down, ducking away from the fierce airflow stirred up by the decelerating blades.

The whine of the blades decreased in pitch as he moved away. The police captain followed him out, and then stood for a few moments, waiting until the noise had died down sufficiently for him to speak in a normal tone.

"The men who were in your house have all reported back in," he said. "They were told to leave everything as they found it. If there's any damage, anything missing, let us know. I'm afraid that there's bound to have been some degree of disturbance. If you need any help . . ."

"There is no need," said the alien. "I have all the time I need."

The official looked uncertain for a few seconds, as though he felt that he ought to say something more, but he decided, instead, to retreat from the situation and let Sisyr fade away into his forgotten corner of the Earth. He raised his hand in an odd mock salute, and then clambered back up into the belly of the helicopter.

The rotor blades were still whirling. The moment the captain was back inside, they began to pick up speed again and the whine began again.

Sisyr moved back, and then watched the helicopter dance away into the sky, swinging round to head away into a bank of dull gray cloud that was moving in from the north. The alien waited awhile, seeing the snowclouds filling half the sky, and then three-quarters. The first thick flakes were tumbling out of the sky, settling in his clothing, before he finally turned away and walked slowly to the door.

Sisyr's house was very large by the standards of Euchronia. Through well hidden in the higher slopes of a mountain range, with the towering islands of the old surface all around, it was an imposing sight when glimpsed from the flat platform plain below. It suited its ancient surroundings, like an ancient castle or palace.

For the most part, the houses used by Euchronia's citizens were small, rarely accommodating more than a handful of people. There was no reason why a citizen of Euchronia should not have as much space as he required, but the acquisitive habits of the prehistoric ages had not, for the most part, been recovered by the people of the new world. There were many collectors in Euchronia, but they tended to be selective and discriminating. The old compulsion to accumulate for the sake of accumulation, so common among the prehistoric leisured classes, had been one of the things frowned upon by the Movement in its earliest days.

Sisyr, however, had provided for himself a vast dwelling with a multitude of rooms. His priorities were rather different from those of mortal men. The scope of his projects and pastimes had to be so much the greater.

He made his way to a room with one wall made completely of glass—a great window positioned so that he could stand by it and see the extent of the mountain slopes on either side of him, and beyond them the great cornfields which stretched for hundreds of miles across the platform, tended only by machines. Today, though, he did not stand, but brought up to the window a high-backed chair. He got food and drink from the cybernet, and he seated himself to take his meal in the shadow of the storm which gathered about his home.

It was not a violent storm, by the standards of the region, but there was some thunder and lightning, and the snow drove hard against the glass wall and tried to stick, to build a curtain of white which would close out the world.

As he finished his meal, he heard someone enter the room by a door behind him. He did not look round, but simply waited. He was aware of the intruder walking across the carpeted floor, to stand just behind the chair.

"I've never seen snow," said a voice. "That's rather strange, isn't it? So much happens in the world that we remain unaware of. For instance, I never knew about the mountains. I suppose, in my brain, I must have stored the fact that some mountain peaks from the old world project beyond the platform, but I really never *thought* about it. It never occurred to me that some of the Underworld is actually above the Overworld. Pieces of the prehistoric past. Is there, perhaps, a lost race of Second Dark Age people lurking somewhere nearby?"

In the glass before him, Sisyr could see a faint reflective image of the man who was speaking. He had seen the man before, if only on a screen. In a sense, this man and he had been involved with one another for a considerable time.

His name was Jervis Burstone.

He was holding a gun.

"I was informed that the police had left," said Sisyr, calmly.

"They did," replied Burstone. "When they left, we came in."

"We?"

"There are a dozen of us. There may be more. We're still making contacts . . . preparations . . ."

"Preparations for what?" Sisyr still did not turn. Burstone inched forward, until he was beside the alien, and he made sure that Sisyr could, by the merest sideways glance, see that he held the weapon.

"This is a weird place to build a home," said Burstone. "It's cold and bleak. Or is that more like home, to you, than the temperate zone? Perhaps you come from a cold, bleak world, full of bare rock slopes, with a snowline right down to the sea."

"Perhaps," said Sisyr. He had lived on many worlds.

"And the house," said Burstone. "So many rooms, full of so many things. A museum. All those books . . . you must have as many as the main depository. All that store. And, of course, all your plunder from the Underworld. How far into the mountain do your cellars extend?"

"Far enough," said Sisyr.

"What are you?" asked Burstone. "Some kind of custodian, holding the history of Earth's two worlds in trust? I often wondered what I was doing, in the name of the Plan, trading garbage with the Underworlders."

"You did it because you wanted to," said Sisyr. "You felt that you were doing something worthwhile. And you were."

"You tricked us. You made us believe that it was all part of the Plan. You made use of what we believed, of the *need* we had to be doing something for the Plan."

"Is that why you've come?" asked Sisyr. "To confront me with your righteous rage? To gain your revenge? Because you're frightened, as you've never been frightened before?"

"I'm not frightened," said Burstone. "I've been into the Underworld fifty times and more. I'm not afraid of it."

"Of course," said Sisyr.

But Burstone was afraid of the Underworld. Part of the reason why he went back, again and again, was because he was afraid. He fed on fear—it was almost a kind of pleasure. But from the Underworld, there had always been a return —a return into the utter safety and security of the Overworld. In a sense, Burstone was a man who had spent his life in a ritual parody of return to the womb: the mechanical womb of the host cybercomplex. But now the fear upon which he had fed was feeding on him. The Underworld was threatening to invade his womb. And Burstone had found a gun to hide behind. He had found someone to blame.

Still Sisyr watched the blizzard beyond the window. Burstone moved round still further, until his back was pressed up against the glass wall and he could look at Sisyr's blue eyes.

"You helped the people of the Underworld," he said. "You kept them alive. And now they're going to destroy us."

"I didn't keep them alive," said Sisyr. "I kept them self-aware. I preserved some measure of humanity, not only in the men, but in the others. I helped them keep communication and some degree of civilization. I helped to smooth the path of change, to give them some small degree of *control* over that change. At the pace of evolution with which they live, you see, they could so easily have lost everything, and had to start all over again, without really becoming anything new. I wanted to give them the chance of becoming something new—of making use of the tschytelic evolution without falling prey to its demands. But that was the Plan."

"Your Plan."

"If you choose to believe that, you will. But the Plan was neither wholly mine, nor wholly the Euchronians'. At least in part, it was the Plan of the men on the ground. Without some degree of assistance from men on the ground, the platform could not have been built. Surely you realize that."

"It's not true," said Burstone, flatly.

"It doesn't matter," said Sisyr, after a pause. Burstone could almost imagine the sigh which might have preceded the remark, if Sisyr had been human.

"No," said Burstone. "Not any more."

"Why have you come here?" asked the alien.

"We want your help," replied the human.

"Everyone wants my help," said Sisyr. "For more than a hundred years, I have hardly spoken to a human being. And now, all of a sudden, they are flocking to my door, asking for help. I will do all that I can. I have promised you this again and again. But what you want is always something different. You always want the help that I cannot give, and you always want it with a gun in your hand."

"We *need* your help. We must have it. We're prepared to do what we must in order to get it."

"What help?" asked Sisyr. For the first time, he moved. His head bowed, as though he had suddenly become too weary to support it. His spidery hands clenched beneath his chin.

"We want the starship," said Burstone.

40

Iorga backed up the staircase slowly. No one came after him. That frightened him, because he knew that the Cuchumanates would not give up. If they were not following him, that almost certainly indicated that they knew another way up.

He knew that he and Nita, at least, were trapped. Unless they killed all their enemies, they would not be able to get out of the building. If the Cuchumanates were so inclined, they could simply wait. But that was not the way of the Cuchumanates. Ahrima might have done that—Men Without Souls certainly would have—but the Cuchumanates would make every effort to find and kill the fugitives.

The best thing to do, he decided, was to gain time—to go upwards. There was every chance that he could separate the attackers, spread them out while they hunted him on ten or a dozen different levels.

He felt Nita touch him on the arm. She was feeling her way. It was so dark now, even to his sensitive eyes, that sight was almost useless.

"Up," he murmured. "Keep going."

"Huldi?" she asked.

"I don't know." He hoped that she might, perhaps, have evaded the attackers and got away outside, but it seemed more likely that the Cuchumanates had caught and killed her.

While they continued the ascent, there was a steady susurrus of noise around them as the larger creatures inhabiting the corridor moved away from them. Much of the clicking and faint buzzing came from insects too small to be worrisome, but they both knew only too well that there might be creatures here as dangerous as the Cuchumanates. Nita remembered the coenocytic creatures which had come out of the blackland to destroy the armored vehicles from the Overworld.

Iorga felt Nita suddenly flinch, and she swayed back toward him, her fingers grasping at his clothing. The steps were overgrown, and it was easy to fall, so he reached out immediately to steady her. When she was safe, he let her guide his hand out to touch the obstruction from which she had recoiled.

The passage was blocked by a soft, warm substance. It had the stickiness of the trailing spiderwebs, but it was solid. It yielded slightly to pressure, like a heavy curtain, but it did not tear. He ran his hand from side to side, and then reached upwards, to confirm that the barrier extended all the way across the corridor.

"Take the left wall," he said to Nita. "I'll take the right. Go down slowly until it opens out."

They descended together, very cautiously, staying level with one another by adjusting to the scraping of each other's hand along the wall. Thus they arrived together at the level beneath the barrier. One way seemed to lead towards dim light—perhaps to the external face where there had once been a window. The other way, Iorga could see nothing.

"This way," he said, pulling Nita to him, and moving toward the distant gleam.

He had spoken in a whisper, but he had betrayed his position nevertheless. He did not know from which direction they came, but they were suddenly upon him—at least two, perhaps more. He felt a knife cutting at his head, though it scraped his shoulder blade and only ripped his clothing, and he felt hands grabbing for his arms, trying to stop him bringing the gun into play.

He swung the gun round, trying to clear space, tracing a full circle at a height which should hit a Cuchumanate's shoulders but miss Nita's head. He collided with one body, but at least one had ducked under the swing, and he felt the blade of a bone weapon sink into his abdomen.

He fired once, and hit the one who had stabbed him. The gun fired without a flash, and still he could see nothing. More hands groped for purchase and fingers fastened on his wrist while he kicked viciously to dislodge someone who had grabbed at his waist. He managed to draw his own knife, and slashed wildly, lefthanded, while he moved rapidly to the side. He grappled desperately with the attacker who was forcing his gun hand outwards, and fired off two shots, without any hope of hitting anything, but trying to startle his assailant into letting go.

Then, for the second time, a blade went into his belly, and this time was driven home hard. It was not a metal blade, but he felt it tearing inside him, and the pain was so intense that he doubled up. With a convulsive jerk he freed his right hand, and drew it in to his body. He fired twice from the hip, at the places where he judged the attackers to be.

He waited for another touch, ready to fire again, but no other touch came. His legs buckled under him, and he fell to the ground. For a moment, he tried to sit up, then he allowed himself to sag until he was resting on the full length of his left side. He drew up his knees, trying to confine the gashes in his belly from which blood was coursing, trying to smother the pain.

A minute passed, and there was no sound save for the buzzing of flies. He was very still. He felt two light touches on his face, then three and four, and he realized that a cloud of small insects was gathering around him. He tried to remember which direction the nearest wall might be, and reached out an explorative hand. His fingers found something soft—the body of one of the Cuchumanates. At his touch, the flesh quivered, but she did not move away, and he guessed that she must be near death. As his fingers explored further, a hand tried to push him away. The hand was hot and wet with blood.

He whispered: "Nita!"

There was no answer.

41

"You want the starship," echoed Sisyr.

"We want to get away," said Burstone. "We want to go to a new world."

"That's not what you want," said the alien. "And if it were, the starship would be no use to you. No use at all."

"It can take us away from here," insisted Burstone.

Sisyr stared out at the swirling snowflakes for a few moments, and then, abruptly, stood up. Burstone made a defensive gesture with the gun, jerking its barrel up to threaten the alien. But Burstone's hand was shaking. Sisyr strode away from him, toward the keyboard which controlled the input to the house cyberunits.

"Don't touch it," said Burstone.

Sisyr reached out a hand, and tapped the keys with the thin, hard fingers. The window blanked out, becoming a solid face of gray—a screen. Burstone moved away from it.

"Come away!" he commanded.

Sisyr looked over his shoulder at the man with the gun. "On that screen," he said, "I can show you the worlds of your neighbor stars—the world that my ship could reach in twenty or fifty of your years. There are only a handful. Wouldn't you like to see? To have a choice of destinations?"

"No."

"No," said Sisyr. "You wouldn't. Because you know, in your mind, that you aren't going anywhere. Humans are not equipped for star travel. The experience would probably kill you, and there is, in any case, nowhere that you could go. Not one star in a million has a planet where you could live. There are a great many such planets, but the distances between them are immense. My starship is not a miracle-machine which defies physics. It cannot travel at the velocity of light—in fact, its acceleration is so slow that it takes many decades even to attain a velocity close to that of light. Once such velocities are reached, subjective time begins to slow down, relative to elapsed time here on Earth and on the planet of destination. But long before then you are old, and the period of deceleration is as long as the period of acceleration. The nearest known world capable of sustaining your kind of life—and mine—is centuries away from here. You could not live to see it. And what if you could? What does an alien world have to offer you that makes it worth going to? What makes it worth all those years of confinement within a tiny metal bubble, sensory starvation and utter loneliness?"

"You tell me," said Burstone.

"I am immortal," said the alien. "To my kind, the centuries do not matter. The distortions of time do not matter. We are equipped, mentally and emotionally, for the interstellar gulfs."

"Then you must make us immortal, too," said Burstone doggedly. "You have the science."

Sisyr shook his head deliberately. "It is not a matter of science," he said. "Do you think that I have some secret elixir of youth? Do you think that the constant renewal of my body is merely a matter of medicine? It is inbuilt. My kind do not age. Our bodies have defense mechanisms which destroy all parasites, all disease. Our faculties of self-repair following physical injury are almost unlimited. If I were cut in two, one part would regenerate—if the cut were precise enough, perhaps both. There is only one way that I am likely to die, and that is by surrendering life—willful death. Perhaps, if every cell were burned—if my ship fell into a star . . . but these are not likely events.

"You must see that my mind is adapted to these circumstances. Time means very little to me in itself—it is only the rate of experience which is important. During a star-journey I am hardly aware of the passing of time. But your mind is adapted to *your* circumstances. You live at a faster rate, a constant rate. While you are awake, you are the subject of time, not its commander. A star-journey would destroy you, mentally and physically.

"You do not want the starship. Perhaps, for the moment, that is what you imagine. You are afraid, and you feel a desperate need to escape. You feel, because of your fear, that to stay here—to stay anywhere on the Earth—may mean death or the destruction of your mind. But the starship is useless. Death, and the destruction of the mind... the very things which you are afraid of... are all that the starship has to offer you. You must know that."

Burstone's composure suddenly broke. He lifted the gun high and brought it's butt crashing down on the back of the chair which Sisyr had vacated. The plastic splintered, and a jagged edge ripped the heel of Burstone's hand. He clutched it to his chest, still clutching the gun. Moments later, he leveled the weapon once again at the alien. There was a small red stain on the front of his tunic.

"Then what *can* we do?" He spat out the words as if they tasted foul in his mouth.

"Wait," said Sisyr. "Whatever happens will happen in any case. There is no way you can exempt yourself. You may die, but it is not something that you can avoid. Sooner or later, you will die anyway. All that has changed, in these last few days, is that you have come to realize how little control you have over the moment of your death. But the change is in you, not in the world. You have never had the power to determine the length of your life, save within the limits permitted by chance and other men. Your fear comes from discovery, not from circumstance. You must learn to live with what you know."

"You've got to help us!"

"You don't want help," said the alien, quietly. "You demand help which simply does not exist, and you know that. What you want is to avoid responsibility. You want to blame someone for what has happened. You want to pretend that the world has suddenly turned against you, and wants to destroy you, though all that has happened is that you have encountered reality.

"You didn't bring that gun to compel me to give you the

starship, or to make me take you to another world. You
came here with that gun because you wanted to shoot me,
to hurt me, to kill me. You need someone to blame. Rafael
Heres wanted exactly the same thing, but he found, in the
end, that he couldn't blame me enough. Perhaps you can.
I've played a bigger part in your life. It's easier for you, and
the others who shared your work. They're waiting for you,
aren't they? But what are they waiting to hear? Are they
waiting for you to tell them to load their possessions into the
starship, and prepare for a great voyage, or are they waiting
for you to tell them that you've killed me?"

Sisyr turned his face back to the deck, and his fingers
dwelt in the air over the controls, as though hesitating,
while he chose between courses of action.

Just as his fingers descended, to begin punching out an
instruction, Burstone fired. Three of the bullets hit Sisyr in
the back—the rest went wild, smashing into the control
deck and setting red warning lights flickering.

As Burstone ran, he saw that the blood pouring from the
alien's wounds was brown, like the brown of human skin.

42

When Nita felt the touch of a Cuchumanate hand on her
face, she leaped back from it. In so doing she passed behind
Iorga, whose large body sheltered her for a moment.

Had there been more light, she would have stayed to
fight, but in the darkness, she had no thought but to get
away, to escape. She ran the only way she knew—back up
the staircase toward the soft barrier.

As she ran, she heard—or thought she heard—the sound
of pursuit. At least one of the attackers, she fancied, was
at her heels. When she came to the barrier her knife was already raised to slash the curtain.

The soft substance resisted the bite of the blade for a
second or two, then yielded. Once cut, the tissue tore easily,
and Nita dragged her blade down in a great arc, then
brought it up again to slash sideways, rending the skin of
the barrier so that the slit became a yawning hole.

She had no way of knowing how thick the barrier might be, or what lay beyond it, but she had no sooner opened an access when she shoved herself through it. The rubbery tegument through which she had cut was no more than a containing membrane. Beyond it was a loose liquid substance which filled the corridor with foam. It was like walking into a mass of soap bubbles. As she waved her arms before her face, trying to clear a space from which she could breathe, her feet slipped, and she stumbled. The steps were wet, and swarming with vermiform creatures. She fell forward, catching herself on her hands, and the hands, too, crushed the wriggling things. They were several inches long, and three or four in girth, and they were very soft. Wherever her weight fell upon them they burst into liquid slime.

There was air enough in the foam for her to breathe, though it smelled rank, and as she tried to suck it in her mouth filled with the bubble fluid. Its taste was not bitter, but she had to cough to stop the liquid following the air into her lungs. Desperately, she clambered to her feet, and staggered on through the froth, squashing the larvae to death as she did so. Her passage would probably result in the destruction of the whole nest, in any case, as the gaps she had made in the protective membrane would allow predators to come in and feed on the succulent, but helpless, creatures.

Within seconds, she was at the second curtain, and again her small weapon was already hacking at the air as she reached it. Her movements were frenzied as she pulled and tore a way through and into the corridor beyond, where the air was once more dry and dust-laden. Still coughing, she did not pause for an instant, but continued to scramble her way up the overgrown steps with all possible speed.

Her skin and clothing were wet, her feet and hands bemired with the soft protoplasm of the crushed larvae. There was not an inch of her skin which did not seem to have been tainted in some way by this colossal organism through whose bowels she ran. All the great building seemed to her to be a single entity—a gigantic corpse in which parasites ran wild. All the worms and the insects and the multitudinous algae and fungi which competed to fill up every chamber, use up every surface, seemed to her akin to the tiny organisms which swarm over every corpse, inside and out, greedy for every last vestige of its decaying substance. And she, with them, felt herself reduced in size to a mere insect, something well-nigh invisible, almost unreal.

Without sight, she could have no real idea of the size and nature of things. There was only touch and smell and hearing, and what these told her was that she was swallowed up by this gigantic creature, that she was one with the cockroaches scrabbling at the walls around her and one with the maggots in their balls of spittle and one with the slithering worms.

Without sight, there was nothing to tell her that she was human.

Living in the moment, as she did, with past and future submerged in the subconscious continuity of her life, she was totally subject to unreasoning panic. Once in the grip of the compulsion to run, to surrender everything in flight, she was completely captive. Her brain ceased to think, and merely let her act.

She was no longer a creature of choice, a thinking being, but only a thing of arms and legs, with a single claw of animal bone.

She drove herself upwards.

Up and up.

A mere handful of compound eyes followed—or tried to follow—the direction of her flight. Most of the creatures who made the staircase—the spinal column of the concrete corpse—their home had no eyes at all. Only the fugitives, the creatures who crept in from outside to shelter and hide, had eyes. There were not many of them. Few sighted creatures will voluntarily venture into a blind world. It is an adaptation which is almost invariably permanent. An organism which is *temporarily* blind is at a great disadvantage.

And so a million vibrating membranes recorded her coughing and the scuffling of her feet. The smell of her was heavy in the air with her sweating and her fast breath, and the warmth of her, too, was there for the feeling. The creatures of the darkness were very much aware of her as she scuttled through the lacunae of their world.

And they reacted. The heat of her flesh drew them. Where she had passed by, her essence lingered in the thick air, an irresistible bait. She ran so fast that she did not signal her coming very far in advance, but every time she passed from one level to the next she sucked something out of the caverns into the zigzag column behind her. They scratched the stairs and they rustled and clicked, but the sound of their hurry meant nothing to Nita, who was simply running.

Up and up.

The whole collective organism which had grown on the bones of the great tower could feel her, like a crumb stuck in a gullet, an indigestible fragment of gristle alarming an intestine . . . the kind of thing which, in a human, might begin a nightmare . . . just as rats in the walls may haunt a home. The multidimensional creature was, in its way, conscious of her. It knew her. Impassively, it gathered itself around her and contained her.

She was very tiny.

As Nita's mental inertia carried her up and up, and began to relax while the panic ebbed away, sensory impressions of a vague character began to seep into her consciousness again. Her mind lingered in the fringes of wakefulness. She sensed the organism almost as it sensed her. She sensed the whole being as a unit, as a crouching beast.

She had no destination. There was no meaning in her frenetic action. She had lost the past and the future was a blank wall pressing against her face, in which there was no moment save the one where she was trapped. Time was not passing. Nothing changed, everything was still, constant. The furious effort by which she hurled herself along and up was nothing—merely a steady leakage of energy from her system. As though her lifeblood was flowing steadily away through an open wound, pumped out pulse by pulse with the beating of her faithful heart.

But she went higher, and still higher. Ultimately, unless the edifice extended forever . . . even beyond the Face of Heaven, she had to reach the top.

43

In the meantime, Iorga's situation was not very different. She moved, and he lay still. Otherwise . . .

His heart beat steadily, and the blood leaked slowly away from his abdomen. Very slowly, mingling as it ran with the acid juices of his stomach, which was ruptured.

He hovered on the borderline between consciousness and unconsciousness. He was not wholly aware of the insects which settled on his skin and crawled into the crevices of his clothing. In time, they would use him up: suck out his juices and lay their eggs by the million in his rotting flesh, but for now they were waiting, letting him die in his own time. However, while his awareness of reality was slight, his mind was still active and there was a strange clarity in his thoughts, a definition about his ideas and images which was unusual. He felt little enough pain, though he knew that it would be a brief respite before the burning in his belly as his lights began to dissolve. That would come, in its own time, and dragging death somewhere behind it.

The gun was in his hand, and it would not have been beyond his power to raise its barrel into his mouth and fire through his brain, but he really could not remember whether there was a bullet left. In any case, the mental image which he still carried of Randal Harkanter's head exploding stood between himself and any such action. The pain would mean little enough to him when it came, and he was content to live with it, for a little while.

He felt that he was dying rather easily.

He knew, somehow, that it should not have been so simple. A couple of cuts with a rough-hewn knife wielded by a savage should not be sufficient to destroy a man like himself. He felt that if the need were more urgent he could shrug off this mortal lassitude, and bring life back into himself by the energy of will. He felt that he still had the power to refuse death. This once, and perhaps several times more. But that power was blocked by an overwhelming indifference—a sense of loss. The creative force that might bring to bear the effort of will and the power of life was not there. The *need* to create was missing.

If Iorga had been an animal, he would have crawled away, and if the predators had not taken advantage of his weakness, he would have survived. There is nothing in an animal except that kind of need.

But Iorga was a man, and between himself and the outside world there was a mind whose decisions were taken according to a whole network of needs and systems. Iorga remembered Aelite, and a long struggle in the Swithering Waste to save her from the cloak-fungus which had grown on her like a cancer. He had that image clear in his mind, and at the same time there were others. The stars in the limitless sky of the Overworld. The blight crawling slowly through the blackland.

There was no doubt in his mind that Nita and Huldi were

dead. Intellectually, there had to be doubt, but in his feelings there was none. He felt that it was ended, and so it was.

His life had been emptied of all that it contained, and opened to things it could not and would not contain.

And so Iorga allowed himself to die.

44

Nita, disgorged by a circular aperture that growth-upon-growth of fungus had not managed to close in thousands of years, stood on flat roof, in the middle of a metal-railed arena, with a hundred thousand ghost-moths startled into the fluttering flight of clamoring alarm making a living halo about the crown of the tower. Likewise, a hundred thousand thoughts hovered in the margins of her startled consciousness. The running was finished, the panic dead, and while her heart roared and rattled in a futile attempt to pay back the energy debt owed by her muscles in her limbs, she felt a sudden tremendous sense of presence. Aliveness surged inside her like sunlight.

She had never been so close to the stars. Not one of her ancestors, back to the beginning of consciousness, nor their cousins, had ever come so close to the bleak inner face of the world above, the higher world, the world which engulfed her own.

From where she stood now the stars were each as large as the face of the moon which the heaven-born knew. And they shone so brilliantly white, so completely composed of pure radiance, so steady and so secure. There were ten, or twenty, drawn in a great flat arc across the sky whose black solidity was so close that she felt almost able to feel its metal coldness. Beyond those few, in either direction, they began to blur, to distort, until—ultimately—they faded into a thick line declining to either horizon. Even from a height such as this, she could see no end to the road of stars, in either direction. There was no dead end, and there was no marriage with a radiant horizon. The road of stars was simply swallowed up by the darkness in the maw of the curved world.

She went to the rail, staggering like a corpse whose brain has somehow failed to understand the message of mortality carried by its servant nerves. She dropped the knife, the better to grip the metal cylinder with her tiny hands. She looked up, and out . . . and then down.

She was seized by intense vertigo, and her mind was abruptly spun into a gyroscopic whirl. She tried to snatch herself back from the lip of the abyss, but her hands were convulsed, the ligaments frozen and unyielding, and she was sealed to the rail. She shut her eyes tight, and tried to gain control of the electrical turbulence in her brain.

Only when she had fainted did her hands let go and leave her lying in the gutter, protected by the raised edge of the roof. She lived for a few moments with the giddy madness of herself before awareness began to return.

She realized then that tiny clawed feet were swarming all over her, that a living wave had spilled out of the aperture in her wake as, once, she had seen a great worm evert its gut over one of her companions in the Swithering Waste. A living vomit, coppery in color, bright as though burnished in the brilliant light of the beautiful stars, was pouring on to her body, rushing at her from the mouth of the great beast.

She tried to regain her feet, but it was hopeless.

The centipedes clung to her, wrapped themselves around her limbs, her neck, dangled from her hair. They were innumerable, and many were several feet in length. They were eyeless, but their heads roamed ceaselessly, the jaws moving with frantic eagerness as the palps guided them to flesh into which they spewed their poison. They covered her, and they covered one another, the heads perpetually burrowing while the myriad legs and the long, segmented bodies writhed like gorgon's hair around her.

45

Julea was sitting up in bed, listening to music. On the opposite wall film of birds in flight filled an area some eight or ten feet square. The music and the film were unconnected —there was no attempt to synchronize or symbolize. The music was a somber symphony, muted and leisurely. The birds were mostly gulls, soaring on cliff-face updrafts. The combination might have been restful, almost sedative, but Joth found somehow that it conflicted with his mood. It annoyed rather than soothed. Looking at Julea, however, he was uncertain of its effect on her. She seemed completely diffident.

She had hardly reacted when he had come into the room. It seemed to make no impression whatsoever on her state of mind. It was as if a stone were dropped into a viscous liquid: a brief stir of recognition, a turgid ripple of attention, and then relapse into quietude.

Ravelvent had warned him in advance that it would not be easy. According to Ravelvent, Julea was emotionally bankrupt. She had stopped caring. She was content simply to live on, without investing anything of herself in anything which might happen or offer itself.

"It's settled now," said Joth, gently. "It's all over. I'm sorry it couldn't end when you wanted it to end, but now it's finished. There's nothing more."

"No," she said, absently. Her eyes were following a gull round and around in long, slow arcs.

"At last," said Joth, "they're beginning to understand. They're beginning to see the need to understand, and they're beginning to want to understand. What my father wanted to do . . . it's just beginning now."

"It was all because of him," she said. "All of this. If only he'd taken his sleeping pills . . ." She laughed, faintly, at the irony.

Joth was pleased to see the reaction.

"And no one would have cared," said Joth. "No one would have done anything . . . until the platform collapsed."

"In a thousand years . . ." she murmured.

"Our children's children's children," said Joth. "But that's what the Movement stood for. That's what our civilization meant . . . the willingness of men to protect the future instead of the present, the surrender of personal objectives to the objectives of the race. Isn't that what we were taught to believe in—isn't that what they tried to force us to believe in? And we do believe it . . . but only in our heads. It's only an idea, a rule of the game we play . . ."

He paused. She said nothing—he had completely lost her attention again.

"What are you going to do?" he asked her, his voice sharpening a little to cut into her isolation.

"When?" she said, turning briefly to look at him again.

"When you get out of bed," said Joth. "And after that. What are you going to do . . . ever?"

"Stay here," she replied.

"With Ravelvent?"

"Abram," she corrected him.

He shrugged. "He has something against me. Not just what happened to you . . . there's some other reason why he doesn't like me. Do you know why?"

She didn't answer. Instead, she said: "What are you going to do?"

"Work."

"In the Underworld?"

"Sometimes. A great many people will have to work in the Underworld for periods of time. Maintenance of the platform's supporting structures is only a part of it—the easy part. Contact with the people is something else. That will take time, and it won't be easy."

"And that's what you want to do?"

"I want to work on the project which will grow out of what Burstone was doing. I wonder what happened to Burstone . . . they questioned him, I know, but there was never any mention of a trial. I think they must have let him go. He might be useful to the new Hegemony."

"He tried to kill you."

Joth shook his head. "I'm not sure," he said.

The music finished, and for a few moments the gulls flew on in a dead, unnatural silence. Then Julea reached out to the selector panel beside her, and another piece began to play.

Joth nodded toward the film, and said: "How long does this go on for?"

She smiled, very slightly. "It's synthesized," she said. "A basic pattern, repeated with variations. Almost infinite. It can go on forever . . . just as long as we watch, and our children, and our children's children . . ."

Joth stared at the images of the birds. There seemed to be so many. It all seemed so real. But on the wall, it was only a pattern of light. With the faculties of the cybernet, there was no reason why a pattern of light should be any more than that. A computer simulation. No more limit to its scope than real gulls flying near real cliffs had limits to *their* scope. The gulls on the film, even though made of light, could dive for fish, could mate, could lay eggs, could fall

prey to hawks. But why should they? They could fly forever, if they wanted to.

"Are there others like that?" asked Joth. "Ones with people? Are there whole catalogues full of pattern-of-light people who can be put up on the screen and then set in motion forever, living pattern-of-light lives?"

She shook her head. "It only works with things like gulls,"
she said. "When it's people, it becomes absurd."

"I wonder why," he said, drily.

He watched the wheeling birds in silence, for a few more
minutes. He was quite fascinated.

"I never saw anything like that before," he said.

"It's always been available," she told him. "The net can
do so many things . . . you simply don't realize."

"No."

The music suddenly swelled into a loud, dramatic sequence. For a moment, the music seemed to be carrying the
birds. Then it died away again, but the birds were still
there, drifting and darting on the unreal air currents.

Suddenly—almost absurdly—Joth thought of Enzo Ulicon.
He almost laughed, but then lost the humor of the juxtapo-
sition of ideas as he realized why the image had come into
his mind. Trying to put it into words, he drew Julea's attention with a quick gesture of the hand.

"For the last few days," he said, speaking slowly, feeling
his way, "I've been trying to convince Eliot Rypeck and
Enzo Ulicon that they must stop the plan to destroy the
Underworld. I talked to them endlessly, and in the end, I
went through a kind of experiment, trying to make contact
with someone or something in the Underworld, to prove that
such a contact could be made, and was only an extension of
the kind of thing which is already happening in our dreams.

"When all that was over, Ulicon questioned me. I thought
. . . I was convinced . . . that he was trying as hard as anyone
possibly could to find out exactly what had happened, and
how, and why. But when it was over . . . when he'd asked
the questions he had to ask . . . he just switched off. Just like
that. All of a sudden, he began talking and thinking about
something quite different—Heres' removal and Dayling's
takeover. And the way he talked, and what he said, suddenly seemed to me to be so utterly child-like, so completely detached from reality.

"I suppose I might have seen the same thing a hundred
times before, but that particular moment I was completely

wrapped up in what I'd been trying to do, trying to understand and to remember and to evaluate. I thought he was,
too. I thought that what we were saying and doing was
vitally important. But it wasn't—not to him. He just wasn't
involved with it . . . not really. When he wanted to, he could
deliberately involve himself—throw himself into the problem
—but he could just as easily disassociate himself again.
And that, just at that moment, appalled me. I just couldn't
see *how* . . .

"But I think I do, now. Perhaps. I think I may have
been just the same, once, but what happened to me in the
Underworld changed me. Permanently. It wiped out the
person there used to be, and made a new one, and even
coming back to the machine and the i-minus drug couldn't
change me back again.

"You see, to Ulicon, reality is just patterns of light. It's
all superficial, all a matter of appearances. There's no difference, so far as he's concerned, between those gulls on the
wall and real ones. The quality of his experience is precisely the same in either case. But I feel a difference. I don't
see it, in the film, but I feel it.

"And . . . as you say . . . I can't help feeling that when it's
people, it's absurd."

She looked at him blankly. She had not even tried to follow the argument. It would have been no use if she had.

"It's just that . . . he doesn't seem to live inside his head.
He lives . . . inside the machine. The cybernet's senses are
more important than his own."

As the words drained away, he looked into her eyes. He
tried to look through them, into her mind. He tried to see
what she was thinking. But he couldn't. Her life, like Ulicon's, like Ravelvent's, like all the rest, was contained in the
four walls which enclosed her and the electronic brain which
made them what they were.

46

The roofs of gleaming silver, domed and arched, peaked and
tented, stretched endlessly away into the distance. Sunlight

glittered in windows scattered like flotsam over the rippled surface. In grooves and slits, and over threads and bridges, moved tiny vehicles. Like ants in a hill, they seemed integral parts of a great system, whose logic and strategy was too vast, too god-like, for the entities themselves even to suspect.

The sun hovered near the spires of the western extreme of the complex, tinting them with red and casting dappled shadows in the furthest streets. The room in which Dayling stood was circular, its windows curved. It was easy to forget the direction of weight, provided only that he stood very still, and lost himself in the illusion that the world was tilting this way and that, the gleaming complex spinning like a great metal plate, with himself as its center, and his vantage its cockpit.

Dayling was not afraid of falling. He was master of the illusion. He felt, in this particular moment, that he was master of the sky as of the city, and that the thin, languid clouds were his to command.

This was a city—one of several cities on the face of the Earth—but it was a city where no one lived. Men worked here, in their thousands, each of them engaged in the basic task of instructing the machines, but the city was *for* and *of* machines. No one lived in cities—cities were held to be unfit for human habitation. Houses stood alone. The cities were the organs of the cybernet.

This particular organ was the brain. It was the largest, the most complex, and the most vital. It was here, in Euchronia's brain, that the personality of Euchronia was determined, that the thoughts of the human race happened, that the self-awareness of the human race was contained.

Dayling looked out from the crown of Euchronia's steel skull, and rejoiced in being, now—and perhaps for a long time to come— the *idée fixe* within that brain. The dominant idea . . . the delusion of grandeur.

The mundane functions of the Euchronian organism went on as they had under Heres, and under the kingpins of a thousand other Euchronian councils. The hunger of the race was satiated, the thirst, the need to rest, to excrete, to receive occasional stimuli of excitation. Even the sense of identity which the brain of Euchronia possessed was very little affected. The body was the same, and the face. Its state of health was not changed.

In a way, the alteration which had taken place was the

most trivial possible. Only the very highest, most abstract functions of the brain and mind of Euchronia had been affected. What had taken place was a kind of religious conversion, a sudden reinvestment in a new set of ideas, a sudden rediscovery of purpose and ambition.

But Dayling felt all the triumph, all the exultancy which such a conversion inevitably brings. He felt the power, and the pleasure. He felt the confidence of the newly faithful —the confidence that the great organism whose brain contained him was *immortal*, and *ultimately meaningful*.

To him, these concepts went hand in hand, inseparable, just as they had to Heres, and to the first Euchronians. But Dayling, it will be remembered, was a mortal man. Like the patterns of electric discharge forever forming and decaying within his own brain, he was transient . . . a ghost in the machine.

He was thinking, as he looked out over the glistening panorama of his power: "Now is the time to build, to clear away the sterile ideas of the Movement and build a real world . . . a world adapted to mankind . . . a perfect world. We have the instrument, if only we have the mind . . ."

47

There was Festival in Cynabel, in the heartland of Shairn. More than twenty thousand people were in the town and the fields around: fields to which the blight had not yet come but which were stripped bare nevertheless. Even so, of twenty thousand people more than half were starving.

Only a fraction of the vast assembly could gather before the long house for the Festival. Cynabel was a large town, by Shairan standards, but refugees from the north had swollen its numbers eightfold. Thousands more might be in the marshes and the bare hills, but they too would have to travel southward as the blight came.

The crowd around the throne-stone had never been so vast nor so dense—and perhaps never so quiet. They waited anxiously, desperately, not so much for the confrontation with their Gray Souls, but because they were in dire need of guidance from the priests, from the wise men, from the strong men, and from the prophets. They had to be told what to do. Their lives—their whole way of life—was being eaten out from beneath them. In such a time, prophets are needed. They are more necessary than any other breed of men.

The Shaira had confidence in their prophets, for they knew them to be more intimately in contact with the Gray Souls than other men, and they had implicit faith in their Souls.

Chemec the crab stood close by the throne-stone, waiting. Of all men in Shairn he was, at this moment, the most important. His greatness had been thrust upon him by chance, by the Souls, and by the priests. He was a puppet to all these things, and he was the focal point of the destiny of Shairn.

The drums beat with the slow, steady rhythm which all men knew. The beat was no louder, but it seemed, perhaps, a little *larger*. There was something massive in the way the sound swelled and spread about the town. The drummers were beside the long house, and in the shadow of the earthen wall. They were Cynabel's drummers, but they were also Kerata's and Myrmeleon's, Asica's and Fiera's, and others from the north and the east. When the horns blew, they seemed to fill the air and the land with mournful crying—the wailing of Shairn.

There was not one fire, but fifty, each confined within a ring of stone and huddled round with silent people The embers burned red and spat sparks, and no flames danced in them. No smoke clouded the air.

Only a fraction of the assembly possessed enough of the leaf-like fronds from which the pulp used in the festival derived. The small, lichenous plant had suffered from the blight as had everything else. For the rest—rather more than half—this would be a barren Festival in terms of spiritual comfort.

The elders, the Chemec with them, stood with eyes closed, absorbing the rhythm of the drums and the strange cadence of the horns, reaching for the inner sight, as always, without the aid of the pulp. They would contact their Souls, because they had faith. The others, used to the crutch provided by the drug, would not.

There was no clear space around the throne stone for the dance of the Star King. On this occasion, the ritual would be practiced in another fashion. There was to be no transfer of power, no death. This was to be a Festival without secular leaders. The robes which the priests wore had one sleeve black with sequins of silver, the other golden yellow. Each one, therefore, had taken into himself the roles of sun and stars.

The pace of the drums grew slower and slower, and the metabolism of each of the listeners, attuned to the rhythm, began to slow down. The crying of the horns melted into the low beat, and became almost constant—the notes tortured, dragged into indefinite extension.

When the moment finally came, Chemec was very calm inside himself. His senses were relaxed, and he was in a light trance. The power which took hold of his voice was not under his conscious control, but it was nevertheless his voice and not that of the Gray Soul within him. He knew what he had to say, and as long as it was said, it did not matter what power guided the words: his, or the Soul's, or the elders'. The message was the same.

He told the people that Shairn was dying. He told them that they must leave Shairn, and go west-of-south, into the lands where the Men Without Souls lived. They would not be welcome, and the journey would be hard, because the Men Without Souls were poor farmers, and lived mostly out of the wilds. The Children of the Voice, too, would have to live on the wild country, and they would have to fight, even to do that. The Ahriman horde which had passed through Shairn had also gone into that country, and it might be that the Shaira would have to face the Ahrima a second time.

For the Children of the Voice, said Chemec, there would always be war, wherever they moved. But the Children of the Voice would win, because they would move together, in an army so vast as to be unconquerable. They would live like Ahrima, but they would not die so fast, because they had more to sustain them in life.

He told them that this was not a matter of invasion. They could not and would not try to take the lands into which they moved in order to settle there. They would have to move on, and on, because the blight which killed Shairn would follow them wherever they went, and though they would stay ahead of its relentless march it would always be moving, always behind them.

They must keep going, he said, while they died, and

while their children died, and while their children's children died. No one would see the end of the march, nor would their children.

And then began the prophecy:

Though Shairn died now, it would not die forever. Though all that lived was perishing of the blight, new life would spring up again. In time, the new life would spread throughout the land, and make it good again. So, too, would all the dead lands flower and flourish once again, in their turn.

There would be a time, he promised, that the Children of the Voice would return to Shairn. They would not find their villages and their homes, but they would find new life throughout the land. Though no man living and listening would ever see his homeland again, the children of his children's children's children would return, and find it a new home, and make it once again the land called Shairn.

Before then, there would be hardship. Though thousands would begin the journey, and tens of thousands, perhaps only hundreds would return. Some, no doubt, would be lost on the way, and might live on in other lands, as different people. But the true people of Shairn would be guided, not by Chemec, who must die, but by their Souls, and by the hero Camlak, killer of the Harrowhound, who had seen Heaven. The people of Shairn would be one people, and they would come home one people, in due time, no matter how many or how few lived, no matter how many or how few went their own way.

Thus Chemec gave to the people of Shairn not only a purpose, a goal, and hope, but also an identity, and a unity. He was a prophet, and he gave them a saint: a dead hero, who lived nevertheless, who was both guardian and guide to the Shaira.

Those who saw, during that Festival, their Gray Souls knew that what Chemec said was true. But even those who did not—those without the pulp or the inner strength—*believed*. When the great trek began, there was no one who stayed behind. A handful, perhaps, could have scraped a living out of what the blight left, might even have protected some tiny area from the blight, driving it out with fire as some of the northern villages had tried to do, with limited success. But no one chose to try. When the twenty thousand left Cynabel, and became thirty and forty thousand while they passed through the remaining villages and towns of Shairn, none stayed behind them. All followed, secure in the knowledge that one day, in some manner, the children of their children's children's children would bring the name of Shairn back to the reborn land.

48

Having failed to make contact with Rafael Heres through the medium of the cybernet, Eliot Rypeck sat back in quiet contemplation. There was, he supposed, every reason why Heres should not be accepting calls, especially from himself.

Rypeck knew full well that Heres would consider himself betrayed, and he was not at all sure that he did not agree. He *had* betrayed such trust as Heres had put in him. He had released not only the secret of the i-minus project, but also the news concerning the corrosion of the pillars. In so doing, Rypeck had dealt a death blow to the Euchronian Movement as a political monopoly. And in going further, committing himself to the new government under Dayling, he had—almost entirely by his own action—destroyed the Movement even as a political entity.

And the pity of it all was that Eliot Rypeck still believed in Euchronianism. He still believed that there could be a Millennium, if only the right historical route could be discovered, and if only the right social evolution could take place. Rypeck still wanted *everybody* to win. But he had come to believe in Euchronia for all the people of Earth, not just Euchronia for the Euchronians. The strength of his faith had made him into a heretic, as strength of faith always tends to do.

He could not help feeling a kind of relief at the fact that he had been unable to reach Heres. He had felt it his duty to try—to face the man he had deposed, and be accused—but he had not really known what he could say, or whether there was anything to be said at all. The gulf which had now opened up between himself and the ex-Hegemon was not something which could be healed, by words, by time, by any human action. Rypeck had smeared Heres' image of the world, and nothing could cancel that.

Rypeck felt sorry for Heres, and he also felt shame in

himself. But he stood by what he had done. If, in time, it was proved to be a mistake, he would still stand by it. He did not lack trust in himself. For a moment, though, while he thought of Heres, he wished that all that had happened could be wiped out, cut away from the thread of history, and the clock turned back so that all the choices might be taken again, by wiser men.

Then he put Heres out of his mind.

Much later, he discovered that the reason he had failed to make contact was that Heres had hanged himself.

49

When Warnet came back to see him a second time, Sisyr was feeling a great deal better in himself. The pain had been controlled, new growth was replacing the destroyed tissues.

They had taken the bullets out of him, because they dared not leave them inside. The surgeons had been very much afraid, in performing the operation, that through ignorance they might kill the alien rather than helping him, but they had been even more afraid that the same result might accrue through inaction. Sisyr knew that what they had done was neither dangerous nor necessary, but he understood, in his mind, the conflict which must have taken place in *their* minds. He was grateful for their decision.

He had been in pain for some considerable time, and he had slept deeply while much of the internal repair work had been carried out. But this was simply an incident that had to be lived through, and he had been content to live through it, allowing it to take the time it took without anxiety or any other kind of mental turmoil. Warnet had tried to talk to him before, and had found communication difficult. Now, however, all was well again . . . or becoming well again.

"Burstone went into one of the Sanctuaries," said Warnet. "If and when he decides to return, he will be isolated."

"It is not necessary," replied the alien.

"Why did he shoot you?"

"I think," said the alien, "that you might call it a lack of instinct. His mind was altered by changing circumstance, and it had no ... capacity to steer. The action was a product of the distortion. It was futile, without meaning."

"He meant to kill you."

"Yes—but it does not matter."

Warnet stared for a while at the inhuman face, still finding it strange to his eyes, though he had looked into it so many times before.

"What will you do now?" he asked. "Will you stay, or will you leave us to our miserable inheritance? We can't really protect you."

"If you will let me," said the alien, "I will stay."

"Why?"

"This is my home."

Warnet eased forward. "You once told me that you had no secrets. But you do. Perhaps you are not absolutely determined to conceal things from us, but there are things which are concealed, nevertheless. Will you reveal those things, if I ask you?"

"I will tell you anything I can," said Sisyr.

"The trouble is," said the Eupsychian, "that I'm not quite sure what it is that I want to know. I can only ask you again: why do you stay here on Earth?"

Sisyr considered the question. Eventually, he said: "You understand, I think, why that is such a difficult question. I do not think as you do. My reasons would not necessarily sound like reasons to you. The way I see reality and the way you see it are not the same. Obviously, you would consider it frivolous if I were simply to say that I have to live somewhere—here, or on another world—and that I am here. You would want to know whether I might not find it more pleasant living with others of my kind. I would not. It is, in fact, necessary that I live apart from others of my own kind. We ... meet ... occasionally, and that is good. But we cannot stay together. We are, by nature, solitary."

"Shall I tell you why I think you are here on Earth?" asked Warnet.

"It may make things easier," said the alien. "Or more difficult."

Warnet smiled. "I think you are here because Earth is your experiment. I know that for many centuries you have been observing life in the Underworld, and I think that during the same period of time you have been observing the

Overworld also. Discreetly, of course, with the help of the machine you helped to create.

"I think you are—playing Hoh. I think you understand what I mean by that. Perhaps even playing god. I think you came to Earth in the beginning because you were looking for it, and I think you stay because you are still looking. You are waiting for something to happen—something which is important to you by virtue of what you are."

"There is truth, of a kind, in what you say," said Sisyr. "You see me, perhaps, as a lonely wanderer adrift in the universe, searching for some ideal . . . a holy grail. And perhaps that is what I am. But there is a flaw in that idea, just as there is a flaw in every analogy you might draw. You think, you see, in finite terms. You think of experiments and results, of searches and goals. You know that I am immortal, and you see this planet as a stage in my life, something with a beginning and an end. A game of Hoh reaches a conclusion—inevitably, for that is the kind of game it is. The conclusions may be widely various, but there is always an end-point of some kind. In all your games there is some state which you play *toward*.

"All the games that my people play are infinitely extended in time. There is never beginning, and never end, but only change. I am involved in the quality and nature of eternal change, whereas you—an ephemeral being—are concerned with abstractions from that change.

"You have a concept called infinity, but you are not infinite. Your infinity is a logical artifact. Mine is a reality. You cannot discover an end or a beginning to time—so far as you can imagine, the universe always has existed and always will. But you experience duration as finite. There was a time before you existed, and there will be a time after you are dead. You accept this, but you do not experience it. That is your nature.

"By virtue of your nature, you cannot comprehend mine. I do not wish to claim that I understand yours—perhaps the way I see you is only a logical artifact. But you must be able to accept the idea that what time is to me is not what time is to you. And because time is different, so is space. And because space is different, so is the very nature of existence.

"I will offer you another analogy. You are a three-dimensional being. I am a four-dimensional being. What you see of me is only a cross-section through me. You perceive me as an actor in your reality, an actor who can interact meaningfully with you on your terms. But there is more to me than that. I can attempt to simulate your kind of consciousness, and succeed—to some extent. I am not sure whether you can attempt to simulate mine. Perhaps not.

"You ask me: why am I here? What is your world to me? I can only begin to make an answer.

"Your scientists have put a great deal of effort into the extension of the human life-span. That research shows results—you might expect to live twice or three times as long as your prehistoric forefathers. Your social philosophers—most especially the Euchronians, but also the Eupsychians, to a lesser extent—have embraced similar aims: they have tried to design and make societies with longer life-spans, for the long-lived people. You have always fought for stability, because in stability you see the antidote to death.

"But even within your own people, there has always been a dissenting voice—or its echo—which holds that a longer, more stable lifetime is not—and cannot be—any richer in experience than a shorter, less stable one. I do not wish to say that this dissenting voice contains the truth, because your truth is not my truth, and I cannot judge. But consider my viewpoint.

"I am not merely long-lived, but eternal—if I so choose. I can accept death if I wish, and many of my people do. We are a declining race, ever becoming fewer. You may find an irony in that—the idea of an immortal race dwindling slowly into extinction. But this is so. The reason is stability. Once life becomes stable, it becomes empty—that is what we think and that is what we *feel*. Those of us who elect to die do so because of an overwhelming feeling that they have exhausted life, that it has nothing more to offer them, and that it is pointless to continue.

"You think that I came to Earth in search of something. I came in search of instability. But you will, perhaps, be able to understand that instability is not a goal, in the sense that you have goals. In searching for instability, it is not enough to find . . . one has to keep on finding, forever. The discovery has to be made over and over again, with each new day and each new year. For me and my people, it is not enough that the universe should be infinite in extent, either in time or in space. It must also be infinite in *experience*—for otherwise, how can we find a purpose in our infinite lives? Perhaps there is no such purpose. Perhaps we are doomed to failure in the search for it. Perhaps, in a million or a million million of your lifetimes, we will all have chosen mortality, and died. But in the meantime ... the effort continues.

"My kind have lived so much longer in the universe than yours that you find it almost inconceivable that we have little more scientific knowledge than you. When your people have lately come to me demanding help, they have taken it for granted that any miracle they could ask, I could perform. It is not so. My kind have no more scientific knowledge now than we had billions of years ago, because we found that science had very little to offer us beyond the tools to move about the universe. Beyond that, we found science an embarrassment. Science, you see, is founded upon the basic assumption that the universe is an ordered and systematic place, whose principles of organization are both rational and comprehensible. But what good was that assumption to us? What *we* needed was not science, but anti-science. We needed to proceed on the exactly opposite assumption that the universe was *not* wholly ordered— that there was an element of irrationality. Without that element of irrationality, you see, there could be no ultimate escape from stability.

"We had to abandon religion as well as science, for the fundamental assumption there is not so very different—it argues rationality but incomprehensibility. The last god which my people worshipped, so very long ago, was an insane god. There seemed to be no other trust that we could place in a god beyond the hope that he was insane. But we find too much rationality to believe in such a deity. Our best hope seems to be the flaw underlying scientific philosophy, a wholly secular belief that beneath the façade of reason and natural law the universe, in the final analysis, does not make sense.

"I think that you may be able to see, now, what I am doing on Earth. It is, if you like, my experiment—an attempt to test my belief. But you will notice that it is an experiment that can only fail. If it succeeds, it proves nothing beyond the fact that I can continue.

"I helped your people to build the Overworld, knowing that it would fail ... ultimately. I helped to make the Underworld what it is: a cauldron of evolutionary turmoil, where change is near to its most extreme. I will confess to you now that I contributed to that change by genetic engineering. The Children of the Voice are a collaboration between myself and chance, just as the Overworld is a collaboration between myself and order. In the end, I *must* believe, chance and change will win. They cannot be defeated. They must win, not only on Earth, but *everywhere*.

"Having said that, I must risk your anger. This, you will say, is interference . . . I have been intruding into the substance of your lives, threatening the very pattern of your existence. You may, perhaps, feel that what I have done—what I am doing—is evil. But I must say this: that I am dealing with factors which belong to a far greater time-scale than the one by which you live your lives. What I have done is negligible, in your terms. *Your* quest for stability is a purely temporary thing. You can find stability, if that is what you want, within a historical pattern which, from my viewpoint, is eternally chaotic. Because you ask so little, you have every chance of success. Because you are so transient, you have the opportunity to make whatever you want out of your lives: you do not have my limitations.

"Perhaps you will be unable to understand what it is that I have been trying to achieve here on Earth. I do not know that there is any way I can tell you which will help you to understand, because it is something which has virtually no meaning so far as you are concerned. But I will say it this way: what I have sought to gain from Earth is a glimpse of infinity—some hint of evidence that the universe is not only infinite in size, but infinite in incident. I have tried to find something new, in pursuit of the faith that there is *always* something new . . . something beyond. Beyond the shape and form of the universe there has to be shapelessness and formlessness, and there had to be a way to see and to know that chaos here on Earth. That is what the Children of the Voice mean to me: they may give me a glimpse of infinity.

"Perhaps I should add just one more thing, with reference to that point, and it is this: for you, too, what has happened and is happening may provide a window into new possibilities. Your people, unlike mine, have so many choices, so many opportunities. But here are more, opening up before you.

"You cannot know how much I envy you."

50

The road went over the edge of the world. Joth braked, and got out. He went to the brink of the Overworld, and looked down, following the sweep of the highway as it slanted down the metal face in a vast, shallow arc. The face was concave—headlands to north and south carried spurs of the overworld out beyond the expanse of sandy beach, and only dissolved into irregular masses of bare black rock some way out to sea. But the road curved out and looped back on itself, disappearing into a black semicircle cut out of the steel cliff.

The sun was setting into the sea, its light turning the sea gold and the hazed air pink. The great wall which enclosed the Underworld was fiery with reflected glare. Joth watched the garish display until the sun was gone and the colors began to drown. He knew that the afterglow would last for a long time, and even when he looked back over his shoulder to the eastern horizon, he could see no stars. Nor was there a moon.

He went back to the car, and drove it over the edge of the world, following the long decline. There were no seabirds—they found the metal cliffs too inhospitable. Seabirds lived almost entirely on uninhabited offshore islands—miniature sanctuaries.

Gradually, the sky darkened, and he switched on the headlights of the car. Cut into the saline dirt which had been deposited on the road over a great many years he could see the imprints left by Germont's ill-fated convoy not so very long ago.

When he reached the bottom, he switched off the lights and got out of the car again. He did not drive into the tunnel. He did not even look at the tunnel, at first, but walked off the causeway on to the sand, and looked out over the sea. The weed and detritus which marked the last high tide was only thirty or forty feet from the edge of the road, and he walked out to stir the stinking wrack with his feet. Tiny crustaceans squirmed in the wet sand he exposed. He looked at them, and wondered which of Earth's two worlds they belonged to: the old, or the new. Perhaps they, and everything within the ocean, were part of a third world, neither old nor new, neither Under nor Over—an eternal womb of life undisturbed by magnificent Plans and huge steel follies.

Overhead, the stars began to shine through. The night was cloudless, and they shone in their thousands. Behind him, his footprints, imprinted in the wet sand, gradually filled up with water, and their edges began to crumble. The footmarks lost their shape, and became mere puddles. He walked on a littel way, toward the sea, looking for small pools held by the rippled sand and the thin ridges of rock. But the loneliness and the darkness quickly became oppressive, and he turned back.

From the back of the car he collected a heavy flashlight, and armed with this he directed his attention to the tunnel into the Underworld.

Curiously, although this was undoubtedly the end-point of the road of stars, there seemed to be no light in the great corridor for the first few hundred yards. Without the beam of the torch, he could see nothing in the tunnel except the merest gleam of distant light. There was nothing that might attract a man—or even an animal—into its depths. From *inside*, though, the red glow of the setting sun might be clearly visible during certain seasons.

Joth walked into the tunnel mouth, playing the light of his torch all around and up above. He did not go far. He intended to wait—perhaps sitting in the car—for an hour or two, and then drive away. He would return, at the same time of day, in a few days time, and he would continue to return again and again, until something happened, or until he became convinced that nothing ever would. He had chosen evening, and the hours that followed twilight, because he knew that people waiting within would only venture out after the sun was gone.

But these intentions were not necessary. He did not have to wait, because someone was already there, waiting for him. She came to him cautiously, with her weapon drawn, because she could not see him while he stood behind the light, and she could not be sure that it was him. But she allowed herself to be caught by the beam, so that he could see her.

Only when he spoke, saying "Huldi!", did she know for certain who it was.

He questioned her. She told him all she knew about Iorga and Nita—the encounter with the Cuchumanates... her fall... and her recovery to find herself alone. She had not dared to go into the building in search of the others. She had waited outside until she was sure that they were not coming. She had killed the last of the Cuchumanates with her knife. And she had followed the road of stars to its ultimate end.

Joth led her outside, and showed her the stars in the sky. But she was so frightened by the ocean and the towering metal face, and the illimitable depth of the sky, that she really saw very little. Iorga had seen so much more, and Nita, if only she had lived...

But the merest glimpse of infinity was, to Huldi, a terrifying thing.

She would not get into the car, and so they went back into the tunnel, together. He asked her what she would do now, and she could not tell him. She had not thought, but had merely followed the road to its end. He wanted to take her to another part of the world, to deliver her into lands which were lighted by many stars, where people of her own kind lived, but there was no way that he could do that. The only way she would go was back, into the blacklands. He told her to go south rather than following the road east, because his map assured him that there were lighted lands that way, and not too far distant. He gave her the flashlight. Whether she would take his advice, he did not know. She said she would go south, but he did not know whether she was telling the truth.

Before they parted, they made love—for the second time.

51

The sentence of exile which Heres had passed on Sisyr was confirmed, and he left Earth. He never returned.

52

In time, all Chemec's prophecies came true.